LOST truth

Dawn Cook

ACE BOOKS, NEW YORK

THE BERKLEY PUBLISHING GROUP
Published by the Penguin Group
Penguin Group (USA) Inc.
375 Hudson Street, New York, New York 10014, USA
Penguin Group (Canada), 10 Alcorn Avenue, Toronto, Ontario M4V 3B2, Canada
(a division of Pearson Penguin Canada Inc.)
Penguin Books Ltd., 80 Strand, London WC2R 0RL, England
Penguin Group Ireland, 25 St. Stephen's Green, Dublin 2, Ireland (a division of Penguin Books Ltd.)
Penguin Group (Australia), 250 Camberwell Road, Camberwell, Victoria 3124, Australia
(a division of Pearson Australia Group Pty. Ltd.)
Penguin Books India Pvt. Ltd., 11 Community Centre, Panchsheel Park, New Dehli—110 017, India
Penguin Group (NZ), Cnr. Airborne and Rosedale Roads, Albany, Auckland 1310, New Zealand
(a division of Pearson New Zealand Ltd.)
Penguin Books (South Africa) (Pty.) Ltd., 24 Sturdee Avenue, Rosebank, Johannesburg 2196, South Africa

Penguin Books Ltd., Registered Offices: 80 Strand, London WC2R 0RL, England

This is a work of fiction. Names, characters, places, and incidents either are the product of the author's imagination or are used fictitiously, and any resemblance to actual persons, living or dead, business establishments, events, or locales is entirely coincidental.

LOST TRUTH

An Ace Book / published by arrangement with the author

PRINTING HISTORY
Ace mass market edition / December 2004

Copyright © 2004 by Dawn Cook.
Cover art by Jerry Vanderstelt.
Cover design by Rita Frangie.

ISBN: 0-441-01228-0

ACE
Ace Books are published by The Berkley Publishing Group,
a division of Penguin Group (USA) Inc.,
375 Hudson Street, New York, New York 10014.
ACE and the "A" design
are trademarks belonging to Penguin Group (USA) Inc.

PRINTED IN THE UNITED STATES OF AMERICA

10 9 8 7 6 5 4 3 2 1

For Tim

acknowledgments

I'd like to thank my writers' group for their moral support; my husband, Tim, for listening to the rewrites; and, of course, Richard Curtis and Anne Sowards.

I

The half-dozen chicken eggs cradled in her ridiculously long, clawlike fingers threatened to slip. Alissa drew them close to her body, knowing she wouldn't be able to catch them before they hit the ground, even from this height. She flicked a glance down. Below, the tallest outcrops of the mountains slipped soundlessly under her, gray in the morning light. The fog was beginning to rise with the sun, making a patchwork with low areas peeking out from under flat-topped white clouds and high crags sharp in the clear air.

Damp and clinging, the breeze tugged at her as she flew, and Alissa felt her secondary, nictitating eyelid shut against the wind. It was spring, and she was restless. This was the best she had felt all week—headed west, with the rising sun sending the shadow from her batlike wings to scare the occasional deer or goat into panicked dashes.

This morning, before the stars had vanished, she had flown across the mountains to her mother's abandoned farm in the foothills with the excuse of gathering eggs from the chickens that remained there. In truth, she was seeing if the snow was gone and all the passes were open. They were, thrilling her to no end. Now perhaps she could convince Useless to let her leave and find her mother.

In all his scheming wisdom, her teacher, Useless—or Talo-Toecan as everyone else properly called him—had decided that having been raised in the foothills, Alissa would adhere to foothills traditions concerning marriage. Her mother needed to show favor to one of her suitors before she could wed. But her mother had returned to her desert homeland, leaving only a tear-marked note on the abandoned stove.

Alissa knew Useless didn't care one whit about foothills traditions. He was just using the situation to keep Strell and Lodesh at arm's length from her, hoping she would lose interest and turn her attentions to a match more suitable to her new Master standing. His scheming only made Alissa all the more determined to marry one of them. The question remained, though, as to which one.

Slowly on the thin updrafts of the morning, she glided toward the Hold. The energy of the rising air currents stained the perfect sky with upwelling shades of a darker blue, visible through her raku eyes. To her right, a stark rock face threw off a steady stream of violet, swirling heat. Alissa's stomach clenched as she found herself angling toward it.

"Do you want to try rising on it?" came a thought that was hers, but not. It was Beast, and Alissa grimaced.

"No," Alissa answered shortly in her mind, peeved Beast would even ask. *"You do it."*

"You need to learn to fly," her alter consciousness said.

"And you need to learn to hoe your own row of beets."

Beast smugly withdrew her control over their level glide. Finding herself responsible for their motion, Alissa panicked. Immediately they stalled. They hung motionless for a heartbeat. Wings flailing, they dropped.

With a snort of laughter, Beast resumed command to catch their fall in an elegant swoop.

Alissa's tail brushed against the top of a dew-wet hemlock. *"Burn it to ash!"* she shouted in their shared thoughts, clutching the eggs close as her racing heart slowed. *"Don't do that!"*

Beast twisted her thoughts to give the impression of a smirk in their shared mind.

Glancing down, Alissa shuddered, knowing from experience how hard the ground was when one barreled into it at this speed. *"I've been stuck at the Hold all winter,"* she thought, sending a trace of rueful emotion to Beast. *"Now that the passes are open, I want to find my mother."*

"You want to go," Beast said suddenly. *"I like to fly. The sky is clear. Let's go."*

Alissa nervously shifted the eggs. She hadn't known her very real—and often annoying—alter consciousness felt the same. *"I can't,"* Alissa said. *"After the fiasco in the plains last summer, Useless said I had to find her thought signature first. My range isn't that good yet."*

"It's an excuse," Beast said shortly. *"I don't think even he could pick one person out from thousands. Not half a continent away."*

Alissa bobbed her great head, and Beast easily adjusted for the shift in momentum. *"Even so, I can't just fly away."* Alissa's mood turned soft and content. *"Strell and Lodesh can't keep up."*

"Oh." Beast's thoughts were tinged with disgust and a grudging confusion. *"I understand love. It grounds you when you want to fly."*

"No, Beast," Alissa insisted. *"You don't understand at all."* She sighed, hearing the exhalation come out in a primitive, guttural sound. Despite the nights spent trying to explain, Beast didn't seem to have the capability to comprehend what Alissa felt for Strell and Lodesh. It wasn't as if she could ask Useless for help, either. Only two people knew that Alissa had broken the Hold's oldest law and kept the bestial consciousness that evolves when a Master learns how to shift forms. If Useless ever found out, he would rectify the situation with a savage vengeance that would destroy Beast and probably leave Alissa bruised and battered—and less for the lack of her alter consciousness.

A sudden tightening at the back of her sinuous neck where it met her shoulders sent a wash of tension through her, driving her idle thoughts away. Something wasn't right.

"We're being followed," Beast said in unconcern. *"Connen-Neute has been behind us since we left the ground. You're just now noticing him?"*

Vexed, Alissa snaked her neck around and saw a golden form, twin to her own, a valley behind. Connen-Neute knew

of Beast, accepted Beast, and was admittedly a little afraid of
Beast. But as a fellow student Master, Connen-Neute was her
only peer. Seeing him, Alissa spurred Beast into a faster pace.
She had no problem sharing the sky with Connen-Neute, but
his skulking made it obvious that Useless had sent him to
shadow her.

"Bone and Ash," she muttered into her thoughts. *"Doesn't
Useless trust me?"* Then her annoyance hesitated, shifting to
a rising anticipation. *"Beast,"* she asked, *"can we lose him?"*

Beast made a short puff of scorn. *"Do updrafts rise?"* Still
she waited. Beast moved by instinct; all decisions were de-
ferred to Alissa.

Anticipation sent a shiver to set her wing tips to tremble.
Alissa modulated her thoughts so Connen-Neute, a valley behind, could hear her. *"Tag,"* she sent loudly, tingeing it with
expectation to let him know she wasn't angry. *"You're it."*

Alissa gasped as Beast took over with a frightening intensity, dropping them into a steep dive. A thrill of alarm struck
through Alissa, mirrored by the faint excitement she felt from
Connen-Neute. In three breaths, they had raced over a valley
that had once taken her two days to traverse on foot. Skimming
over a lake, she looked back to see Connen-Neute in hot pursuit. A slow thrum from in her mind told Alissa that Beast was
enjoying the chase far too much. Alissa's feral side angled
them high as if to climb, and when Connen-Neute matched
their path, Beast dove to the side into a mature forest of beech
and elm.

"Beast, no!" Alissa cried, remembering the shame of tearing her wing, but Beast found an opening into the clear un-
derstory. An ancient beech loomed before them. Alissa cried
out, her hind foot bending forward to push off it. The barrel-
sized tree snapped. She ricocheted over a patch of wild black-
berries sweet with flower. Birds flew and branches crashed.

Lungs heaving, Alissa looked back at the destruction.
Connen-Neute was stuck in the briars. Scratches made red
lines on his wings. His golden eyes focused intensely on her
as he struggled to get free. *"Go up!"* she demanded of Beast.
"The trees are too close. Go up!"

But Beast ignored her. Alissa felt her lips pull back from
her long canines as Beast's excitement grew. No one had ever

brought her down but Useless. Wings half closed, Beast jumped them through an opening and out over a fast mountain river. Her wings sprang open. Beast flew them downstream, taking advantage of the open space to gather speed.

Risking a quick look behind, Alissa saw Connen-Neute hop awkwardly to the river's edge. His feet pushed off from the rocky ground, wedging a boulder the size of a horse into the soft bank. She had a gap but not much of one. His eyes widened with excitement.

Alissa looked forward, her enjoyment suddenly faltering. The river had grown wild. Spray made her belly chill and her long tail cold. The rumble of water had grown loud. They were flying downstream to a waterfall.

The banks closed in and the flight space grew tight. *"Ah, Beast?"* Alissa quavered, seeing a dead end before them. They might have been able to fly out over the waterfall and into space but for the surrounding growth of forest that made the river a dead-end tunnel only water could escape. Branches and vines made an impregnable wall on every side. Over them, the trees arched and intertwined. The water frothed and railed against the boulders, and trunks jammed against the drop-off. And Beast showed no sign of stopping.

"Beast, we can't get through that!" Alissa warned. She glanced up, imagining the pain of breaking through the thick ceiling of branches. Her wings beat in time with her heart.

"Then we will go under," Beast thrummed, exalting in the chase.

"Beast!" Alissa cried. *"You don't know what's under the water!"*

"Water, wind, they all move the same," Beast said. *"He'll go around. We'll gain the span of a hundred wing beats."*

Alissa's confidence in Beast's abilities faltered. *"I changed my mind. He can follow us."* Alissa hesitated. *"Beast?"* Fear gripped her. *"Oh, no-o-o-o!"* she shrieked as Beast took a gasping breath and dove them under the water to follow it over the cliff.

A rush of bubbles carried the rumble of the river. The thunder of water beating the bottom of the cliff pounded through her. It was the roar of the earth's pulse. Her second eyelid closed to make everything green, black, and gray. Pebbles abraded her skin. Unseen forces buffeted her as boulders appeared and vanished behind her. Beast swam through the currents as if they were air. The water flung them down, and Alissa's eyes widened. Her stomach dropped. They had fallen over the edge! They would be crushed!

"Beast!" she screamed into her mind, frightened by Beast's savage desire to fly. Her haunches bunched. As they fell, Beast pushed off from the wall of the cliff behind them.

Green light flashed to gold as Beast shoved them out of the waterfall and into space. Heavy with water, they dropped. Her wings sprang open, and they rose on the cold, violent updraft from the upwelling mist. Alissa shrieked aloud, hearing her triumph come out as a savage roar. *"You did it!"* she cried.

"Burn you to ash, Alissa!" came Connen-Neute's thoughts from above and behind them. Alissa snaked her neck back to see him clambering awkwardly through the branches. *"Beast is going to kill you someday!"* he shouted at her.

"See you at home!" Alissa called back, finding herself doing a barrel roll.

Beast shook them, and they flew through a rainbow. *"And we still have your breakfast,"* Beast thought smugly.

Eye ridge rising, Alissa glanced at the cluster of eggs still secure in her grip. They still had the eggs. Alissa puffed out her air in disbelief, letting Beast take whatever updraft she wanted on the way home. Gradually her pulse slowed as the excitement from their flight eased. Alissa didn't think she would ever learn to fly. To let go and trust the wind was asking too much. Perhaps as much as asking a beast to understand love.

ב

The wind had dried Alissa by the time she passed the abandoned city of Ese' Nawoer. The thick walls that encircled it directed the rising heat into a soft upward blue swirl that she imagined looked like restless souls rising to heaven. She skirted the updraft, feeling eerie, even though all but one of Ese' Nawoer's ghosts were gone. Just ahead lay the Hold. The nearly empty fortress rested snug against a towering crag. Behind it, the mountain dropped in a sheer cliff, plunging down to the floodplain that led to the distant sea.

Once the Hold had been a hidden place of learning where raku Masters taught select humans, Keepers, how to use their stunted-by-comparison magical abilities. But of all the Masters, only Useless and Connen-Neute remained. Twenty years ago, Bailic, a Keeper, had convinced the Hold that a map Alissa's father had drawn led to a fabled lost colony of Masters. But it was an argument between Useless and his wife, Keribdis, that prompted the strong-willed, self-proclaimed matriarch to take the rest of the conclave and fly across the sea to find them. She had been hoping to cause a shift in power. What she did was empty the Hold and make it vulnerable.

Bailic murdered the Keepers that remained, Alissa's father

among them. With the Hold empty and Useless trapped in its cellar, Bailic was free to set his plan in motion. He wanted to force the ghosts of Ese' Nawoer to spread their madness among the foothills and plains, stepping forward as the land's grand and glorious redeemer when he deemed the plains and foothills punished enough for having shunned him.

Between Alissa and Lodesh, they had stopped him, but the skies had been empty of all but feral rakus for almost twenty years. Despite Useless's searching by wing and mind, he had never caught a glimpse or whisper. The rest of the raku were dead, perished in their search.

The Hold's tower glinted yellow in the sun just now reaching the surrounding fallow fields and hearth-wood forest. But it was to the walled garden surrounding the Hold that Beast angled them. Wings moving in a flurry of backward grace, Beast put down in a clearing Alissa would have said was too small to land in. The chaos that twenty years of neglect had wrought in Useless's garden brought a grimace to Alissa: tangled fruit trees, beds of flowers overwhelmed by grass, pathways overgrown and moss-covered. It was a mess.

Fatigue fell upon Alissa as Beast seemed to disappear. Only flight, fear, or Beast's newest preoccupation with dancing would bring her to the forefront of Alissa's thoughts. Weary, Alissa settled the eggs on the grass so as to not accidentally incorporate them when she shifted to her original, human form.

Alissa sent a thought into her source, instigating the loop of power that gave her wards strength. She set the tracings in her mind to glow with the proper pattern. A touch more energy, and the disconnection of time plucked her as the ward jumped from her thoughts to her body.

In a heartbeat, the tangled garden vanished. She dissolved to a thought, changed that thought to her human form, then made the thought a reality. At the last moment, she added a second ward to the first to ensure she would be clothed when she reappeared. She swirled back into the physical world, her ill-made shoes standing in the large oval she had pressed out in the wet grass. Alissa straightened as the chill of the spring morning shocked her awake. Clutching her arms about herself, she looked over her Master's garb.

It had taken her all winter, and more attempts than she would like to admit, but she had finally fixed another thought-form into her memory. Smiling in satisfaction, she shook out her floor-length skirt. It wasn't the elaborate attire Connen-Neute and Useless could fashion, but it adhered to the basic outline that designated her a Master instead of a Keeper.

A knee-length, dark green sleeveless vest was bound tight about her waist with a black scarf whose hem brushed her ugly shoes. Below the vest was a matching green skirt edged with a gold ribbon. A blouse the color of sand finished the outfit, its sleeves deep enough to serve as pockets if she wanted. The shadows of ivy leaves were woven into the fabric of both the vest and blouse. Connen-Neute had patiently spent two months teaching her the pattern.

Lips pressed, Alissa ran her hand over her hair. It had gotten down to the middle of her back this winter. Strell had threatened to punch Lodesh in the mouth if Lodesh gave in to Alissa's pleading and cut it for her. Strell was from the desert plains, and long hair was synonymous with status. Alissa had been raised foothills, and long hair was synonymous with irritation. Being fair as it was, it didn't make her look any more like a plainswoman, and she saw no use for it. Her features were a scandalous mix of foothills and plains. Strell said the coastal people were much as she was, and she would love to be able to walk down the street with impunity.

Wondering what time it was, Alissa bent to retrieve her watch from the ground, where it had fallen when she shifted. Metal was too dense to break down and so remained unchanged. The oversized bland ring with a hole in the band was too large to wear as a ring in her smaller form, and Alissa dropped it into a pocket. When dangled in the sun, the ring would show her what time it was by where the light fell upon the hours scratched on the inside of the band.

The repeated thunk of an ax into wood drew her attention, and she gathered her eggs into the flap of fabric her sleeve made. They made a comfortable weight as she picked her way through the damp grass to the overgrown path. Useless's formal gardens were too extensive to keep up with by herself. In its prime, Useless had kept all his Keeper students out here.

Now it was just her and occasionally Connen-Neute when he did something to irritate Useless—which wasn't as often as she wished.

She slowly made her way to the kitchen, mindful of the eggs. The rhythmic crack of wood grew louder, and the banter of two voices brought her to a standstill. She peeked around the corner of the path to see both Strell and Lodesh before the door to the kitchen, splitting wood for the fire. Her heart gave a lurch, and she drew back into the shadows.

Strell had stripped to his waist. The morning sun had yet to find him, and his dark skin glinted in the shadow-light. Though he looked too thin and tall to be able to wield the heavy metal, he moved with a confident precision, striking the wood Lodesh was setting up for him with almost a vengeful force. His muscles slid smoothly as he swung the ax. Sweat trickled down his shaven face, catching into drips at the cleft in his chin. His shoulder-length hair was tied out of his way, the loose waves all the darker for being damp from his sweat.

Her eyes traveled over his lanky build as he worked, and she warmed from her thoughts. Strell had spent much of his life as a minstrel, and his occasional, worldly-wise comments attracted her as much as his exotic plains appearance. They had met by chance: she traveling to the Hold, he fleeing the pain of learning that his family had died in a freak spring flood. That they had fallen in love while struggling to survive Bailic had been a shock to both of them. Useless wasn't timid in expressing his unhappiness with the situation, but Strell and Alissa didn't care. They had not overcome the scorn of two cultures to be held back by a third. Especially when it was one neither of them cared anything about.

Beside Strell, Lodesh was a study in opposites. Dressed in traditional Keeper garb, he carried a refinement that spoke of an easy nobility and confidence. His green eyes glinted more often in mischief than anything else, standing at great odds to his past responsibilities as Ese' Nawoer's Warden. Shifting forward and back, he wove between Strell's strikes with a well-earned dancer's grace. He wore a sturdy but elegant cloak against the morning chill, and a hat covered his short, blond waves. His cheeks, too, were clean shaven after Alissa had pointed out last winter the beard he was growing made him look old. He was Ese' Nawoer's last ghost, brought back to life to absolve his curse.

As Warden of the once populous city, he had denied entrance to the long-ago refugees from a plague of madness. Turning a deaf ear to the people as they cried for succor, or at the very least, a clean death, he and the other citizens of Ese' Nawoer had watched in horror as the women and children outside tore themselves apart against the gates. For so heinous a crime, a onetime friend condemned Lodesh and his city to an eternity of servitude until they made amends. The city's population had since found their rest, but as the one making the decision to keep the gates closed, Lodesh remained.

A whisper of regret tinged with guilt swept over her. It had been over a year since Lodesh—driven by a love she had yet to experience—had betrayed her, allowing her to go 350 years back in time to a Hold that was alive and flourishing. She met him anew as an innocent youth, balanced on the cusp of becoming the Warden and beginning the inexorable slide to his fate. Thinking that a return to Strell was impossible, she had been captivated by his ardent desire and her wish to spare him his tragic future. But she had found her way back to Strell, complicating her ties to both of them. She could not bring herself to hate Lodesh for what he had put her through, but neither could she trust him completely.

"You're wrong," Strell said to Lodesh between blows. He was speaking with a hard plains accent, as he did when agitated. "She loved me first." The ax bit deep, with a dull thunk, to cleanly split the wood. "That means more than you want to admit."

"Loved you first?" Lodesh answered, his careful speech making Strell's accent sound even more exotic. "That depends on your point of view. And what can a plainsman know of love? You all marry for gain. Love has nothing to do with marriage in the desert. Nothing at all."

Alissa hesitated on the path. They had fallen into one of their noncombative jousts with words. The winter had been painfully full of such conversations, calculated to start when they knew she was near. Each believed he would be the one

Alissa wed. Tensions between the two men were as strong and hidden as the current of a deep, fast river.

Strell chuckled. "Marry for gain? Not by choice. But perhaps we understand love better for having it unrequited most of the time." He lifted the ax and brought it down a bare hand's width from Lodesh. The well-dressed Keeper started, then looked up askance at him. His lips pressed together as he put another chunk of wood in its place, boldly keeping his hand upon it.

The ax rose again. "I know for a fact she will choose me when it comes to the sticking point," Strell said as he swung. *Thunk.* "I've saved her life more times than a beggar goes hungry." *Thunk.* "A woman won't throw that aside for fancy manners and sweet words that melt with the morning sun." *Thunk.* Strell paused, leaning against the handle as he wiped the sweat from his forehead. It was cold, and steam rose from his bare shoulders.

Lodesh brushed the bark from his sleeve as he straightened. "She doesn't need your protection, Piper," he said, and Alissa felt a flush of gratitude. It vanished as he added, "Not with Talo-Toecan looking after her. Shake the sand out of your ears and listen. A woman wants a man who can move her body and soul. A man with power, my desert friend." He grinned, but she could see the seriousness behind his green eyes.

"Power?" Strell blew as he caught his breath. "The last time I looked, your city was empty. And if you're talking about your Keeper skills, she makes you look like a commoner—my *dead* friend." Strell sent the ax into the wood.

"I'm not dead," Lodesh asserted, sounding hurt as he set another log in place.

Grunting with effort, Strell brought the ax down. "You're not all-living," he shot back.

"I'll outlive you," Lodesh said, and Alissa drew herself up, thinking the Warden had stepped over the line. But Strell laughed, leaving the ax stuck in the block as he kicked the split wood from his feet. Though their words were light and their manners civil, it was obvious their underground competition had grown fierce.

Still breathing heavily, Strell looked at Lodesh. "The extra years your curse gives you won't mean a thing after Alissa weds me, and she will." He yanked the ax free. "Love stretches beyond the grave. Your patient waiting will mean nothing."

Anger flickered across Lodesh's face, then vanished. He straightened to his full height and ran a hand under his elegant hat. "No," he said, shaking his head as if explaining something to a child. "Despite her human beginnings, Alissa is a raku. They live in the present. Once you're gone, she'll forget." His manner shifted, becoming lighter. "But I'll tell you what. We'll switch off, if you like. I get her for the first fifty years. You can have her the next."

A small sound of outrage slipped from Alissa.

"Untie your tent and blow away," Strell said with a chuckle. "I get her the first fifty years. After that, it won't matter to me."

She stiffened. Angry, she strode forward, her shoes crunching on the gravel Useless had set down just this week. The men spun to face her. Lodesh found his voice first, carefully brushing his short Keeper's vest smooth. "Alissa! Can I help you with those eggs?"

She pushed between them, her temper worsening as she tripped on the scattered wood. She had no idea that it had gotten this bad. With one hand, she yanked the door to the kitchen open. Leaving them to stare at each other in a masculine bewilderment, she slammed the door.

"*Alissa?*" came Lodesh's mental question, and she blocked him out, thinking it was unfair the Keeper would try to talk to her through the walls when Strell couldn't.

Fuming, Alissa felt her way across the Hold's kitchen to the dry sink as her eyes adjusted to the dimmer light. A globe of warded light glowed in a corner, setting her tracings to resonate when she came within a raku length of it. "Good morning, Useless," she said sullenly, sensing his presence with a quick mental search. There was a welcoming chitter of noise from the open rafters, and she wasn't surprised when Talon, her pet kestrel, dropped to her shoulder.

The small bird's claws dug painfully into Alissa, and she moved her to the back of a chair. Alissa ran a finger over the bird's markings, long since gray with age, as she snuck a glance at Useless to estimate his reaction to her less-than-respectful greeting.

"Good morning," the Master said slowly as he looked up from his work. By the stench, she guessed he was mixing up a batch of masonry paste to repair another crack in the Hold's twenty years of neglect. Her teacher was in his human guise, seeing as a raku couldn't fit in the Hold's kitchen. As her eyes adjusted, she took in his gold, floor-length, sleeveless vest, cream-colored shirt, and matching trousers. He had the same black scarf around his waist as she did. The light from his ward made odd shadows on his white eyebrows and his short hair, cropped so close it was almost nonexistent. Wrinkles edged a serious-looking face and a hawklike nose.

More old than young, he nevertheless appeared to be in his sixth decade, not his eightieth. The fingers gripping the stirring rod were abnormally long, with four segments rather than the usual three. They, along with his golden eyes, gave away his raku origins even when in his human form. But Alissa returned without fail to her original short fingers and gray eyes when shifting from raku to human. Even as a Master, she didn't quite fit in.

Avoiding his questioning look, Alissa washed and stacked the eggs in a bowl. One was cracked, and she put it on top. Still upset, she slumped at one of the narrow black tables. Talon hopped close to bump her head under Alissa's fingers. Fingers moving aimlessly over her bird, Alissa stared at nothing. She had to get Strell and Lodesh sorted out in her mind. Soon.

The chirping of sparrows intruded as the kitchen door opened and closed. Alissa didn't look up, knowing it was Strell and Lodesh. The soft and certain sounds of wood being stacked intruded.

Lodesh busied himself at the smallest of the three hearths. "Would you like some eggs with your toast, Alissa?" he asked cheerfully.

Alissa looked up, thinking his courtly figure looked odd with the heavy pan in his hand. "Of course I want eggs," she said. "Why would I bother to bring them back if I didn't?"

Useless hesitated in stirring his paste. His eyebrows

bunched, and Alissa added contritely, "Sorry. I'd like some eggs. Thank you."

Her gaze fell upon Strell, noticing he had put his shirt back on. His shoulders pulled at the brown fabric as he stacked the wood. There was a click as Useless set his stirring rod down. "Are you feeling well, Alissa?"

She flicked her gaze up and away. "No. I mean, yes. I'm fine." She took a slow breath, settling her eyes and fingers on Talon. She wasn't going to tell Useless what she had overheard. He would only put more restrictions on her. Rules were his answer to everything. "It's spring," she said impulsively. "I want to go to the plains."

"Have you found your mother's thought signature yet?"

"No-o-o-o," she moaned. "But—"

"Then you know your answer."

Alissa's brow furrowed. There was a soft flutter as Talon retreated to the rafters. Strell and Lodesh glanced at each other uneasily, but Alissa's forthcoming complaint was interrupted as Connen-Neute pulled open the garden door. In his human guise, he was tall and scholarly, dusky of hair and solemn of manner. His long face was pinched in apology as he gave Useless a sheepish look. Connen-Neute wouldn't meet her eyes, and she was pleased to see him sweating under his black and gray Master's vest and trousers.

Talo-Toecan sighed and pushed out a chair across from him. "Come here, Alissa. I'd like to speak with you for a moment. Alone, gentlemen, if you don't mind?"

A quick breath of worry and defiance shifted Alissa as Lodesh pulled the pan he had set over the fire off the flames. "Not again," he said sourly under his breath, avoiding her gaze as he headed for the open archway and the rest of the Hold.

Strell was a soft blur of brown as he brushed past her, "I'll be at the firepit, Alissa," he murmured, taking the opposite direction of Lodesh and going back into the garden.

Connen-Neute rose with an effortless movement, but Useless cleared his throat. "Connen-Neute? Stay," he said, and the young Master blanched.

From the dining hall came Lodesh's voice: "Well, why didn't you just say no humans?"

Alissa didn't move, shunning the chair Useless had pushed out for her. She hated his rules, and she didn't appreciate the way he kept trying to get Connen-Neute and her together.

Connen-Neute hovered by one of the unused hearths, his tall frame hunched and nervous looking. He exchanged a weary look with Alissa that told her he, too, guessed this was going to be one of Useless's matchmaking exercises.

Alissa cleared her throat. "No," she said clearly. "I'm not going to pick berries with Connen-Neute or dig a pond with him or go hunting poor defenseless sheep, or even go down to the holden and copy texts from the pillars onto paper. I want to go to the plains and find my mother. You promised I could once the passes were open."

Connen-Neute's eyes widened, but Useless kept his reaction to a slow breath. "No," he said. "I said you could go once you pinpointed her location."

"But you can't search past the curve of the earth," she protested. "I didn't know that when I agreed to it. She's too far away! At least let me get close enough so I have a chance."

Useless rose. Moving with a predatory slowness, he eased himself down across from her. The irate firmness in his golden eyes made her more angry yet. "It's time for you to put your fancies aside and accept that you can't follow your heart," he said, his few lines seeming to deepen. "There are bigger issues here."

Alissa's stymied emotions bubbled over. "You don't think I know that Strell will die before my first wrinkle?" she said, keeping just enough presence of mind to keep her tone soft. "You don't think I know that I can never have raku children with either of them? I hate it. But maybe I'm supposed to be the last. Ever think of that? Maybe it will be better this way."

"Alissa . . ." he cajoled. His eyes flicked to Connen-Neute in apology. "What, by my sire's ashes, is wrong with Connen-Neute?"

"Nothing," she admitted. "But I don't love him." The words were easy to say as she knew it wouldn't hurt the sensitive Master at all. He was the only eligible raku left. But Connen-Neute was frightened of Beast and wouldn't think to pursue Alissa, much to Useless's confusion and bother.

Useless leaned back in his chair with a heavy sigh. "Alissa," he tried again. "We are talking about the real risk of extinction. You may not care, but are you going to deny Connen-Neute the chance to live a full life? Yes, I know right now he's bound and determined to have nothing to do with you, but he is young. Give him a chance."

Connen-Neute cringed. *"Sorry. Not my idea,"* he whispered privately into her mind.

Alissa said nothing, her eyes sullenly on the table, her ankle tapping the leg of her chair.

"Be patient," Useless said softly. "Someday you will be free to go where you want. But not yet. You are too young, too inexperienced. Last fall, you got out of the plains by the skin of your teeth." Clearly frustrated, he raised his abnormally long hands in explanation. "You can pass for human. I can't. For all my strength, I'm useless. I can't come rescue you, and I won't let you risk your life again until I know you can handle yourself."

"I can take care of myself. I'll be fine," she muttered.

"You'll be staying here." Useless crossed his arms, making him look more like a dignified teacher than usual. "Sometimes," he said in a serious voice, "you learn more by not doing something than by doing it."

Alissa took an angry, frustrated breath. "What the Bone and Ash does that mean!" she exclaimed as she stood up.

"Alissa," Useless said, the first hint of real anger crossing him. "I'm going to be very clear about this. I am confining you to the Hold. I don't want you even in the foothills."

For three heartbeats, she stared at him. "But you let me go before—"

"Not anymore." Useless's jaw was set firmly.

Her breath came fast, and her body demanded action. Heart beating wildly, she stood. "You overgrown, snotty, know-it-all lizard!" she shouted, sending Connen-Neute staggering backward in fright. "You're hiding behind rules invented for your convenience. Rules were made to be broken. Only the law must be obeyed!"

Frustrated, she spun to the garden. She took three steps, gasping as she jerked to a halt when a ward snapped over her. Her thoughts white-hot and angry, she burned the ward aside.

Shocked Useless would even try to bind her that way, she spun round to find him right behind her. "I'm going into the garden," she said, hating her sudden fear.

He reached out and gripped her arm. "Where did you hear that?"

Frightened, she jerked away. "What does it matter?" She stormed out, slamming the door behind her.

Her steps quick and stilted, she stomped down the new gravel path to the firepit. Arms clasped tightly about herself, she fumed. Useless was being overprotective. Getting confined in a plains jail for dissident behavior hadn't been her fault. And she had gotten out on her own.

The door to the kitchen opened behind her, hitting the supporting wall with a bang.

Alissa whipped about. Her eyes widened. Useless stood tall, framed by the archway. His usually placid face was fierce. His golden eyes were intent, as if on prey. He caught sight of her. "Alissa!" he all but shouted, striding forward.

In a surge of fear, she shifted to her raku form. Beast stirred to life, the full awareness of the insults Alissa had heaped upon Useless crashing down on both of them. *"Fly!"* Alissa shrieked into their shared thoughts. She had pushed Useless too far and finally found his limits.

Beast took over. Haunches bunching, they leapt into the air. An almost crippling tug on her thoughts told her Useless had shifted to his raku form as well. Fighting for height, Alissa circled the tower. Her wings struggled to beat faster. She had to outdistance him. He would thrash her. He would ground her and not let her read anything for a week!

"Alissa!" came Useless's thought. *"Wait!"*

She didn't. Frantic, she looked behind her. Useless was following her wrathfully. His golden wings were almost a third again as large as hers. "Fly!" she shouted out loud, hearing her cry as a terrified, guttural sound. He was the only thing that could catch her, the only thing that had ever brought her down. The only thing she was afraid of.

They reached the top of the tower. Alissa clutched at it, her long, clawlike hands scrabbling. She propelled them forward. Still flying, Beast ran them across the top of the flat roof.

They reached the edge. Beast gathered them for a mighty leap to add to their speed.

"Go!" Alissa exclaimed. Haunches bunched, breath gathered, and they leapt.

She shrieked as a savage claw gripped her ankle. Jerked to a halt, Alissa fell. Her chin smacked into the railing, and she cried out. Tears of pain and fear blurred her vision. Wings flailing, she cowered, backing her bulk into a corner. The long claws slipped from her. Her tail whipped around her submissively, and she lowered her head almost to the paving stones. Beast vanished from her thoughts, leaving her alone to suffer what her mouth had gotten her into.

"I'm sorry!" Alissa thought frantically. *"I'm sorry! I'm sorry! I'll never talk back again. Please, Useless,"* she pleaded, afraid he was going to hit her. She had said so many disrespectful things. *"I'll stay here. I'll be good!"*

"Where did you hear that?" he asked, the intentness of his thought shocking her.

Head on the paving stones, she peered up at him. Her wing tips quivered. She had forgotten how much bigger he was as a raku than she was. Useless towered over her, the sun glinting through his great wings as he was clearly too agitated to fold them.

"What?" she asked. He took a step forward. She gasped as his shadow fell over her. Hind legs scraping at the stones, she tried to scrunch her great bulk farther into the corner.

"Where did you hear that?" he asked. *"Who told you that only the law must be obeyed?"*

She let out her held breath, holding the next one as well. Frightened, she snuck a quick look at him. She wasn't very good at reading raku expressions, but she would be blind not to recognize his agitation from the way his stubby, truncated tail whipped the air.

He reached out one clawed forearm with incredible suddenness. Her breath came in a panicked sound as he pinned her wing to the paving stones. *"I'm sorry!"* she cried out. *"I won't do it again. I promise! Useless, I'm sorry!"*

She cowered, watching his shadow tremble. *"Alissa,"* he said, his thoughts precise and impatient as they slid into hers.

"I'm not going to strike you. Though the Navigator knows you deserve it."

She angled her head up, disbelieving. Useless's triangular head dropped to hers. *"And if you ever speak to me like that in front of Connen-Neute again,"* he intoned into her thoughts, *"I will lock you in the holden for sixteen years."*

"Yes, Useless," she stammered, her pulse slowing. She released the breath she'd been holding in a quick sound as he lifted his grip on her and backed up a step. With a tug on her thoughts, he disappeared in a swirl of gray, coalescing back down to his less formidable, human shift. He squinted in the sun as he came to stand by her head.

"Now," he said, able to talk as he again had vocal cords. "Who told you that?"

"Silla," she said. *"Silla told me that."* He paced forward, his eyes fever bright. Alissa jerked her head up out of his reach. *"I'm sorry!"* she cried. *"Is it wrong? I won't say it again!"*

Useless jerked to a stop. He clasped his hands behind his back and took a slow breath. His lips pursed. "Who is Silla?" he asked, his voice deceptively soft.

"Just a dream," Alissa said, mystified. *"I used to dream about her when I was lonely. Before I became a Master."* Alissa felt herself blush. Looking down, she noticed her gold color had shifted to almost pink. It was embarrassing to admit that she had dreams so real that Silla seemed like a friend.

Useless made a slow, strength-gathering blink. "Raku or human?" he asked softly.

"Ah . . . raku," Alissa said, remembering Silla's long fingers and golden eyes. Alissa had first dreamed of Silla even before she had found the Hold, catching the young woman halfway out her bedroom window during a dream of her father. Her imaginary friend had since found her occasional way into several other dreams, usually when Alissa was unusually tired or upset, coming to cheer her up with tales of her own trials and frustrations with her own teacher.

Alissa slowly lowered her head, easing into a more comfortable crouch. It suddenly struck her as odd that she would dream of a girl with a raku's long fingers and golden eyes even before she knew Masters had them in their human shift.

"How—how old is she?" Useless asked.

He was pacing, and Alissa stared until he slid to a halt before her. She had thought she was going to be beaten, or at the very least chastised severely. *"Younger than me,"* she said. *"But not much."* She felt her pulse slow. *"Should I not say it?"* she questioned.

He ran a quick hand over his short white hair. "That would make sense. That might explain it. Do you dream of her every night or just sometimes?"

Bewildered, Alissa lowered her head to his height. *"Hardly at all anymore. I dreamed of her a lot when I was recovering from that burn across my tracings three winters ago."* Her pulse slowed, not believing that he was more upset about what she had said than her insults.

"The daytime," Useless said, alarming her with the intentness of his words. "You dream of her in the daytime."

Alissa nodded, just now realizing it.

"What does she wear?" he demanded. "You said she was a raku. She can shift to human form, yes?"

Alissa drew back, wondering if Useless might be losing his grip. Slowly she looked over the edge of the railing, wishing Connen-Neute would appear. *"Master's attire."*

"No," Useless said impatiently. "What color?"

"Purple, with a red sash."

Useless's eyes lit up. *"Connen-Neute!"* he shouted with his thoughts, and Alissa winced at the strength of it. *"Come to the roof!"* A smile, looking not out of place but rather giddy, blossomed over him. "They're alive," he said almost to himself as he went to the edge and looked down into the garden for Connen-Neute. "They're alive! And you have again done the impossible."

3

Alissa anxiously blew out her breath, ruffling her hair with her exhalation. "But I'm not sleepy," she complained, her eyes darting from one man to the next.

Useless settled himself to the back of his chair in exasperation. Running a hand atop the bristles of his short white hair, he scowled over the curtain-darkened dining hall. Strell and Lodesh were in separate corners, trying to stay out of the way. Connen-Neute sat sideways on a hard-backed chair, looking sullen that she was being taught a new ward and he wasn't.

The fire was high and the room was stuffy. Redal-Stan's old chair before the fire seemed to cradle her, and she drew her legs up under her, pushing herself back farther into the cushions. The overstuffed monstrosity was a salute to comfort, and Alissa always felt near to the gruff, fatherly Master from the Hold's past when she sat in it.

She ran a nervous thumb across the faded pattern, wishing he was here. He would understand, and if not, she would feel comfortable enough to tell him why she was afraid to put herself into a trance. The old Master had helped her when she found herself shifted into the past, accepting with a shocked wonder who she was and where she had come from, trying to help her when it was clear she was going to slowly lose her

mind from her jump through time. Though she had known
him for only a short time, she missed him. Inhaling deeply,
she imagined she could smell book paste.

Talon chittered soothingly from the arm of her chair, and
Alissa brought herself back to the present with a sigh. Her
tension returned as she met Useless's gaze. "It doesn't matter
that you aren't sleepy," he said with a mix of understanding
and impatience. "You aren't trying to sleep. It's a trance, a
deep state of concentration. You've done this before—"

"Not on purpose," she interrupted, showing a questionable
lack of common sense. Eyes dropping at his sudden frown,
she whispered, "Sorry."

Her thoughts swung wildly back to Bailic and the trance he
had lulled her into three winters ago. The insane Keeper had
been more powerful than she, fluent in the skills Alissa was
only just learning. She had been helpless in his grip; with his
voice alone he had unknowingly opened the way for Useless
to enter her mind and speak through her. It had ultimately
saved her life, but looking back on it now, it frightened her.

She put a hand to her middle. To do as Useless asked
would put her where the ground might fall out from under her
feet. Bad things happened when she lost her volition. She had
gone feral when her book of *First Truth* had taken over her
mind to teach her how to shift. When Bailic had lulled her into
a trance, the evening had ended with her burning her mind so
deeply she almost died. Beast had once unwillingly taken her
over when Alissa loosened her grip in an instant of anger. And
to voluntarily put her will in another's hands again, to allow
them to manipulate her at their whim, was too much to ask.

Useless adjusted his sash, obviously not seeing the problem. "As I was saying, you've done this before. You can do it
again. I'll run the ward for you, if that's what concerns you."

"No!" she exclaimed, unwilling to admit the reason for her
reluctance. "I'll do it myself." She hesitated. "Maybe we
should wait and try tonight. The sun is nearly crested."

"That is the whole point!" Useless burst out. Taking a slow
breath, he set his hands on his lap. "I don't understand all of
it," he said calmly. "But you said when you dream of Silla, the
beach is white sand, not gravel. You dream of her only when
the sun is up. Silla is a Master, born to those that left twenty

years ago. They're alive, and I think they're so far away that it's night there when it's day here."

Alissa arched her eyebrows in disbelief. Even Connen-Neute, usually able to accept anything on faith, cleared his throat in doubt. "You—ah—can't send thoughts beyond the curve of the earth," the young Master protested meekly, flinching when Useless gave him a black look.

"Perhaps Alissa is bouncing her thoughts off the bottoms of clouds," Useless said in a bother. "Perhaps because they are both asleep they only need to go halfway. Perhaps it's because Alissa was born a human instead of a raku. How should I know what she is doing? But Silla is real, and she knows Keribdis. My wife was forever throwing that phrase about rules and the law at me. Every burning-ash time we argued."

Connen-Neute moved uneasily in his chair. Brow pinched, he fingered the red sash around his waist. Alissa went slack in thought. Silla wore a red sash as well. Sashes were marks of teaching lineage. Her eyes widened. Keribdis had been Connen-Neute's teacher?

"Alissa," Useless said, jerking her attention back. "You've memorized the pattern needed to maintain a trance without sacrificing your lucid state. Just set it up and run it. I've tried to reach both Silla and Keribdis. I can't do it." His expression was fierce with longing.

Anxiety tightened her shoulders, and she glanced at Strell and Lodesh. Lodesh gestured she should try, but Strell had a helpless, knowing look. Miserable, she met Useless's golden eyes, the fire setting the brown flecks within them aglow. His pain was obvious. For two decades he had believed Keribdis was dead, and their last words to each other had been harsh and unforgiving. "I—I can't . . ." she said, ashamed to admit she was frightened.

"Why not?" he shouted, gesturing wildly.

Her eyes widened. Staring fiercely at the fire, she refused to cry. She wanted to run, but the memory of being pinned to the Hold's tower kept her unmoving.

Seeing her obvious misery, Useless fell back against his chair. "Please, Alissa," he amended softly. "I'm your teacher. Tell me why you can't?"

Still she wouldn't say anything, keeping her hands tight in

her lap and her eyes riveted to the fire. The silence in the dark, stuffy room became uncomfortable.

"Um," Strell offered, his low voice hesitant. "Can I talk to Alissa for a moment?"

Useless jerked himself to his feet. Clearly in a sour mood, he gestured for Connen-Neute and Lodesh to precede him out. The well-dressed Keeper seemed as bothered as Useless, clearly not liking Strell imagining he could help when Lodesh could not. Useless's long vest swirled as he stomped out. She listened to their hushed voices echo as they went into the great hall.

Talon chittered, and Alissa took the small bird, finding comfort in running a finger over her grayed markings. Ashamed of her cowardice, she glanced at Strell, relieved to see the understanding in his eyes.

She gave him a thin smile as he pulled his hard-backed chair over to sit facing her with their knees almost touching. Talon chittered aggressively at how close they were to each other, and Alissa set her aside. He hadn't yet shaved, and the prickly black looked awful.

"I know what's bothering you," Strell said softly, and she slumped.

Leaning forward, she dropped her forehead to his shoulder. The scent of dry sand filled her senses, and she felt the prick of tears. Strell leaned forward as well to rest his head against her. They sat for a moment, Alissa taking strength from his silence.

"I can't do it, Strell," she whispered, her fingers running over the calluses on his fingers. "What if I lose control? What if I—"

"You won't," Strell soothed, interrupting. She took a breath to protest, halting as he put a finger atop her lips. "Alissa, listen," he asserted gently. "When you're in a trance, you haven't given your will to another, just freed your inhibitions. You're no more likely to do something you don't want to do than when you're fully awake. I'm a minstrel. Trust me on this?" Strell tucked a strand of hair behind her ear, his fingers rough and warm against her neck.

She nodded, miserable, as she wiped the moisture from her eyes. Shame for her cowardice filled her. Useless had spent twenty years away from his wife, his colleagues, everyone he had known. And now her weakness was keeping them from coming home. She was being foolish. No one in the Hold would hurt her. No one.

Alissa took a steadying breath. "You'll stay here with me?" she asked.

Strell's brown eyes glinted with what looked like pride in her. "Yes, I'll even keep everyone out until you wake up, if you like." He ran his hand over his hair and gripped the clip that kept his dark hair back. "If that's all right with you?"

Her heart gave a pound at his last words, and she searched his anxious expression. *Ashes,* she thought, her heart going out to him. He wanted to help, and as a commoner incapable of working wards, he thought there was nothing he could do. He had no idea the strength she took from him simply being there, keeping her from being alone.

Unable to hold his gaze, she nodded. Taking three slow, practiced breaths, Alissa felt the tension drain from her. She focused on Strell and his encouraging smile before she closed her eyes and prepared to set up her newest ward.

Deep in her unconsciousness lay a glittering, silver sphere of power, a gift from her papa before he died. It had been given in love, and therefore she was left in the unique situation of owing no one a debt of allegiance for her strength. Not even Useless. He taught her to pass on his knowledge, and she put herself under his direction out of respect alone.

The glowing sphere was her source, the beginning of everything. Surrounding it to bind it into shape were uncountable threads. The arrangement gave Alissa the impression of a loosely wound ball of wool. Glimpses of force eked out, making the sphere glow brighter than a star. Never had Alissa been able to form any impression of what lay encased by the threads. Useless once told her it was because limit-bound thoughts balked at infinity.

Alissa slipped further into her mindscape, enjoying the slow immersion instead of the usual dash and crash she used to instigate wards quickly. As the fire hissed and popped, her thoughts slowed, and her tracings, a close companion to her source, seemed to melt into focus behind her mind's eye. A twisted chaos of blue-black lines spread in all directions about the glowing sphere. The lines were nearly invisible against her thoughts. Dewdrops of a more intense blue marked where tracings met and fractured. A gold shimmer followed the tracings in wisps visible only when she looked at them sideways.

Alissa sent a thought to pierce her glowing source. A silver-lined ribbon of energy shot out and made the jump to her tracings. Touching at a single juncture, the energy made a curving arc back to her source, crossing over itself to make a twisted, crossed loop. It was the primary circuit, according to Useless. Alissa preferred to call it "nothing," as that's exactly what it did.

Her awareness focused as she brought back the memory of the ward Useless had shown her earlier. Double-checking as she went, Alissa allowed the energy from the primary circuit into selected tracings. The pattern of lines looping in and amongst themselves was what made a ward. It wasn't magic, she still contended, but it didn't hurt to let everyone think it was. It was easier than trying to explain what really happened.

The pattern filled with a hissing energy, lighting her mindscape with a brilliant glow that wasn't gold or silver but somehow both. Assuring herself again that nothing would happen to her as long as Strell was near, Alissa set up a field within herself to give the ward a place to act. She allowed a tinge more energy to flow into the completed circuit. Her tracings went dark as the ward made the jump from her tracings to her field.

The warmth of the fire on her face seemed to increase as *something* slowly settled over her. It was the ward, and though similar to being asleep, it was different at its most basic level. The ward sharpened her thoughts, and Alissa intentionally imagined herself in the Hold's garden in the snow. Silla liked snow, and in her dreams they had often compared the snowflakes that fell upon their sleeves. Alissa shivered in the imagined chill, feeling a gust of wind in her hair. She waited in the moonlit garden, watching the stars grow sharp as the air cracked in her lungs. Still, no Silla.

Perhaps, she wondered, *I should try to find Silla?* This was harder, and Alissa had seldom managed it. Relaxing further, she felt herself settle deeper into the cushions. The snowblanketed garden vanished. Again she felt the stuffy warmth of the dining hall. This, too, she worked to block out, believing she should feel nothing, emptying her thoughts so she could find Silla's.

In her dream state, she closed her eyes to listen with her entire being the way Beast had taught her. Slowly she recognized the wind. It was steady, and with it came an increasingly familiar scent of salt. In her dream, Alissa opened her eyes and gasped.

She was dreaming. She knew that. She was also standing at the edge of a cliff overlooking more water than she had ever seen. It was flat like a tabletop, and so far below her that its motion was lost. "Alissa!" came a high-pitched voice.

Alissa turned, smiling in recognition. "Hi, Silla." Alissa pulled her hand up to shade her eyes from the imaginary sun. With new understanding, she looked at the young Master in her human form. Silla was almost as tall as Alissa, not yet having grown into her full height. Thin with late adolescence, her face angled to a small chin, its shape accentuated by her cheekbones.

Silla smiled in greeting as she held a wisp of black hair out of her eyes with an overly long hand. Her cascade of ringlets were held off her neck and shoulders by ribbons, and the arrangement gave Silla a regal demeanor only strengthened by the golden eyes Masters had, even in their human form. Alissa's gaze dropped to the red sash about Silla's waist, comparing it to Connen-Neute's. They were the same.

Silla grinned as she saw Alissa's new Master's attire. "I like it," she said, taking an expansive sleeve in her hands and running a thumb across the shadow of ivy leaves woven into the fabric. "How long did it take you?"

"All winter. Two months to learn how to weave the ivy leaf pattern. After that, it was easy." Alissa turned to the drop-off. "This is nice. Why haven't you shown me this before?"

Silla shrugged, looking embarrassed. "I come up here sometimes to sit. It looks like a good place to learn how to fly."

Alissa sat down on the conveniently placed dream rock. "Don't you know how, yet?"

Silla turned away. "Of course. I'm just not that good yet."

Seeing her obvious embarrassment, Alissa winced. "Sorry.

I'm not that good yet, myself," she added, and Silla flashed her a quick, grateful smile.

"Listen," Alissa said. "I'm glad I found you today, or tonight, rather. You're real. I mean, I'm real." Silla's heart-shaped face went slack in astonishment, and Alissa added, "You remember me telling you about the Hold?"

"Yes," Silla said cautiously. "That's where we came from. It's cold there."

Alissa stood up in excitement. "Cold. Like snow! Remember I showed you that? That's where I am. With Useless. I told you about him. But his real name is Talo-Toecan." The proper name for her instructor sounded odd coming from her lips.

Silla's eyes widened. "Talo-Toecan? He's—he's Kerib-dis's—"

"Yes!" Alissa cried. "Her husband. Is she all right? Useless—I mean Talo-Toecan—has been trying to reach her ever since he realized you were a real person, or raku rather, and that it was possible to reach another from so far away." Her words tumbled over themselves.

"You're—real?" Silla looked ill. "I thought you were a dream."

"And Connen-Neute and Lodesh are here," Alissa said as she took Silla's hands.

Silla drew her hands from Alissa and backed away. "Connen-Neute is feral."

Alissa grinned. "Not anymore. I accidentally brought his sentience forward from the past. It was sort of my fault he went feral in the first place. But listen. I'm a Master, just like you. Talo-Toecan says these aren't dreams but a communication that's possible when the mind is relaxed and free to believe in the impossible. It's fantastic that we can reach that far."

Face white, Silla took another step back. "I saw you dream of your father," she said. "He wasn't a Master. How can you be one? You don't look like one."

Concerned at Silla's fright, Alissa stepped forward. "I've got ancestry from the plains, foothills, and even the coast somewhere. I made the jump from Keeper to Master," she said. "Wait. I can prove I'm real," she pleaded. "I know your teacher is Keribdis. You never told me that. Connen-Neute wears the same red sash you do. She taught him, too."

Silla's head shifted violently in denial. "Connen-Neute is feral. I heard the stories. You're a dream, telling me things I already know. Keribdis said I shouldn't think of you. That you're madness. That I might go feral if I listen to you!"

"Silla!" Alissa cried, seeing in her the desire to flee. "Ask Keribdis about Lodesh Stryska. He's a Keeper. He's here at the Hold. Blond hair, green eyes, always trying to get me to blush. Keribdis will remember him. He makes really good tea," she finished weakly.

Silla looked terrified, and Alissa scrambled to find a way to prove neither one of them was insane. "Ask Keribdis about the cups he can make from his thoughts," she said suddenly. "They're the size of two fists! No one ever told you that, did they?"

"But he's dead," Silla whispered. Eyes wide, she gazed at Alissa. "He was the last Warden of Ese' Nawoer." She backed to the small footpath leading down.

"Silla! I'm real," Alissa cried. "Talo-Toecan wants you to come home."

"I can't fly!" Silla shouted. "It's my fault we can't get off the island!" Her face shifted back to fear. "You're a dream. You're madness. Get out of my dream! Get out!" she shrieked.

Alissa started awake, gasping. Her heart pounded, and she almost rose from her chair. Strell was gripping her shoulder, his eyes crinkled with worry. Useless stood behind him. He glowed with hope, but it turned to ash as he took in Alissa's cold face.

She swallowed hard as her pulse slowed. The fire's warmth felt chill after the balmy strength of the sun on Silla's cliff. She glanced at Strell, and he let her go. "She thinks . . . She thinks I'm a figment of her imagination," Alissa said, shaking inside. "She thinks I'll make her insane. I'm sorry, Useless," she whispered. "I found her. I tried to tell her I wasn't a dream. I told her about Connen-Neute—"

"The last they knew, he was feral," Useless interrupted. "She didn't believe you." Face gray and pained looking, he closed his eyes as if unable to tolerate the heartache.

"And trying to convince her with Lodesh was just as bad. And it didn't help that I'm a transeuent; I don't think she even knows it's possible for a human to become a Master," she added, thinking of Silla's long stares at Alissa's short-by-comparison fingers.

Talon hopped to Strell's shoulder, peering at Alissa with an odd, unbirdlike intensity.

"We'll try again tomorrow," the old Master said softly as he turned away to hide his grievous disappointment.

Somehow, Alissa didn't think it would make any difference.

4

"It's not working," Alissa said in exasperation, trying to hide her frustration as Useless sighed. "We should just fly out there and get them." Slumping in one of the kitchen's chairs, she pushed her plate of stew away. Strell, halfway across the room, stiffened. Alissa closed her eyes at his abhorrence of wasting food, then gestured he could have it.

Useless said nothing, his attention upon repairing a bowl that would be easier to replace than fix. His usual upright countenance had degraded over the last few days, worn down as their attempts to convince Silla that Alissa was real failed. His craggy features remained quiet as his abnormally long fingers manipulated the blue-glazed shard of pottery into place.

Connen-Neute fidgeted—he was hiding in a corner, if the truth be told—and it rankled Alissa that his nervousness was because she had found fault with Useless's plan of action.

There was a scrape as Strell pulled her stew across the table and retreated with it to the hearth. His travel-worn pack rested by the garden door beside Lodesh's far newer one. Alissa eyed the packs in frustration. Strell was ready to go to the coast and charter a boat to find Silla. And as Silla believed Alissa was a dream-demon, someone would have to go fetch them.

Useless set the mended bowl down with a soft clink. His eyes meeting hers across the table were tired but held a daunting determination. "We'll try again tomorrow," he intoned.

"But she's scared of me," Alissa insisted. "She wakes herself up when I find her. Ever since she told Keribdis what I said, the poor girl is convinced that I will make her go feral." Alissa's lips pursed. Silla never would have come to that conclusion by herself. Keribdis must have told her that, and Alissa wasn't pleased to have been shelved with dream-demons and nightmares.

Useless made a noise of disagreement. They all looked up as Lodesh burst into the kitchen. "Where are my other shoes?" the elegant Keeper muttered. His green eyes were pinched as he riffled through his pack. "Has anyone seen my other shoes?" he asked. Waving his hands in bother, he strode out before anyone could answer.

"Tomorrow, I'll share your trance," Useless said as Lodesh disappeared. "If I pickaback my consciousness on yours, we'll share the same vision. I'll calm Silla down and convince her she's not going feral." His expression darkened as he looked at Lodesh's pile. "There's no need to leave the Hold."

"No," Alissa said. "I won't pickaback. Not again."

Surprise pulled Useless straight. The blatant defiance would normally earn her a severe lecture and a withdrawal of privileges, but pickabacking was a dangerously close sharing of mind and emotion. She was within her rights to refuse.

"You pickabacked with Connen-Neute," Useless protested. I'm more skilled than he is in keeping my thoughts to myself. If anyone should be worried, it's me, not you."

Thinking of Beast, Alissa glanced at Connen-Neute. The young Master solemnly shifted his head. The subtle movement told Alissa volumes. If she allowed such a close contact, Useless would see Beast, just as he had. That was a bed of worms she had no wish to hoe. "No," she said.

Lodesh breezed in with a bundle of blankets over his arm.

Never acknowledging them, he threw the blankets beside his pack and strode out. He was humming a dancing tune, his steps smacking the floor loudly in time with the beat.

Useless leaned across the table as Lodesh's footsteps grew faint. "I haven't given anyone permission to leave. Strell is the only one who doesn't need it. You and Connen-Neute are students, and have already demonstrated an incredible inability to keep your mouths shut and your skills to yourself when caught by surprise. Lodesh is on probation because he allowed you to become trapped in the past. No one leaves without an appropriate escort, and I'm not going."

Alissa frowned as she recalled Useless's aversion to large bodies of water. She took a deep breath. The memory of him pinning her wing to the tower's roof flitted through her. Her eyes dropped, and she tried to disappear into the hard kitchen chair. "If it weren't for all the water, we all could fly out and find them," she muttered.

Useless stiffened with an audible breath. "It's not the water, Alissa," he said coldly.

Alissa's first feeling of alarm shifted to overconfidence at his relatively mild response. She glanced at Connen-Neute. Eyes frightened, he shook his head, telling her to stop. Her foot tapped as she weighed her options. She was disagreeing; she wasn't being disrespectful. "We should take a boat," she said. "After all, Strell and Lodesh want to come."

"It's not the water." Motions jerky, Useless stood. He turned his back to her. The hem of his baggy trousers trembled. The warning was clear. Alissa ignored it.

"Besides," she continued, "I wouldn't risk flying off to the horizon without a place to land." She hesitated, knowing that's exactly what Keribdis had convinced the entire Hold of Masters to do. "That's foolish."

"It's not—the water," Useless said, his soft voice tight. He turned, and Alissa was surprised to see an old pain hiding in his weary gaze.

"Then what is it?" she pleaded, just wanting to understand.

Useless took a slow breath before coming to sit across from her. His head drooped, and he stared at the black evenness of the tabletop. A hand ran over his white, short-cropped hair.

"I swore I wouldn't chase after Keribdis this time, and I won't." He looked up, his few wrinkles looking stark. "Not this time. She went too far, and I won't go after her. Not again. Not ever."

Alissa blinked. *Pride?* she wondered. Useless was too proud to go after them? After all this time?

Lodesh entered the room, soft and subdued. He wedged a tin into his pack and gave Strell a quick, sideways jerk of his head. Strell stared blankly, his spoon halfway to his mouth. Lodesh grimaced in meaning, and, grunting, Strell unfolded his long legs and ambled after him with his plate of unfinished stew. Connen-Neute looked at her in pity, then bolted out after them.

Alissa swallowed hard. Alone with Useless, she waited until even the faintest sound of footsteps vanished. "Your pride?" she asked carefully. She hadn't known him long enough to cast judgment, but someone had to pull Useless's head out of the rabbit hole, and she was the only one who might get away with it. "Your pride is going to keep the Hold split?"

"You've been alive for twenty years," he said, his eyes on his mended bowl. "Berate me about pride when you have eight hundred behind you."

"Since when does age have anything to do with foolishness?" she said, knowing she was stepping over the line. But he was hiding something from her—or she was too dense to see it.

"Keribdis is . . ." he started, his golden eyes tired. "Even before we wed, Keribdis was the accepted matriarch of the Hold," he said softly. "Better liked than I, which means more than it should." He hesitated, his long fingers running over the repaired crack in his bowl. "She has an uncanny ability to persuade. I'm the only one who ever stood up to her, telling her when her plans were immoral and not allowing her to break our laws with impunity. If I seek her out, I will be saying her ideas to continue manipulating the plains and foothills are just. She won't listen to even me anymore." He frowned. "And she needs to understand her desires are wrong before she commits any more atrocities."

"Does it matter?" Alissa exclaimed. "Is it worth all this?"

He grimaced, his white eyebrows bunching. "Perhaps it would be best to show you," he said, and her stomach tensed. Useless had never shared any of his memories with her. Ever.

His golden eyes were sad as he read her surprise. "I'm sorry, Alissa," he said as her tracings began to resonate in response to him setting up a ward to trip the lines and relive a memory. "This is a wisdom I had hoped you would never need to learn. It might have been easier had the rest of the Masters stayed lost for a few hundred years more."

"Wisdom isn't bad," Alissa said, worried at what he might show her. "Only the way you use it."

He smiled faintly, settling himself with his hands laced across his front. "Perhaps."

Useless waited until she had her tracings alight with the proper pattern and nodded her readiness. With a surprising ease, she slipped into Useless's memory.

Talo-Toecan stood three steps above everyone upon the stairway in the great hall. As they argued in useless debate, he slammed his hand upon the banister in frustration. It was an unusual display of temper. Only Keribdis noticed, pursing her lips in a derisive admonishment. The tumult of sixty-plus strongly opinionated Masters trying to outdo each other in voicing their opinions continued. "Qui-i-i-iet!" he bellowed, his voice resonating from the ceiling of the great hall. It was four stories up, and there still wasn't enough room for all the egos.

Keribdis's look was ripe with a patronizing disgust, but slowly it grew still. The whoosh of the pendulum overhead, marking time and the spinning of the earth, cut through the tense air. "Yes," Keribdis said into the last murmurs. "Let him dig his own grave without interference."

Talo-Toecan refused to frown. "The only grave is continuing to ignore that scores of recessive alleles have escaped unnoticed and unrecorded," he said with a practiced restraint.

"Yes!" came an impatient shout. "We all agree on that."

Ruen-Tag pushed to the front, his golden eyes bright with agitation. "We must regain control of all three populations, slowing down the occurrence of Keepers," he said, and Talo-Toecan nodded for him to continue. "I like them and all, but I have five students already. One came from a line it shouldn't. It made chaos of my records. I had to go back three generations to find where her family line picked up a recessive coastal allele, of all things. All my charts had to be modified, years of work. I don't have the time—"

"Yes, yes," Talo-Toecan soothed, his hands upraised. "We're all running into the same problem. It only strengthens my position that we need to loosen control further, remove all the barriers, both physical and psychological, and let them mix as they will."

The hall roared into controversy. Talo-Toecan let them rage, turning to the thin, tall windows and the sky beyond. It was a perfect morning for flight: the updrafts steady and strong, the clouds thin and high. What he would give to leave the touchy sensitivities and stubborn tempers and soar away.

But rakus loved to debate. They could be decades deciding what to do, and their callous disregard for their weaker kin disgusted him. They hid in their mountains, the people they surreptitiously manipulated duped into believing rakus were only winged beasts. Ashes, even their Keepers held the secret, bribed into silence with the promise of "magic."

He turned from the sky when a strong voice cut through the subsiding turmoil. "Letting them mix will make things worse," the voice accused. "You admit it yourself, Talo-Toecan."

"For only a short time," he agreed, but they weren't listening. "Two centuries, perhaps."

There was a tug on his sleeve, and he looked down at Wyden. She was flushed for having interrupted him, and his anger softened. "It's impossible to keep track of the pertinent alleles in a homogenous population," she protested gently. "That's why our ancestors divided them in the first place."

"We'd be overrun with Keepers in fifty years," another stated.

"Septhamas and shadufs would be popping up like mush-rooms in a foothills dungheap," came a voice from the back, and there was a chorus of agreement mixed with nervous laughter.

"We could have a transeunt, and not even know it," Kerib-dis said.

Talo-Toecan settled his gaze upon her, thinking she looked splendid in her proud, impassioned defiance. She stood on the floor, her low position in relation to his stance only adding to her inner strength. The babble went still, and Talo-Toecan's brow furrowed. Keribdis had an uncanny, ir-ritating talent of finding the slightest drawback to his ideas and twisting the knife. It wasn't the assemblage he had to convince, it was his wife. The rest would follow her. They al-ways did.

"Yes, Talo-Toecan," someone accused. "What if we had a transeunt and didn't know it? Do you really want one show-ing up at the Hold thinking they were a Keeper? Who knows what we would get?"

He said nothing. Were they all blind?

Ruen-Tag, forever Keribdis's bootlicker, tugged his yellow sash straight as he turned to the assemblage. "We must regain control, if only for that reason," he said, glancing at Keribdis for approval and flushing when she smiled at him. "A transe-unt must be nurtured with discretion and prudent wisdom," he all but oozed, "or they'll have no reason to follow our direc-tion upon reaching their Master potential. They must be painstakingly created, a careful blending of chosen family lines watched through the generations, so we get what we want. You can't allow them to come into existence like a squash from last year's refuse pile."

"Coward," Talo-Toecan muttered. His roving gaze landed on Redal-Stan leaning against the far wall. The old Master had a hand over his eyes as Talo-Toecan ruined what was left of his reputation. By voicing his radical beliefs so stridently, Talo-Toecan had just destroyed what little chance he had left to be allowed to teach a student Master. It didn't matter, he thought dryly. There hadn't been any raku children to teach for almost three hundred years.

"The next transeunt isn't planned for centuries," someone broke in. *"We're wasting time. The question is how to regain control of the three alleles necessary to create a transeunt, and the easiest way to do that is purging the plains of the recessive coastal allele."*

"No," came a hot protest. *"The contamination is minimal in the plains. It's the foothills. They're beginning to breed outside their population again. It doesn't matter if recessive coastal alleles have infiltrated into the plains or foothills if we can just keep them from interbreeding."*

"Reinstate the animosity between their cultures," came a strong voice. *"It's easy, fast, and maybe we can remove some of those coastal alleles in the process. A famine? Diverting the main snowmelt for three years ought to be enough."*

Talo-Toecan closed his eyes to gather his strength. Purging alleles? Reinstating their animosity? What they meant was killing half the world's human population.

"No," Keribdis said, and his eyes flew open. She had put herself into a beam of morning sun, knowing it would glow through her hair like glory itself, knowing exactly what it would do to him. *"We should reduce all three populations to a manageable level. When the dust clears, we can pick up the remaining family lines, make minor cullings where needed, and move forward from there. Everyone will get a needed break. My sabbatical is up in eight years, and I'm not looking forward to having the overabundance of students everyone else has."*

Talo-Toecan divorced himself of the thoughts Keribdis had stirred. *"You don't understand,"* he whispered as he tugged the black sash around his waist straight. *"Limiting the populations isn't a viable option anymore,"* he said loudly. *"It's too late. The recessive alleles have escaped. The populations are mixing. There are too many people to instigate a continent-wide plague or war again. It would be inhuman."*

"Inhuman," Keribdis said, tossing her head. *"Listen to yourself. They don't live very long—and they breed fast enough. In a few centuries we will have Keepers again. And at a manageable level."*

Talo-Toecan's breath came fast in anger. *"I'm not con-*

cerned with the temporary lack of Keepers!" he exclaimed. "Keepers, commoners, you forget they are of us. To treat them as we have in the past is wrong! Killing half the human population to regain control is not management. It's murder!" He was shouting now, trying to finish, but his voice was drowned out in the uproar his claim of equality provoked.

"Your personal views on the matter," Keribdis said, her mocking words cutting through the noise, "don't amount for a fledgling's chance in a windstorm."

"I wouldn't know," he said bitterly. "You never cared enough to give me a child."

The hall went silent. Keribdis drew herself up, glaring magnificently at him. Feet scuffed, and gazes dropped as the rest of the assembly cringed, embarrassed to be witnessing one of their frequent arguments so openly.

Talo-Toecan's hands clenched at his sides. "Killing half the human population to free your morning from work is unacceptable, Keribdis. We should encourage their genetic histories to mix. Masters have been manipulating the human population for the last five thousand years, and what happened? Our numbers have dropped to sixty-four. Sixty-four!" he accused, spinning about. "Only one raku child has survived to maturity in the last three hundred years, and even he went feral! Doesn't that tell you anything?"

He gestured over the assembled Masters in frustration. "They are us! Look at yourselves. It isn't coincidence theirs is the only form we can shift into and return back from. Why do they frighten you?" He pursed his lips, frowning. He had said more than he should.

Keribdis gave him a withering look. Turning, she sedately walked out the front door and into the sun, lightly warding it open as she went so he would be forced to see her shift into her raku form and leap golden and shimmering into the light, a vision of grace untamed. Someone coughed, and Talo-Toecan looked back.

"Meeting adjourned?" Ruen-Tag stammered.

Without a word, Talo-Toecan spun on the stairs to rise to their empty room. He would give her a generous head start, he seethed. Already he could feel the tension building, an undeniable desire for flight, for chase. Nothing else mattered.

For all her well-thought-out protests, Keribdis didn't care about this morning's meeting. But she knew he did. All her spiteful words had been to goad him into chasing her.

And chase her he would, as he always had, thrilling in the hunt as much as she, even as he despised himself for succumbing to her wiles. Despite his years of gently refusing the quiet offers of companionship extended by his female associates, he clung to the hope that Keribdis would someday find within herself the same feelings he held for her.

But he knew he waited in vain. She was too much a beast and too little a Master.

5

Alissa sat cross-legged at the western opening to the holden, brooding in the warmth of the setting sun. The Hold's tremendous cavern of a cellar was hard to get to unless one had wings. The only other way besides flying was a long, cramped tunnel that started in one of the Hold's closets. The capstone was currently warded shut. She knew; she had checked.

Possessing tremendously high ceilings and pillars decorated with the Masters' script, the holden was both a ceremonial chamber and a prison. Masters went feral while learning to shift to a new form, and the holden had been used to confine them until sentience was returned or deemed lost forever. Bailic had perverted its use, cleverly trapping Useless within it for sixteen years while the cowardly man searched for a safe way to put the plains and foothills at war. It had been Strell who had freed him. Alissa came down here when she wanted to avoid Useless, knowing the large cavern made the usually unflappable Master uneasy, even though he had torn the enormous western gate from its hinges shortly after regaining his freedom.

Shadowed and still, the only sound besides the wind was the measured drips of water falling into the cistern behind her.

Alissa had once spent an afternoon trapped here herself, scratching her pet name for Useless upon the cistern's wall next to his real name, Talo-Toecan. Afterward, she had fallen in to nearly drown herself. Alissa flushed at the memory. Lodesh had fished her out. But that had been before she had really known him.

She had come down here to sulk, as only Useless and Connen-Neute could reach her. "And you, Talon," she said, soothing the small bird as Talon worried Alissa's fingers with a gentle beak. Sighing, she looked out over the tremendous drop-off and to the unseen sea. Sunset had turned the clouds pink, and they stood out sharp against the deep blue of the evening sky. The sun had beat upon the flat rock face all afternoon until even her human eyes could see the updraft as a shimmering waver.

She was packed, Alissa thought glumly. Connen-Neute was packed. Strell was packed. Even Lodesh had managed to whittle his pile down to something he could carry. But Useless wasn't budging, having cloistered himself in his room the last two days to avoid everyone.

The kestrel chittered a welcome as the shadow of wings covered the shattered remains of the western gate. It was Useless, and Alissa listlessly scooted sideways to make room for him to land. Her hair flew wildly as he back-winged before her, expertly clearing the low opening and finding the floor. There was a tug on her thoughts as he shifted from a raku to his human form.

Alissa ignored him. Knees pulled to her chin, she clasped her arms around herself. She had nothing to say he hadn't already heard.

Useless tugged his black sash around his waist straight until the tips of it brushed the floor. Saying nothing, he sat cross-legged beside her and watched the sun set. Slowly the sound of the dripping water became obvious again. Alissa squinted at him from the edge of her sight, then looked away. "Let me go find them, Useless," she said. "I'm the only one who can."

"I know," he said shortly.

"I'm the only one who can hear Silla this far away," she asserted.

"I won't argue that with you," he agreed, not giving way at all.

"I'd be very careful. I'd follow your rules," she pleaded. "I wouldn't complain."

"That," he said dryly as he turned to her, "would be a miracle in itself."

Frustrated, Alissa exclaimed, "I am not Keribdis! I'm not running away from you!"

His eyes closed against the sun, and he took a slow breath. "I know."

A miserable puff of sound escaped her as she slumped. "Then why are you here?"

Useless opened his eyes. For a long time, he was silent. "You know you are the only Master I've taught?" he finally said, and Alissa nodded. "Over eight hundred years old—five hundred years of teaching experience—and never granted the opportunity to take a raku child for a student, only Keepers. At first, they said it was because I was too busy or held too many responsibilities. Later, there were no children to teach. But I always knew it was because they were afraid I would pass on my strong beliefs, shifting the balance of power in the Hold."

The grievous hurt in his eyes froze her words of sympathy.

"The only thing I was ever allowed to teach a raku child was how to fly," he whispered.

Alissa said nothing, almost frightened at what he might say next.

"I would like to teach Silla how to fly," he said softly, and she felt a stirring of hope.

He was silent for the span of three heartbeats. "Go," he said.

Astonished, she took a breath and held it. Shoes scraping on the floor, she turned to face him, reading the worry behind his decision. "Go," he repeated, his jaw muscles clenching. "All of you. Bring them back to me."

Her heart leapt. "We can go?"

A faint smile broke over him, somehow making him look old as his white hair and few wrinkles did not. "Did you ever doubt it? Lodesh didn't."

"We're going!" she shouted in her thoughts to Connen-

Neute. His enthusiastic response resonated in her mind as Alissa flung herself at Useless. He gave a startled grunt as she hugged the imposing Master. "Oh, Useless. Thank you!" she babbled, putting herself at a proper distance again. "We'll find them. You'll see."

"I fully expect you will," he said, a worried frown passing over him. "Let's all have a good dinner," he said as he rose to his feet in an effortless motion, "and then you'll leave tonight by starlight. From here."

"Tonight!" she exclaimed, getting to her feet.

Useless nodded, squinting at the lowering sun. "The up-drafts coming off the cliff face are strong enough that you, Connen-Neute, and I can manage Strell and Lodesh's weight in a slow glide most of the way. We can set down a day from the coast in the salt swamp. It will save you weeks of travel. I'll leave you there, and you can continue on alone."

Alissa tucked her hair behind an ear in worry. "I can't carry the weight of a man."

"Which is why you will have the packs—in case you drop one." Useless moved forward until his toes edged the drop-off. Surprise crossed his features as Connen-Neute's massive wings eclipsed the light. "What are you doing here?" Useless asked as he took Alissa's elbow and moved them to the shadows so Connen-Neute could land.

"We're going," he thought excitedly as his claws scraped the opening. *"I wanted—"*

"You aren't," Useless interrupted.

Alissa turned to him in surprise, and the old Master sent a terse, *"Hush,"* into her mind.

Connen-Neute's head drew back in surprise, and his wings drooped. With a tug on her awareness, he shifted, vanishing into a pearly mist to coalesce down to a tall, thin man standing with his heels hanging over the edge. His long face was pinched in distress, and Alissa looked at Useless in surprise. He had just said Connen-Neute was going.

"I'm going," Connen-Neute said. His breathing was fast, and his solemn face looked frightened as he tugged his red sash. "Technically, you're not my teacher. Keribdis is. I should rejoin her now that I know she lives."

Useless crossed his arms. "You never wanted Keribdis as

your teacher. You only accepted because you knew she would be instructing the next transeunt."

The rims of Connen-Neute's ears reddened as he flicked a glance at Alissa. "She is still my teacher." He adjusted his long sleeves, pulling his arms into them so the hem covered his fingers. "I can hide my hands and wear a hat," he said.

"It's too risky." Useless shook his head. "I'll not be responsible for starting a panic with the appearance of long-fingered men with golden eyes abroad to steal children."

There was another tug on her thoughts as Connen-Neute crafted a red scarf matching the one around his waist. He bound it about his head to cover his eyes. "I have been burned," he said softly. "And I've wrapped myself so no one has to look upon my ruined face and hands."

Useless sighed and turned away. Alissa thought she saw him hide a pleased smile.

"I'll wear them all the time," Connen-Neute persuaded. "Even on my hands. It will be safer than sending her alone with a wandering piper and a cursed Keeper. And if I'm with them, I can call you when Alissa eventually hurts herself."

Peeved, Alissa smacked him lightly on the shoulder with the back of her hand.

Useless made a soft groan. "All right," he said. "You can go."

"What?" she cried. "I had to beg for three days. I cleaned your shoes. I made candied apples. I swept your balcony. He gets to go with only that?"

Useless coughed to hide a chuckle. *"There was never any question as to whether he was going,"* he replied mentally, the tightness of his thought telling Alissa she would be the only one to hear. *"As he said, someone has to keep an eye on you. But if he couldn't find the courage to ask himself, then he ought not go."*

Alissa smiled, seeing the slow but honest building of Connen-Neute's nerve.

"I just hope he doesn't lose his new confidence when he finds Keribdis," Useless added sourly, and Alissa went worried. Keribdis was trained to spot Beast, and Alissa would have to work hard to keep her second consciousness hidden.

"Go tell Lodesh and Strell," Useless said aloud. "They can

bring their packs down the tunnel. I've unwarded the capstone already. With any luck, Lodesh will decide to stay once he knows he's going by air."

Alissa grinned. Lodesh was terrified of flying, but she knew he wouldn't risk Strell traveling alone with her. Brimming with enthusiasm, she almost danced to the drop-off to prepare to shift, wanting to tell them in person. Toes edging the deadly fall, she hesitated. "You'll let me go halfway across the world, but you won't let me cross the plains to find my mother?" she asked.

The amusement in Useless's face was easy to read in the orange light of the setting sun. "You can get in less trouble aboard a ship than if I let you loose on an entire continent again."

"Useless . . ." she cajoled, and his eyes narrowed.

"Not another word," he cautioned. "Or you'll be staying here with me."

Her mouth snapped shut, and she stared at him, thinking the situation grossly unfair. The Master was driven entirely by his egotistical urges—but she wouldn't say anything this time.

"This is a courtship excursion between you and Connen-Neute, as far as I'm concerned," he continued, and Alissa and Connen-Neute exchanged tired looks. "Or would you rather pick berries—"

"No," Alissa quickly said.

Useless turned pointedly to Connen-Neute.

The tall, awkward Master seemed to jump. "No," he agreed belatedly, the dullness of his words standing in stark contrast to his excitement slipping unbidden into her mind. "This is fine."

6

The wind slipping over her was chill, and she imagined she could smell salt in it as she flew. The sun was long set. She moved like a ghost, hidden from the superstitious coastal folk by height and shadow. Her frustration that Useless would let her go across the ocean to find his kin yet refused to give her leave to find her mother had settled to a familiar, dull irritation. Going anywhere was better than being stuck at the Hold.

Clutched in her hind clawlike feet were the packs. They were slung in a tarp hanging from her mirth-wood staff. Alissa squinted into the night to find Connen-Neute ahead of her. The young raku was clearly straining, more from worry that he might drop Lodesh, Alissa thought, than from the weight of the Keeper dangling from a taloned hind foot. Behind her was Useless with Strell. Alissa had fallen appreciably in altitude, and at her soft inquiry, Beast beat their wings three times so as to rise and match Connen-Neute's path.

"Set down, Connen-Neute," came Useless's thought into hers, and Alissa winced. *"We're close enough."*

"I'm fine," Alissa contended, feeling her wing muscles ache all the way to her tail. *"Just a bit farther, and we can make the coast by tomorrow afternoon."*

"Which is why we're setting down now," Useless said, and Connen-Neute obediently turned into a downward spiral, disappearing in the tall vegetation. She angled to join them, glad to see the black ribbon of a stream only a stone's throw away. As she hovered, Connen-Neute vanished in a swirl of mist to coalesce down to his smaller form. Lodesh hunched against the wind from her wings, and the young Master pulled him out of the way for her to land.

Alissa dropped the tarp at the edge of the pressed oval of grass, quickly following it down. The wind didn't abate at all when she landed. If anything, it became worse. She squinted up to find Useless hovering with Strell. Immediately she shifted to her usual form to give her teacher space to land.

The air felt colder as she reappeared, and she held the hair from her eyes and tried to find Redal-Stan's watch and get out of the way before Useless landed on it or her or both. Bits of vegetation and tufts of grass flew wildly, and her hair tangled. She gasped as Strell hit the ground next to her in a smooth crouch. Squinting from the raku-made wind, he took her elbow to move her to the edge of the flattened grass. Useless, though, simply landed to press out an adjacent area.

The wind suddenly ceased. Relieved, they all straightened. As a raku, Useless held his head high above the grass and scanned the black horizon as if expecting trouble. Alissa flashed Strell a smile and bent to look for her watch. "Here," he said, taking her hand and dropping the ring of metal into her palm. Her smile deepened. One of these days, she was going to lose it.

She slipped it into a pocket, thinking the night was completely different through her human senses: the shadows were darker, the buzz from the insects was louder, and the distant rolls of thunder that wouldn't reach them until tomorrow had vanished. Even the grass was taller than she had imagined, waving high above her head where it hadn't been flattened. Peering into the dark, she looked for Talon. The small bird hadn't been able to keep up. Alissa wasn't worried. Talon had found her in thicker surroundings than this.

There was a tug on her tracings as Useless shifted to his human guise. Another tug—this time subsiding into a steady pull—and a head-sized globe of light came into existence.

Useless set it down as if it were a campfire. Hands hidden in his expansive sleeves, he ran his unsatisfied gaze over her clothes. She knew he wasn't happy she had appeared wearing her sturdy, more practical Keeper garb rather than the refined Master attire she was capable of.

"I'll head back to the Hold now," he said, giving her a final, sour look. "I won't slap at insects and sleep on dirt when I have a bed a short flight away."

Alissa's breath caught. He was leaving already? She thought she'd have all night to say good-bye. "Um, Useless?" she said, hating the way her voice went up at the end.

Lodesh drew his leather hat down and shifted from foot to foot. "I think I saw a dead tree on the way in," he said, pointing. "Help me get some wood?" he asked Connen-Neute.

"I thought your eyes were shut," Connen-Neute said, and Lodesh frowned. "Oh! That tree!" the young Master exclaimed.

Lodesh sighed in exasperation, giving Useless a respectful nod of farewell before striding into the tall grass. Connen-Neute followed, hesitating briefly as he, too, said his good-bye to Useless. A faint buzz of private conversation drifted at the edge of Alissa's awareness, and she grew worried when Connen-Neute smiled wickedly at her before vanishing into the grass.

Strell took a step after them, then mumbling something about water, yanked an empty sack from the pile of belongings. Slapping at the returning insects, he went the other way to the stream. Alissa turned to find Useless rummaging among their packs. "Here. These are for you," he said, extending a small pouch to her.

Alissa's brow rose as she peered inside the palm-sized sack. She shook it upside down, and three silver bells fell ringing into her hand. A delighted smile came over her. "Thank you, Useless," she said, nudging one with a finger. "They're beautiful."

Useless's white eyebrows were gray in the dim light. "You wear them. On your ankle."

She warmed at the idea of drawing attention to her feet. "My ankle?" she questioned.

"It's a harmless tradition. Everyone wears them on the

coast. The women, I mean. Put them on a string or something."
Running a hand over his short hair, he winced. "M-m-m-m, if
everything is settled, I'll go."

Alissa tucked the bells in her pocket. "Useless . . ."

"Tell everyone good-bye for me. I expect to hear from you
every night at sunset until you are so far away we can't reach
each other. With any luck, we won't lose contact at all."

"Useless, I—"

"Keep Connen-Neute talking aloud," he said, his eyes
searching the thin updrafts. "Don't let him slip back into his
usual thought-speech. I expect him to be fully verbalized
when you get back. No shifting to raku once you find people.
And you burning-well better not do anything to link rakus to
Masters. Who knows what they will do if they figure that
out?"

They had been over this at dinner, and she took his long
hand so he would stop. A heavy sigh escaped him, and he
dropped his gaze. "You're the first Master I have taught," he
said as he drew his hand from her and put it on her shoulder.
"Don't let Keribdis make you feel as if that leaves you lacking. You're an excellent student."

Alissa's stomach clenched at the reminder of the woman,
and he stepped back. In a swirl of gray fog, he shifted. He
towered over her as a raku, his color almost amber in the dim
light of his ward. *"But I wouldn't let on that I've already
given you some of the more complex wards,"* he added soundlessly, and he leapt into the air.

She covered her face as the grass hissed and waved. The
camp went black as he reached a raku length above the
ground and his light vanished. Arms clasped tight about herself, she watched him gain altitude, wings pushing against the
still air strongly. No more than a shadow against the dark sky,
he angled east to the Hold. Only now did he whisper, *"Good-
bye, Alissa,"* into her thoughts.

Her throat tightened, and she turned to find Strell watching
her from the edge of camp with knowing eyes. Sniffing once,
she made a light to replace Useless's. The rich scent of river
muck pulled her attention to Strell. He was soaked to his
knees, and her eyebrows rose.

"The bank was softer than I expected," he said as he set

the water sack down. Shaking the muck and slime from his
hands, he gingerly reached into the inner pocket of his coat
and pulled out his pipe wrapped in a roll of leather. He carefully set the instrument aside on his pack. "Least these didn't
get wet," he said, more to himself than her. Dropping to the
ground, he tore a hank of grass from the earth and tried to
clean the mud from himself.

A smile that was almost a smirk came over Alissa as she
set her light down. Her hair swung forward, and she impatiently tucked it out of the way. Her eyes fell upon the roll of
leather, widening as she recognized it. It was her papa's old
map, the one that showed the way to the Hold. He was using
it to wrap his pipe with? Her lips parted in surprise, and she
glanced at Strell, flicking mud from his hands as he scraped it
from his worn boots. He had gotten the map years ago in a
trade with Alissa's mother for a length of coastal fabric, and
Alissa had been trying to get it back ever since.

Her envious gaze lingered on the copper-colored hair ribbon binding it to the length of mirth wood. That had been
her mother's, too. Strell wouldn't trade that to her, either.
Standing silently before him, she arched her eyebrows hope-
fully. Seeing where her attention was, he shook his head.
Disgusted, Alissa glanced at her pack and the ribbon her
mother had used to tie her cup to her pack over three years
ago. The once-bright copper color was grimy and stained. It
was too filthy to wear, but she needed something to tie her
hair back with. "Strell?" she questioned. "Trade me the ribbon at least?"

Strell rubbed the back of his hand over his ugly, infant
beard. "No," he drawled.

Frustrated, she came close, wrinkling her nose at the rank
smell of mud. "Please?"

Strell's eyes grew mischievous, making him look more
like a vagabond than ever. His newest preoccupation with fa-
cial hair didn't help. "Only a cad gives away a woman's heartfelt sign of affection. Besides, you might shift while wearing
it, and it would be gone forever."

Alissa took a breath to argue, letting it out in a puff of
sound, deciding he was probably right. Grumbling, she fought
to tug the tarp from under the packs, taking her frustrations out

on the well-oiled cloth. The entire situation reminded her of when she and Strell had met. Ashes, he had been more irritating than a wasp bumping the ceiling. Nothing had changed since then.

She glanced at him as he industriously scraped at the mud. His sharp features were blurred under the shadow of the old hat she had given him when Talon shredded his original one. Slowly her anger eased, and a smile crept over her. Struck by an idea, she scuffed the ground with the toe of her shoe until she loosened a handful of dirt from under the thick mat of grass. Grinning, she extended half to Strell.

"What?" he questioned, peering up at her and wiping his hand before accepting it.

She smiled. "Rock in the east, keeps away the beast," she said with a mocking seriousness, throwing a clump in the proper direction. It was a charm from the coast he had once used to protect their camp for the night—though he insisted he never believed in it.

Strell's mouth turned up. His eyes glinted in her warded light as he stood. Gaze fixed to hers, he chose a rock from the cup his hand made and tossed it to his right. "Stone in the north, spirits won't come forth," he said, his low, musical voice soft with the sound of remembrance.

Taking a step closer, she dropped a rock. "Pebble in the south, seals the raku's mouth."

The dirt sifted through his fingers. Strell took her elbows to pull her willingly closer. The pungent smell of river mud filled her senses. Her pulse sent tingles to her toes. "Sand in the west, will protect you best," he whispered.

His hands were warm on her, and a wave of emotion sent her heart racing at what might follow. The remaining dirt fell from her hand. The stiff bristles on his face made him look more unkept than usual. "What's this?" she said, smiling as she ran a nail over his prickly cheek.

"A hobby." His eyes were as soft as his voice.

"I don't like it," she said mischievously, not moving from his arms.

"You will."

Her heart pounded. Twin feelings of desire and common sense flashed through her. She couldn't. If she changed the distance she had been keeping between them, the rivalry between Strell and Lodesh would turn ugly. "I don't want anything to change," she whispered, watching his brown eyes for any sign of anger.

"Nothing changes if only you and I know," he answered. He was poised at the moment of pulling her closer—waiting.

She closed her eyes to find the strength to make her hands fall from about his neck. Taking her hesitation as acquiescence, he drew her closer. "Strell . . ." she protested, wanting nothing more than to willingly respond. But she looked down, putting her forehead against his chest to hide her frustration as well as ease the sting of her refusal. "I can't."

A *harrumph* startled her into taking a step back. Strell's hands fell from her with a guilty swiftness, and she spun. Connen-Neute stood at the edge of the flattened grass, his white teeth glinting in the glow of Alissa's warded light. Mortified, she flushed. "Strell," the young Master said, "you're supposed to be Alissa's and my chaperone, not the other way around."

Alissa's blush deepened as Lodesh pushed around him. The Keeper let his scanty armful of wood clatter to the ground. "It's not sand *in* the west," he said sourly as he brushed his immaculate clothes clean. "It's sand *from* the west."

"When did you become a minstrel?" Strell said, frustration soft in his voice.

"I was there when Redal-Stan wrote it." Jaw muscles tight, Lodesh tried to scuff through the thick mat of grass to make a spot for the fire. "Bone and ash, do you know how well sound carries out here? Show some restraint, desert man."

Face burning, Alissa became very busy with the tarp. Strell's motions were sharp and abrupt as he dropped back to the grass and continued to clean the cuff of his trousers. The smell from the new mud on her shoulders was obvious, making her more embarrassed. Connen-Neute shifted, and as a sleek raku the size of a small house, he edged Lodesh out of the way and cleared a spot for the fire down to bare earth with a single swipe of his taloned hand.

"Thank you," Lodesh said, clearly peeved as he went to rummage in the packs. With a tweak on her awareness, four gray cushions made from the same cloth as Connen-Neute's vest winked into existence. Clearly put out, Lodesh sat on one as he pulled his pack closer and found his striker rocks and charred tow.

The bells tucked in her pocket made a soft chime as she slapped at the insect on her neck. She started as she felt a large field sweep over her. Eyes wide, she turned to Connen-Neute. *"It will keep the insects out,"* the raku thought, sinking down into a comfortable crouch.

As Strell continued to scrape at his trousers, Lodesh arranged what sparse wood he had found into the shape of a fire. Making a nearby nest of tinder, he pulled a spark from his striker rocks and set the charred tow glowing. There was a tug on her thoughts as Connen-Neute warded the wood alight. Lodesh closed his eyes in a suffering blink. "Can I make tea?" he asked Connen-Neute as he patted his tiny fire out. "Can I make the tea all by myself?"

The young Master blinked his great eyes good-naturedly. Frowning, Lodesh pulled a double-wrapped packet of tea from his belongings.

Alissa's eyes widened; she hadn't thought to bring tea. "Is there enough for everyone?" she asked, and Lodesh's frustration dropped from him like a mask.

"You'd like some tea?" he questioned, beaming as he moved to sit on the cushion beside her. "I'll make you some."

Strell made a rude noise, and Lodesh turned. "Piper," the Keeper mocked, "you smell."

Strell froze, his stubbled face looking worried. "I—uh—didn't have room to pack a proper change of clothes," he said. Alissa winced. She could carry only so much. "I was going to buy something at the coast," he finished, making her feel worse as he moved himself to the edge of camp and continued to scrape the mud from his lower legs.

Alissa frowned at Lodesh, but her anger stopped short and fell to ash at the surprising, heavy look of promise she found in his eyes. Her thoughts flashed back to him catching her with Strell, and she became worried. She had said no, but she knew Lodesh wouldn't stand by and do nothing. He looked so young, it was hard to remember he had a lifetime of sly wisdom to draw upon. She had once heard him tell Strell that he had no qualms about waiting Useless out. He had bided three centuries for Alissa. What were a few years more?

He smiled, and her pulse leapt as she recalled their dance under the mirth trees the fall before last—or three centuries ago, depending upon how one looked at it. The wild, desire-filled emotions he had stirred that night had all but persuaded her to abandon Strell. She knew Lodesh's love was real and that he would never hurt her again, but the memory of his betrayal haunted her. Being trapped in the past had been a confusing mix of heartache and joy. The younger Lodesh, innocent and unaware of who she really was, had been an unexpected anchor, keeping her sane. And she had fallen in love with him, just as the wiser, older, world-weary Lodesh had planned.

"Um, Lodesh?" she stammered, flicking her attention between him and Strell.

"Your tea is ready," he said softly, his eyes unmoving from hers.

Taking a quick, disconcerted breath, she resettled herself upon one of Connen-Neute's cushions. The raku had curled up like a great cat at the edge of camp. His second eyelid drooped to turn his gold eyes to red as he drowsily watched the heat stream from the fire.

Lodesh poured her a cup of tea. His gaze never left her, and Alissa nervously flicked her attention between his eyes and the rising level of liquid. But he knew exactly when to stop. "Thank you," she said, and he leaned forward, tucking a strand of her hair behind an ear. He smelled like mirth wood, all pine and apple.

"You're welcome," he said, his light words standing in contrast to his body language.

Her gaze went unseeing as images of Ese' Nawoer's grove sweet with blossoms swirled through her. Alissa felt her resolve weaken. "Lodesh?" she stammered. He took her hand, testing to see if she would lean into him if he, by chance, pulled. His grip was warm, and his green eyes made her forget.

"By the Wolves, stop it, Lodesh," came Strell's irate voice from the shadows, and she pulled her hand from Lodesh's. "Have the decency to wait until I'm not watching."

Connen-Neute's eyes slitted open, and he rumbled an agreement.

Grinning, Lodesh gracefully eased back from her, and Alissa breathed easier. Shifting suddenly, he dug awkwardly in a pocket. "Here," he said with a surprising formality as he extended a closed fist. "I'd like you to have this. You wear it. On your ankle."

Alissa held her hand out, and with a soft chime, a tiny bell weighted her palm. Her eyebrows rose, and she set her cup aside. *Another bell?*

"It's a traveling-to-the-coast present," Lodesh said, his green eyes shining. "The last time I was there, all the affluent women had them. Will you wear it for me?"

"Yes. Yes, of course," she said softly as she brought it close. "Thank you, Lodesh." It was smaller than the ones Useless had given her—barely the size of her pinky nail—and by the amount of tarnish, older as well. Its sound, though, was sweeter, like water over rocks, and she couldn't help but smile. Two of them, now, had given her bells. What were they for?

There was a strong pull on her awareness as the massive shadow of Connen-Neute vanished in a mist of pearly white, swirling down to his human shift. "I've got one for you, too, Alissa," the young Master said as he reappeared, sitting down upon the cushion that had just held his head and dragging his pack to him.

Sure now something was going on, she held out a hand across the dying fire to take the bell as he extended it. The cool sphere was much like Useless's, tinkling merrily as it rolled in her grip.

"You're supposed to wear them on your left foot if you aren't married," Connen-Neute said. "Isn't that a quaint tradition? It's nice you have two of them."

Strell came forward, his pack in his grip as he knelt at her other side. "Alissa? I was going to give this to you tomorrow, but—"

She turned, eyebrows high. "Another bell?"

Saying nothing, he fished a bell out from his pocket and handed it to her. It was appreciably bigger than the others, the dent in it making an inharmonious clink. "I—uh—made an ankle strap for you, too. See?" he stammered, his neck red.

He held it out, and when Alissa refused to take it, he set it cautiously beside her on the ground. It looked like the strap he had once tried to fasten around Talon's feet, and her eyes narrowed at the comparison.

Lodesh leaned toward Connen-Neute. "Where did *he* get a bell?" he whispered loudly.

Strell's face darkened. "I bought it. It took me two winters, but I *bought* it. Where did you get yours? A drawer in the citadel?"

Alissa took a breath. "All right. What are these for?" Not one of them met her eyes in the suspicious silence. "You all gave me one. They must be important. What are they for?"

"I told you," Connen-Neute said with wide, innocent eyes. "It's to show the marital status of a coastal woman. I didn't want you to be stared at. I know how you like to fit in."

Lodesh topped off her tea. "They make a lovely sound when you dance."

She turned to Strell. His gaze had dropped. "Bells are used to show status on the coast, Alissa," he said softly. "I bought it for my sister. I'd—like you to have it."

Alissa's anger vanished. His entire family had been lost years ago in a rare desert flood. That he would think to give it to her touched her heart. "Status?" she questioned. "The more bells, the higher your standing?"

Strell's mouth opened in obvious surprise. "You aren't angry?" he asked. "I thought you'd think it was demeaning to ask you to wear a bell to show your worth."

"Uh, no." She laced his bell onto the strap, embarrassed she cared about something so fleeting as status. "Everyone shows status somehow. The plains by how long the women grow their hair and the number of children they can keep alive. The foothills by how many sheep they have and the amount of trinkets they buy from the plains. I haven't figured out how status is shown in the Hold." She thought for a moment. "Perhaps by how far up in the tower your room is?" she said, and Connen-Neute shrugged. "Anyway, I've—uh—never had any status." She winced upon recalling the misery of market day when she covered her fair hair with a scarf and tried not to talk for fear of revealing the accent her plains mother had instilled in her. "It might be nice—for a change?" she finished.

Strell and Lodesh looked at each other, their surprise that she cared about status making her ashamed, almost. But burn it to ash, it was hard to hold her head up when whispers of "half-breed" trailed behind her like hungry curs.

His face slipping into understanding, Strell said, "A man's status on the coast is that of his mother's until he marries; then it becomes that of his wife's. It has given rise to the state that though men earn the money, the women generally have it all. Their husbands give them everything to heighten their own status by association. With three bells, I'd say you're equal to a merchant's daughter, or perhaps a small ship holder." He ducked his head, smiling as he met her gaze from under his shock of dark hair. "Congratulations, Alissa. You're rich."

Returning his grin, Alissa jiggled the strap to make them chime. Alone they were nice, but together they made music. Tomorrow, when no one was looking, she would put them on her ankle where they belonged, adding Useless's three as her secret.

Strell looked decidedly relieved as he took up his pipe and ran through a quick scale to warm the mirth wood his pipe was made of. "What would you like to hear, Alissa?" he asked. "I need to practice, and it won't hurt to have a little money to spend on you. Seeing as you're now wealthy and all," he added, his eyes glinting.

Her eyebrows rose at his rare offer to entertain requests. Feeling magnanimous, she tossed a careless hand and said, "Your choice."

Clearly pleased she let him decide, he sent the first phrase of "Taykell's Adventure" into the air. Her breath caught, and her eyes went wide. Her eyes darted to Lodesh, blushing as she recalled the bawdy verses they had composed together under his mirth trees while she had been trapped in the past. "Anything but that!" she amended.

Connen-Neute all but snickered, and Lodesh grinned at her obvious fluster. Strell paused, clearly knowing something was going on but not having a clue as to why one of her favorite tunes now made her blush. Slowly he began to play a lullaby, eyeing Lodesh warily.

Alissa settled back on her cushion. She gave the three men an honest smile, content to sip Lodesh's tea while Strell played what he would.

7

Alissa inhaled deeply, thinking the scent of dead fish and too many people was almost an assault. The combined sights and sounds of the coast were overwhelming, but she smiled, insufferably pleased with them. The afternoon's rain had slacked to a faint mist, disappearing under the strong sun. Moisture glistened on the planked road—a landlocked dock, really.

The way had been covered to keep the busy thoroughfare from turning into a slurry of mud from the rain that Strell said fell daily. Whereas the wooden road would be an extravagance anywhere else, here, made of wood too inferior for shipbuilding, it was a commonplace luxury. And over it all was the faint chiming of tiny bells to draw her eyes downward to feet demurely covered, teasing as to what might be hiding about the women's ankles.

It had come as a shock to Alissa to find that not everyone wore shoes. Since sighting her first pair of mud-covered, hairy-toed feet, she had kept her horrified eyes firmly above knee level. Strell and Lodesh had banded together to tease her, exchanging clever plays on words and sly descriptions until she was red-faced and tight-lipped. She had been more than a little peeved they hadn't warned her, but it was nice to see them drop their rivalry for a time.

Even so, the coast fascinated her. Strell had once said everyone looked different at the coast, and he was right. Though he stood taller than most, the difference wasn't unduly great. Her skin was lighter than theirs, but not so anyone would stare. And a few people had hair as fair as she did, so she didn't feel out of place. Everyone was different, the only unifying feature being the wide-brimmed hats made of reeds that everyone wore to keep off the rain. She walked confidently on Strell's arm as the passing people eyed her with varying amounts of interest.

Alissa thought the attention might be from Talon safely perched on her shoulder inasmuch as from her odd dress and jangling walk. Her bells put out a recognizably louder noise than most, and she suspected Strell knew she had more than the three they had given her.

The looks might also be attributed to Connen-Neute. He was nearly a head taller than everyone except Strell. His eyes and hands were bandaged in several of Alissa's black sashes such that he could still see through the thin fabric. Lodesh was making a great show of leading him by the elbow as if he were blind. Together they must make an odd sight, strolling down the wood-planked road in the slackening mist.

Bringing up the rear was a rattling pushcart with their belongings. Upon reaching the outskirts of the busy coastal village, Lodesh had rented it and the services of a young boy for the day. He had claimed they would raise too many eyebrows if they carried their belongings on their backs like paupers. Alissa thought he was being lazy, but it was nice to feel important.

"Look, Strell," she said, pointing at the barren trunks of trees clustered above and behind the roofs of the surrounding buildings. "What do you think happened to those trees?"

Strell leaned close, amusement in his eyes. "Those are masts," he whispered. "From the ships and boats. See the ropes hanging on them? And the bound sails?"

She winced, feeling stupid, but she had no idea they would be that tall.

"We'll go down for a look before it gets dark if we have the chance," Strell added. "I want to try to find a clothier before we get a room."

"Maybe I can find a hair ribbon, too," Alissa added as Lodesh snickered. Her tone hinted at an accusation, and Strell stiffened.

The scent of mirth wood filled her senses as Lodesh appeared at her side. "Let me buy you a ribbon, Alissa," the well-dressed man graciously offered.

Alissa beamed. "Why, thank you, Lodesh. You are the gentleman."

Strell's grip on her arm tightened. "I'll buy you a ribbon," he said, his neck reddening.

"Lodesh wants to get me one," she said, pleased it bothered Strell.

"Look," Strell said, pointing. "Let's ask that man where the nearest clothier is. I want to get you a ribbon." Pulling Alissa away from Lodesh's grasp, he angled them across the street to where a man stood with a cart of late bread draped with a cloth to keep off the weather and flies. Halfway there, a piercing shout of recognition brought them to a halt.

"Strell?" a woman called exuberantly. "Strell! By the Hounds. You're back?"

Surprised, Alissa spun. A tiny woman with a child on her hip was striding across the street with no regard to her safety. The chimes on her ankle seemed to magically open a path. Alissa dropped back, falling into a stunned shock as the woman flung herself at Strell. Turning to keep the child on her hip out of the way, she wrapped one arm about his neck and pulled him down to her height, kissing him soundly on the mouth.

"What the Wolves —" Connen-Neute whispered into her mind. The intrusion jolted Alissa out of her surprise, and she shot a black look at Connen-Neute's grin.

"Look at you!" the ribbon-decked woman scolded fondly as Strell tried to disentangle himself. He was flushing, and his embarrassment only made Alissa all the more peeved. "You said you were leaving," the short woman scolded. "Have you been down-coast all this time? Was that just one of your tales to put me off? Ashes, what happened to your finger? It's half gone! And this?" she cried, tracing a ringed finger across his whiskered cheek. "Wolves and hagfish, a beard? You'd never grow one for me, you cad. Where are you staying? I'll have your room aired out, and—"

"Lacy!" Strell cried, placing a hand over her tiny, pretty mouth. "Let me talk."

Eyes wide, the small woman glanced at Alissa, Connen-Neute, and Lodesh as if only now realizing they were with him. She stepped back and put her free hand to her hat. It made her look all the more comely, and Alissa felt herself warm. Strell had spent six years on the coast. Of course people would know him.

"Lacy," Strell said, pulling Alissa stumbling forward as if a shield. "This is Alissa." He ran a hand over his chin, and a puff of what Alissa thought was disappointment escaped the woman. "She's traveling with me, as are Connen-Neute and—ah—his guide, Lodesh."

"Guide?" Connen-Neute muttered into Alissa's thoughts, and she frowned, not liking Strell's introduction. A traveling companion? Was that what she was?

"Good tide," Lacy murmured to Alissa. Her gaze ran from Talon on her shoulder to the mud on her shoes peeping out from under her damp hem. Something in her expression carried a mocking question, and Alissa suddenly realized she was far out of her element, not knowing the first thing about the devious subtleties of society.

"Steady wind," Alissa said tightly, remembering the proper response Strell had told her this morning. Her jaw clenched as she refused to let this tart of a woman make her feel lacking.

Lacy turned to the two men. She smiled, her teeth standing out against her dark skin. "May the Hounds keep from your heels," she said formally to Lodesh and Connen-Neute, her eyes shifting from Connen-Neute's bandages to Lodesh's yellow hair.

Lodesh beamed, stepping forward to take her hand. "And the Navigator's Wolves from your dock, mistress ship-holder," he said, touching the top of her fingers to his chin.

Alissa's mood darkened further. *Lodesh, too?* she thought.

Strell started. "Ship? How would you know—"

Releasing Lacy's hand, Lodesh stepped back and made a grand flourish. "By the music of her steps," he said. "Such a melody can only mean she has a ship."

Not liking Lacy at all, Alissa retreated to take Connen-Neute's elbow. If Strell and Lodesh wanted to make fools of themselves, that was fine with her. This woman with her bells and child was no threat. Clearly distressed by her withdrawal, Strell fidgeted. Lacy, though, was beaming, probably thinking she had scored points in whatever game she was playing.

"Ma'hr Lodesh is right," she said, giving her foot a shake under her skirt. Alissa smugly thought the sound wasn't nearly as nice as her string of bells. "I have a boat," Lacy said. "A boat and a husband to pilot it. She's a small vessel, but large enough to make it up-coast in winter, if need be." Lacy leaned closer, her eyes going sad. "It's what I thought I wanted, but if the truth be told, I miss the comfort of my husband much of the time."

Strell's face went slack in alarm, and he took a step back. "It doesn't look as if you're ailing too badly, Lacy," he said, glancing at her daughter. Then he hesitated, looking closer at the child. Seeing his brow furrowed, Lacy subtly shook her head. Strell took a relieved breath, and Alissa's eyes widened at the unspoken question. Suddenly Lacy's game had an entirely new significance.

"You're hurting me," Connen-Neute said into her thoughts, and Alissa forced her grip on his arm to ease.

The child on Lacy's hip began to fuss, and the woman jiggled her. "I married the spring after you left. This is little Mantia, born the next fall. Had I known you were staying—"

"I did leave," Strell protested. "I never intended to come back."

"You named your daughter after a fish?" Alissa asked.

Lacy smiled, and Alissa forced her breath to stay even. "A very fierce devilfish," the tiny woman said proudly. "Just like she is going to be. She's a terror on the docks already. Her singing reaches high street when she's hungry." Another jump and jiggle, and Lacy beamed from her child to Strell. "I have accounts to settle yet today, but I can send Tia to get your room ready. Your friends are welcome, too, of course."

Strell rubbed his chin as his smile went stiff. "Well, ah, we were planning on staying at a public house. It's easier to earn a coin there."

Real disappointment dimmed Lacy's eagerness. "Oh. I understand. Where are you staying? I'll stop in and buy a tune

from you." Her smile turned devious, and Alissa felt a wash
of ire. "You know the one I want, Strell."

Strell flicked a glance at Alissa, his smile going stilted at
the pointed look she knew she wore. "We, uh, haven't decided. Has Kole fixed his ceiling?"

Lacy nodded, and Connen-Neute pried Alissa's fingers
from around his arm. "I happen to know he doesn't have anyone playing there, either," the woman added, clearly aware
Alissa was upset. "And even if he did, Kole would throw
them out when he finds you're back."

Strell bobbed his head once. "Then that's where we'll be."

Alissa stiffened as Lacy ran a finger over his beard again
to brush the rain from it. "I wish it was for me," she said. She
reached to give him another embrace, and Strell took a step
back. Lacy bit her lip in the awkward silence, and her daughter began to cry from the brightening sun. "Good fortune,
then, Strell," she said, forcing a smile as she touched his arm.

"Good fortune, Lacy. And I'm happy for you."

Alissa grew smug. Gathering her skirt up, Lacy hitched her
child up higher and walked away. An adolescent girl Alissa
hadn't even noticed before trailed behind them with a large,
leather-bound book. Almost cowering, she moved silently
with nothing on her ankle but a simple band. Suddenly conscious of her bedecked ankle, Alissa frowned at the disparity.
The girl clearly had no status, walking with the stance of a
beggar.

Strell cleared his throat nervously, and as one, Lodesh and
Alissa turned to face him. The crowd moved around them like
water past a rock.

"Make up your room?" Lodesh drawled, reminding Alissa
why she was angry. "A hole in a tavern's ceiling? I don't think
we knew our good minstrel until just this moment, Alissa."

His face grew closed as Strell looked everywhere but at
her. "It was winter. I was icebound. Her father enjoyed long
desert ballads. I was a guest until the weather broke, that's all.
And the hole in the ceiling wasn't my fault. Let's find a clothier on the way to the Three Crows." He reached for her arm,
and she pulled away. She didn't know what she was feeling
right now, but it wasn't pleasant.

Strell hesitated, then drew himself straight. "I don't need

to explain myself," he said, his brown eyes taking on a glint of anger and worry. "Look. Kole's tavern is up there on the right. You can see it from here. I'm going over there." He pointed. "I need to get a hat. I'll meet you at the Three Crows, all right?"

"What's wrong with the hat I gave you?" she said, unable to keep the hurt from her voice.

He paused as if to say something, then, swallowing whatever it was, he strode away. His back was hunched, and his steps were sharp. The boy with the cart behind them hesitated until Lodesh gestured he stay with them. Alissa's mood went more sour still. Strell was going in the same direction that Lacy and her little drudge had gone. And there was nothing wrong with his hat. "Make up his room," she muttered, knowing she had no reason to be jealous of something that had happened before she met Strell. That she was made her angry with herself.

Lodesh took her arm, and they continued to the wide porch of the tavern. His steps were noticeably lighter, and he bobbed his head at everyone who met his gaze. Connen-Neute sighed, stoically making his way behind them without help.

They slowed as they approached the tidy inn. Its roof was of red tiles, and it had brightly painted shutters to keep out the winter's cold. A preadolescent boy was sweeping the damp off the raised porch. At the sound of Alissa's anklet bells, he hustled over and pulled a rag from his belt. "Let me clean the bottom of your shoes, Ma'hr," he said, kneeling before her.

Alissa stopped short, never having had that particular title of respect aimed at her before. "Uh," she stammered, glancing uneasily at Connen-Neute and Lodesh.

Lodesh grinned. "What's the matter, Alissa?"

"He wants to clean my shoes," she said, giving him a helpless look.

"Well, they're muddy, and that's his job. If you walk in like that, he'll get his ears boxed." He eyed the boy. "Isn't that right?" he asked, and the boy nodded emphatically.

She lifted her skirt a touch higher and peered at her shoes. "They're all right," she said, and the boy looked scared.

"Let the boy clean your shoes," Connen-Neute asserted. *"I want to sit down."*

"Let him clean your shoes," Lodesh whispered, and she shivered at the sensation of his breath on her neck. "It comes with the bells. How many do you have down there, anyway? It sounds like more than three. Did Talo-Toecan give you one as well?"

"He gave me three," she muttered, and he made a small grunt of surprise.

"Six?" he breathed. Instead of answering, she extended first one foot, then the other, balancing with Lodesh's help as the boy wiped the mud from her soles. Looking relieved, the boy got to his feet and opened the door for them.

"Touch the top of the sill," Lodesh said as he drew her to a stop before the threshold. "It keeps the bad luck you might bring in from entering."

"How quaint," she grumbled, thinking the only bad luck would be if Connen-Neute hit his head on the low lintel. Her fingers brushed the wood as she passed. It was worn and black from use. Talon chittered as they entered, and they hesitated just inside the doorway as their eyes adjusted. It was quiet, with only one man sitting at the tables, hunched around a mug in the corner. He looked up at them before going back to staring at nothing.

A man with badly gnarled hands was knocking a spoon against a pot over the hearth. There was a rag tucked into his belt, and by his gaze, half-wary, half-expectant, she guessed he was the innkeeper. Alissa ran her attention over the ceiling to find one corner by the hearth had the bright finish of boards that had only seen a few winters' worth of soot. Her brow furrowed, and she wondered if she really wanted to know.

"Afternoon, and good tide," Lodesh said as Alissa made a show of leading Connen-Neute to a table. Her bells were almost silent as she tried to walk quietly, uncomfortable with the deference the boy outside had shown her. Perhaps she ought to remove one or two bells. She had imagined she would have liked the attention but was now having second thoughts.

"G'd tide," the man said, eyeing them up and down as she sat beside Connen-Neute. The innkeeper was short and stocky, not even as tall as Alissa. His hands looked twice as old as the rest of him. "You aren't from around here," he said shortly. "What do you need? A room? Supper? I can arrange for an introduction to a merchant."

Lodesh smiled, taking off his cloak and shaking it dramatically to get the last of the rain from it. "We need a room for four, and possibly board."

"I only see three of ya."

"My associate is shopping," Lodesh said dryly. "Apparently, he needs a new hat. Your establishment came highly recommended. I hope you have something."

Lodesh's words were well-schooled in comparison to the innkeeper's, and the man with his earthen mug in the corner began to take notice. Wiping his hands on his rag, the innkeeper slipped behind the end of the counter to become taller. Alissa guessed the floor was raised there. "How long, then?" he asked, all business.

"A few days, if all goes well. Can we pay by the day?"

Again he nodded. "It will cost you more."

"Fair enough," Lodesh said. "Room and board for four." He pulled a small sack out from his belt and shuffled through it.

"I'll be back," Alissa whispered to Connen-Neute as she rose. She hadn't had much opportunity to see coinage before, all her dealings having been by barter. Careful to keep her movements slow, she made the trip with barely a chime. Lodesh smiled briefly as she came even with him. Alissa peered over his shoulder, watching him put a few coins on the counter. He somehow knew how much, and she was glad he was here to take care of it.

"That's two nights," the man said gruffly. "You can have an upstairs room, but the bird stays outside."

"Outside!" Alissa cried, her hand going protectively to her shoulder. Sensing Alissa's alarm, Talon chittered and raised her feathers.

"Or in a cage. I won't have it loose in my tavern," the innkeeper said.

The man slumped in the corner was now watching with bloodshot, tired eyes.

Lodesh put another coin on the counter. "Perhaps if we confined the bird to our room—"

The taverner shook his head tightly. "The mess. The flies. No animals in my inn."

"But Talon is the eyes of the blind man," Alissa lied.

"Then why is he on your shoulder?" the innkeeper asked.

"Talon is a she, not a he," Alissa said, stiffening. "And she stays with me."

The man kept his pointing finger just out of Talon's reach. "Then ya both stay outside."

Lodesh shifted uncomfortably. He hesitated when light spread over the floor and Alissa turned at Strell's familiar footsteps. He still had on his old hat, and Alissa sourly wondered what he had really been doing.

"Have a heart, Kole," Strell drawled, making his accent unusually thick. "It's not like you to make a woman sleep on the porch. Besides, the bird belongs to me. Part of the minstrel costume. You won't begrudge me that, will you?"

The innkeeper started, his black eyes lighting up. "Strell!" he bellowed to shake the dust from the ceiling, and the man in the corner winced. "Strell Hirdune! I thought you'd left."

Alissa exchanged a weary look with Lodesh as the innkeeper strode to Strell. The boy with the cart was quietly unloading their packs just inside the door with the help of the boy who'd cleaned her shoes.

"You said you were leaving!" the squat innkeeper said as he pounded Strell on the back. "Where've you been? Upcoast? There's been no mention of ya."

Strell grinned and pushed his old hat back off his forehead. "Here and there. I made it through the mountains all right, but I got sidetracked before reaching home." Strell held a hand out for Alissa, and she came forward, still miffed. The jingle of her bells was loud, and the innkeeper went red as she came to a chiming halt. "Kole," Strell said formally, "this is Alissa."

"Ma'hr," he said, his eyes dropping to her unseen ankle. "I do apologize. Your steps were so soft before. Of course you may keep your bird loosed. Is there anything I can get you for her? Mice? Snakes? We don't have any in my inn, but I can find you some."

Alissa managed a wry smile. The difference wasn't Strell but the bells on her ankle.

"And that is Connen-Neute, there, and Lodesh," Strell added as Lodesh cleared his throat.

"Not alone anymore, eh?" Kole bobbed his head. "Good. That's good." He eyed Alissa, and she flushed as he glanced at her unseen feet again. "Sit. Sit, sit," he said, gesturing. "Let me get you something. I have a cask I've been waiting to open. Stay here." He pushed at the air with his palms. "I'll be right back."

The squat man hustled to a back room, cheerfully mumbling about a six-bell woman in his inn, and how pleased his wife would be.

Hearing him, Strell turned to her. "Six bells?" he asked her, his long face going dark as he looked at Lodesh.

Connen-Neute put a restraining hand upon Strell's shoulder. "Talo-Toecan gave them to her," he said softly, and Strell went easy.

Before they had finished arranging themselves at the table, the innkeeper was back with a cask no bigger than a pumpkin. He tapped it right there at the table, making more of the ordeal than Alissa thought was necessary. Strell closed his eyes in delight as he sampled it.

"Your best yet," he said, but Connen-Neute coughed violently at the first sip. He set his tall mug aside, making a face as he reluctantly swallowed.

"What's the matter, Connen-Neute?" Lodesh said merrily, topping off his own mug. "I thought you liked blueberries."

Alissa reached for her shallow cup, eager to know what it tasted like. *"Don't drink it, Alissa,"* Connen-Neute warned in her thoughts, still coughing and rubbing his eyes through his scarf. *"It's fermented. Too much will block your ability to make wards."*

"Lodesh doesn't seem to care," she said, eyeing the Keeper as he downed a mug, showing his appreciation with watering eyes and pounding the table once with a closed fist.

"Lodesh can't fly, either," Connen-Neute answered dryly.

She pretended to take a sip, nodding at the innkeeper's expectant expression. It tingled on her lips, and when she licked them, they tasted of blueberries and warmth.

"You can have a room, no charge," the innkeeper said, topping off Strell's mug. "But for it, I want you here after sunset." He settled back and ran a hand over his greasy hair. "And you will take requests this time, desert man."

Strell nodded. "I can promise one night," he said, and the innkeeper's brow bunched.

"Leaving already? Stay. When word gets out you're back—"

Strell shook his head. "As soon as I find a ship, we're away."

The innkeeper's eyes brightened. "I knew it!" he shouted, making Talon chitter and the man in the corner groan. "I knew the sea called to you. Just sit apace, a week maybe, and I'll have you your choice of destinations. Though I'll be sorry to see you ruining your hands at sea."

Eyes distant, Strell ran his thumb over a rough spot in the mug's glazing. "I'm not looking to crew," he said. "Passenger, only. But if it lowers the fare to entertain, I don't mind."

"Just passage?" The innkeeper turned devious, his thin lips curling at the corners. "Lacy's got a boat now. Her husband— sorry, lad, but if you leave 'em, they jump ship—her husband is up-coast getting the first of the leather, but he'll be back in a week or so, the Navigator willing and the winds stay right. You can room here in the interim." He glanced behind Strell to Alissa, Lodesh, and Connen-Neute. "All of you. Strell, you can eat what you will, but the rest of you will have to make separate arrangements."

Alissa blinked. A room and food for Strell's music? A room worth more money than she had ever seen in exchange for Strell's promise to lure people in with his music?

Strell took a long drink, setting the mug down with a satisfied, contented sound. "I ran into Lacy outside." He flicked a glance at Alissa. "We need a bigger boat than what she has. I'm looking to see deep water. I want to see that blue current you all tell me about."

Satisfaction warmed Alissa. Lacy's boat was too small. How tragic.

Kole frowned as he turned his attention over Strell's shoulder to a noisy group that had entered and arranged themselves at the counter. Alissa couldn't help but notice their shoes were wet with mud. "Now?" Kole said as he looked back. "The silvers are spawning in the shallows, and the leather is ready up-coast. Strell, you know as well as I you won't find a ship willing to forgo the usual runs for a pleasure sail out to the current. There's too much money to be made the usual way. Not unless you can meet the profit of a regular run."

Strell smiled confidently. "Put the word out anyway?" he asked as the innkeeper rose.

Kole bobbed his head. "Aye. I'll do that." He looked to the back of the room where the dark blackness of a hallway beckoned. "Take the last room on the left if you want, on the ground floor. It's the largest, and my wife has a curtain over half of it. There's a bed that ought to be long enough for even your legs. Help yourself to the stew." He nodded to Lodesh. "I'll let you know when you've run out of what you gave me already. Though if you eat like Strell, here, it'll be tomorrow." He was smiling when he said it, and with a nod to Alissa, he returned to his counter and the newest patrons.

Alissa turned to the dark mouth of the hallway. *A curtain?* she wondered. She would have preferred a door. Strell had leaned back on two chair legs, a very satisfied look about him. "Now what?" she asked him.

Grinning, Strell thumped back to an upright position. "Now we eat and wait."

Lodesh set his mug down, his gaze fixed upon it. "Room and board for a song," he said softly. "Perhaps I went into the wrong profession."

Strell smiled, but Alissa thought there was a trace of sadness in his eyes. "For a song. For now," he added. "By next week, the novelty will have worn off, and it won't get me even a bowl of bilge slop." His gaze met Alissa's, filled with an emotion she couldn't place. "But I don't mind moving from place to place." He set his hand atop hers. "Not anymore."

8

Alissa balked in the dark of the hallway, her toes edging the arch of lamplight in the inn's common room. It was astonishingly quiet for the number of people crammed into it to hear Strell perform. Only Strell's voice shifted the hush, rising and falling with the cadence of music.

Beyond the gaping front door was the night-black street. Alissa wondered what time it had gotten to be as she fingered Redal-Stan's watch on its cord about her neck. Forcing her hands down, she rubbed the red scratches on her knuckles. It had taken all her guile to lock Talon in their room, and she felt more alone than usual without the bird on her shoulder.

Earlier this afternoon, Alissa had been lulled to sleep by the damp heat. The cool of evening and the noise of song had awakened her. Actually, Beast had woken her, pulled to the forefront of Alissa's thoughts by the rhythmic thumps of a dance tune. It had since stopped, but Beast drifted at the edge of Alissa's awareness, should it start again, comforting and familiar.

Alissa was glad Beast had woken them. Quite by accident, Alissa had reached Silla's thoughts while asleep. As before, the young Master had startled herself awake upon catching wind of Alissa. Perhaps next time, Alissa thought, she ought to try to appear as a raku. She never had before. Alissa sighed, running a hand over her head to try to smooth out the wave her pillow had put into her hair. She didn't like being the Navigator's night demon.

As if drawn by her motion, Strell's gaze met hers from across the room. His beard had grown in over the last few days to make him look more like one of the sailors surrounding him. He nodded his distant greeting, his intent, spellbinding speech never hesitating as his hands gestured expansively. The only other movement was from a few subdued women and young boys tending the astounding variety of coastal people who had come to hear Strell.

The seamen, their skin dark from the sun and leathered by salt, leaned forward with an honest anticipation. They rubbed elbows with well-dressed women who chimed with every move, their eyes wide with alarm and their delicate hands covering mouths more often than not. With them were men in carefully tailored garments, their upright stance as much as their clean fingers saying they dealt in goods they didn't make themselves. Most tried to hold a faint air of disinterest, but it was obvious they were as caught up in Strell's magic as everyone else.

Alissa smiled. Apart from the few requests Strell had honored, the last two days had been stories and songs extolling the rewards to be found in chancing a path the timid shunned. It was obvious to her that Strell was trying to sway his audience. So far, no one was budging from well-traveled paths and known profits.

Strell's familiar voice was compelling. The intensity of his gaze and the sound of his spellbinding voice seemed to touch her core, sending a shiver of emotion through her. Flustered, she turned in a sudden commotion, finding Lodesh making his careful way across the room.

"Did you have a good rest?" he whispered as he came up beside her.

"Yes, thank you," she said. He took her arm and led her to a small table almost behind a support post. Her bells sounded loud in the hush, and she winced as heads turned. The basin-sized table held only one man, and after meeting his eyes for permission, Lodesh edged out a chair for her. Alissa gratefully sat as she recognized the old man who had seen them arrive several days ago. Immediately one of the serving boys was at her elbow.

"Tea?" she whispered. The boy nodded, slipping away with the stealth of a servant. She glanced at the man, relieved he wasn't ignoring her but not bothering her either. Lodesh stood behind her as there were no more chairs. His hands rested upon her shoulders, and the scent of mirth wood slipped over her like a balm. Alissa breathed it in, feeling herself relax into that odd tautness he seemed so adept at pulling from her. She tugged at the hem of his shirt, and he dropped to a crouch beside her. "Any luck finding someone to take us out?" she asked softly.

"No," came his vexed whisper. "Strell and Connen-Neute spent their afternoon arranging what we need for an extended voyage while I went through every tavern in town and even one under the docks. No one will risk deep water if there's a sure wage to be made near shore." He sighed. "I don't want to go home because of someone else's good business sense." His smile was charmingly lopsided. "I'll never hear the end of it."

Alissa returned his smile, and he stood back up. She simply had to find Silla if only to convince the girl she wasn't going insane.

"What about Keribdis?" Beast intruded. Alissa started, not knowing her second consciousness had been listening. *"They go together, you know,"* Beast added, sounding frightened.

"I know." Alissa pushed her worry aside to concentrate on Strell's story. It was one of her favorites about a raku learning how to sail. She had taught it to him, actually, hearing it from her father before he died, and she was delighted at the rapt attention of the crowd.

Her roving gaze found Connen-Neute sitting alone in a corner surrounded by a respectful distance his supposedly blind status conferred. He looked decidedly uncomfortable. The rims of his ears poking beyond the scarf were a shade of red she could see over the distance. *"What's wrong?"* she sent privately across the crowded room.

Connen-Neute turned his scarf-wrapped eyes to her. *"I nearly lost my fingers when I got them caught between a rope and a winch,"* he said.

She blinked. *"That story is about you?"* she asked, and he shrugged glumly. His hand trembled as he lifted his drink, and her brow furrowed in concern. Lodesh had said he had been shopping. Alissa thought it looked more like he had been working the fields all afternoon. *"You look tired,"* she said, thinking haggard might be more accurate.

Connen-Neute's shoulders shifted in a sigh. *"I found a shaduf today,"* he said, his thoughts tinged with a remembered pain.

Alissa's lips parted in surprise, but before she could say anything, the young Master's thoughts came slipping into hers with a guilty swiftness. *"I gave him a mercy burn. Turned his tracings to an unresonating ash. I had to, Alissa. The boy was on the edge of suicide, not knowing why he was having visions of death that always came true."*

She went cold, and her thoughts turned guilty. Shadufs were an unhappy accident that arose when there was too much mixing between the coast, foothills, and plains. Their tracings were almost complex enough to make the jump to Master as she had but were tragically malformed. Even so, they could do something no Master could: trip the lines of time forward instead of back. The talent would have been prized except that only death was strong enough to force itself backward through time. It had almost been her fate, missed by a very narrow margin.

"You should have woken me," she admonished, reaching up to touch Lodesh's hand as he placed it upon her shoulder. It was obvious the Keeper knew they were talking but was too polite to intrude. *"I could have helped carry the pain."*

Connen-Neute pushed his cup of drink farther from him. *"I managed. Besides, if Talo-Toecan finds out, I'll be the only one in trouble."*

Alissa flicked her gaze to Strell and back again. *"You should have called me anyway,"* she repeated, almost angry. Her hand dropped from Lodesh's at the thought of the agony he had endured to help the boy. Phantom pain or not, it hurt as if the Navigator's Wolves were ravaging one's soul when one burned another's tracings, even in mercy. *"Are you all right?"*

"I will be tomorrow," he thought faintly as he slowly spun

the glass in his grip. *"At least there were no septhamas in his family. That I'd have to tell Talo-Toecan about—and then he would investigate—and then he would want to know how the boy got burned in the first place."* He shuddered, the motion visible across the distance.

"How could you tell?" she questioned. *"I thought the only way to find them was to work back from an upsurge of Keepers in a family line that should be commoners."*

Connen-Neute leaned to run a finger between his boot and his leg. *"I asked the boy if any of his family could see ghosts. He said no."*

Alissa made a sour face. Sometimes the simplest tests were the ones she overlooked.

Septhamas were a rare group of people—almost as rare as her. Unlike shadufs, they were largely undetectable until their children all became Keepers instead of the expected commoners. Like shadufs, they were caught between Keeper and Master. But their misaligned tracings allowed them to exorcise ghosts.

Useless had spent an excruciating three days giving her the technical explanation, spouting terms like psychic imprints and ether frequencies. From what Alissa had picked out from his twaddle was that a tragedy often left behind an invisible imprint of the event. When a similar emotional state was reached, even hundreds of years later, it set up a resonance, setting the first imprint to relive itself, hence ghosts. Septhamas could change the frequency of the imprint so it no longer was capable of resonating.

The Hold largely ignored septhamas as they had yet to find a use for them. It would be extremely improbable to run into one as—like a shaduf—they needed a background hailing from the plains, foothills, and coast. To find one, though, would mean the Masters' carefully contrived division of humanity into three separate groups had come dangerously close to completely breaking down.

The serving boy cut between her and Connen-Neute, and she straightened, dismissing her worried thoughts. There was a second cup for Lodesh, and she poured tea for him first. Lodesh crouched beside her to take the hot cup as she offered it to him. "Was Connen-Neute telling you about the boy?" he

asked, his face frighteningly grim. She glanced at Connen-
Neute and nodded. "I'm glad he did it," Lodesh said. "His life
was a living hell."

She couldn't meet his eyes, relieved when he stood back
up. The cup of tea was hot in her hand, but she didn't drink.
Though she had nothing to do with the Hold's policy of capi-
talizing upon the shaduf's abilities, she still felt guilty. The
Hold had refused to prevent Lodesh's first love, a woman
named Sati, from turning shaduf. Watching his future bride
turn bitter and cold, losing even her ability to return his love,
had nearly killed him. That Alissa had been the one to end
Sati's torture seemed a pale restitution for the Hold's collective callousness.

From behind her, Lodesh shook his head in amazement.
"Bone and Ash," he said, his tone carrying a respectful awe as
he clearly tried to change the subject. "Look at them. Every
single one hanging on his words, wealthy and poor alike. I've
never seen anything like it—and I've seen my share of story-
tellers." He shifted his weight to his other foot, his eyes on
Strell. "I'd wager he could convince a queen into giving him
her firstborn," he said softly.

"I don't think there's anything he can't do," Alissa said as
Strell met her gaze.

Lodesh made a muffled groan. She glanced over her shoulder, finding him pushing his fingers into his forehead as if he
was in pain. "Are you all right?" she asked, concerned he
might be still thinking about Sati.

"Yes." He set his cup down and edged away. "I need some
air is all."

"All right." Concerned, she watched him move through the
crowd. His steps were unusually loud, and he vanished into
the blackness beyond the open door. Alissa turned to the old
man, giving him a noncommittal smile before going back to
her tea. It had come with a hard biscuit, and she nibbled at it,
surprised at the sharp, tangy taste.

Strell's voice wove up and down, and Alissa listened to the
murmur of it rather than the words. It took her by surprise
when Strell finished and the room collectively sighed. Chairs
scraped against the floor and loud calls for service rang out
over the new chatter. Alissa peered over the rising heads to see

Strell taking a well-deserved drink. Mug tipped up, he simultaneously swallowed and waved a hand to forestall any more requests. "Later!" he shouted cheerfully when he came up for air. "Give me a breath!" he added as protests were raised.

The innkeeper bustled out from behind the counter, looking more pleased than a farmer who had finished bringing in his hay before the fall rains. Alissa had all but forgotten the tired man sitting across from her when he leaned toward her and muttered, "He can see, can't he."

Startled, Alissa turned to him, hardly noticing when someone bumped her elbow in the press of people. "Beg your pardon?"

He gestured with his chin across the room crowded with motion. "The tall one you came in with. He's not blind. I've been watching him. And you."

Alissa glanced up to find Connen-Neute hidden behind a wall of people. "Yes, he can see," she said. "He wears the scarves to cover his, ah, burns." She frowned, not liking the lies. "He doesn't want to frighten anyone," she added to give some honesty to her answer.

The man's head bobbed. "Aye. Unless you beg, a burn is a mark of shame."

Alissa didn't know what to say. She wished she could graciously excuse herself to make her way to Connen-Neute, but the room was too crowded. Fortunately, the man seemed satisfied, and she snuck glances at him as she waited for the room to settle. His hands gripping his mug had almost no nails, so worn were they, and his fingers were thick. She breathed deeply, deciding he smelled like wind, as Useless did. Her eyes closed, eager for her nightly talk with her teacher. It was still too early. Later, when most of the coast was sleeping, it would be easier.

"Is he the one who gave you your bells?" the man said suddenly. "The blind man?"

Alissa opened her eyes. "Ah . . . one of them," she said hesitantly.

"One?" He took a drink and brushed his mustache. "You must feel very secure to wed a burned man who can give you nothing more in the future."

"I'm not marrying Connen-Neute," she said, glancing at

Strell. He was deep in conversation with a man in an expensive-looking coat. The man was shaking his head vigorously. "He's more like a brother," she continued. "He's here because he said I needed all the help I could get."

The old man shifted his chair to put both his elbows on the table. His eyebrows were shot with gray, but his eyes were clear. "*You* are going on the water?" he asked.

Alissa slumped, picking at the glazing on her cup. "If we can find someone to take us."

"You *want* to go?" the man repeated.

"Of course. I'm the only one who can—" Biting her lower lip, she dropped her gaze.

There was a short silence, and she winced as the man leaned over the small table. "Just what are you looking for, Ma'hr?"

She said nothing. Strell had warned her how superstitious the coastal people were and that it would be best to approach their real goal carefully. Seeing she wasn't going to say more, the man leaned back, and Alissa's tension eased. "Why don't you take one of your ships?" he said around the lip of his mug. "You have two or three hangin' about your ankle, there."

"If I had a ship, I'd be on it," she said, judging that the room was still too crowed to make her escape. "Maybe I could buy one, though. How much are they?"

The man laughed. "It would cost you a pretty bell, that would. And then there's a crew to be found, and someone to pilot it . . ."

Excited, Alissa leaned across the table. "Really? Is that all?" Not thinking, she reached to untie her anklet strap and set it jangling on the table. "Which one would do it, do you think?" She went cold as she saw his wide eyes, and she wondered if she had broken one of the coast's many superstitions. But the man's hand went out and took up her bells with a professional interest, not a voyeuristic one. The people nearby, too, seemed not to care, being more intent on procuring more ale than about her bells on the table.

The man's brow furrowed in thought, and a hand touched his short beard. "This is an interesting chain," he said, and Alissa exhaled. If they couldn't charter a ship, they'd buy one.

"Is there one worth a ship?" she asked, feeling a flood of relief when he nodded.

"Aye. The question is, which one would you be willing to part with?"

She blinked. "Does it matter?"

The man flicked his gaze to hers and back to the bells. Instead of answering, he laid the strap out flat and touched the bell Strell had given her. "This one," he said. "This was your first?"

Alissa shook her head. "No. These were." She pointed to the three bells from Useless.

The man grunted in surprise. "Three at once?" He eyed her sharply, then tapped Strell's. "No matter. Whoever gave you this one loves you. Shame to sell one given in love."

She put the back of her hand to a warm cheek. "How can you know that?" she asked.

The man rolled the bell on the table to make it clank. "It's not very old, about thirty years. Originally it was probably the first bell of a merchant's daughter or perhaps a sailor's wife. It's ugly, hear that rank jangle it makes? Not much of a bell, almost as bad as the bells the dock chulls wear, but it's a bell, which is saying something. And it's the bell of a poor man. One who has little to spend on anything he can't eat, drink, or wear. It was given by someone who loves more than he can afford. That he gave it away shows he loves you more than his life."

Alissa stared at the bell, never having imagined it could tell so much.

The man shifted his shoulders, turning his attention to the bell Connen-Neute had given her. "Now this one here, this is the gift of a young man who has status but isn't in the habit, or perhaps the position, of using it yet. Perhaps the sole heir of an old man?"

She blinked in surprise. "Connen-Neute gave me that one," she admitted.

"The burned man?" he asked, his brow raised in question. "I thought it was the one who can't shut his mouth." He gestured to where Lodesh was sitting with Strell and Connen-Neute. She hadn't noticed when he had come in, and all three were scowling, clearly not liking her talking to a stranger but unwilling to intervene just yet.

"It's new," the man said, regaining her attention. "You can

tell because of the ridge on the edge and the ting it makes."
He lifted the strap and tapped the bell in question to send a
solitary chime to mix with the sound of conversation. "New,
well-made. Whoever gave you this holds you in great esteem
but no romance."

Alissa's gaze went distant. That was Connen-Neute, all
right.

"This one," the man said, his brow furrowing as he pointed
almost reverently to Lodesh's bell. "You couldn't have been
given this. It must have been inherited. And it tells me you
have wealth in your background, Ma'hr. This bell is very old
and very rare. No one could put this on the market without
there being a stir over it. I'd wager a season's haul that it's the
most valuable of the lot, enough to get you three boats and a
crew for them all."

She swallowed, not knowing she had been carrying that
much wealth on her ankle.

"Aye," the man said dryly, clearly reading her sudden dis-
quiet. "I've only seen one like it, and it was said to have been
over three hundred years old. Originally it was probably a gift
to a young woman of status comin' of age. Now, it's far more
valuable." His mustache moved as he worked his upper lip
between his teeth. "So who died and left it to you?"

"No one," she whispered. "It was a gift."

He grunted. "Then you got it from your loudmouthed
pretty boy?"

She nodded, feeling her face go white as she looked at
Lodesh. His expression had softened, and he was holding up
a finger to forestall Strell's urgent words. "Yes," she said.

"Well, he loves you, too, for I'm sure he had many other
choices available to him despite his present status of—wan-
derer? His choice shows great taste as well as great desire. He
won't be deterred for much longer," he warned.

Alissa broke her uneasy gaze from Lodesh. Almost frightened, she watched the man arrange the last three bells. "And
these must have been a gift from your father," he said.

"My papa died when I was five," she said softly. "Those
were a gift from—" She stopped. "From the man who taught
him his craft," she finished.

"And this man is now your guardian?" he continued.

"I suppose," she said, watching Connen-Neute, Strell, and Lodesh argue.

"Well," the man huffed, "anyone who can give his ward three bells for a trip to the coast must have a vast amount of wealth—"

"I've never seen it," she interrupted.

"And not a lot of time," he continued, "or they wouldn't be all alike. These were bought in a hurry, uncaring for their worth, only concerned you'd have something about your ankle."

Her slight ire washed away in embarrassment. That was Useless to the last word.

His eyes narrowed, and he leaned back with his arms crossed. "You aren't from the coast," he said. "And even my brother-in-law wouldn't believe your story about wanting to see the current. What are you lookin' for, Ma'hr?"

Gulping, she looked at Strell, Lodesh, and Connen-Neute. Immediately Strell rose, and all three began to make their way to her. Seeing their resolute stride, the man's eyes narrowed. "Jest drop your sails," he almost growled. "If you want me to take you out, you'd best tell me what you really want."

"You're a captain?" Alissa exclaimed, tearing her gaze from the three approaching men.

"Used to be," he muttered, then louder added, "I'm the captain of the *Black Albatross*. It used to be a fine boat—before my damn wife dragged it down. What is it you're lookin' for that you'd be willing to spend a man's fortune on?"

Alissa tensed in a wash of warning. She felt the support of Strell, Lodesh, and Connen-Neute as they stood protectively behind her. Lodesh had told her they had to be circumspect about their real desires, but Alissa couldn't bring herself to lie to the man. Deciding to be out with it, she turned to the unseen water. "My never-seen kin," she said, feeling the strangeness of the words. "Lost on a sea voyage—a long time ago."

The captain's wind-leathered face went slack. Leaning back, he flicked his eyes to the men behind her. "Ah," he breathed. "You're lookin' for the Rag Islands."

Hope went through her. There were islands. He knew where they were! But her flush of excitement flickered as the older man shook his head. "I'm sorry, Ma'hr. They're just a desolate chain of rock and sand if the rumors are right. No one even knows if they really exist. If your kin was lost on the sea, then you should pray to the Navigator and all his Hounds that they perished in the waves. If they washed up on the Rag Islands, it was a slow death they endured."

"I have to try," Alissa pleaded. "Will you take us out?" she asked, her eyes falling to her string of bells still on the table.

The man sent his gaze up and over her shoulder to the men behind her. He chewed his lower lip to make his mustache dance. "Aye," he said slowly, and anticipation pulled her upright. "I'll take you on your fool's errand." He nodded to the men behind her. "I'll take you for the price of your man's entertainment and your other man's boots." He glanced at Lodesh's feet. "I like your boots. Never seen anything like them."

Lodesh's mouth dropped. "You'll take us out for my boots?"

Connen-Neute hid his bandaged hands in his long sleeves. "Why?" he said softly.

The captain squinted in the light behind Connen-Neute. "Why? Why do you care why?" He abruptly pushed Alissa's bells across the table and stood. "Be on my deck before the second tide shift tomorrow. The one after sunset." His eyes pinched. "And keep it quiet. I need time to find my crew—if there's any left of 'em," he finished sourly.

"Wait!" Alissa called as he walked out, but he was gone. "We have a ship?" she asked.

Lodesh grinned as he sat in the vacated chair. "You got us a ship, Alissa," he said. "I told Strell all we had to do was let you ask."

Strell's eyes narrowed. "I believe I was the one who suggested that."

Their argument was interrupted as the innkeeper brought Strell a bowl of potato soup. It seemed as if it was all Strell had been eating the last few days. "But why?" Alissa said as Strell pulled a chair around to sit and enthusiastically started eating. "He didn't even want money."

The innkeeper made a small noise. "It was spite," he said, taking Alissa's empty biscuit plate. "Captain Sholan caught his wife dallying with one of his crew on his last trip up-coast. He stopped short of keelhauling the man and threatened to divorce her. Backed out of it as, if he does, he loses his boat."

Alissa's breath slipped from her in understanding, and Strell hesitated at his soup.

The innkeeper's lips pressed together disapprovingly. "He took a one-bell chull from under the docks and made her a two-bell woman." He shrugged. "Sometimes bringing 'em up from bilge scrapings works, sometimes it don't. Captain Sholan is taking you out because there's no profit in it. He wants to ruin her before divorcing her. She may own the boat, but he decides where it goes." He added as he turned away, "You were lucky."

"Lucky," Strell breathed. "I don't believe in luck."

"And Alissa doesn't believe in magic," Connen-Neute said as he took a seat beside him. "Even when it slaps her in the face." He grinned from under his scarves. "Let me tell Talo-Toecan, Alissa? He wagered me a week's worth of firewood that you wouldn't be able to find a ship in less than a month."

Strell laughed and bent his head to his soup. "He should have known better than to wager Alissa can't do something. It only insures she will."

9

The breeze was damp in her hair and the sound of bells gave away her footsteps as Lodesh escorted her down the wide dock. Sunset was past, making the ocean a black expanse of hidden motion and scent. Scattered fires in metal kettles sat along the dock or bobbed on the small, one-masted boats rafted out from each other. The boats sat five deep in places, the outermost people having to clamber over their neighbors to reach the dock. She thought it looked risky. If one caught on fire, they'd all go up. Out in deeper water were the merchant ships, the *Albatross* among them. Oil lights showed the ends of the otherwise dark vessels.

"Watch your step, Alissa," Lodesh cautioned, taking her elbow as she stumbled on a board. She gave him a quick smile and returned to her gawking, trusting him to keep her from tripping. Connen-Neute and Strell were before her with the inn's boy and their cart of belongings. Talon was pinching her shoulder, grousing for having been locked up all day.

The smell of cooking bacon and fish was strong. Surrounding the fires on the docks were sullen people occupied in conversation and small tasks. Their singsong accent rose and fell like the waves they lived on. Blankets and cushions were arranged on the dock in a careless disarray that told of a deep-rooted self-confidence. Children ran from group to group, heedless of the possibility of falling in. Old men fished, and young couples had private conversations at the edge of the light. It was nothing like her excursion through the streets, but rather like walking unnoticed through someone's house. It made Alissa feel like a ghost.

The docks were populated by what seemed an entirely different people than in the streets. They were shorter, darker, and carried mistrust with them like a shield. "There are more now than this morning," she said, referring to their first trip out to the docks to get a glance of the *Albatross*.

Lodesh gave her hand a squeeze to bring her attention to a wide crack in the dock. "Most were out fishing. They live on their boats all the time. Even in winter."

"Sounds miserable," she said, eyeing the nearest shadowy boat in passing. It was no bigger than a small shed, the ceiling so low one would have to crouch when inside.

"I don't know." He flicked his yellow curls from his eyes and smiled. "They keep to themselves. Marry within their own. To be honest, they look down upon anyone not their kin. Even so, Captain Sholan has a few on his crew."

Alissa frowned. "You said they don't like anyone but themselves."

"They'll still work for others," Lodesh said. "The young men especially, as they need money to buy materials to make a boat. The girls, too, will hire themselves out as crew before they come of age to build up their worth to rank a better husband. It's said they make the best sailors, fearlessly jumping about the rigging of the larger ships like birds. They use bells to show status, too, but theirs are coarse, not the beautiful works of art you have."

She dropped her gaze. "Thank you. But I haven't done anything to deserve them."

Lodesh gave her hand a squeeze. "I think you have."

She ducked her head, knowing she hadn't. A deep sense of bound tension filled her as she stopped at the end of the dock. Her toes edged the drop-off. Behind her, the lives of the dock people continued. Before her lay the black expanse of ocean, the wind and water moving under their separate but intertwined forces. The wind tugged a strand of hair from the white ribbon Lodesh had bought her, pulling it into her eyes.

Alissa gazed at the lights on the water where the larger ships rested at anchor. "How are we going to get to our boat?" she asked, looking down to where several empty rowboats rocked in the rougher water outside the shelter of the dock. "Can we borrow a dinghy?"

"No," Strell said with a quickness that frightened her. "Someone will come."

Uneasy, she fidgeted, realizing she might have committed a grave error without meaning to. Soon the soft padding of feet came from behind them. It was a short, thin dockman. Not meeting their eyes, he stepped into a rowboat, fixed the oars to the blocks, and waited.

Shrugging, Lodesh nimbly stepped to the center of the boat. He held out a hand, and Strell and the inn's boy began handing their things across to him. Connen-Neute forgot he was supposed to be blind and stepped into the boat without help. He balanced with no effort as Strell tossed the remaining packs to him. But it was the surly dockman who took Alissa's staff, peering at it intently in the dark before setting it aside.

"It's mirth wood," she said, knowing it would mean little to him. "From the mountains."

"It would make a fine boat," he said, his musical voice startling her. Only now did the man look up, grunting as he saw Talon on her shoulder. He pushed his red cap back to show the tight black curls under it and held out a wiry hand to help her cross the short expanse. Alissa accepted it gratefully, surprised at the easy confidence in his grip.

She made the short hop, clutching his hand when the boat shifted. He eyed her intently as he rocked with the waves. Instinctively she followed his lead as he maintained his balance. Their eyes met, and he smiled before he let go of her, knowing she had found the knack. It was dancing. Dancing with the wind and waves.

Alissa moved to sit on a bench beside Connen-Neute, more sure of herself as she found the pattern in the boat's motion. The boy with the cart quickly rattled away, leaving Strell. Lodesh stood with his hands on his hips. "Coming?" he asked, and Alissa frowned at the mockery in his tone.

Strell visibly swallowed. He ran a hand under his dilapidated hat and touched his pocket where his pipe and her father's old map lay. Talon crooned encouragingly from Alissa's shoulder. Taking a resolute breath, Strell stretched his foot out to find the floor of the boat. He lurched, sending them rocking violently. Alissa gasped and clutched the railing.

Lodesh chuckled and rode the shifting out with a dancer's grace, but the dockman looked at the laughing Keeper with a dark, irritated expression. Awash with empathy, she touched Strell's arm. He gave her a forced smile. Dead center of the small boat, he sat on the floor and clutched his pack.

"Are you all right?" she whispered. He nodded tersely, and her heart went out to him.

Lodesh brought out his coins, but the man shook his head. "Paid for already," he said. "I bought my children a song. Bought it from the man from the desert where it never rains."

Alissa went still as she remembered now having seen him in the streets. Strell had interrupted their shopping to play a request: a song from his desert. The dockman had his three children arranged before him like stairsteps, listening with solemn eyes and serious faces. He had bought his children a song. Her eyes pricked, imagining the pride he carried for having given his children a glimpse of a larger world the only way he could.

A sound of annoyance slipped from Lodesh as he tucked his coins away and sat down.

Connen-Neute leaned close to the Keeper. "For someone with no money, he certainly seems to get what he wants," he whispered loudly, and Lodesh frowned all the more.

The dockman stretched to unhook the rope keeping them to the dock. Hunching his back, he began to row. A thrill went through Alissa as the dock fell away in rhythmic surges. They had no light, and she felt the dark slip about her as if it were something solid to be forced through. Slowly the shape of the *Albatross* became distinct, lit at both ends by oil lamps. Alissa felt a frown of concern come over her.

It had looked fine from the dock this afternoon, but the closer they got, the more unkept the *Albatross* became. It wasn't a derelict—and vastly larger and nicer than the boats the dock people called home—but it carried an air of run-down abandonment. The varnish was worn, and the eyes painted under the waterline were encrusted with barnacles. Alissa's eyebrows rose as she realized the shadows on the statue of a woman on the bowsprit were actually hack marks.

"Perhaps he wanted to leave at night so we couldn't see how bad his boat looks," Strell said, his voice strained.

"It's a sound boat," Lodesh said.

Strell pulled his gaze from the *Albatross*. "What you know about boats could fit into a thimble, Lodesh."

The Keeper sniffed. "I never said I knew about boats, but there are three dockmen among the crew, and they won't set foot on a vessel they don't trust."

A light burst into existence amidships upon the *Albatross*. Captain Sholan stood at the railing, a torch in his hand. "Get them on deck!" he shouted, gesturing merrily at them. "Pull up the anchors. All watches on deck!" he bellowed. "I want those sails up! We're ready to go!" There was a flurry of motion on the shadowed deck. Dim figures tugged on ropes, and with the sound of sliding canvas, white triangles blossomed in the dusk, rising up along the two masts.

Lodesh leaned toward Connen-Neute. "He's in a better mood," he said softly. Alissa silently agreed, thinking he looked nothing like the tired man she had met in the tavern.

The sound of water slapping the side of the *Albatross* grew loud, and Alissa looked up the tall expanse as they bumped into it. A rope ladder rolled down, and she stood, swaying for balance. Talon left her shoulder and vanished to chitter unseen from the top of one of the masts. At Lodesh's gesture, she grasped the ladder. The cord was damp and cold in her hands. Heart pounding, she abandoned the bobbing rowboat for the slow, ponderous swaying of the *Albatross*.

Dark thin hands reached down for her, helping her over the railing. Connen-Neute was next, shortly followed by their supplies arching over the railing to land in a jumble on the deck.

Captain Sholan was standing with his hands on his hips, squinting in the dark at the sails flapping noisily. A skinny man in a red knit hat was beside him. He caught Alissa's eye and said a few words to the captain. Immediately Captain Sholan turned, beaming as he came forward. He was still

smiling as he halted before them, a contagious good humor
flowing from him.

"I need to thank you, Ma'hr," he said, touching the brim of
his faded hat by way of greeting. "It's because of you I got my
boat back from my poor excuse of a wife."

"Former wife!" the skinny man called loudly from the
wheel, grinning, and Captain Sholan bobbed his head and
smiled.

"Me?" she said as she picked her pack out of the growing
clutter. She glanced at the sails. They were making a terrible
amount of noise, but no one but her seemed to notice.

The man solicitously took her pack from her. "She is a bad
woman, Ma'hr. Disguising her wants with pretty words and
thin kindnesses that come from her greed and not her heart.
She didn't believe me when I told her I was going to sink the
fortune I made for her into the waves if she didn't stop dock-
ing her boat in another man's bed." He bit his upper lip to
make his mustache dance. "There's only so much a man's
pride can take. But when I told her I was taking you out for a
pair of boots, she gave me back my boat and sundered our
marriage before I made good on my promise to drain our accounts to buy hats for harbor whores."

Alissa's face burned, and she was glad it was too dark for
him to see it. With a small grunt, he directed her to a small recessed dip in the deck where the ship's wheel was. The skinny
man had the wheel, his arm muscles bunching as he managed
it. Benches lined two sides of the recessed deck, a hatch leading down into the black behind it. Her bells chiming, Alissa
followed. "She's broken your marriage because of me?" she
asked, feeling guilty.

"Aye, and I owe you deeply for it, Ma'hr. Me and my crew
both. My regular crew," he amended. "Not the dock chulls I
had to take on to replace those that got work elsewhere while
I was—ah—waiting for a run suitably worthless to tip her
over the edge."

He stepped easily into the recessed pit, turning to extend a
work-leathered hand to help her down. It reminded her of the
firepit at the Hold, though it was vastly smaller. Calling out,
he tossed her bag to a swarthy man wearing an apron standing belowdecks.

"Hayden will show you where you can bunk," he said, indicating the dark man who had caught her things. "Best get everything belowdecks before we get out of the harbor proper and the spray starts to come over the deck."

"Yes, of course," she murmured, glancing up at the noisy sails as Strell, Lodesh, and Connen-Neute joined her. Their arms were full of packages, and even in the torchlight, Alissa could see that Strell looked positively ill.

"Iron's on deck!" someone exclaimed. "Comin' about!"

Alissa felt the boat turn, and a strong hand pushed her shoulder down. "Watch the boom, Ma'hr," the captain said as the heavy beam of wood holding the bottom of the sail swung over the deck where her head had been. A thump rattled under her feet as the sails caught the wind and landed firm against their ties. The sudden cessation of noise from the sails was shocking, and the boat began to move.

"Over the deck?" Strell whispered, clutching his pack before him.

Lodesh grinned. "Yes," he said merrily. "Great waves of spray going up and down for weeks on end."

His voice rose and fell as did his hands in explanation, and Alissa swallowed, feeling slightly ill. "Do stop," she chided him, and Lodesh and Connen-Neute exchanged curious looks.

"This might be the shortest voyage on record," the young Master said. "I do believe our Alissa may be prone to seasickness."

10

"Ma'hr?" the galley man said, his lyrical, dockman accent attracting Alissa's attention like a chirping bird.

She smiled as he wiped his hand on his apron and held out a thick-walled mug of tea. "Good morning, Hayden," she said happily as she accepted it on the flat of her hand. The time she had taken it by the handle, he had angrily thrown it overboard, cup and all, much to the disgust of Captain Sholan. According to the superstitious dockman, she had given wandering spirits permission to drink out of it.

Hayden ran a hand not yet gnarled by the sea over his bearded chin. "Saw a bird on the mast afore dawn," he said, his brown eyes serious. "That's good luck."

"Almost as good as a cat sneezing on you before you get up, right?" she questioned.

He smiled, wrinkling his otherwise young face. "You're learnin'. Now, don't take my tea up to the bow. A man died there from a fall, and he won't take kindly to you wakin' him up."

Alissa nodded, shifting the hot cup in her fingers. The dockman was slowly warming up to her. The other two maintained a suspicious distance; the ship's boy wouldn't talk to her, and the other was on the night watch. She didn't even

know his name. Taking a sip of the cooling tea, she watched
Hayden wedge another notch out of the wall support with his
knife. There were three cuts so far, one for each sunrise they
had seen since leaving.

One hand on the mug, the other gripping the rail fastened
to the low ceiling, she made her bell-chiming way to the
bright square of light at the end of the aisle. The floor was
slanted under her feet, and the dip and swoop was soothing.
"Comin' about!" a muffled voice called, and she tightened her
hold. They had been tacking back and forth since leaving the
harbor. If the captain was right, they would find the current
today.

The angle of the sun on the wall began to shift, and she felt
the boat turn. Seeming to hesitate in its rhythmic motion, the
deck under her feet leveled out. The sound of flapping sails
came from overhead. Alissa took advantage of the level floor
and scrambled halfway up the wide stairway to the deck.
Head poking out, she watched the violent flapping of sails.
Like magic, the noise ceased and the sails filled. The floor
tilted the other way, and Alissa leaned into the wall supporting the stairway.

Timing her moves with the boat, she lurched up onto the
deck. Noise and motion engulfed her. The wind caught her
long hair, pulling it into her eyes despite it being tied back
with Lodesh's ribbon. A smile came over her. To be going
somewhere with no effort was extremely satisfying. *"It would
be grand to fly,"* Beast whispered unexpectedly into her
thoughts. *"I know I could teach you to fly when there was
nothing you could run into."*

Alissa grimaced. *"There's the water,"* she answered, and
she felt Beast sigh.

From her position by the midhatch, she looked to the bow
where Connen-Neute was standing on one foot, balancing
against the motion of the waves and the push of the wind.
Talon was perched beside him on the railing. The young Master made an odd sight with his hands and head bandaged, the
front sail outlining him on one side and the sky on the other.
The ship's boy was watching him with uneasy glances as he
went about his work, occasionally touching the tattoo of a fish
on his shoulder to ward off evil.

Behind her in the recessed wheel deck were the captain and Lodesh. Her eyebrows rose as Lodesh had the wheel in his hands—again. He looked grand with the wind tugging at his tailored clothes and the hat jammed on his head. His green eyes were squinting up at the top of the mast and the flag fastened there. The captain was pointing at it, explaining something. It was obvious the sun and wind agreed with Lodesh. She had a sudden desire to be next to him. Warming, she looked past him to Strell.

Strell was at the very back of the boat, slumped against the railing. He looked awful, giving Alissa a weak wave before turning away, clearly wanting to be left alone. Her own ill feeling had vanished the first day out, and she felt bad for him.

"Alissa!" Lodesh called, his voice faint from the wind. "Come here. The captain is explaining about the direction of the wind and why we have to zigzag."

Not caring why, Alissa nevertheless made her grasping, halting way to ease herself down on one of the built-in benches. She could have made the same trip under the deck and come up at the wheel pit hatch, but it smelled down there. Glancing at the captain, she sipped her tea. "Thank you for agreeing to take us out," she said.

Captain Sholan beamed. He was wearing Lodesh's boots, and his feet were spread wide against the boat's motion. "It is my pleasure, Ma'hr. I'm in debt to you." He smiled, showing bad teeth. "The longer I stay out of port and away from that woman, the happier I'll be. As it is, I can only take you out for three weeks, more is the pity."

"Three weeks?" Alissa questioned. "You said we have enough food and water for two months!"

The captain eyed her darkly. "We do. One month out and one month back. I'll cart you about wherever your little heart desires for three weeks. Then I start back. Besides," he said, fidgeting, "I've got three dock chulls—beg your pardon—on my boat." He grimaced. "That's almost half my crew. Keep them on the water too long, and they'll cause trouble. No. Three weeks is all I'll give you."

Alissa took a breath to protest, desisting at Lodesh's subtle shake of his head. Her brow furrowed as she grasped the significance of the marks Hayden had made in the galley. Perhaps she and Connen-Neute could make the rest of the journey by wing. She wasn't going to come all the way out here just to turn around and go home. But as her eyes went from Strell to Lodesh, she wondered if she could do it.

Putting his hand to shade his eyes, Captain Sholan chewed on his upper lip to make his mustache dance. It was a nervous habit, and Alissa wondered about the food stores. "Got the wheel all right?" he asked, and when Lodesh nodded, he added, "Keep her steady." The captain levered himself out of the recessed deck. He strode to the first mate preparing to go off watch, his shoulders hunched in what looked like concern.

Her gaze shifted back to Lodesh, and she hid a smile behind her mug of strong tea. He looked taller with the wheel in his hand and the strength of the boat under him. The breeze tugged at the yellow curls peeking from under his hat. With his eyes on the distant horizon, he looked more relaxed and content than she had ever seen him. "It must be easier than it looks if he's willing to let you steer the boat alone," she said.

"It is," he said. "And if I shift too far off course, the sails start flapping." He loosened his hold on the wheel and immediately they turned into the wind. The pitch of the deck lessened, and the sails began to rattle. The crew going off watch looked up from their breakfast, and Lodesh pulled the boat back where it ought to be. From across the deck, the captain shouted, "If you can't hold 'er, I'll get someone else to do it!"

Lodesh grinned and waved. Scowling, the captain followed the first mate belowdecks.

Alissa took another sip of her tea, warming what was left back to near boiling with a quick ward. Her eyes were drawn to the bow and Connen-Neute and Talon. When the bird noticed Alissa's attention on her, she launched herself into the air.

A stab of fright went through Alissa—undeserved and embarrassing—as Talon circled the boat. She was heavy with the weight of something as large as herself. With a sliding hush of feathers, the bird landed to pin a dead rat between her feet and Alissa's shoulder.

"Oh, Talon," Alissa exclaimed in disgust, shuddering as she moved both the bird and rat to the bench. "How wonderful. You eat it. I'm *definitely* not hungry."

Lodesh laughed, but Alissa saw nothing amusing. "Has she always brought you her catches?" he asked as Alissa pushed the rat toward her bird and Talon nudged it back.

"Always." She frowned. "I liked it better when all she could catch was grasshoppers."

"Hm-m-m-m. How sure are you that Talon is a her?" he asked, and Alissa gave him an odd look. "What I mean is, I've seen birds do that to a prospective mate."

Alissa flushed. "She just wants to share her catches, that's all. And look at her markings. Males are more striking than that."

"True." Lodesh glanced at the yellow flag at the top of the mast. "But how old is she? Perhaps she's a he with her feathers going gray?"

"Birds don't go gray," Alissa scoffed. "Talon is a she." But her thoughts went back to when she had found Talon flapping ineffectively on the forest floor in an attempt to get into the air. Talon's markings had been darker then. Actually, the only reason Alissa had decided Talon was female was because of her larger size. It had only been the last few years—the last few years of a suspiciously long life span—that her feathers had become so dull.

Quiet in thought, Alissa ran a finger over Talon. The small bird jumped to her shoulder, tugging at her hair until the white ribbon fluttered free. Alissa made a grab for it, but it was gone, over the side and into the water. "Talon!" Alissa cried in exasperation, then turned to Lodesh. "I'm sorry. And you had just gotten it for me, too!"

"I'll get you another," he said, his eyes warm with emotion.

Chattering as if insane, Talon snatched up the rat and struggled into the air. Alissa put a hand to her head as Talon circled the boat three times to gain height, then landed atop the highest mast to eat her breakfast. "That's it?" Alissa shouted up at her bird, not caring that the ship's boy was staring at her. "You lose my ribbon for me and leave?"

Talon's response was hardly audible over the wind, and Alissa slumped into her seat. Lodesh touched her shoulder, and she jumped. "Want to try piloting the boat?" he asked.

Her jaw dropped. "Oh, I can't," she said, imagining the

clatter of the sails and the harsh looks of the sailors if she put them off course.

He grinned. "Just for a moment? It would be a shame if you came out all this way and never really found out."

"Found out what?" she asked, hearing the challenge in his voice.

He hesitated, teasing as he adjusted his hat. "The wind and the water meshing. That's what a boat does. It harnesses both, and you can feel the strength of them only when holding the wheel." He shifted to hold the wheel with one hand, the muscles in his arm bunching. "Here. Slip in ahead of me. I won't let go until you have the knack of it. Promise."

She eyed the small space he had offered her, then glanced behind them at Strell looking out the back of the boat. "Ah," she stammered, thinking if she got that close, Strell would see and try to do something to prove he wasn't ill. "Thank you, no. I want to talk to Connen-Neute."

His crestfallen disappointment convinced her she had made the right decision, and taking her tea, she made her wobbly, hesitant way to the bow and Connen-Neute. She gave the crew hesitant smiles as she passed them as they assembled in grumbling knots before the captain and first mate. Unlike the first mornings when there had been an almost seamless change, both the day and night watches were present. The three dockmen were clustered before the first mate as he questioned them. No one looked happy.

"Morning, Alissa," Connen-Neute said silently as she stumbled closer.

"Excuse me?" she said slyly, remembering Useless's charge to keep him talking aloud.

"You heard me," he said, his voice just above the noise of the wind.

Grinning, she sat down and peered up at him, wondering how he could keep his balance on two feet, much less the one he was standing on. Arms spread wide, Connen-Neute slowly pulled his leg higher. "Would you like some tea?" she offered, extending the amber brew.

"No, thank you. Hayden's tea is worse than Lodesh's used to be." His Master's vest furled in the wind, and the wrap around his head fluttered like a kite tail. Pulling his limbs back toward himself, he gracefully sank down to sit cross-legged before her.

Alissa dropped her eyes, the mention of Lodesh's tea recalling her time trapped in the past. She had tried to make changes so that he wouldn't have to endure the pain of watching his beloved city go empty under a friend's curse. But the only thing she had managed to change was the quality of his tea. Oddly enough, the only person who remembered it was bad before was Connen-Neute.

"How are you this morning?" Connen-Neute asked.

"Fine." Her thoughts went melancholy upon Lodesh and Strell. "Not fine," she amended. He said nothing, and she silently picked at the fraying seam in her shoe. "Connen-Neute?" she asked, wondering about what Useless had said the evening before they left the Hold. "Why did you want to be schooled with the next transeunt?"

A puff of amusement escaped him. "I didn't want him or her to believe we were all like Keribdis," he said. Glancing past her at the distant crewmen, he slipped the wraps from his hands and eyes.

Keribdis, Alissa thought, feeling a stab of anxiety. Her thoughts went to Beast, helpless and vulnerable. Alissa had been hiding Beast for almost two years, and Useless had never caught on. But Keribdis had been trained to spot such abnormalities. "Is she that bad?" Alissa asked.

Connen-Neute's long face reddened. "She's strong-willed, refusing to see a path to an end other than the one she came up with. Like you, in that way." He ran his fingers through his short dark hair to free it from the shape the scarf had pressed into it. "But the real reason I wanted to be schooled with the next transeunt was that Redal-Stan told me it would be a sure way to shift the balance of the conclave. I could gain the trust and ear of someone who would probably hold a great deal of sway." He shrugged sheepishly. "I work better by stealth than bluff and bluster. Keribdis is hard to confront. I can never remember what I wanted to say."

"Hold sway with the conclave?" Alissa said, feeling a trickle of alarm through her.

Connen-Neute folded his scarf. "They simply listen more to some than others. To me, not at all. I'm the fledgling of the

Hold. And if you join with someone who isn't a Master, they'll never take you seriously, either. Transeunt or not."

She frowned, not liking that. "I'm going to marry Strell or Lodesh," she said. "I don't care what Keribdis or anyone else says. I just can't decide whom," she said petulantly.

"I think you already have decided," Connen-Neute said softly.

"What?" she exclaimed, tensing.

He shrugged his thin shoulders, looking far too young to know what he was talking about. "Lodesh is obviously the better of two bad choices. By not coming out with it, I think your heart has already decided on Strell. You're simply too frightened to admit it, knowing the storm of trouble it will cause."

She put the back of her hand to her warm cheek. "I just haven't decided is all."

Connen-Neute held out a long-fingered hand. "Strell?" he said, ticking off his fingers as he spoke. "Commoner. Very short life span. Can't make a ward to save his skin. Last member of a family line half the Hold has been trying to surreptitiously wipe out. Capable of begetting only common children—"

"Stop it," she protested, not wanting to hear it said aloud.

"Lodesh?" He put the other hand out, pantomiming weighing their qualities. "Keeper. Carries a curse to keep him alive until he breaks it. Children who will be Keeper, possibly Master. Past administrator to a city of thousands. Knows the same people they do. Been to the same weddings, parties, funerals . . ." His second hand had fallen appreciably, leaving his first high in the air. "Need I go on?"

She sighed. "No."

"As I said . . . trouble. And to top it off, Strell gets seasick."

She glanced to the stern, wondering if he was right and she was too blind to see it.

"I think you're frightened," Connen-Neute continued. "You know Keribdis will forbid you from marrying a commoner, forcing you to either stand up to her or live a lie."

"How can I be afraid of her?" Alissa said with a false anger. "I've never even met her. And I haven't decided only because when I do, I know the other will leave." Her eyes dropped to her shoes. "I don't want either of them to be alone."

Connen-Neute gave her a wry look. "Them? Or you?

Alissa said nothing, unable to raise her eyes to his as he bound his scarf around his head again. "So will you follow your heart and bring about your end," Connen-Neute said as he hid his golden eyes, "or follow your logic and marry Lodesh? He loves you, and you love him. Either way, you had better decide soon, or they will decide for you."

"Who do you think would win out?" she asked in a small voice, wondering if she was so cowardly as to let them decide.

Connen-Neute shrugged. "Logic says Lodesh, seeing as he has a lifetime of experience to draw upon and is a Keeper. But Strell has survived Bailic when no Keeper could, charmed a feral raku, and defied the boundaries of logic to bring you back from the past through a memory." Connen-Neute tucked the end of the scarf under itself and hid his bare hands in his sleeves. "Lodesh underestimates him. So does Talo-Toecan."

There was a scuff behind her, and she turned to see the first mate approaching with Lodesh. "How so?" she asked softly.

"Strell was raised in the desert," he said soundlessly as Lodesh and the nervous-looking crewman came close. *"He has a core of savage ruthlessness no one but I seem to see."* Folding his hands peacefully in his lap, he turned his cloth-wrapped head to Lodesh.

Alissa followed his gaze, her mild concern as to what they wanted shifting to alarm when Lodesh asked, "Have either of you seen crewman Farrin? He was on night watch, but no one has seen him since midnight."

11

Connen-Neute's plate threatened to move as the boat ran down an especially tall wave. Peeved, he grasped the edge with a scarf-wrapped hand. Gravy sloshed to stain his bandages, and he frowned. In a wash of irritation, he ran a mental search of the boat. The crewmen not on watch were clustered together in the bow. *Still gossiping about the missing sailor, most likely*, he thought. Deciding if worse came to worst he could snuff the oil lamp, Connen-Neute slipped his hands from his wrappings and undid the binding from around his eyes.

"Do you think that wise?" Lodesh asked, not meeting his gaze as he continued to sop up his leftover gravy with a crumbling biscuit.

Connen-Neute ran a long-fingered hand through his short hair to free it from the folds the scarf had pressed into it. "I know where everyone is," he said softly.

The Keeper shrugged, seeming not to care. "Where's Alissa?" he asked as he sipped his drink. "She promised to play cards with me tonight." Glancing at the black rectangle of the night at the top of the ladder, he took a strip of salted meat with a guilty swiftness.

Connen-Neute reached across the table and commandeered

what was left in a show of quiet possessiveness. "You told Alissa you wouldn't eat meat anymore. You and Strell, both."

"I said nothing of the kind." Lodesh grinned mischievously from under his yellow curls. "I simply stopped when she brought it to my attention she didn't like it. That she would make a conclusion from that is her prerogative."

A small sound of warning escaped Connen-Neute. He was sure the distinction would mean nothing to Alissa. Shredding the last wedge of meat, he ate it piece by mocking piece. He rather liked that Alissa stuck to her foothills upbringing and didn't eat meat. It saved possible wear and tear on their friendship. And since he had no designs on pursuing her, she didn't care what he ate. "Alissa is asleep already," he said, answering Lodesh's original question as he washed the meat down with gulp of tepid water.

They had gone through almost half the casks of water in the boat's hold. What was left was showing signs of going bad. Perhaps the captain was right. Perhaps they should start back tomorrow. At least the humans . . .

A scuffing at the top of the ladder broke into his thoughts. He quickly hid his hands in his sleeves, sending a questing thought to find Strell shakily descending. Blowing in relief, Connen-Neute reluctantly picked at the potatoes Alissa had made the cook boil up.

"Strell!" Lodesh called companionably. "Potatoes tonight. Your favorite."

The haggard man hesitated, swallowing as he glanced at their plates and quickly away. "Maybe later," he said. "I came down to get my blanket." His usually dark skin was pale in the amber light from the swinging lamp. "The Navigator help me, I can't stay down here." A panicked look came into his eyes as he lurched to his pack.

A frown pulled Lodesh's brow tight. Leaning across the narrow table, he whispered to Connen-Neute, "Can't you ward him to sleep? For one night? He's doing better, but look at him." He went silent as Strell gripped the ceiling support. "He's been on deck every night," Lodesh continued. "A good sleep might be just the thing."

Connen-Neute nodded. Reassuring himself that none of the crewmen were near, he set his tracings to glow. The pattern for a ward of sleep was difficult, and as he set his field about Strell in preparation, the plainsman started, dropping his pack. As Connen-Neute and Lodesh watched in surprise, Strell looked behind him. "Ashes," the piper whispered. "Now I'm seeing them down here."

"Them?" Connen-Neute questioned cautiously.

Strell grimaced. "Ghosts. The plains are full of them. So is the Hold, and I don't even want to think about Ese' Nawoer." He made a mocking shudder, turning to dig in his pack again. "Talo-Toecan taught me some exercises to ease the scar tissue across my tracings. He thought it might help me reach Alissa when she was—" He hesitated, flicking a dark look at Lodesh. "When she was trapped in the past. I don't do them anymore as it makes the ghosts all the more clear. Sometimes, I don't notice them at all. But when I'm tired or worried, it's worse."

"Really . . ." The idea Strell was sensing ghosts was thin at best, but the piper's response had been a classic reaction to a novice catching his first resonance. Connen-Neute glanced at Lodesh, reading in his uncomfortable expression that the Keeper had guessed the same. "Strell," Connen-Neute asked cautiously, "would you like me to ward you to sleep tonight? So you can get a good rest?" He smiled. "We'll need all your piping skills to calm Alissa tomorrow when Captain Sholan announces we're turning back."

Strell looked ill. "No. Bailic warded me to sleep once. I couldn't wake on my own."

"How about a ward of calming, then?" he asked. "If you'll allow me to look at your tracings, I can tailor it as strong or weak as you like."

Lodesh opened his mouth—undoubtedly to point out that it wasn't possible to tailor a ward in such a way—and Connen-Neute shot him a warning look. He didn't care what ward he put on Strell; he just wanted to get a good look at his tracings.

"Why not?" Strell draped his blanket over his shoulder and straightened. "Ward away."

Lodesh's mug of water hit the narrow table with an accusing thump. His arms crossed before him, and he leaned back against the narrow bench.

"Good," Connen-Neute said, not liking being caught in a

bald-faced lie. "I'll set it up, and you tell me when you sense it. That should be strong enough to do you some good but weak enough such that it won't incapacitate you. And, ah, I'd appreciate it if you don't tell Alissa about this. Talo-Toecan wouldn't approve if I told her it was possible to tailor wards this way."

Lodesh snorted, and a faint smile came over Strell mind. "She won't hear it from me," he said.

Settling himself, Connen-Neute glanced at a wry-faced Lodesh before easing a thought into Strell's mind. He had been invited under a lie but invited nonetheless. He stifled a wince as he viewed the chaos. It was hard to see anything as Strell had no source to light his mindscape, but it was obvious the piper's tracings had no cohesion. It would be impossible for Strell to have caught a resonance. Especially as everything was coated with healing scar tissue. Concerned, Connen-Neute looked closer. The damage looked too old to have been acquired in the short time Strell had been at the Hold. Where had he gained that much scar tissue? And why?

Connen-Neute set up a ward of sleep as he had earlier, careful to keep the energy below the level of invocation. Strell did nothing, standing blankly as he waited for something to happen. There was not a glimmer of resonance from his tracings. Connen-Neute shifted his head slowly, and Lodesh seemed to relax, easing back against the narrow seat.

Wondering what Strell had sensed if it hadn't been his ward, Connen-Neute prepared to put a ward of calming over the plainsman. He could at least do that for him. But as his field touched Strell, the man stiffened. "There," Strell said, his eyes intent.

Connen-Neute looked at him in wonder. He hadn't yet set the ward. "It's the field," he said. "You've become sensitive to the fields that carry wards. That's all."

"A field?" Strell said, his eyes going wide. "Is that . . . normal?"

Connen-Neute exchanged a cautious glance with Lodesh. "There have been very few commoners allowed to stay in the Hold as you have. Perhaps the extended contact with fields and wards could account for it."

That seemed to satisfy Strell, and at his nod, Connen-

Neute set the calming ward in place. Immediately Strell slumped. His face went slack, and his grip on the support post eased from white-knuckled to one only mildly clutching. "That should help," Connen-Neute said, ignoring Lodesh's disapproving look as he noted the piper's breathing had grown slow. He had begun to rock with the boat, too, instead of against it.

"Yes," Strell said around a yawn. "Thanks. It's working. But I'm still going to sleep on deck. G' night, Connen-Neute. See you in the morning." Giving Lodesh a nod, he took the last biscuit from the tin plate and headed to the stairs.

"We should have done that the first night out," Connen-Neute whispered as Strell vanished.

"Uh-huh," Lodesh drawled, a questioning tone to his voice.

Jolted from his thoughts, Connen-Neute flicked a look at him. "You saw him jump. I had to see his tracings," he said. "He might have had a resonating pattern."

"You lied to gain his permission," Lodesh answered.

Connen-Neute met his gaze evenly, refusing to show any guilt. He was a Master of the Hold. Lodesh was a Keeper. "And you've never lied before?" he questioned.

Lodesh took a slow breath, his gaze going back to his plate. "Never mind."

Making a satisfied noise, Connen-Neute picked up his cup and took a swallow. The water was getting worse at the bottom, carrying a sour taste that seemed to stick with him. He set the cup aside, his thoughts going back to Strell's damaged tracings. Strell Hirdune: piper, potter, and heavily scarred. There was only one way to account for it. Feeling a hint of mistrust, he watched Lodesh pick at his biscuit. "Where is the pipe?" Connen-Neute asked.

"Pipe?" Lodesh never looked up.

Connen-Neute leaned forward and pushed the Keeper's plate out of his reach. "The one I warded for you three centuries ago to prevent your sister's children from turning shaduf. Strell is a descendant of your sister, and you know it."

Lodesh glanced up and away. His face showed no emotion. "Of course I know it," he said as he pulled his plate back. "He knows it himself. So does Talo-Toecan."

"Alissa doesn't."

The Keeper frowned. "Strell has chosen to remain silent. But please, I'm sure he would appreciate your telling Alissa before you find out why he hasn't told her himself. I think the man is embarrassed to be my kin. The Navigator knows why." He pulled the plate back, his motions slowing in thought. "Unless . . . No."

A tinge of red came over the man, and Connen-Neute eyed him suspiciously, not remembering ever having seen such an emotion on the usually composed Keeper before. He gestured for him to continue, and Lodesh went sheepish. "I only meant it to get him to leave me alone," he said, "but maybe he took me seriously. Last winter during an—ah—discussion concerning Alissa, I told him the only way I could get rid of my curse was to remove a threat that could save or damn the world, and that if anything like that came up, I'd just leave it to Talo-Toecan. He kept pressing the issue, looking for a way to absolve my curse so I would go away and leave him and Alissa alone. It became rather tedious, so I told him if I got angry enough, I could probably foster it off on one of my descendants. Maybe he took me at my word and is trying to hide his ancestry."

"You'd give another your curse?" Connen-Neute asked, thinking the often self-serving Keeper might someday do just that if he thought it would be to his benefit.

Lodesh looked at the square of night at the top of the stairs as if seeing into the past. "Connen-Neute, you know I never had any children. Besides, why would I want to lose my curse? Especially now?"

Connen-Neute grunted softly at that. Curious about whether his ward had been responsible for the damage, Connen-Neute stretched to pull Strell's pack closer. After searching Strell's mind, ransacking his pack was a small indiscretion.

"I can't believe my ward is still holding," he said as he shuffled about in it. "I'd have expected it to have lost its effectiveness by now." He hesitated. "That's why Keribdis has been trying to wipe out the Hirdune line. She doesn't know my ward has been keeping them commoners when they ought to be Keepers and shadufs. You never told her?"

Lodesh's eyes went tight in anger. "Keribdis began her campaign to wipe out the Hirdunes long after I'd died. Three generations of failure is embarrassing, and for her, it's easier to eliminate an aberrant family line and start over than try to understand why it isn't giving her what she wanted. I see no reason to say anything now. Or do you want to explain to Keribdis why her attempt to nurture a shaduf from the Stryska/Hirdune union failed so spectacularly?"

Tensing in a pang of angst, Connen-Neute shook his head. Giving Lodesh's sister a warded pipe to gently scar her infants' tracings into unusable pathways to prevent her from having a shaduf child had been his idea. If it was found he had secretly worked against the Hold's agreed plan, he could be charged with sedition—even three centuries later.

Connen-Neute stifled a shudder as he dug deeper into Strell's pack. He'd never agreed with the morality of the Hold's policy to capitalize upon the tragedy of shadufs. But as no one listened to him, he always relied upon stealth to make things go the way he thought they should.

A cry of success slipped from him as his fingers found a smooth length of wood. Then he looked closer, frowning. "It's made of mirth wood, but this isn't the pipe."

"No." Lodesh took a huge swallow of his drink, making a face as he set the cup down at arm's length. "He broke it. Which was just as well, seeing he was starting to scar himself worse playing it for Alissa. He made that one from the end of Alissa's staff." Lodesh stacked his plate upon Connen-Neute's empty one. "See the position of the last hole?"

Connen-Neute held the pipe as if to play it. "He put the hole where his shortened finger could reach it." He looked up, his brow furrowed. "Our good minstrel has a pipe of mirth wood that no one but he can play. Interesting . . ."

Lodesh guffawed. "Save me from prophesying rakus."

A sudden thought pulled Connen-Neute's attention from the valuable pipe. "He might be able to engender Keeper children."

"You saw his tracings," Lodesh said quickly. "Talo-Toecan agrees there's no cohesion under the scarring. Strell's siblings might have been Keepers, but Strell isn't."

"Perhaps," Connen-Neute said around a yawn. "Ashes, I'm sleepy. I'm going out on deck to clear my head. I want to try to reach Talo-Toecan tonight."

Lodesh yawned as well. "Alissa said she lost contact with him three nights ago."

"It's worth a try," Connen-Neute persisted. "He might have an idea of how Strell can sense fields. In any case, he'd want to know about it."

Lodesh stood when Connen-Neute did, catching himself against a ceiling support. He hesitated, unusually unsteady. "I'll see you in the morning, then. Alissa will need some cheering up."

"She's trying to convince me to abandon ship with her and fly ahead," Connen-Neute said, watching Lodesh as he rewrapped his eyes.

Lodesh spun, the haze of fatigue vanishing from him. "You won't, will you?"

Grinning, he said nothing, making a pair of red scarves to replace the black ones of Alissa's that he had gotten gravy on. Still silent, he bound his hands and rose up the stairs and into the dark. It would do the cocky Keeper some good to not know everything for a change.

12

"Alissa," a voice hissed, humming in her head like bees. "Alissa, please. Wake up!"

She tried to swallow, surprised at the difficulty. Her mouth had a bitter taste she recognized. *Drugged?* she thought, disoriented. Had Redal-Stan drugged her again? Was he here? She had a word or two to put in his ear about that!

Confused, she tried to open her eyes with no success. Someone was pulling on her hair. *Feathers,* she thought, smelling them. *Blood? No, carrion.* Her thoughts swirled, making the connection. *Talon.*

Her mind cleared somewhat. There was a flush of wind, and Talon was gone. Alissa's head hurt and her arms ached. She thought she was going to be sick. The boat rose with a wave, and the rigging thumped against slack canvas.

Something bumped her, fumbling at her wrists bound before her. "Ashes," Strell whispered, panic in his voice. "Why did I ever agree to this? I knew she was going to get herself into trouble. The girl can't pick flowers without coming home with ghosts."

Alissa felt a laugh bubble up to come out as a soft groan. Strell talked to himself? Why not? she decided, her thoughts weaving. She not only talked to herself, but she answered back.

"Beast?" she slurred into her mind, getting a somnolent murmur of a response. Her alter consciousness was as aware as she was, which meant not at all. But that, Alissa thought, could be rectified—if she could pull herself together long enough to focus.

Struggling to concentrate, she sent a careful thought into her source to put her tracings alight. She set the pattern for a ward of healing, wagering it would cleanse the drug from her as easily as it mended small cuts and sped bruises on to healing. Unsure of herself, she checked the pattern twice before invoking it. Just as she decided she had it correct, someone yanked her into a sitting position by her hair.

"Ow," she groaned, struggling to open her eyes.

"Don't touch her!" Strell shouted. There was a surprised grunt, and the grip on her hair vanished. She collapsed. Her head met the deck with a thunk. Pain shocked through her. Cheek pressed against the sun-warmed wood, she heard a derisive shouting and the sound of Strell retching. Sunlight stabbed her eyes. Squinting, she saw a pair of bare feet pad away. Strell was curled into a ball, clearly having been kicked in the stomach. His hands were tied behind him. Blood smeared his shoulder where his shirt had torn.

"She's still out," the barefoot dockman called out in his singsong accent. "She won't be awake until sunset."

Her eyelids opened a slit, and she fought to keep her breathing slow at the sound of approaching boots. A shadow fell over her. Lodesh's boots, the pair the captain had taken for passage, stopped in front of her. She didn't think Lodesh or the captain was wearing them. There was a soft sound of regret, and the boots and bare feet moved away.

Stomach churning, she closed her eyes and returned her attention to her mindscape. She was pleased to see the pattern had held through the abuse. That was good. She didn't think she had the presence of mind to set it up again. Dizzy, she allowed more energy to flow. Her tracings filled with a soundless force. There was a moment of heavy disorientation as the ward seemed to exist in not only her thoughts but her body as well. Then, with a snap that she swore had to be audible, her tracings went dark. The ward severed itself from her thoughts and acted.

A sigh sounding like a moan slipped from her. Warmth from the ward mixed with the sun. It pulsed in time with the shush of the water against the hull and the rocking of the boat. The mind-slowing taste of the bitter drug dissolved. She stretched languorously upon the deck, basking in the somnolent peace instilled by the ward. It was only when she reached to brush the hair tickling her nose that she remembered her hands were tied.

She jolted awake. Heart pounding, she held herself still, hiding her open eyes behind her bound hands. From her hand span height on the deck, she saw the sails were down. It was late morning. Strell was slumped nearby, his hands bound and his hair wild. What the ashes was going on?

"Get your chull hands offa me!" she heard the captain shout. There was a thump, and her gaze shot across the deck to where he had been dropped near the main mast. The ship's boy and the dockman usually on night watch were checking the ropes about the captain's hands and feet. Captain Sholan was barefoot, his white toes looking vulnerable in the sun. A gash across his skull bled sluggishly to drip into his eyes and beard. He shook his head, scattering clotted blood against the deck and gray sails. Sickened, she wiggled her hands to test her ropes.

"Strell," she whispered, he turned to her. Relief so strong it was painful to see cascaded over his haggard face.

"Thank the Navigator," he breathed, clearly forcing his heartfelt gaze from hers. He licked his cracked lips and glanced at the three dockmen taunting the captain. "Stay asleep," he muttered, scooting until his bound hands shuffled into her view. The smell of wet rope and sand assailed her. And blood. She could smell blood. Fear chilled her through the strong sun.

Immediately she began to pick at the ropes on his wrists. Her fingers were cold and unresponsive. Stifling a cry of frustration, she added her teeth. "What happened?" she asked, her words muffled by the thick cord. It tasted like sweat.

"Captain Sholan was right," he said, leaning so his shadow shaded her eyes. "The dockmen took the boat."

She didn't care about the boat. "Where are Lodesh and Connen-Neute?"

"I don't know. They drugged last night's dinner. They didn't expect me to wake up. I watched them kill the first mate and one of Captain Sholan's regular crew. They probably killed that missing sailor, too. I'm sorry they hurt you, Alissa. Are you all right?"

She nodded. The knots were slick with his sweat. His fingers looked white, with the truncated tip of his pinky showing a stark red. Strell had been seasick and had barely eaten a thing. She had fallen asleep unusually early. They were all fools.

As she worked, she sent her thoughts over the boat. Panic took her as she couldn't find Connen-Neute and Lodesh. *They are dead,* she thought. *They have to be!* Stomach knotting, she fearfully widened her search. Her shoulders slumped as she found them bobbing in a dinghy resting against the boat. They were asleep, too deep to be natural. "I found Connen-Neute and Lodesh," she whispered. "They're in one of the dinghies."

"Are they alive?" he asked, frightened.

"They're asleep," she whispered, feeling ill at his question.

"You're a dog!" the captain suddenly shouted. "I'll see you hanged by your own entrails. Let me up!" he raged. "Fight me. We'll see how brave you are, then. Poison and venom. Dock whores have more honor than—"

His words ended with a sodden thump and a pained grunt. Alissa worked harder. "Almost," she whispered, feeling the knots begin to loosen. With Strell's wiggling, the wraps came apart. He tensed, shifting to sit upon his ropes. "Can you ward them?" he asked, keeping his back to her as he reached behind him for her bound wrists. "Put them to sleep? Still them?"

"Only one at a time. Warding people is hard. Let me get the poison from Connen-Neute and Lodesh first. As long as they are ignoring us, we have time."

"You can do that? From here?" he said. His hands behind his back took her bound hands in his. "How could I have been so stupid, Alissa?" he whispered. "I put you in so much danger. They want to sell you!"

Tears threatened, not at his words but at the love behind them. She kissed his fingertips, then urged him back to freeing her. "We'll be all right. Let me wake them up."

As Strell worked at her bonds, Alissa sent her thoughts to the rowboat. Trembling, she set up her tracings. They were within a raku length, so her wards would reach. Blood rushed into her hands as Strell freed her. Ignoring the tingling pain in her fingers, she first set a ward over Lodesh. A heartbeat later, she warded Connen-Neute. The young Master fell into a natural sleep as he always did after a ward of healing, but Lodesh woke up.

"What the Wolves am I doing down here?" she heard his elegant accent echo up over the side. She met Strell's eyes. He glanced at the three dockmen and shook his head. They were arguing and hadn't heard Lodesh.

"Lodesh," she sent silently as she rubbed her wrists, hidden behind Strell. *"The dockmen drugged you. Strell and I are on deck. We're both free, but they don't know it."*

"Mutiny?" Lodesh thought, his emotions tinged with anger.

"Give Connen-Neute a shake. We need to—"

She cut her thought short as two pairs of bare feet and one booted came toward her. Strell kept his hands clasped behind him to appear bound. She slit her eyes, watching Strell squint up. Sweat trickled over his brow. She tucked her hands under her.

"Alissa?" Connen-Neute blurted into her thoughts. He sounded bewildered. Frightened at how fast things were spiraling out of control, she relaxed to fall into an intense state of connection. Connen-Neute's awareness seemed to stumble, falling past the usual barriers to land deep into her thoughts. The young Master hesitated, then, realizing she was asking him to pickaback his consciousness on hers so he would know what was happening on deck, he agreed.

Alissa stifled a shudder as he lowered his own defenses and their thoughts came close to mingling freely. It wasn't difficult to maintain such a close link with another soul, just highly ill-advised. But they had done this before. And it was easier than relaying everything.

Feeling a glimmer of Connen-Neute's fear, her pulse slowed to match his. Their breathing synchronized. Connen-Neute saw through her eyes, and she felt her lips move as he told Lodesh what he was seeing through her slit lids.

"Look," the ship's boy said, his usual meekness having changed to a bullying scorn. "She's a-talkin' in her sleep." Her lips stopped as Connen-Neute realized what he was doing.

"She looks mighty pretty, just a-lying there," the barefoot man said, and she fought not to move as a work-blackened toe brushed the hair from her face.

"If you touch her," Strell threatened, "I'll kill you. I swear it. Somehow, I'll kill you."

Alissa stifled a shudder at the heavy promise in his voice. Connen-Neute was right. None of them knew the depths to which he would go.

"Shaddup!" a high, rough voice shouted. "Or I'll slit your throat and make her watch."

"No," she heard Hayden, the galley man, say. "I told you no killin' or rapin'. You listen to me this time." Lodesh's boots appeared in her sight to take an aggressive stance. "You don't like it, you can get in the rower with what you left alive," Hayden exclaimed. "Or do you want to settle this right now? Eh, Clen? You and me? I cut you under the docks when you touched my sister. I'll spill your guts right here if you kill anyone else afore I say so! You know I can!"

Her heart pounded wildly as the bare feet edged away with a reluctant slowness.

From the mast, Captain Sholan shouted, "You'll be a murderer sure as slicing our throats if you put us in a dinghy out here. Give me a knife. Let me die fighting. Or are you afraid I'll best you? Worthless dock chull!"

Hayden turned, Lodesh's boots scraping. "It's up to the Navigator if you live or die in a rower, not me." There was a moment of silence. "Clen, we're keeping the piper 'cause he's worth something now that he ain't seasick. And the woman. But you ain't touchin' her. Red runny eyes don't sell as well as angry ones."

"Let me have a bell, then, Hayden," Clen almost whined. "I should get at least one."

Alissa stiffened. Her pulse raced. Not her bells. They couldn't have those!

"Alissa," warned Connen-Neute in her thoughts, his fear

thick. *"I'll buy you new ones. I'm almost free. With all three of us, no one will get hurt!"*

But someone touched her ankle. "Get off!" she shrieked, hearing Connen-Neute shout the same, linked together as they were. Panicked, she flung Connen-Neute out of her thoughts. She lashed out with her foot, hitting nothing. Sitting up, she stared at the three startled dockmen.

"Wolves," she heard Connen-Neute swear.

"Burn it to ash, Alissa," Lodesh thought. *"We aren't ready yet."*

Wide-eyed, she scuttled back to Strell. Her heart pounded. Together they rose. Strell stood protectively in front of her. The dockmen's surprise melted back into confidence. Hayden dropped back a step and fingered the hilt of his knife. "Not so sleepy? It don't matter." He gestured to Clen and the boy. "Tie them back up. And keep them apart this time."

Alissa gasped. She tried to think of a ward, but her mind went blank. Strell dropped into a fighting crouch. Hayden's face went sour as he urged the other two dockmen to attack. The ship's boy looked frightened, not so brave now that they were awake, but Clen stepped close, eagerly swinging his knife in a threatening arc. Jaw clenched, Strell stepped into the swing, ducking the blade. Grabbing the man's hand, he twisted.

"Stop!" Alissa shouted as the boy stepped forward to help. She heard Talon chitter in anger from the mast. Alissa jumped when the bird landed on her shoulder and hissed.

"Don't kill him!" Hayden shouted irately. "He's worth more than both of you!"

"It's nice to be appreciated," Strell grunted, falling back. Blood stained his upper arm, but Alissa didn't think it was his. White-faced, she warded Clen's knife to make it hot. It was the ward she used the most, and the only one she could remember. The dockman dropped it with a curse, staring at the knife on the deck. The boy gasped, backing up as he whispered a chant over and over to ward off evil. She stood blankly, trying to recall a ward of stillness, but her swirling thoughts wouldn't slow.

"Lodesh?" Strell shouted. "Alissa is a bit preoccupied. I could use a little help up here!"

"That's enough," Connen-Neute muttered into her thoughts. *"I'm tired of masks and scarves. I'm tired of Talo-Toecan telling me what I can and can't do."*

"Wait!" Lodesh cried. "I almost have you free."

"I can do it myself," he snarled into her thoughts, and Alissa felt a pull on her tracings.

"Don't!" she shouted, knowing he had shifted to a raku. They had promised they wouldn't! The deck tilted violently. Talon's nails vanished from her shoulder as Alissa lost her balance and rolled to the edge. Clen's knife slid to a halt beside her. Clawed hands large enough to encircle a horse gripped the railing above her. The dockmen stopped their advance, holding onto the boat to keep from sliding as they stared in fear.

Strell slid down next to Alissa. He took Clen's knife. "Stay here," he hissed. She reached out after him as he half-crawled up the sloping deck to the captain. The crewmen stared in horror at the long, wet tail coiling heavily up onto the deck. Strell knelt behind Captain Sholan and worked at the knots.

The timbers groaned, and the boom swung as the boat leaned farther when Connen-Neute peered over the side of the boat. His reptilian head was larger than the boat's wheel. He grinned, showing canines as thick and long as her arm.

"It's a serpent!" the boy screamed, jolting everyone into motion.

"Serpent?" Connen-Neute roared, not understood by anyone but Alissa as his word was repeated in her thoughts. *"I'm a Master!"* Snarling fiercely, Connen-Neute lurched onto the deck. Alissa gasped as the boat nearly swamped. It righted itself as Connen-Neute found the center of the boat. The boom swung, splintering against his thigh.

"That's a raku!" Hayden shouted, terrified.

Alissa's heart pounded. They weren't supposed to shift. They had promised they wouldn't let anyone know who they were! The dockmen might guess it was Connen-Neute!

Lodesh's arm appeared over the railing. Using the rope tied to the dinghy, he pulled himself up, straining. He was soaked. The rowboat must have sunk when Connen-Neute shifted. Taking everything in with a glance, the Keeper levered himself onto the deck with a sodden splat. "Well, if you're going to do it the hard way . . ." he said, slicking his hair back as he joined her. Strell had freed the captain and was back with them.

Connen-Neute spread his wings and roared magnificently. With his neck extended, he was almost as tall as the largest mast. Even knowing he would never hurt anyone, Alissa was taken aback. The crewmen cowered. Hunched, they retreated to the stern, knives in hand. Lodesh grinned, and Alissa gave him a backhanded whack on his shoulder to be still. "It's not funny," she said.

"They can't fight that," he said merrily as he gestured at Connen-Neute. "We've won."

Her ire shifted to a deadly concern as she saw the captain standing with the mutineers. "Truce?" Captain Sholan said. Hayden nodded, tossing him a dagger.

"Survivor gets the boat," Hayden said shortly. He took a breath. "For your lives!" he shouted. Together, the men raced across the deck, fear in their eyes.

Connen-Neute made a puzzled harrumph. Shocked, Alissa screamed, "Wait!"

Someone set up a ward of sleep. She gasped in relief as the pattern resonated across her tracings, jerking her memory of it into play. Faster than she ever had before, she set her tracings alight. Her sleeping ward dropped the captain two man lengths from Connen-Neute. He fell, sliding across the deck. Her gaze darted to Clen. He was falling as she watched. The boy was brought down by Connen-Neute or Lodesh, or both. It was only Hayden who reached Connen-Neute, and that was by stealth.

"Above you!" Alissa cried as the man dropped from the rigging.

Connen-Neute leaned out of the way. Hayden hit the deck in an ungraceful fall. His limbs splayed awkwardly, and he groaned. The dagger rolled from his slack fingers. Alissa took a breath as Beast reminded her to breathe. Her feral consciousness had watched it all with an amusement that baffled Alissa. She took in the blood-splattered deck and the four men sprawled upon it. It was over?

Connen-Neute picked up Hayden's dagger with an awkward claw and dropped it over the side. The man's eyes opened, widening in fear at the raku towering above him. *"Gnat,"* Connen-Neute thought, raising a foot over him. *"That would have hurt."*

"Don't you dare!" Alissa cried as she stumbled forward.

"I'm not going to crush him," Connen-Neute said at her horrified look. *"Just scare him."*

Alissa blanched as Connen-Neute pinned him under a careful foot, lowering his head to breathe on him. A low growl reverberated up through her feet. Alissa swallowed, imagining his fear, but Connen-Neute's teeth were bared in what she recognized as a grin. *"Come and tame me,"* he thought cheerfully. *"It'll make a grand story!"*

"Oh, no," she said, backing up into Strell. "I couldn't."

Strell took her elbow. "Couldn't what?" he asked, unable to hear Connen-Neute.

She winced as Hayden started chanting another of his charms. "He wants me to pretend to tame him."

Lodesh snickered, and she spun. "Stop it!" she shouted. "The man is frightened!"

"Go tame him, then," Strell said, clearly wondering at her hesitation.

She took a resolute breath. Lips pressed tight, she stomped to Connen-Neute. "Get off Hayden!" she shouted up with a real anger as she pushed on his foot.

Connen-Neute roared, gnashing his teeth at the sky. In her mind was his laughter, peeving her all the more.

"I'm already dead," Hayden said, his eyes wide and glazed with fear. "The Navigator sent one of his Wolves for me."

Alissa blinked. She had never heard rakus referred to like that. "I said, 'Get off!' "

Connen-Neute took a breath to roar again, hesitating as her eyes narrowed. "Now," she quietly threatened, and Connen-Neute looked to where Lodesh was leaning against the wheel wiping his eyes. Strell, at least, was taking the situation seriously, searching the sailors and gathering the scattered weapons. Reluctance in every motion, Connen-Neute lifted his foot. "Go on. Give him some space," she demanded as she extended a hand to help Hayden rise.

Frightened, Hayden scuttled back to his fallen comrades. His gaze darted from them to her in terror when they didn't move, felled by nothing he could see. "Mirim save us. Mirim save us," he panted, for the first time loud enough for Alissa to hear what his charm against evil was.

She felt a wash of shock at the name. Mirim? That was the name of the Hold's first transeunt. "They're all right," she said, snapping herself out of her surprise. "They're asleep."

"You're—you're its master," he stammered. He sent his gaze high over her head to where Connen-Neute was gnashing his teeth and weaving his head as if chained by unseen ropes.

"Stop that," she said into his thoughts. *"You look foolish."*

"I look fierce!" he answered, clearly enjoying himself.

"Then why is Lodesh laughing?" she said, and he paused, his wings drooping as he saw the Keeper chuckling as he helped Strell with the weapons. *Is he a fool?* she wondered. They would have been dead had Strell not woken her. "Look," she said, taking a step forward. Hayden backed up, fear and panic making him look old. She hesitated. "We never meant to hurt you. But you took over the boat."

Hand pressed to his shoulder, he mumbled and backed away.

Alissa sighed, frustrated. "What if we—uh—I wake everyone up?"

He licked his lips. Fright made his eyes wild.

Alissa's stomach was in knots, and her knees felt weak. There had to be a way to calm him down. She took a dramatic pose. "They will wake when I say the proper words," she said, glancing meaningfully at Lodesh. If they could synchronize their actions, it would look as if she was doing it all. So far, they had done nothing to link rakus to Masters. As she didn't have the long hands or golden eyes, they wouldn't even know she was one.

Alissa hesitated, thinking. Edging from foot to foot, she tugged at her dress and adjusted her stance.

"What's the matter?" Connen-Neute asked.

"I can't think of anything to say," she muttered, embarrassed.

The raku laughed, and Hayden chanted louder at the savage sound. *"Ashes, Alissa. Just make something up."*

She nervously brushed the hair from her eyes. Taking a

firm position, she lifted her arms to the sky, feeling like an idiot. "By the power of the sea, awaken before me!" she said loudly.

"Wolves. No more," Lodesh said, turning away with his arms clutched around himself.

"And you thought I looked foolish?" Connen-Neute said.

Flushed, Alissa almost forgot to break her ward upon the captain. The two men and the boy woke more or less as one, rolling to their feet to gather in a frightened knot. "She's controlling the raku!" Hayden shouted as he joined them. "It's her! Her!"

Alissa shivered at the fear and hate pouring from them, especially the captain. Strell gestured for her to continue. "We're going on," she said, glad she kept the shaking from her voice. She wasn't used to people being afraid of her. "We're going to find the Rag Islands."

"We aren't doing anything," the captain said, then spat at her feet. Lodesh's mirth dropped from him. He stiffened, and Strell gripped his arm to keep him unmoving. Alissa didn't move, used to being spit at.

"We're going on," she insisted, conscious of Connen-Neute's shadow about her. "Or my beast will tear your boat apart," she bluffed.

The captain's eyes narrowed. His hands clenched on nothing, clearly wanting his knife back. "We're already dead," he said, and Hayden muttered his agreement. "There's not enough water to get home with the boom broken."

She took a breath to fight off the shakes. "There's enough water now that half the crew is dead," she said bitterly. "And the Rag Islands must be closer than the coast."

The men before her moved uneasily. In response, Connen-Neute rumbled, edging forward until his talons were both to the right and left of her. He towered over her, as substantial as a mountain. *"I don't know, Alissa,"* he warned. *"Maybe we should just let them have one of the dinghies? They're going to run the first chance they get. I know how to sail."*

"They'll die out here," she protested. Face pinched in worry, Alissa put a hand upon one of his claws. "We are going on!" she said louder. "Why did you all have to go and ruin everything?" she shouted. "All I wanted was to find

them!" Depressed, she watched the four men band together. How could she convince them there was nothing to be afraid of?

"Maybe if I shift back?" Connen-Neute thought. *"They aren't afraid of me as a human."*

Alissa looked up at him as she rubbed her wrists. The burn from the rope was gone, thanks to the healing ward, but it still felt as if it marked her. *"I don't know. They would know rakus are Masters, then. Talo-Toecan said—"*

"They'll die if they flee," he interrupted. *"They won't be as afraid if they know it's me."*

Still unsure, Alissa nodded.

The sailors gasped as Connen-Neute vanished in a swirl of pearly white. The boat eerily rose as his weight left it. "The Navigator help us," Hayden stammered as Connen-Neute reappeared and put a long-fingered hand upon Alissa's shoulder. "It's one of them. They've come back! He's one of them!"

Alissa's eyes widened. If their fear was strong for the raku, it doubled when seeing Connen-Neute's long hands and golden eyes. "Maybe this wasn't a good idea," Connen-Neute said, hiding his long hands in his sleeves and trying to look sage.

"Let me go!" the boy cried, pushing at the hands that kept him from jumping overboard. "Let me go! Please! He'll take me!" He was crying, and a cold feeling slipped though her. The raku he would fight. The Master he would run from. What had the Hold done to the coast to warrant this reaction five hundred years later? Connen-Neute mirrored her bewilderment.

Her eyes widened as the three older seamen gathered themselves, lunging. Frightened, she set a ward upon the closest, freezing him into immobility. Connen-Neute and Lodesh got the other two. The boy collapsed in a huddle, sobbing on the deck.

"Stop trying to kill Connen-Neute!" she shouted. "We're going to the Rag Islands, whether you like it or not!"

She released her ward, purposely turning her back on them, trusting their fear and Lodesh to keep her safe. "Bury the dead and get the sails up!" she demanded, stomping away.

Inside she was weeping harder than the boy. Vision swimming, she went to the bow so no one would see her tears. Behind her, the dockmen were invoking the protection of Mirim. *Mirim,* she thought bitterly. They didn't even know they were putting their trust in a Master.

Talon dropped from the mast to her shoulder, and Alissa ran a finger over the claws pinching through her shirt. Despondent, angry, and frustrated, she kept her attention on the horizon as the sound of the men's funeral whispered up from behind her. The smell of the blood on the deck made her ill. She stood by herself, refusing to take part, not wanting to acknowledge it. How was she going to keep the crew from killing them the first chance they got?

They left her alone as they raised the jib around her. The smallest mainsail behind the wheel pit was brought tight, and they began to limp forward. Her stomach clenched at the sound of bristles against wood as the boy scrubbed the deck free of the blood of the two men who had died. He was still crying, his tears mingling with the water on the deck.

She didn't turn when Lodesh joined her. For a long time he said nothing. "How close are the islands?" he finally asked, his concern obvious.

"Close enough to fly if I knew exactly where to go," she said, her voice flat. *Close enough to dream of Silla every night,* she thought. Close enough to frighten the young woman from sleep every . . . single . . . night. She looked at Lodesh. His eyes held a shared pain.

"I only wanted to find them," she whispered, feeling the hot swelling of tears. "Now three men are dead, and the coast will know Masters and rakus are the same." She wiped her eyes with a corner of her sleeve. "Why am I even doing this?"

"To make Talo-Toecan happy," he whispered.

She nodded, and Lodesh put a steadying arm over her shoulders. There was no sly underlying feeling in his touch, so she leaned her head against his shoulder as he steadied her. To make Useless happy. Yes. But she was sure he wouldn't be happy with them now.

13

Alissa sat at the bow of the boat, dismally waiting for Connen-Neute to return from his morning search for land. Her knees were drawn up to her chin, and her arms were clasped about her legs. Talon was perched on the railing to keep her from being alone. A bright red square of silk fluttered from the back rim of her hat. It had been a gift from Connen-Neute to help keep the sun off her neck, but it didn't matter. After this many days, her skin was as dark as Strell's.

To her right was the gray of the jib stretching tall enough to make her dizzy; to her left was the blue of the water and sky. It was the same sky, the same water, the same boat. But now the joy was gone.

Connen-Neute's daily flights had turned up nothing. Mental searches were shouts in the dark. Her dreams of Silla had become fragmented at best as Silla's fear jolted them both awake whenever they managed to touch thoughts. Alissa had been counting on Silla's help to pinpoint them exactly, and that wasn't going to happen.

The soft sound of conversation rose behind her, but she didn't turn, recognizing Strell and Lodesh at the wheel pit. Strell's seasickness had improved dramatically. He was piping an odd tune on his instrument, trying to cheer her up from a distance, as nothing else seemed to work.

A faint smile curved over her as his music drifted out to mix perfectly with the hazy morning. Slowly her smile faded. Her eyes dropped from the empty horizon to her shoes, salt-stained and beginning to fray at the seams. They had been under water rations ever since Clen and the ship's boy had absconded with most of the water in the larger of the two row-boats. As she had feared, they had chosen to take their chances with the elements. That had been six days ago. The captain and Hayden had refused to flee. Each wanted the *Albatross*. Greed, Alissa mused, must be stronger than fear.

Between the six of them—two reluctant, three inept, and one who knew what he was doing much to the surprise of all concerned—they managed the boat. It had been Connen-Neute's idea to put himself and the captain together on night watch. It seemed to be working, as the captain's mood of mistrust had markedly shifted. Alissa thought it might be from their late-night conversations about star movement. He seemed ready to consider that Connen-Neute was neither going to eat him nor steal his soul. Hayden was reserving judgment, but at least his constant diatribes on the evils of Masters had ceased.

Despite the rationing and the moisture Strell was collecting from his desert water traps, she was worried. They had been out on the ocean so long. She was starting to wonder if the captain's loud and daily predictions would hold, and they would indeed perish. Thinking she had led them all to their deaths, she fingered Redal-Stan's watch on its cord about her neck.

Strell's music drifted off into nothing, and she slipped into a hazy drowse, lulled by the heat and the motion of the boat. Connen-Neute's mental hail struck through her like a whip, jolting her upright and awake. *"I'm coming,"* came his oddly tense thought as her pulse slowed. *"Get the jib down."*

"Did you find land?" she asked, but he didn't answer.

Her eyes widened in anticipation. He hadn't said no like every other morning. Feeling hope for the first time in days, she rose to her feet. "Get the jib down!" she called as she hastened to the wheel pit. "He's coming in!"

Strell ran a slow hand down his neatly trimmed beard as he took in her obvious excitement. "Did he find something?" he asked as he held out a hand to steady her as she hopped into the pit.

"He didn't say." The boat turned into the wind, and there was a sliding crumple as the jib fell to give Connen-Neute room to land. She scanned the horizon. "Do you see him?"

Hayden had joined them at the mention of land. He stood coiling up the jib line as his eyes roved the sky. Suddenly he stiffened. "There he is," he said, going uneasy. "Give me the wheel," he grumbled, dropping the rope and pushing Lodesh out of the way. "You aren't facing into the wind enough. You want him to swamp us?"

Lodesh gestured flamboyantly, and Hayden took the wheel. The first time they had tried this, Connen-Neute had nearly torn the small mainsail from its ties from the force of his back-winging. Now they knew they had to have the sails utterly slack to keep everything on an even keel. After so much practice, Hayden's worry was unfounded.

The boat's motion slowed, and the sound of the waves grew louder. Alissa followed the dockman's gaze to a bright spot of gold. It rapidly grew larger, and as Hayden made muttered oaths of protection, the young raku awkwardly landed.

The boat tipped forward for an instant as it took his weight, then Connen-Neute vanished in a swirl of white. He reappeared in his Master's best, looking distracted and upset.

Alissa's anticipation faltered. Her worry grew when Connen-Neute made his hurried way to the fore hatch and vanished belowdecks. Eyes wide, she turned to Strell and Lodesh. "He didn't say anything!" she said, stating the obvious. "He never even looked at us!"

Lodesh's green eyes were pinched as he adjusted his hat.

"Get the sails up!" Hayden said brusquely, as if the *Albatross* was his boat when the captain was asleep. "We won't get anywhere with the canvas on the deck."

Lodesh took her elbow and pulled her close. "Let me help Strell get the sails up, and then I'll go see what's the matter."

"He found land," Alissa said, her stomach clenching. "I know it." She glanced at Strell. His motions to raise the sails were slow and dejected.

Lodesh's lips pressed together in worry. He suddenly looked tired, his entire tragic history falling upon him in an instant. She had almost forgotten his curse, the guilt of an entire city's populace upon his soul. The reminder of the pain he carried now shone from him. But under it was the clear indication that he knew something she didn't.

The lost Masters are dead, she thought, her stomach clenching and her skin going cold.

"I'll ask him what he found," she said, determined Lodesh wouldn't shield her from the truth. Lodesh took a breath to argue, and she frowned. "Strell needs your help," she added, turning on a quick heel. Leaving them without a backward glance, she headed to the galley hatch, backing downward on the ladder as she went belowdecks.

The sudden absence of wind accentuated the closed-in feeling. Squinting as her eyes adjusted, she found Connen-Neute standing in the galley, a flaccid waterskin in his long hands. He was drinking, his throat moving rapidly as he downed the contents in one go. "Connen-Neute?" she said softly.

He came up for air, coughing violently. His eyes were watering, and she took a step closer in concern. "Oh, Wolves," she swore. "You found them. Are most of them dead?"

Not looking at her, he put up a hand to forestall her from saying anything more. Alissa's heart sank. Her eyes closed as she thought of Useless. It was done. It had all been for nothing. Better she had never come out here than to have given Useless a false hope. Above her on deck she could hear Hayden shouting instructions. The muted sound of wind and waves grew stronger, and the boat began to move. She reached for a handhold as the floor shifted.

"But Silla," she said, refusing to believe the worst. "Someone has to be alive."

Connen-Neute took a ragged breath as he lowered the water sack. "You should wash your hair," he said. "Wash your hair, wash your face, wash your feet." He took a breath. "Mend your stockings. Clean your nails. Scrub your back ridges." His long finger pointed as he spoke, and his focus wavered.

Alissa peered at him, her lips parting in surprise. Taking

the waterskin from him, she brought it to her nose, recoiling. It wasn't water, it was Hayden's stash of rum! Her jaw dropped as he took the skin back and tried to eke out another swallow.

From above them came Hayden's muffled, excited call. "Land! I see land!" Alissa stood torn between joining the jubilation on deck and shaking Connen-Neute until he told her what was wrong. "What are you doing!" she questioned angrily as his golden eyes suddenly struggled to focus. "Why didn't you tell me you had found them? You did, didn't you?"

"Found them," he said slowly, blinking at her like an owl. "They're there. All of them—mostly. I found their thought signatures."

Frustrated, she clenched her hands. "Then what are you doing? We should fly out there and tell them we're here!"

Connen-Neute shook his head. She tried to grab the empty sack, but he wouldn't let go. He stumbled as he fought to keep it, falling to slump at one of the galley benches. His long face took on a mix of fear and defiance. "I like who I am," he said, and she drew back in confusion. "I like everything the way it is. I didn't want to find them. I only came with you because—" He hesitated. "I won't let her hurt you," he said suddenly with the fierce loyalty of a big brother.

"No one is going to hurt me," she said, and he shook his head dramatically. He had gone from stone sober to drunk in the time it would take her to tie her shoes.

"Not that hurt. Inside hurt. I like you. Maybe together—we can stay the same?"

She was very confused. Connen-Neute tried to rise. He quickly gave up, leaning toward her on an elbow with a conspiring expression. "She's devious, Alissa. She picks at your foundations. She finds the gaps in your updraft and steals your wind."

"Keribdis?" she whispered, feeling a pang of fear. Connen-Neute nodded, settling back to look wise despite being drunker than a sailor newly in port.

"I don't like her," he admitted. A shocked expression came over his wide, innocent eyes. He took a breath, as if seeing the sun for the first time. "I don't like her," he said firmly as if Alissa might tell him he was wrong. He plucked at his red sash, trying to pull it from around him. "They called me dead when I turned feral," he said, his words slurred. "I don't have to wear her sash anymore."

"Connen-Neute, wait!" Alissa said, thinking he should make the decision when he had all his wits about him, but he had fallen asleep, the scarf undone but not removed. Worried, Alissa tightened his scarf back up. She gazed at him for a moment, her concern growing. He had done it on purpose. He wasn't drinking to forget. He was drinking to cloud his tracings so he couldn't shift and fly, knowing she wouldn't go ahead by herself.

"Keribdis can't be that bad," Alissa whispered as she pulled a blanket over him. But a thick sense of foreboding filled her. This was not like Connen-Neute at all.

14

Alissa sat in the bow of the dinghy beside the captain and tried not to fidget. Her stomach hurt, and she wished she hadn't eaten anything. She was dressed in her Master best, and the heavy winter outfit was miserable in the afternoon sun. Strell was at the oars, the lean muscles in his back sending them quickly through the water. His loose brown hair shifted in the breeze from under the dilapidated hat that had once been hers. She had yet to see the supposed hat he had bought on the coast. She had a suspicion there wasn't one.

Connen-Neute was in the stern, his long fingers tapping restlessly. Talon was on his shoulder, and he cringed every time she screamed at the gulls flying overhead. Despite the healing ward Alissa had run on him—he had been too drunk to do it himself—the Master was still shaking the last of the rum's effects and wasn't feeling well. Though he could shift, he couldn't fly yet, which might account for some of his mood. Lodesh, though, was cheery, standing up in the back of the dinghy despite Strell's muttered complaints about balance.

Hayden and the captain had been emphatic about remaining on the boat while the rest searched for water and survivors, but when Connen-Neute took the *Albatross*'s rudder off to keep them from leaving, Captain Sholan decided he would accompany them. "To keep an eye on ya, nothing more," he had said sourly as he clambered down the rope ladder and into the *Albatross*'s remaining rowboat. The rudder was currently tied to the back of the *Albatross* like a raft. It would be impossible to reattach without Connen-Neute's help in raku form.

Much to Alissa's surprise, Connen-Neute had shown only anticipation since throwing off his drunk. The closer they got to the cove, the more impatient he became. "I thought you didn't want to find Keribdis," Alissa said as the young Master cracked his knuckles at their pace.

His long face went solemn. He and Lodesh exchanged a look, piquing Alissa's curiosity. The two of them had cloistered themselves in a long conversation while Captain Sholan looked for a good anchorage. "She's my teacher," the young Master said, not meeting her eyes. "Why wouldn't I want to find her?"

Alissa frowned at Lodesh. *"Telling him to hide his feelings is a mistake,"* she said to him alone. *"Especially when it was so hard for him to admit to them in the first place."*

Eyes on the approaching cove, Lodesh said, *"You should meet her before you start pointing fingers. She's a hard woman to argue with."*

"I don't want to argue with her," Alissa protested. *"I don't even want to know her."*

"But that doesn't mean I have to like her," Connen-Neute said, unwittingly interrupting their private conversation. "For all her shortcomings, she is highly experienced. I can learn a lot from her. But I won't allow her to sway me any longer when the conclave votes."

The captain grunted as if surprised Connen-Neute might have someone to answer to.

Having to be satisfied with that, Alissa watched the approaching shore and the odd trees. Slowly the sound of surf came over the wind. She peered down at the ocean floor, their shadow giving no clue as to how deep the water really was. The black patch following them grew suddenly larger. A thrill went through her as the dinghy scraped onto the beach. "Sand," she whispered, squinting at the glare of white expanse between her and the greenery. "Just like in my dream."

Lodesh was holding his hat on his head against the breeze. "What's that, Alissa?"

"Nothing." Pulse quickening in anticipation, she gripped the gunwales as the boat rocked. Strell and the captain jumped into the surf and pulled them farther up. Strell held his arms out to Alissa in invitation. Gathering her skirts, she half fell into his grip, enjoying the feeling of being cared for as he lifted her over the last of the waves to the shore. Her bells jingled as he set her down. Strell's hands tightened about her waist before letting go. It pulled her gaze to his, and she wondered why his brown eyes were pinched in worry.

Lodesh and Connen-Neute both jumped from the bow to keep their nicer clothing clean. "It's hot," she said, feeling the sand's warmth through her thin soles. Strell bobbed his head, clearly glad to finally have something firm under his feet again. As she took it all in, the captain and Connen-Neute pulled the dinghy past the high tide mark. One hand gathering her skirts, the other holding her hat to her head, Alissa took awkward, tiny steps in the loose sand. Behind them stomped Captain Sholan with a small pack.

There was an almost impossibly impassable band of vegetation, but once they got through that, the undergrowth thinned. Birds called from within the forest to join the noise of the gulls on the beach. Talon called back, and Connen-Neute soothed her. It was all vaguely familiar but possessed a sense of permanence that Silla's dreams lacked.

The captain frowned as he peered into the greenery. "I hope there's hardwood in here," he said softly as he adjusted his pack. "We need something to repair the boom with."

Lodesh took her arm as she stumbled. "We should've sailed around the island until someone noticed us," he said cheerily.

"Lazy citadel man," Strell said half under his breath as he held a vine out of Alissa's way. Her footing improved once under the trees, but her skirts kept snagging, making her twice as slow as everyone else. Slowly hardwoods began to appear, but none of them were thick enough for Captain Sholan's liking. His mood eased dramatically when they found a small stream, and it was here they stopped to rest at Strell's insistence.

Alissa sat down gratefully atop a fallen tree not too badly decayed. Sweat had made her forehead damp, and she knew her face was red with exertion. She had drastically underestimated the thickness of the island's vegetation. Her long sleeves and full-length skirts were proving to be almost impossible to get around in, and the heavy fabric was making her hot. Lodesh, too, looked warm, but at least he wasn't snagging on everything.

Alissa took off her heavy Master vest to leave only her nondescript shirt and skirt. Immediately she felt better. Setting it aside, she fanned herself with her hat. Strell sat with her, and she accepted a gulp from his waterskin. Lodesh immediately put himself on her other side.

"Would you like something to eat?" the Keeper asked solicitously, bringing out one of the ship's hard biscuits from a pack. Feeling ill from the heat, she shook her head. The sudden tension between the two men rose. She took a steadying breath. Feeling like the last candied apple on the tray, she put her hat back on and went to help Connen-Neute fill the waterskins.

"See what you did?" Strell muttered.

"I wish I had worn something else," she complained to Connen-Neute, wanting to fall into the creek and let it wash right through her. Talon chittered from his shoulder, and she wondered how he tolerated her sharp claws through his lightweight summer outfit.

"We have time," the young Master said, crouching as he refilled a second waterskin. "Why don't you splash off?"

Alissa's eyebrows rose. "You don't mind waiting?" She turned back to Strell and Lodesh. They had gone to stand at opposite ends of the temporary camp. "I'm going to go wading," she said. They stared at her blankly, and she added, "In the stream, to cool off." Not wanting them to see her bare feet, Alissa headed upstream. "I'll be right back."

"Not too far!" Strell called, and Talon chittered as if in warning.

She stifled a sigh of bother. Jerking her skirt free of another stick, she followed the bank until their voices grew faint. A final pause to listen, and she leaned against a tree to remove her shoes.

"Are you all right?" Strell called distantly, and her head came up.

"I'm fine!" she shouted back, tugging at a lace. "Don't come up here!" Ashes, couldn't they leave her alone for even a moment?

"Come on back," Lodesh called. "You're too far away, Alissa."

There was a soft gasp at her name, and a twig snapped. Alissa's head came up. Breath held, she stared across the running water. Beast surged to the forefront of her thoughts, looking through Alissa's eyes at the surrounding vegetation. *"There,"* Beast said, and Alissa's heart pounded. A quick shadow darted away. Purple, with a red sash.

"Silla!" Alissa cried, her fear shifting to excitement. She lunged across the shallow stream. Her shoes filled with water, and her wet skirts tangled about her ankles. Heart pounding, Alissa scrabbled across, slipping to fall into the water. Beast animated her, getting her up. Snatching control back, Alissa ran.

"It's Silla!" she shouted as she found the opposite bank. "I've found her!"

"Alissa, wait!" she heard faintly. She didn't.

Silla's heels vanished behind a clump of decaying roots. "Silla!" Alissa gasped, scraping her palms as she swung around it. "I'm not going to hurt you. Let me explain!"

The girl was fast, darting around fallen logs like a deer. Alissa scrabbled up an incline. Rocks bit her palms. She lost her footing, and her face went into the dirt. "Silla!" she cried, spitting leaf mold from her. "Wait!"

Alissa reached the top of the hill. A path ran along it. The red of Silla's sash showed through the vegetation, disappearing. "I just want to talk!" Alissa cried. Gasping for air, she ran after her. Alissa's hair caught on a branch. Making a frustrated cry, she tore free. Her pulse pounded. The path was hard under her feet, making her way easier.

Finally she seemed to be gaining. At the forefront of her awareness was Beast, warning Alissa about low branches and dips in the path. Together they made progress.

"Silla, please!" Alissa called again. She was almost close enough to touch her black hair. Alissa's hand stretched out, and Silla surged ahead. Feeling the heat of the chase, Alissa grinned, finding more speed. Her lungs burned and her muscles hurt, but she would catch her.

"*Get her,*" Beast exclaimed. "*Now!*"

Alissa lunged. She missed, reaching out even as she fell. Her fingers found a shoe as she hit the ground, and she gripped it tight. "Got you!" she wheezed, stretched flat on the ground.

Elated, Alissa took a huge gulp of air. She looked up from the dirt and went cold. It wasn't a shoe. She was holding the ankle of someone in sandals. And the foot was facing her.

She let go as if burned. Alissa looked up to find a red hem embroidered with the likeness of grapevines. Panic coursed through her.

It wasn't Silla.

15

Heart pounding, Alissa looked up from the dirt path. A lightweight, red linen skirt stretched upward, bound about a slender waist by a red scarf decorated with black, twisting vines. The dark Master's vest was open over a sleeveless shirt lying loosely upon narrow shoulders. Gulping, Alissa peered up to see long black hair arranged with ribbons, high cheekbones with red spots of anger, and flashing golden eyes. There were dark eyebrows very unlike her own, furrowed in anger. The hands upon the woman's hips were abnormally long, her fingers having four segments instead of three.

"Who are you?" the woman said, her voice musical and hard.

Alissa scrambled to her feet. She hastily brushed herself off, mortified to see she was damp and covered in leaves. Silla was hiding halfway behind the stately woman. Alissa looked at her, and the girl, a young woman, really, shrank back with wide eyes.

"Why were you chasing her?" the woman said, her Hold accent clipping the words.

"It's her," Silla said, tugging at the woman's arm. "I told you I wasn't going feral."

"Don't be a goose," the woman said, one hand gentling Silla. "We've got a marooning is all." She sounded irritated. "I really don't know where we are going to put her." She pursed her lips, and as she pushed back her hair, Alissa noticed it was shot with gray. Her face, too, was lined. She was older than Alissa's first estimation, but it made her no less formidable.

"No," Alissa said. "We were trying—"

"We?" the tall woman interrupted. "There are more of you? Burn it to ash." She sighed. "Just go to sleep," she said absently.

There was a tug on Alissa's awareness as a ward of sleep went up. Her eyes widened. Taking a gasping breath, she broke the field before the ward had time to coalesce. "Wait a moment," she exclaimed. "Would you listen to me?"

Surprise cascaded over the woman's face. "You're a Keeper?"

"Not exactly," Alissa said, peeved. She was hot, out of breath, and had sticks in her hair. And where had her hat gone? She wasn't about to be put to sleep.

"Uh, Alissa," Beast whispered, deep in her thoughts.

"Shut up, Beast," she thought. *"I don't care how angry you get, don't say anything."*

Silla came out from behind the woman, her fear replaced with a wide-eyed awe. "You're real," she said to Alissa, her relief so obvious it was almost painful. "All those dreams?" she exclaimed. "They were real? The snow? Bailic? The Hold? Everything?"

Alissa found herself grinning. Silla believed. Finally, Silla believed. Perhaps they could be friends again. "Yes. I'm sorry I chased you—". She hesitated as a sudden shadow covered them and was gone. She looked up to see Connen-Neute in his raku form making a sharp turn.

For the second time, the woman seemed shocked. "Connen-Neute?" she stammered, a long-fingered hand over her mouth. "No! You're feral!"

"I told you!" Silla shouted, pointing. "I told you it wasn't a dream!"

The wind buffeted them as Connen-Neute landed on one of those odd trees, bending it down to make room for him to land. It unexpectedly snapped, the loud pop pulling a gasp from Alissa. "I thought you couldn't fly yet," Alissa said, and he shrugged.

"How—" the older woman said, taking an involuntary step back. "You were feral . . ."

Connen-Neute shifted in a swirl of white. As a man, he jumped from the broken tree to the ground. "It was Alissa's fault," he said merrily, and Alissa's jaw dropped. Her fault?

The woman stared at Connen-Neute. "But how?" she said, reaching forward to run his sleeve through her long hand as if to prove he was real.

"Alissa," he repeated, flicking glances at Silla. "She brought my sentience forward in time, leaving me to go feral back then." All trace of his morning's reluctance was gone.

"But . . ." the woman said, her eyes wide and confused.

The sound of Talon's wings pulled Alissa's hand up just in time. The small bird landed, smacking Alissa in the face. Sharp nails dug into her, but she wouldn't give up the strength she took from Talon for anything. She brought the raptor close, soothing the bird as much as herself with gentle murmurs.

There was a padding on the path behind them, and Alissa turned. "Hey! Connen-Neute?" Lodesh called. "Did you take down the entire forest?"

The Keeper jogged around the path. Strell and the captain were behind him, and Alissa felt a knot of worry loosen. Lodesh slowed, a delighted smile on his face. "Keribdis!" he called.

Alissa went cold. *Keribdis?* She felt Beast quiver, only now understanding why her second consciousness was hiding. Captain Sholan was as pale as she felt, frantically crossing himself from his shoulder to his chest to ward off evil at the sight of three long-fingered Masters.

Lodesh stepped forward to take Keribdis's hands. His clothes and hair were perfectly in place except for an artfully arranged curl drooping roguishly before his eyes. "Bone and Ash!" Keribdis said, her cheeks pale. "Lodesh?"

"Good afternoon, Master Keribdis," Lodesh said, his eyes twinkling with mischief as he brought her limp hand to his chest. "You're looking extre-e-e-emely well."

Keribdis's mouth opened and shut, but nothing came out. "You're young?" she finally managed. "No. You're dead! I was there."

"That's what they tell me," he said. "I heard you gave me foxgloves. Thank you."

Keribdis shook her head. She glanced at Connen-Neute and Lodesh, then turned to Silla. "You were right," she said, her face slack. "But it sounded so impossible."

Lodesh released Keribdis's hand. "You'll find Alissa is adept at the impossible."

A flicker of unease went through Alissa. The last thing she wanted was to draw attention to herself. She silently took her folded Master's vest from Captain Sholan as he handed it to her. Behind her, Strell shifted from foot to foot. Connen-Neute had gone suspiciously quiet. He was staring at Silla, and his ears were red. Alissa thought she was going to be introduced, but Keribdis was looking expectantly at Strell and the captain.

Seeing the direction of Keribdis's gaze, Lodesh beamed. "Keribdis," he said formally, "the man on the right is Captain Sholan. The plainsman beside him is Strell Hirdune."

Saying nothing, Strell nodded stiffly. Alissa knew he had come to blame Keribdis for the flood that killed his family, and he was reacting with more grace than she could have found.

"Hirdune?" the woman breathed. "We finally got a Keeper out of the Hirdune line?"

"Ah, not exactly," Lodesh said. "Strell is a commoner. But he's the Hold's piper. Given a room in the tower for his past services."

"The Hold has no such position," Keribdis snapped, and Talon chittered at her harsh tone.

Alissa's brow pinched as the woman found fault with Strell's accomplishment. He had earned it. She took a breath to protest, and Lodesh interceded with a professional, soothing charm. "It does now," he said. "You see, Talo-Toecan thought—"

Keribdis took a quick breath. "Is he here? Did he come?" she interrupted, her face alight and glowing. It turned her more beautiful than anyone had the right to be.

"No," Lodesh said softly. "He is minding the Hold."

The woman's eyes went cold, and her manner became stiff. "Well, he's done a bone-cracked poor job of it!" she said. "I leave him alone for twenty years, and what happens? Feral rakus regain their sentience, commoners are given tower rooms, the dead return to life—"

"Actually," Lodesh interrupted, "I'm not entirely alive, just cursed."

She stared at him in disbelief. "Talo-Toecan woke you?"

"No. Alissa did, sort of," Lodesh added, not sounding at all apologetic.

"And where—by my teacher's ashes—is this Alissa?" Keribdis said tightly.

Lodesh glanced at Alissa, his brow raised in an honest confusion. "I'm sorry. I thought you'd already been introduced."

The woman's face went colder still. Alissa tensed as she watched Keribdis's thoughts coming together as she looked at Alissa's hands and eyes. Taking a quick breath, Alissa held it, grateful for Strell's hand on her shoulder. "Silla has been dream-touching with you?" the woman said, the word overflowing with scorn. "You're a transeunt. I thought you were a Keeper."

The silence was pained. Alissa was acutely aware of her dirty clothes and wild hair. "I'm Alissa," she said, her chin raised. The tightness of tears threatened, and she savagely pushed them away. She didn't have to like Keribdis. Keribdis didn't have to like her.

"The worm!" Keribdis exclaimed, and Connen-Neute and Silla both took a startled step back. "He brought about the next transeunt without me? I'll flay the skin from his wings!"

"Keribdis . . ." Lodesh stepped forward. "Talo-Toecan had nothing to do with it. Alissa was born before you left. She's Meson's daughter. Remember him? He joined with a woman from the plains. This wasn't planned."

"I'll say." The proud woman ran her eyes over Alissa disapprovingly. Alissa stiffened, remembering the same look from the women in her village, as if she were a vagrant who might steal the clothes drying on their line or teach their children unsavory words. Strell's grip on her shoulder tightened, and Talon's nails dug into her until she had to move the bird to her other arm.

Keribdis shook her head. "Wait until I get to my books. Who was responsible for charting Meson's signature? Someone is at fault, and I'm going to find out who." Her lips pursed, and she crossed her arms before her as she ran her gaze over Alissa. "Well, at least you did one thing right," she said, speaking to Alissa. "Abandoning that shortsighted dreamer and seeking me out for tuition shows you have at least an ounce of brains."

Keribdis turned and headed down the path. "Come along," she called out confidently. "I can hardly wait to see everyone's faces when Connen-Neute and Lodesh walk into the village behind me. And we'll have to hurry if we want to get there before it rains."

"Rain?" Captain Sholan muttered. "There's not a cloud in the sky."

Silla and Connen-Neute automatically took a step after Keribdis, Connen-Neute bringing himself to a halt with a look of self-disgust. Alissa was frozen to the ground, anger making her fingers tingle and her knees shake. "You are not my teacher," she said clearly.

Keribdis jerked to a halt. Connen-Neute fingered his red sash nervously. The woman turned on a heel. "Yes, I am," she said, her shoulders stiff. "I'm teaching the next transeunt. That's you. I'm your teacher, whether you want it or not."

"No, you aren't," she said, feeling herself go pale. Beast quivered, hiding, but Alissa had seen enough of the woman's theatrics and wouldn't be bullied. "Talo-Toecan is my instructor," she said, despite Lodesh's frantic motions for her to be still.

"He's teaching you?" she questioned. Lodesh seemed to collapse in on himself. "The ash-ridden worm. I'm teaching the next transeunt, and he knows it!" She spun about and stalked down the path, clearly not caring about Alissa, only that her perceived rights had been stolen.

"That went well," Lodesh muttered. Giving Alissa an apologetic look, he started after the angry woman. "Keribdis," he cajoled, jogging to catch her. "He thought he had no choice. He thought you were all dead!"

Silla hesitated, seeming to want to say something to Alissa, but then she headed quickly after Keribdis, her long, black hair swinging. Captain Sholan followed her, muttering of Masters and women with hot tempers and how they were the same as snakes.

"You never told me," Connen-Neute whispered as he stared after Silla.

"Told you what?" she said, her voice shaking.

"That Silla was so . . . graceful."

Alissa watched him hasten after Silla. The backs of his ears were red as he came even with her. Silla slowed, glancing up at him as he matched her pace.

Her pulse hammered, and she wanted to sit down. Strell's hand dropped from her shoulder, and she gave him a thankful look. Shaken, she took a cleansing breath.

"You got your shoes wet," Strell said softly, handing her hat to her.

"Thanks," she whispered so her voice wouldn't quaver. "Where did you find my hat?"

"Right where you told me." Taking her elbow, he started them down the path. "By the tree with the red berries. I nearly twisted my ankle when your thoughts slipped into mine." His smile grew soft, and he wiped a smudge of dirt from her chin. "I don't mind, though. I wish it would happen all the time."

Red berries? she thought, confused, not even remembering a tree with red berries, much less asking him to fetch her hat.

"You were busy catching Silla," Beast whispered, and Alissa glanced at Keribdis's back, worried that she might hear. But the incensed woman never slowed. *"It took you three months to make that hat,"* Beast added. *"And you stabbed yourself with the needle twice."*

"Beast!" Alissa hissed into her thoughts. *"Strell might have realized you weren't me!"*

"He didn't, though, did he?"

Alissa fumed, not liking that Beast could speak soundlessly to Strell without her knowledge. She slowly fell into step, her fingers calming Talon. It hadn't been the best impression she had ever made, but at least Keribdis hadn't seen Beast. As long as she kept her wits about her, she could do this.

16

Bells chiming, Alissa tromped behind Strell, hot, sticky, and worried. As foretold, the skies had erupted with towering clouds. She hoped the village wasn't much farther. Though the path was smooth and well-maintained, Keribdis's pace left her panting and hot under her heavy Master's attire. Pride—and a painful awareness that her skirt was stained from falling into the stream—kept Alissa's mouth shut and her long Master's vest on.

So lost was she in her uneasy thoughts that she nearly ran into Strell when he halted. Jerking to a stop, she edged around him. Alissa's eyes widened as she took in the village. "Sweet as potatoes," Strell murmured, and she agreed, craning her neck upward to look into the trees.

Captain Sholan came to stand beside her. "They live in ash-ridden trees?" he whispered. He was crossing himself again, though Alissa thought it was more from habit than fear.

Tall, wide-girthed trees spread their canopy far above clear-swept ground. The smallest was wider around than three people could reach. They made a shady space that looked eerily like the holden with its stately pillars. Wedged among the branches were platforms and shelters. Alissa could tell they weren't big enough to hold a raku. The few Masters she noticed on the ground were in their human shift, and she drew back, suddenly shy.

"Do you think they stay in their human form all the time?" she asked Strell in a whisper.

"Of course not," Keribdis said, making Alissa feel like a fool. "But there's little to eat on the islands. If we stayed as rakus, we would soon strip them of food."

"They're mirth trees!" Lodesh exclaimed softly, and Alissa brought her hand to her mouth, now seeing the resemblance. "But why don't they smell like mirth trees?"

"Most of them are male," Keribdis said. "The ones in your city are female. That's why it's so seldom you get a fertile seed. The pollen has to cross the ocean."

"Fantastic," he breathed.

The Masters on the ground had noticed them, and Keribdis straightened. "Look who I found by the far beaches!" she called triumphantly, leading the way into the village.

Alissa took a steadying breath. "Do I look all right?" she whispered to Strell.

His smile was comforting. "You look like a Master," he said as he shifted the fabric on her shoulders.

Alissa nodded, nervous as she started after everyone. Beside her, Captain Sholan was muttering charms and clutching his hat to his chest. His eyes were wide and afraid. The change in Keribdis from angry wife to self-satisfied finder of lost children was obvious. Her resentment was still there. It remained to be seen how it would express itself.

"Wolves of Ash," one of the approaching Masters exclaimed. "It's Connen-Neute. It's Connen-Neute! And he's not feral!"

"Connen-Neute?" another called, and Alissa's head echoed with the mental shout. Immediately she set a ward in place to dull the noise. Rakus began to spiral down from the trees. Upon landing, they became courtly dressed men and women. The air was full of wings and noise, and Alissa stared, wondering how they didn't hit each other.

"Keep it verbal!" Keribdis exclaimed. "I can't keep you straight that way!"

The mental echo vanished, but the confused babble of voices grew as long-fingered men and woman clustered around them. Connen-Neute was grinning, his long, solemn face lost in pleasure. Beaming, he reached for the hands stretching out toward him.

Alissa felt a moment of panic. Thirty? Forty people? She couldn't tell. They were all old. Not as old as Useless, but as old as her mother would be, perhaps. She stepped back, clustering herself between Strell and Lodesh to try to stay out of the way.

"Too many," Beast whispered, her fright building. *"Alissa, it's too many! Get us away!"*

Talon flapped her wings and called loudly. She refused to leave Alissa's wrist. Alissa let her make all the noise she wanted. It kept a ring of space about her that both she and Beast needed. The bird's claws pinched painfully, and Alissa crafted a black scarf to wrap her wrist. Her heart pounded as more and more Masters appeared. This was what she had come for, she told herself, trying to smile whenever a pair of golden eyes met hers. This was what she wanted. But she hadn't thought it would be like this!

"Connen-Neute!" a short woman cried, pushing her way to the front and pulling him down to her height so she could hug him around the neck. "By the Navigator! It's you!" she cried, her eyes bright with tears. "You left us." She whacked him on his shoulder, having to stretch to do it. "Don't you ever do that again!"

"My aunt," Connen-Neute explained in a private thought to Alissa, darting his gaze to Alissa and back to the woman. The young Master grinned, his white teeth showing strong against his tan. "I don't plan on it," he said aloud, and the crowd cheered.

"He talks!" someone cried. "Connen-Neute returns to us better than he left!"

"Mirim. Oh, Mirim save me," Captain Sholan chanted as he retreated to the outskirts.

"But how did you get here?" Connen-Neute's aunt asked, hugging him again.

Connen-Neute glanced over his shoulder at the unseen cove. "By boat."

"A boat!" she cried. "Hear that, Keribdis? They have a boat!" The joyful woman glanced over the rest of them. "And you brought Keepers." Connen-Neute's aunt sighed, her entire body moving. "It's been so long since I've taught anyone. I never thought I'd miss it."

"Not just Keepers," a loud voice said. "Wipe the sand from your eyes, Neugwin. That's the Warden."

Connen-Neute's aunt peered at Lodesh, her face brightening. "Lodesh Stryska?" she said, beaming. "By the Wolves. You're supposed to be dead!"

Alissa's eyes widened as the crowd was pushed aside by a rotund but refined looking man. *A fat Master?* she thought as she saw the traditional vest made up of acres of fabric.

"Lodesh, is your city awake?" the Master asked, his gaze intelligent and sharp from his round face. "Who woke you? Talo-Toecan?"

Lodesh grinned. Knowing all eyes were on him, he made one of his extravagant citadel bows. "Returned from the dead, Beso-Ran," he said. "My city finally sleeps, and my people are free of the curse that bound us, but I'm here. I'm not done with the world just yet." He gave Alissa an intent look, and she dropped her eyes.

"Connen-Neute woke the city!" someone shouted, and a cheer went up.

"No." Lodesh's eyes went soft on her. "Alissa had something to do with it."

"Ah," Connen-Neute's aunt said as she came to stand before Alissa. "You must be Alissa. I'm Neugwin. It's a pleasure to meet you. How did you manage to wake the charmer?"

The sound of approaching thunder rumbled through Alissa as she crossed Neugwin's hand. She went shy as Neugwin's brow rose at Alissa's Master's vest. Her heart was pounding, but they all seemed friendly enough—if rather intense. "I'm not sure how I managed to wake Lodesh," Alissa said. "And this is Strell Hirdune, and Captain Sholan is there by that tree."

"Hirdune?" Neugwin said, her brows rising. "Keribdis, I should've taken your wager. I told you we'd get a Keeper out of the Hirdune line. You have to have faith, dear."

Keribdis touched her ribbons. Alissa thought it was a move designed to draw attention to her rather than to check her hair. "Then you would be making me breakfast for the next ten years," Keribdis said, her mien just shy of haughty. "He's not a Keeper."

"No?" Neugwin eyed Strell sharply.

"He's a commoner," Keribdis said sourly. "But it gets better. Talo-Toecan gave him title to a tower room. A commoner. The Wolves know why."

Alissa felt a pang of worry at the crowd's uneasy murmur. Lodesh's eyes opened wide in wonder. As she watched, he seemed to become larger than life, balancing against Keribdis's dramatics as if it were second nature. He wore a confusion Alissa knew was designed to divorce himself from the blame Keribdis would put upon the bearer of bad news. "Silla hasn't told you what has happened?" he said, his hands spread wide. "Why we've come? Why feral rakus return to sentience, ghosts take up life, and commoners are granted title to the Hold?" Silla looked nervous, Keribdis rather poisonous. "Silla and Alissa have been dream-touching the last six months," he finished. "Haven't you been listening to her?"

"Actually," Alissa said softly, "it's been longer than that."

As one, the assembly turned to Keribdis. Their faces wore frowns ranging from accusing to frightened. "No," Neugwin said, her voice unreadable. "We knew Silla hadn't been sleeping well. But only Masters can dream-touch. How—" The matronly woman's eyes lit up, and she took Alissa's hands, staring at her normal fingers. "You're the Hold's next transeunt," she whispered. A stab of angst went through Alissa, but Neugwin's eyes were dancing with delight. "But how, love? We hadn't planned any such as you for another fifty years."

Keribdis cleared her throat dryly. "Obviously there's been a mistake," she said, doing an ill job of concealing her displeasure. "It's almost worth the trip home to check my books as to who calculated the probability chart on her parents' union."

"Then we're going home?" Neugwin asked. "Now that we have a boat?"

Keribdis blinked. "Whatever for? I don't need the Hold to begin schooling her."

"But I came to bring you home . . ." Alissa said, bewildered. She'd never considered they wouldn't want to leave. She reddened, embarrassed. Strell, too, wore a blank look. But no one heard her over the buzz of agitated conversation.

An annoyed, calculating look flickered over Keribdis. "Nothing has changed!" the woman asserted; then, seeing the cross expressions in the crowd, she smiled. "But of course we will discuss it in detail later. Tonight we celebrate one of the lost returning to us. Connen-Neute's name is circled no more!"

They cheered at that, and Alissa had to soothe both Beast and Talon. Keribdis's smile had no feeling. Cold slipped through Alissa. Keribdis was playing them as if she had been doing it for her entire life. Unsettled, Alissa carefully scanned the faces before her, seeing who among the crowd realized Keribdis had intentionally distracted them. Lodesh, too, was making meaningful eye contact with several people. She felt a rush of gratitude knowing Lodesh, at least, could effectively move in the conclave's political circle.

The noise eased, and a clean-shaven Master in a simple gray tunic lined in purple said, "You mean, of course, we will be celebrating Alissa's appearance as well as Connen-Neute's."

"Of course." Keribdis made an expansive gesture. "So prepare what we have in the stores. Make everything ready. And leave them alone!" she said with a friendly tone of exasperation. "They're tired. You'll hear their stories tonight."

17

The crowd obediently broke into smaller groups, talking loudly as they dispersed. Talon started at the sudden, combined movement and launched herself from Alissa's wrist to vanish into the mirth trees. Alissa rubbed her arm and smiled uneasily at those who met her eyes in passing. A few people clasped Connen-Neute's hand warmly before they left, making promises to talk later. Alissa watched in relief as the fifty or so Masters dwindled to their original group plus the fat Master, Neugwin, and the somber Master in gray who had suggested they celebrate Alissa's presence as well as Connen-Neute's.

Strell leaned close to Alissa as Keribdis started across the open space under the trees. "They don't want to leave?" he asked, his brown eyes holding a defensive cast.

Lodesh shook his head. "Some do. Keribdis doesn't. Most follow her." He gave Alissa an encouraging smile. "It will make for an interesting party tonight."

Keribdis turned on the path, seeming surprised they weren't following her yet. "You're tired. Let's get you settled."

Connen-Neute hastened forward with Silla. Alissa stepped to follow, hesitating as Captain Sholan took her elbow. "Ma'hr," he said. "I'm goin' back to my boat." His frightened eyes tracked a Master who had shifted and was flying up into the trees. "I have to tell Hayden."

Alissa found enough empathy in her scattered confidence to smile. A part of her wanted to follow him to the boat and skate across the waves back to Useless. "Fine," she said, not caring that Keribdis's waiting stance had grown impatient. "You know the way?"

"Aye," he said, visibly relieved she wasn't asking him to stay. "There's the water to restock and the boom to repair. We'll be ready when you want to leave." His brow furrowed in warning. "She's a manta ray of a woman, Ma'hr," he whispered. "A devilfish. Be careful."

"Thank you, Captain," she said, taking the time to touch his arm in parting despite Keribdis's obvious irritation. Though she knew it was ill-advised, Alissa obstinately kept her pace slow as she joined Keribdis's small following. Connen-Neute's eyes were wide at her defiance. The increasing wind of the approaching storm pulled at her hair, and she relished it.

"Lodesh?" Keribdis said as Alissa joined them and they moved forward. "We have a few huts on the beach. We use them for various tasks, but perhaps you would like to put your people there? No need to climb into the trees when there's lodging on the ground."

"Actually," Lodesh drawled as he took Alissa's arm, "this is Alissa's affair. I'm along to keep her company. You ought to talk to her about such arrangements," he finished lightly.

"Alissa's?" Keribdis's voice carried a hint of mockery. "Forgive me."

Alissa stifled her frown. This wasn't going well. Strell looked sullen, and Alissa knew it was from Keribdis's not-so-subtle slights.

"Warden," the rotund Master said as they moved. "I'm dying of curiosity. How did your people absolve their curse?"

Keribdis cleared her throat. "Tonight. He'll tell us tonight," she said as the wind increased. A few patters of rain encouraged them to walk faster.

Lodesh glanced slyly at Alissa. "It was a Keeper. I think you know him. Bailic?"

"Bailic!" Beso-Ran exclaimed. "If I had the little worm

before me right now, I'd toast his toes good for sending us on a fool's errand the way he did." He puffed at the new pace. "But I thought you said Alissa woke you."

"Bailic didn't wake me," Lodesh said, "but when he found the people roused, he made the improper assumption that he had. He was going to send them into the foothills and plains to bring about another plague of madness, punishing them for having cast him out. My people tore his soul apart to prevent him from starting the same plague that caused their own plight. It was enough to free all of them or singly me." He shifted his shoulders, clearly not upset. "I'll find another way to free my soul." He gave Alissa a knowing smile. "But not anytime soon, I think."

From behind her came Strell's indistinct mutter. There was a buzz in Alissa's mind of a private conversation, and Keribdis sighed. "Your huts need some repair," she said. "You can wait out the rain at the community shelter until they're ready. Quick. You don't want to be caught in it." Not waiting, she turned sharply and headed for a large covered structure. It was the only building Alissa could see on the ground, open on all sides and thatched with huge leaves.

Alissa looked behind her as a hissing roar came faintly. Several calls of warning came from the trees above. Her mouth gaped as she realized the roar was from an advancing wall of rain. Strell tugged at her arm, and, giving up any pretense at decorum, everyone ran.

Patters of rain struck her shoulders as they all rushed under the shelter. Silla was laughing, and Alissa spun to watch as the world turned gray and sound thundered down upon them. It was almost deafening, and she could do nothing but stare. The wind drove the rain under the covering, and they clustered together at the center. She wondered how Hayden was doing. The downfall was so heavy, it seemed as if they were underwater, and Alissa took a deep breath to assure herself she could. She hoped Talon was all right.

The deluge slackened almost as quickly as it had advanced, slowing into an easy cadence. "That's it?" she said, invigorated by the short run and the new coolness to the air.

From beside her came Beso-Ran's deep harrumph. "It does that every day," he said.

Only now did Alissa turn to look at the shelter. A large central hearth kept it lit, presently filled with ash-dusted coals. Just above her head nets were strung between the supports, and she wondered if they dried food there. Strell had settled at one of the benches surrounding the coals, and she moved to sit beside him. Immediately Lodesh took her other side.

She smiled at the sight of Connen-Neute easing himself nervously down between Silla and his aunt. The two women were chattering happily around him, leaving the young Master with a bemused expression. Beso-Ran had taken up a bowl of berries, offering them to everyone before settling himself to eat when they all refused. Alissa became distant, reminded of how Redal-Stan used to do the same in his attempts to get her to try his beloved ham rolls.

Looking across the hearth, Alissa blinked. Keribdis had taken a position directly opposite her, arranging her clothes carefully as if to point out Alissa's simpler attire. "Forgive me," the woman said, her words precise and clipped. "I must excuse myself. I'm anxious to plan out where I'm going to start with you." Her black eyebrows arched mockingly as she looked at Alissa. "Neugwin can show you the shelters when they're ready."

"Connen-Neute can stay with me," Neugwin bubbled, and Connen-Neute flushed at his aunt's enthusiasm. "But I'll show you the shelters. They're just down the path to the beach. Warden, you and Strell can have the larger one if Alissa doesn't mind."

"I'm not Warden any longer, Neugwin," Lodesh said as he pilfered a berry from Beso-Ran's bowl, tossing it into his mouth in apparent unconcern. "Just Lodesh. Keeper of the Hold."

Beso-Ran made a harrumph of dissatisfaction. "Nonsense," the large Master grumped. "Once a Warden, always a Warden. I don't care that you've been dead."

Lodesh's gaze flicked to the distant trees. "Talo-Toecan struck my title—"

"That takes an entire quorum!" Keribdis exclaimed. "You're still the Warden."

"It was deserved." Lodesh raised a hand to forestall any more argument.

Neugwin ceased talking with Connen-Neute, and an uncomfortable silence descended. "What could warrant such a punishment?" the matronly Master asked in wonder.

Lodesh met her gaze evenly. "I kept silent when I should have warned him of a coming danger. That my betrayal was to further my own desires made it twofold the crime."

Alissa felt Strell's breath quicken. Lodesh had betrayed her in the name of love, wagering Useless's trust and her friendship that she would grow to love him in the past as he had fallen in love with her. She had, but the cost had been very high. She had forgiven him for his betrayal. To forget was harder.

It was obvious volumes were being unsaid, but the surrounding Masters respected his new silence. Keribdis, though, seemed to know that Alissa was behind this effrontery, too, and her eyes tightened. "Don't enjoy yourself too much tonight," she warned Alissa. "I want you on the beach at sunrise. That's Silla's usual time for lessons, and I imagine you're anxious to learn what a Master your age is expected to know. We'll start with how to find your tracings and source. Silla could do with the refresher."

Silla cringed, and Alissa felt a wash of empathy. It wasn't pleasant being asked to slow to someone else's pace. "I already know how," Alissa said softly.

A puff of amusement came from Keribdis. "Re-e-e-eally?" she said, her voice so heavy with sarcasm, Alissa was surprised she couldn't see the vowels rolling along the ground.

Beso-Ran looked up from his berries. "Talo-Toecan has begun your studies?" he questioned. His gaze went to Keribdis. "That was your task."

"Yes. I know," the woman said vindictively. "Well," she said to Alissa, "if you think you've *mastered* that, we can move on to nonverbal speech." Keribdis stood.

"I already know that, too." Alissa hated herself for flushing, and pride prompted her to add, "I can speak to Keeper as well as Master."

Keribdis's high cheekbones showed a tinge of red. Stomach tight, Alissa looked up at the consternation on the surrounding Masters' faces. The last Master—the quiet one in gray—was the only one who didn't look surprised. Arms crossed, he leaned against one of the shelter's supports and watched Keribdis, not Alissa. His Master's vest had a very simple cut, reminding her of Redal-Stan's attire. His sash was yellow.

"I don't think you understand what I'm asking, poor child," Keribdis said. "Be on the beach tomorrow. Sunrise." As if that ended it, she gestured for Silla to accompany her as she walked into the last drops of rain glittering in the newly unveiled sun.

Beso-Ran nodded to them, and with more grace than Alissa would have credited him, got to his feet. "Keribdis?" the fat Master said. "A word with you?"

Alissa's mouth turned down as he paced quickly after Keribdis with the bowl of fruit. What did Alissa care what they thought? Her studies were none of the woman's affair.

Strell rose to his feet. Alissa became alarmed at the determined clench of his jaw. "No," she said, pulling on his sleeve to get him to sit down. "I'll explain later. It doesn't matter, and rubbing her nose in it now will only make things worse."

"It does matter," he said roughly, anger making his eyes hard. "She's treating you less than a Keeper, less than me."

"Strell," she pleaded, but he wouldn't be deterred.

Tugging his rough tunic straight, he said loudly to their retreating backs, "Alissa can speak soundlessly to Keepers. She can touch my mind as well. She did so just today, to ask me to bring along her hat she dropped while chasing Silla."

Beso-Ran swung his bulk around. "You were chasing Silla?" he asked, his brow arched.

Alissa tensed. "She, uh, was afraid of me, and I wanted to explain—"

"Afraid." Face tight, Keribdis strode back under the shelter. "I can understand why. You have the manners of a back-hills farmer. We will attend to that tomorrow as well."

Alissa felt her face go bloodless in anger. There was nothing wrong with her manners.

Silla had put herself between Alissa and Keribdis. "I'm not afraid of Alissa anymore," she said, clearly distressed. "You told me she was a dream-demon. That's why I ran."

Keribdis's face went unexpectedly soft. "Hush, Silla," the

woman said. "We'll talk later. Why don't you see if the tide has left any fish in the pools?"

"I want to stay here," she said, her golden eyes going wide.

The Master in gray pushed himself upright from the shelter's support. "Let Silla stay," he said lightly. "We *all* want to hear how Alissa can talk to commoners."

His head tilted in question. Alissa met his golden eyes without dropping them, knowing anger from Keribdis's insult still burned in her gaze. He was silent for a long moment, then, apparently satisfied, he extended his hand. "I'm Yar-Taw," he said formally.

Alissa covered it with her own automatically.

"I'm glad to meet you and Strell." He glanced at Strell, and Alissa's breath came easier after the Master took the time to recognize him.

"Alissa Meson," she said as her pulse slowed.

"Meson?" he asked. "Your father is a Keeper, yes? Talo-Toecan's student. Is he well?"

She looked up at him in wonder. He had known her father. Probably better than she had. "He died after you left the Hold," she said, hoping her bitterness didn't show.

"I'm sorry," Yar-Taw said. "He was a good man and student." He took her hands, his golden eyes intent. "Alissa," he said, "can you really reach the Warden's mind?"

"Yes, and Strell's, too, when my emotions are strong."

Face blank, his hands slipped from her.

Brushing the extravagant length of black hair from her, Keribdis laughed. "She obviously doesn't understand the question."

"She can touch my thoughts," Lodesh said, and Alissa gave him a grateful look as he broke his conspicuous silence. "And don't ask us to perform like trained bears. Talo-Toecan believes because she grew up as a human, her mind was forced to develop around verbal language, not mental, thereby giving her common ground to be able to understand a Keeper's thought patterns. I think it was one of the reasons she was able to wake me."

Neugwin murmured a soft agreement, and Yar-Taw rubbed a hand over his shaven cheeks in thought. Alissa's shoulders eased, but Keribdis ruined it all with a derisive snort. "Look what Talo-Toecan has done to our transeunt," she said bitterly. "She may be a Master, but her mind has been warped by living with humans so long. She should have been isolated until her mind recovered its proper schematic before beginning her studies. Who knows what ramifications this will have? What she won't be able to do?" The woman's lips pursed, making her all the more severe. "This is Talo-Toecan's failing."

Alissa's breath caught in outrage. Keribdis thought her ability was a failing? Strell moved forward a step, and she put a hand on him. "Alissa's mind isn't warped," he said, his eyes hard. But he was ignored. Yar-Taw eased back to the outskirts, watching.

"So," Beso-Ran said as he settled his bulk in Keribdis's old spot and resumed eating his berries. "Talo-Toecan has been teaching you. Has he given you warming wards yet?" His tone was jovial, clearly trying to ease the mood. "Keribdis," he cajoled, "teach Alissa warming wards right away so we don't have to hide them from her. I like my tea hot."

Realizing her only option was to overlook Keribdis's slights, Alissa resolved to ignore the woman. "Actually, that was one of my first wards," she admitted, her pulse slowing. "Talo-Toecan likes his tea hot, too. And it was snowing a great deal of the time we were together."

"How about fields?" Neugwin wanted to know. "Has he taught you—" She hesitated.

"Impervious as well as permeable," Alissa finished for her, thinking Neugwin didn't want to give away anything Alissa might not know about yet. Lodesh had a pained look on his face, and she added, "I had to so as to keep myself alive."

Neugwin glanced at Keribdis, her eyes large. "That wasn't my question," Neugwin said. "I wanted to know how many fields you could hold independently."

Alissa winced. "Oh. Only five. I haven't been at it very long."

Keribdis seemed smug. "Well, he couldn't have taught you any *other* wards of defense. He hardly knows them himself, the pacifist that he is."

The woman's condescending tone fanned Alissa's ire into a slow smolder. "Actually, I saw several when Bailic tried to force Ese' Nawoer to do his will, but Talo-Toecan asked me not to practice them." Her eyes narrowed. "And I haven't," she added, her tone bordering the belligerent.

Connen-Neute grinned. "Alissa can do healing wards, too. And hide one fielded ward within another. She knows almost everything."

Lodesh turned away, his shoulders hunched and a hand to his forehead. Everyone went silent, and Alissa's indignation turned to alarm when the Masters glanced worriedly among themselves. "The Navigator save us," Beso-Ran whispered, the ribbon of fear in his voice making Alissa cold.

"What the Wolves was he thinking?" Keribdis said. "I warned you Talo-Toecan's methods of teaching were dangerous, and this proves it. We were right in confining him to instructing Keepers. He has made our transeunt dangerous and unpredictable. If this is what he does when no one is watching, I would wager that rogue student that put the Hold in an uproar a while back was his, not Redal-Stan's."

"Actually, that was Alissa," Connen-Neute said softly.

"What!"

Alissa's hands were clenched in her lap. Masters had begun to quietly join them as Keribdis's voice drew them like wasps to honey.

"That's how my sentience was returned," Connen-Neute said. His eyes were wide, as if he was afraid to say anything but afraid to stay silent, too. "Alissa accidentally crossed the patterns for tripping the lines and shifting, putting her in the past until, ah, Lodesh and Strell found a way to get her back. She accidentally brought my consciousness back with hers when she returned."

No one said anything, and Keribdis began to pace, stirring the assembling crowd to whispers both verbal and non. "What has he done?" Keribdis said, and Connen-Neute went ashen. Alissa swallowed hard.

"Hold up, Keribdis," Yar-Taw said from the back. "Talo-Toecan has taught Alissa to think past what we accept as possible. Ashes, shifting to the past? What did you use, Alissa? A septhama point?"

Keribdis spun. Alissa blanched at the anger the woman made no attempt to hide. "That's Redal-Stan's watch," she whispered, and Alissa clutched at it hanging about her neck.

"You wore my boots. You rode my horse! That was you?" Her face hardened. "How dare you!"

"Redal-Stan gave it to me," Alissa whispered as she stood in sudden fear. "Tidbit was the only horse I could get on. I'm sorry about your boots."

"Keribdis," Yar-Taw said as he pulled himself upright. "It was over three centuries ago."

"I am not concerned about a horse!" Keribdis shouted, spots of red on her cheeks. "She stole Connen-Neute's sentience!"

Yar-Taw frowned and crossed his arms in front of him. "She only moved it. See? He's not a day older." He glanced between Silla and Connen-Neute. "Perhaps it was a good thing."

Keribdis's red skirts flared elegantly as she paced. "Connen-Neute," she said, and the young Master jumped in alarm. "You said Alissa pulled your consciousness back from the past? How?"

Connen-Neute straightened, and those near him pressed back to make a space around him. "Well—ah—actually . . . I pickabacked my consciousness on hers." He winced. "You see, Strell was playing his music—"

"You pickabacked?" Keribdis exclaimed, and Alissa's stomach clenched. "Talo-Toecan allowed you to pickaback? I'm surprised she didn't kill you or burn your tracings to ash!"

Connen-Neute's eyes were wide. "It wasn't Talo-Toecan, it was Redal-Stan," he rushed. "See, she was in the past, and when we, or she rather, shifted to get back, I was dragged along, my consciousness slipping into my feral skin in the future, or now, rather. It's, uh, not as complicated as I've made it sound. And it really wasn't her fault."

Keribdis shook her head, glancing over the silent crowd. Alissa wondered how many of them recognized she was inflaming the issue. "This is heinous," the tall woman said, and Alissa drew herself up. "What's to stop her from doing it again? Perhaps she might go back and steal Silla's consciousness!" She pointed into the crowd. "Or yours!"

Alissa started to panic. Eyes wide, she looked for a way to escape, seeing only frightened faces with golden eyes. Strell put both his hands on her shoulders, and Lodesh stood beside her.

Yar-Taw laughed into the sudden tension. "Don't be so melodramatic, Keribdis. Alissa isn't going to hurt anyone. Stop frightening the child. You're embarrassing me."

Several Masters chuckled, and Keribdis went white in rage. "You're blind, Yar-Taw!" she whispered intently, her ebony hair swinging. "Don't you see? We have no control over her! She woke Ese' Nawoer. An entire city of cursed souls! Her mind is warped by her own admission. She doesn't know how to properly shift or communicate. She's mixing wards with disastrous results." Keribdis spun to her. "And Talo-Toecan is to blame. The incompetent fool! He should have come for me when the transeunt stumbled in, expected or not."

Alissa's fear vanished, replaced with a hot anger. Keribdis was finding fault in her instructor. They had abandoned him and now blamed him for everything their absence precipitated. No one was standing up for him. Not one.

"He taught me because he thought you were dead," Alissa said, the coldness in her voice drawing all eyes to her. "Bailic managed to kill everyone else. You left Talo-Toecan to be trapped in the Holden. He taught me because he didn't want all of your skills to die with him—"

"Trapped in the Holden?" Keribdis said.

"Bailic—" she said angrily, as the woman focused on her, but Keribdis turned away.

"See what he's done?" Keribdis was saying. "The bungler, the fool of a dreamer? He has subverted our transeunt, making her uncontrollable and a threat to us and our way of life, not to mention single-handedly destroying the Hold."

"That's not what happened!" Alissa said, outraged that no one was listening to her.

"Perhaps we should go back, then," Neugwin offered.

"No!" Keribdis exclaimed, and Alissa wondered at the panic that flashed across the Master. Then more quietly, she repeated, "No. There's no need. If the Hold is empty and the transeunt is here, there's no need." She shook her head as if taking on an unwanted burden. "I'm not going back until I've fixed what he's broken."

Alissa's heart pounded. "I'm not broken!" she exclaimed, shaking off Strell's support. "Talo-Toecan is a good instructor.

He's kind, and generous with his teachings. And I like him. None of my failings are his fault! He, he—" Her words cut off. They were all staring at her.

"Excuse me," she said stiffly. Eyes suddenly hot with threatened tears, she rigidly walked to the edge of the crowd, her bells loud. The people parted before her, and she passed back under the sun without seeing any of them. The air freshened as she left the press of people. Never looking back, she strode down a path to the sound of surf. She felt awkward and ungainly in her Master's clothing. *Why had she bothered?* she wondered, her head pounding as she refused to cry. They would never see her as anything other than nothing.

18

Feeling drained, Alissa sat in the dark on the dew-damp beach and ran her fingers over Talon. The small bird had found her shortly after she left the shelter. No one had followed the bird, for which Alissa was grateful. Everyone respected her desire to be alone. There was an occasional touch on her thoughts as Lodesh checked on her. For this, too, she was thankful.

Alissa dropped her hand from Talon as the wind gusted. Clutching her arms around her drawn-up knees, she stared into the fire. She had coaxed it back to life as the sun set on the other side of the island, and the flames shifted fitfully. Several baskets lay nearby, their contents forgotten in the excitement of their arrival. Alissa had finished stringing the hard berries but wagered no one would notice. Despondent, she rubbed a pinch of sand between her finger and thumb to try to rub out the red stains.

The sand looked like snow in the starlight. Tall and whispering, the stiff grass on the dune behind her added to her feeling of isolation. The surf sounded louder now that the light was gone. Alissa fed the fire another stick, eyeing the tinge of green from the salts in the wood. *How could I have been so innocent?* she thought as she wiped her hand free of grit on her Master's vest. Connen-Neute had warned her. Useless had shown her. Why had she thought Keribdis would treat her any differently?

But at least she was able to hide Beast from Keribdis.

Talon perched upon a basket and kept a silent vigil on the stars as if memorizing their unfamiliar pattern. Depressed and hungry, Alissa rubbed the bump on her hand where the bones had been reset years ago. It seemed an entire lifetime since Bailic had broken them.

She hadn't liked the reminder she could hold only a fraction of the fields everyone else could. Pride prompted her to form a loose, permeable field in the center of the fire. It was an old game. To see a flame curling up the inside of a field was fascinating. Especially when the flame was blue and green.

Slowly the heat filled her field to make a swirling globe of fire. It was difficult to find the balance of making the field strong enough to contain fire but delicate enough not to snuff it out. It had taken her months to learn the skill, but filling her fields with fire was an easy way to visually tell how many fields she could hold at once.

Alissa watched until she was sure enough air was getting through her field to keep the fire alive. Satisfied, she added another, sitting atop the first. It immediately filled to channel the flame higher than usual. The third field she set amongst the coals. Determined to hold six this time, she added a fourth. Her breathing slowed as her concentration built upon itself. Feeling warmer than the fire could account for, she added a fifth.

Talon chittered a warning. Alissa dropped her fields. "Who's there?" she said, hating the urgency that crept into her voice. A shadow drew to a stop at the crest of the nearby dune. It was too broad of shoulder to be Connen-Neute, and she felt a pang of fear.

"It's me, Yar-Taw," came the Master's soft voice. "May I join you?"

Alissa said nothing, wondering what he had seen.

"I apologize," Yar-Taw said as he stood unmoving. "No student should hear another Master find doubt with their instructor. We've been alone so long, we forgot."

Alissa let out her breath in a puff as she turned away. Yar-Taw seemed to take that as an invitation. Slipping to the base of the dune with a good portion of sand, he came to sit beside her, facing the water. She ignored him. She had nothing to say and wanted him to leave. Strell's pipe came faintly over the dunes, and she wondered why he was playing for them.

"Don't think too harshly of us," Yar-Taw said as he stacked the empty bowls to put the strung berries on top. "Most are frightened."

Alissa raised her head in surprise. "Of me? Why?"

Yar-Taw shrugged using only one shoulder. "Student Masters are held in check by withholding wisdom. And you have some very strong wards at your command."

She nodded, but it didn't make her feel any better. "Talo-Toecan believed he was the last. He didn't want your wisdom to die with him."

"Yes, well, we knew we were alive. And the sentiment is that he used our questionable existence to further his beliefs." Yar-Taw hesitated. "His outspoken views concerning . . . ah—" His brow furrowed. "Talo-Toecan holds some very unpopular beliefs concerning how to best bring about a resurgence of our numbers. In order to maintain the balance in the conclave, he was never allowed to instruct any but Keepers, and those were blessedly few, your father among them. He was a lot like you. I see now why he left the Hold. We wouldn't have let him have children with your mother if we had done a proper profile on her signature." His brow rose. "But I don't suppose you know . . ."

Alissa poked the fire. "Redal-Stan told me you divided humanity into three groups to gain control over the traits critical to bring a Master up from a human. And how you did it," she added, her voice hard. They had massacred the coast. They had also been responsible for the plague of madness that cut the world's population by two-thirds and resulted in Lodesh's curse. All for the same ugly reason. Keribdis wanted to reduce the population again, and when Useless had stood against her, she took the conclave and left.

Yar-Taw made a soft sound as he rubbed his chin. "Redal-Stan told you?" he asked, sighing as she nodded. "Then I'm sure he gave you the entire story."

She reached out to soothe Talon's sudden chitter with a gentle caress. "P, C, and F," she said, giving the three traits their designation to prove she knew it all.

"What are we going to do with you?" Yar-Taw said, his light tone softening his words. "Between Redal-Stan and Talo-Toecan, you know almost everything. I noticed Talo-Toecan even taught you pyre fields. I wasn't aware he was skilled enough to even explain them."

He had seen! Alissa thought, her alarm easing when she found no recrimination in his gaze. "You mean making a field that contains fire?" she said, watching him to be sure she hadn't mistaken his emotions. "Yes and no. Talo-Toecan gave me free rein to experiment with fields. I think it was to pacify me, but I took him at his word. He, uh, doesn't know I can make them."

Yar-Taw's face went slack. "You figured it out on your own?"

Alissa winced, hearing his surprise. She had done it again. "Yes," she said softly. "Bailic could sculpt dust in sunbeams using multiple fields. I wanted to do the same, but dust makes me sneeze and gives Strell farmer's fever. So I thought I might be able to do the same with fire." She looked up, finding his face holding that carefully blank look she had seen on Useless so often. "So far I can only make five."

Yar-Taw pulled his legs to sit cross-legged. "The size of your fist, as you were?"

Seeing he had taken a teaching stance, Alissa relaxed somewhat. "Five isn't enough to make anything," she said, willing to show him if he asked.

"Show me?" he said, and she smiled hesitantly.

Settling herself straighter, she made a fist-sized bubble, then another, continuing to stack them until she had a tower of flame rising twice as high as normal. Holding them, she glanced at Yar-Taw for approval. His brow was furrowed in surprise. Thinking she had done something wrong, she dropped the fields and the fire fell to its original shape.

"I didn't know that could be done," he said, his gaze going to her. "Extending the fire, I mean. Pyre fields are usually used only for funerals."

Alissa drew back. "Funerals?"

Yar-Taw's eyes looked like flame in the fire's glow. "That's how we collect the source from a deceased Master," he said softly. "Otherwise it would be lost to the wind and soil. How else could we find enough source for our Keepers?"

She twisted her face in aversion, not liking the idea she had been practicing such a field, even if by mistake. And her source. It was from a dead Master?

"Alissa. Wait," Yar-Taw said, seeming to rush to capture her attention. "You show great potential for them. Not many Masters have the patience to cultivate a field large enough to be useful. I can," he continued, pride seeping into his voice. "I'm the only one, now." His brow furrowed. "I'd like to guide your progress in this area."

A nervous feeling went through her. "I don't know," she said, but pride pulled her gaze to his. "I promised Talo-Toecan I would only take instruction from him. And to take another's source?" She shuddered. "It feels wrong, especially from the dead."

What Alissa thought was a relieved smile came over Yar-Taw's face. Nodding, he said, "I wouldn't be so much instructing you as explaining the philosophy behind such a task. Talo-Toecan isn't in a position to provide this. Exchanging students is a common practice when a student shows proficiency in an area his or her original teacher isn't skilled in. I won't lie to you. It's difficult to steel myself to perform such a task. Much more so than the decades of practice needed to manage a field large enough to be useful."

He dropped his eyes to the sand. "With Talo-Toecan's permission, I would explain to you the philosophies behind the skill. Connen-Neute lacks the patience, and Silla is too involved with—her own battles. Seeing your distaste brings back all my own fears I had thought safely put to rest." His expression pleaded with her. "It's a necessary skill, Alissa, and it will give you status. Status you're desperately going to need."

Alissa ran a finger over Talon. She had promised Useless to take study from only him.

"But if you won't take instruction from me, then . . . listen to me when I sit by the fire—from time to time." Yar-Taw smiled lopsidedly. "And don't stop practicing." He hesitated, then asked, "How big a field can you make if you concentrate on one rather than five?"

A wry smile came over her. For a society so influenced by rules and laws, they certainly had a knack for getting around them. Glancing up, she read his excitement at the possibility of passing on a skill no one else wanted to learn. "I don't know," she said softly. "I've only tried small, multiple fields."

"Try one?" he asked, his eyes seeming to glow. "I'd like to see how far along you are."

Alissa squirmed. It was the first glimmer of approval she had seen in any of them, and she wasn't ashamed to pursue it. Returning her gaze to the fire, she formed a field. Concentrating, she forced the field to widen, struggling to keep the strength of it even as it expanded. Beginning to sweat, she pushed the bubble of thought farther, surprised when she managed to encompass the entire fire. The flames licked up the sides to make curling loops where they reached the edges. She felt the heat grow inside the bubble of thought, and she relaxed the strength to allow some of it to escape.

"Wolves of Ash," Yar-Taw whispered, and she met his pleased gaze. "You have it. You have the balance perfectly! Retain too much heat, and the source is destroyed. Use a field not strong enough, and it escapes."

Alissa dropped the field. She slumped, her heart pounding from the effort.

Yar-Taw glanced behind him to the unseen shelter. Voices raised in song were coming from it. They made her and Yar-Taw seem all the more isolated. "Very good," he said, a smile turning up the corners of his thin lips. "Don't think you have it entirely, though. When done correctly, you won't be out of breath, and you won't be sweating." He reached around the low fire and put a long hand on her shoulder. "But very good."

The presence of his hand was heavy on her. Talon chittered a warning, but Alissa didn't resent his touch, feeling in it the same emotion of pleased instructor she felt from Useless. "Thank you," she whispered, and his hand fell away.

"Come back to the shelter?" he said as he stood. "I'm afraid the gathering has all the signs of degrading into one of Beso-Ran's three-day festivals. He has brought out his latest attempt at ale." He shook his head and beat the sand from his Master's vest. "I think he has it this time. There might be more than a few sleeping on the ground tonight. It's been too long since we've had anything to celebrate." He extended a long hand to help her rise.

Alissa cringed and remained unmoving. How could she just go back? She had walked away from them in the middle of an argument.

Yar-Taw's hand dropped. "Don't be ashamed. You weren't the one pacing dramatically back and forth. Actually, I'm impressed," he added as he looked over the dune toward the shelter. "Usually when Keribdis pins her eyes on someone, she twists their words against them until they lose their temper." He smiled. "You walked away, infuriating her."

Alissa watched Yar-Taw's smile waver from the fire's heat. She had made Keribdis angry by walking away? That, Alissa thought wickedly, had possibilities. No one could find fault with her for not arguing with Keribdis. And if it irritated the woman . . .

Yar-Taw dug the tip of his boot into the sand. "She expects you to be on the beach tomorrow," he said in warning. "If you aren't there, she'll use it against you."

"She's not my teacher," Alissa said as she traced Talon's markings with a finger.

"Don't think of it as teaching. Think of it as evaluating," he said. "Everyone wants to know what wards you have and what they need to be careful implementing around you."

She said nothing. She wasn't going to be on the beach when the sun came up. She would get drunk first. Alissa stiffened, blinking with the idea. She could. It had taken Connen-Neute all of a few moments. How hard could it be?

"Strell has promised to tell us of Connen-Neute's return to sentience," Yar-Taw said, pulling her gaze back to him. "He's already gained the attention of half the conclave with his music. I can see why you brought him. He's very good at subtly twisting emotions."

A puff of amusement escaped her. Strell had three winters to practice on her. She imagined he would soon be friends with most of the Masters, if Connen-Neute's fascination with music was any indication. She was the only one having trouble fitting in. "Um, you go ahead," she said, adding as Yar-Taw arched his eyebrows, "I want to . . . try a larger field."

He seemed to relax. "As long as you aren't avoiding us. Keribdis isn't the only one in the conclave. There are more than a few who are anxious to meet you. Ah, but I would suggest you keep your skills in pyre fields quiet."

Alissa nodded. "It wouldn't help at all, would it."

Yar-Taw glanced at the shelter, a faint smile visible in the starlight. "No. It wouldn't."

She bobbed her head. "I won't be long."

Apparently satisfied, he headed back up the dune with a slow gait enforced by the loose sand. Alissa watched him disappear. Trusting Talon to warn her if anyone else showed up, she bent her thoughts back to the fire. It would be nice to be proficient in a skill most Masters hadn't bothered to cultivate. She would prove she was as good as they were, regardless of having been born to a mother who had never ridden the wind.

19

Yar-Taw settled himself atop one of the abandoned tables of food at the outskirts of the noise, watching Keribdis fume as the balance of the conclave shifted. Though almost everyone was clustered about Strell as he related how Connen-Neute was returned to sentience, there was an almost visible division. Two decades ago, there would have been none. Keribdis knew it as well as he, and he wondered if that was the cause for the tension within her occasional laugh.

Keribdis always had a reason for what she did, even if it made no sense to him. She was being more unreasonable than usual with Alissa, and Yar-Taw hadn't figured out why yet. The collective desire to return home wasn't Alissa's doing. There had been mutterings for the last three years about going back. Not knowing the way, they were marooned as surely as if they lacked wings. But with a boat and a crew who knew the way, Yar-Taw thought Keribdis's reluctance to return didn't rest on safety but pride.

Going back would be an admission that Talo-Toecan was right when he refused to allow her to instigate a continent-wide catastrophe to decrease the human populations. Still, that was no reason for Keribdis's immediate animosity toward Alissa. The girl seemed nice enough. Most everyone else appeared willing to accept her into their small family with little more than a cursory glance. They had several hundred years to form an opinion of her. No need to rush it.

There was a small disturbance as Keribdis rose. She motioned for her followers to stay before making her way to him. Not surprised, Yar-Taw shifted a jug of Beso-Ran's ale to make room for her on the table beside him.

Keribdis didn't look at him as she arranged her Master's vest carefully about herself. He kept his eyes upon Strell as he gestured dramatically, his eyes mirroring the mystery of his tale. Yar-Taw wondered how much of the man's claim that he had given Alissa a living memory to follow through time instead of a septhama point was true. Yar-Taw frowned. The plainsman knew a worrisome amount of Master lore for a commoner.

Keribdis pointedly cleared her throat, and Yar-Taw took a slow breath. Here it came.

"What is she doing?" Keribdis asked, her voice cruel. "Crying in the dark?"

Yar-Taw allowed himself a small laugh. "Hardly. She's practicing her, ah, fields."

"She's still hiding," the older woman said darkly.

Breaking his gaze from the piper, Yar-Taw's turned to her. "Can you blame her? She is little more than a child. She crossed an ocean to find us and is now probably wondering why. What wind ripped your wing, Keribdis? Talo-Toecan taking on your instruction duties is no reason to browbeat the girl. Silla has been exposed to nearly as much, most of it your fault."

"It's hard enough raising an orphan," she said defensively. "It's harder when I have to do it with all of you using wards as if you have no arms to lift wood or fingers to turn a page."

"If you're finding your parental duties onerous, there are plenty who would take that task for you," Yar-Taw said, knowing Keribdis would rather die than allow another to raise Silla. She was the daughter Keribdis was too proud to have with Talo-Toecan, and she loved the girl more than she loved herself. Perhaps, Yar-Taw mused, that was what was bothering Keribdis. That her protégée had someone other than Keribdis to spend her day with?

Keribdis said nothing, her long fingers laced about her drink with a deceptively loose grip.

Yar-Taw could tell she was shaking inside, but from what? "And what about Silla?" he asked, testing the air currents, as it were. "Have you thought about her?"

A flash of fear showed in her eyes, then vanished. "What about Silla?"

Excitement went through Yar-Taw. Was this all it was? He could quell this in an evening. "The two have been dream-touching for some time," he said. "They're friends already. What is Silla going to think if you keep attacking Alissa for no reason other than that she seems to have a lot of wards?"

Keribdis's thin shoulders eased. "Yes. You're right. I'll— I'll be more understanding."

Yar-Taw stifled his frustration. Her admission was too quick. It wasn't Silla's and Alissa's friendship. It was something else. "Please don't tell me this is because she managed to ride Tidbit," he said, thinking it would be like Keribdis to fix upon something as trivial as that.

She frowned. "I'm not angry about my horse."

"Then what?" he asked.

Brow furrowed in thought, Keribdis took a breath to explain, then held up a finger as if to say, *Wait*. Yar-Taw followed her gaze across the shelter to where Alissa had eased out of the dark. Looking proud but unsure of herself, the young woman sat at the outskirts, cross-legged upon a wide bench. The kestrel on her shoulder stared at them, and Yar-Taw felt uneasy.

A smile blossomed over Alissa as Strell caught her eye. Lodesh, too, turned to her, alerted to her presence by the piper's sudden interest in the crowd. Immediately the Warden rose to join her. The flow of Strell's words bobbled, and a brief frown crossed the plainsman's face. Yar-Taw went slack in thought. *What*, he wondered, *is this?*

"Something's wrong," Keribdis said, her jaw tightening.

Yar-Taw ran a hand over his chin, hoping the woman would come out with what was bothering her before it was too late for him to head it off. "There's nothing wrong with Alissa," he said slowly. "She is a transeunt. You have to make some allowances. She's so much like us that the little quirks she has from her upbringing seem twice as obvious."

Keribdis frowned. "That's not it," she said. "Something is wrong." She glared at Yar-Taw as he took a breath to protest. "There is something wrong with her!" she said, hushed but intent. "Look at her thought signature," she added. "Listen carefully."

Yar-Taw made a mental search, easily finding Alissa beside the Warden where his eyes told him she would be. "I don't sense anything," he said, deciding Alissa's thought signature was rather nice: bright and warm like a field of lace flowers at noon.

"Don't look. Listen," Keribdis said. The anger had disappeared, leaving the woman much more attractive. Her eyes were bright with solving a puzzle, and Yar-Taw felt a pang go through him. Once, she had always been like that. "Hear it?" Keribdis said, her usual temperament softened. "It's almost as if—" She looked up, her face going frightened. "It's almost as if there's an echo."

"An echo? What would cause that?" Yar-Taw asked, genuinely concerned.

"I've only seen it once before. I think—" Keribdis cut her thought short, shifting the fabric covering her knees. "I don't know yet, for certain," she finished, but Yar-Taw thought she was lying.

20

"A dance!" someone shouted, and Lodesh smiled. It had been far too long since he had heard a Master's voice raised in so much enjoyment. "Play us a dance, Strell. A Piper of the Hold is a grand idea! Beso-Ran can make ale, but he can't play a tune any more than he can fly."

The rest of them cheered or laughed, their concerns about Alissa soothed by Strell's tales of her woebegone exploits. The piper was better at this political game than Lodesh would have given him credit for. And Strell would be obliged to play a dance tune lest he ruin the Masters' collective good mood. Masters loved to carouse, and he had known it would be only a matter of time until someone wanted to dance. Lodesh felt a jolt of anticipation.

"Alissa," Lodesh said, shifting so his thigh touched hers. She stiffened, and he smoothly moved to put space back between them. "I don't care what any of them think," he said, his voice tinged in amusement.

"I do," she whispered, her voice distant and airy.

"I don't know why. They're a bunch of overpompous, shortsighted, wind-starved, ancient busybodies," he said as he pulled a pitcher close. "Give me some time, and I'll bring them around. I can change even Keribdis's mind." He topped off his cup and took a sip, making a satisfied noise. "No one else but Redal-Stan could do that."

Alissa shakily proffered her own cup made of stone. She had made the small cup earlier from her thoughts when he refused to fill one of the larger glasses with ale. Too much ale did not make for nimble feet, and he did so want to dance with her.

Smiling, Lodesh took the stone cup out of her hand and set it on the table behind them. "Let's dance?" he said slyly. He had retained his grip on her fingers, and he pulled on them.

"No," she said, blinking at him. Moving slowly, she brushed the hair out of her eyes, needing to do it twice to manage it. "I want to go to sleep. Where—where's my bed?"

Lodesh grinned. "It's the ale," he said. "A quick dance will get your blood flowing. Wake you up again." *And remind you of our dance under the mirth trees,* he thought to himself.

"No. I want to sleep." She looked over his shoulder into the night.

"Nonsense." He stood and pulled on her hand. "You haven't possibly had enough to slow your feet, much less put you to sleep."

"Lodesh, stop." Her eyes were suddenly wide. "I can't dance. I don't think I can stand up." She blinked, looking pale in the warded lights at the ceiling behind a strung net.

"Do you know how long I've been waiting for Strell to play something we could dance to?" Lodesh said merrily. Grinning, he pulled her to her feet. Alissa took a deep breath as she rose. Her head swung down to her chest and rose back up in a smooth, unbroken movement. Wide-eyed, she stared at him. Her befuddled state had vanished with a shocking suddenness.

Lodesh felt his stomach drop. This wasn't Alissa. It was Beast. "Burn me to ash . . ." he whispered. Gripping her shoulder, he glanced over at the Masters pushing benches and tables aside to make a dance floor.

"Something's wrong with Alissa," Beast said through Alissa, clearly near to panic. "I think she's sick. She isn't thinking right, and she fell asleep without me. I'm scared—"

"Hush," Lodesh whispered as he sat her back down. His eyes roved the crowd to see if anyone had noticed. Strell had begun to play, and he breathed a sigh of relief as all eyes turned to him. He gave Beast a worried smile. "Alissa is all right," he said. "I think she's inebriated."

The frightened look in Alissa's gray eyes eased. "Inebriated?" Beast seemed to mouth the word, making it sound almost respectable with her odd accent. Her stance changed as she lost her alarm. She became softer, yet a core of strength ran through her. It made her artlessly alluring, and Lodesh's pulse quickened. He had forgotten this aspect of Beast. Wolves, he had to marry this woman. Strell wouldn't know what to do with her.

Still gripping her shoulder, Lodesh gestured for Connen-Neute. He was clustered in the shadows with Silla, having stolen Talon from Alissa earlier with a piece of dried meat, and was now shamelessly using the bird to get to know Silla. Connen-Neute was watching them suspiciously, probably remembering what happened the last time Lodesh and Alissa danced. Lodesh glanced at Alissa as a bittersweet memory surged through him. He had all but proposed, but fear had stayed his hand. If he had, things would have gone differently. He knew it.

Connen-Neute whispered something to Silla. Passing Talon to the delighted young woman, he stood and circled his slow way around the crowd. The Masters had begun to cheer the few dancers on. Someone had a drum, and it was beating into Lodesh like a second pulse.

"All right," Lodesh said. "When Connen-Neute gets here, we'll get you to your bed."

"I don't want to sleep," Beast protested, gazing up at him. "I want to dance. I want to dance with *you*, Lodesh." She smiled, making Alissa's gray eyes smolder.

Taken aback at the sudden change, Lodesh dropped his grip on her shoulder.

"Dance with me?" she asked as she leaned into him.

Connen-Neute came alongside, his long face pinched in worry. "How could you let her drink her tracings into the ground?" he said as Lodesh disengaged himself. Turning to Alissa, he added, "Come tomorrow when your head is exploding, you'll be wishing you had confronted Keribdis instead."

"This wasn't my fault," Lodesh said indignantly. "She

only had one drink. How was I to know what it would do to her? And besides, we have a bigger problem."

"Good evening, wingmate," Beast said, her smile turning seductive.

Connen-Neute stiffened. "That's not Alissa," he whispered, glancing fearfully at the Masters cheering Beso-Ran as he cavorted like a stallion on Ese' Nawoer's field.

Lodesh grimaced. "I know. You take one arm, I'll take the other."

"What are you doing here?" Connen-Neute asked, aghast. "You promised."

Beast's stance shifted from seductress to lost child with an unsettling quickness. "She went away too fast. It wasn't right. I got scared." She swallowed hard. "I don't feel well."

Lodesh scanned the shelter for the easiest way out, his stomach tightening as he found Keribdis staring at them. "The Wolves should tear me apart," he said softly. "We have to get her out of here. Let's go the back way so we don't have to go by Keribdis."

Beast took a breath. "She'll make Alissa kill me," she wailed, fortunately unheard.

"Hush!" Lodesh clenched his jaw. "Can you walk?"

Beast regally extended her hands for help, and they pulled her to her feet. She stood stock-still until she found her balance. "My feet aren't listening to me fast enough," she said.

Lodesh grunted. "That's a new one," he said, not trusting she was as steady on her feet as she appeared. "All right, right foot first." He glanced over Alissa's shoulder to see Keribdis distracted by Strell's music. "We'll get you to your bed, and you can enjoy torturing Alissa for this tomorrow."

At Beast's nod they started their hesitant way to the dark beyond the shelter. Lodesh wasn't sure how they were going to manage the sand, but perhaps once out from under everyone's eyes, he and Connen-Neute could carry her. He took a breath in relief when he felt the open sky over them rather than the thatched roof. "There," he whispered. "Almost there."

The sounds of Strell's music and the singing Masters grew fainter as they reached the path to the beach. The sound of surf rose to replace it, and Lodesh breathed easier when he spotted the two storage huts.

"I don't want to go to bed," Beast complained as they guided her inside the darkness of the first and helped her sit on the small cot. Hayden had brought her pack ashore, and Lodesh was grateful for small favors.

"Yes, you do." Lodesh helped her lie on the bed, and he pulled a blanket over her. Neugwin had made it. He recognized the pattern. Frowning, Lodesh glanced at Alissa's shoes, deciding she would rather suffer the discomfort of waking up with them on than the embarrassment of waking up with them off. Connen-Neute stood in the doorway with a soft, warded light in his hands. Beast stared at him with wide, alert eyes, and Lodesh felt a pang of worry. "Stay here," he said. "Alissa would want you to stay here. All right?"

Beast pushed her blanket aside and rubbed a hand under her nose. Her gaze started to go smoky again, and he took a step back, suddenly feeling he was in danger of taking advantage of her befuddled state whether he wanted to or not.

"Let's go," Connen-Neute said uneasily. "We don't want to be missed."

Lodesh nodded. He gave Beast a stern look before following Connen-Neute out.

The young Master dropped the cloth hanging as a door and exhaled in a long, relieved sound. "She makes my hide crawl when she does that," Connen-Neute said as they slogged their way through the sand to the path.

"I don't mind," Lodesh admitted. He glanced behind them, wondering if he ought to stay and make sure she didn't get up and wander back to the music. "I like it," he added softly.

Connen-Neute frowned, his face looking longer than usual from the globe of light in his grip. "You've never shared the sky with her. Beast isn't tamed, and she isn't charmed. She's feral. She has no idea what emotions she is pulling from you. She would fight you to tatters if you made the slightest move to accept her invitation, despite the apparent indications otherwise."

Lodesh looked askance at him. "You're jesting. How can she not know?"

The young Master shuddered. "If she knew what her body language was saying, she would turn combative. Feral beasts won't allow themselves to be brought to ground. That's why the world isn't overrun with feral rakus," he mumbled.

"Oh . . ." Brow furrowed, Lodesh kept silent on their return trip. There was a way he could turn this to his favor in his pursuit of Alissa. He knew it. He only had to figure out how.

21

Strell jogged down the dark path following Lodesh, Connen-Neute, and Alissa. He was lucky the way was smooth, or he would likely have twisted an ankle. His pace thudded up into his head, and his knees were stiff from holding one position too long. Clearly he would have to establish a tradition of rules, or they would have him piping like this every night.

It had set him aback to find that the Masters raised the Navigator's Wolves with more abandonment than the father of six girls on the wedding night of his youngest. But it made sense in hindsight. Most of them were nearing their eighth century. What else did they have to do?

The temptation to not entertain them had been strong. But he had swallowed his anger, realizing he could do more good with his music than any other way. Requests had been honored, but the theme was of forgiveness and tolerance. He had left under the excuse of stretching his legs, but his knees were the last thing on his mind. Something was wrong with Alissa. It had only been the fear in Connen-Neute's eyes when he and Lodesh had led her away that kept his mouth shut and his distracting music flowing until they were safely out of sight.

A light on the path drew Strell into a slower pace. "Alissa?" he called breathlessly.

The light hesitated, then continued forward. "It's us, Strell," came Lodesh's voice.

Strell felt a wash of bother. Lodesh. The charismatic man had begun to irritate Strell more than usual recently. Strell strode forward in a quick walk as his knees throbbed. He recognized Connen-Neute's dark form next to Lodesh, but Alissa was gone. They had stopped and were waiting for him. Connen-Neute's long face looked uncomfortable in his dim, warded light. But even worse was the calculating, devious gleam in Lodesh's eyes. "Where's Alissa?" he asked, tensing as he realized they were intentionally blocking his path.

"I put her to bed," Lodesh said. "Let's get back before we're missed."

Lodesh put a hand on Strell's shoulder to turn him around, and Strell shrugged it off. Beyond him were the dark huts above the high tide mark. Something was wrong. Lodesh didn't want him to see her. "Is she all right?" he asked, wondering if it would be easier to play along and slip back when they weren't looking.

"She is at the moment," Lodesh said dryly. "I imagine the morning will be different."

"She is inebriated," Connen-Neute said softly, giving the Keeper a dark look.

Strell's brow furrowed. "She only had the one drink. I've been watching her."

"So has Keribdis," Lodesh said. "That's why we got her out so quickly. Come on," he added, putting a companionable arm across Strell's shoulders. "We don't want them to search you out. Hounds, your music has charmed them thoroughly. Quite an accomplishment, Strell!"

The flattery pulled Strell's warning into focus. Again, he pushed the arm from him, refusing to move. The tension grew thick. "Get out of my way," he threatened, his voice dropping.

Lodesh's smile looked false. "She's fine," he soothed. "She's probably asleep already."

"Strell?" Alissa called from the beach, and Lodesh groaned softly.

Strell pushed past them. He moved quickly down the

shadowed path to find her standing by the first hut, holding it as if for balance. He slowed at the odd sound of her voice. It was smoother, more precise, as if she were making a conscious effort to keep from slurring. "Alissa," he called as he came even with her. "Are you all right?"

"Alissa is sleeping," she said, shocking his feet to stillness. "I'm awake, though."

Connen-Neute had come silently up beside him. Strell stared at Alissa, unsure what to do. Lodesh took her arm and tried to lead her away. "Go back inside," the man almost hissed. "You promised you would stay inside."

"I did not," she said, sounding more affronted than usual. The bells on her ankle chimed as she resisted Lodesh pulling at her.

"Stop it," Strell demanded, ready to hit the Keeper and risk being warded into some unpleasant position. But Lodesh desisted, and Alissa tugged free of him. His anger vanished as her gray eyes fastened on his. She was . . . different. It was obvious by her wavering stance that she was drunk, but that wasn't it. "Alissa?" he questioned as he pulled her into the starlight.

"Tell him," Connen-Neute said.

A pang of fear went through Strell at what those words might lead to. "Tell me what?"

Lodesh visibly gathered himself. "Talo-Toecan made a mistake," he said, pitching his voice low. "That afternoon Alissa first shifted and went feral?" he asked, and Strell nodded.

Connen-Neute glanced over his shoulder at the muffled noise at the shelter. "Alissa didn't destroy her beast, she made a pact with it."

Strell went cold. Feral? He dropped Alissa's hands and swallowed hard. He searched her face for any sign of savagery, finding only a look of sly smugness. "You mean . . ."

Lodesh's smile was forced, his concern behind it painfully obvious. "Alissa has been harboring a second, feral consciousness for the last few years. Her arrangement, though questionable, has saved her sanity several times, helped her come back from the past, and I think is what enabled her to reach Silla's thoughts past the curve of the earth. The arrangement seems to work most of the time, though when Alissa passes out, Beast tends to take over."

"I'm not taking over," Alissa said in a huff. "If Alissa was awake, she'd be in control."

Strell stared at her, knowing what Lodesh had said was probably true. Alissa had been subtly different since learning how to shift into a raku: more reserved, less inclined to take advantage of their moments alone. He had attributed it to the shock of learning she was a Master and trying to live up to her new status. But now, seeing her making eyes at him, he wondered. "How long have you known?" he heard himself ask. Wolves, they must think him a fool.

"Since before you were born," Lodesh said, and Strell's jaw clenched. It grated on him that Lodesh had trapped Alissa in the past, almost forced her to live a lifetime there. Lodesh and Alissa may have danced under the mirth trees before Strell's great-grandfather existed, but from Alissa's perspective, it had been the other way around, and that's what mattered.

"Connen-Neute found out when he pickabacked his thoughts on hers," Lodesh continued. "Talo-Toecan doesn't know."

Alissa sniffed. "He can't know," she said plaintively, jerking Strell's attention back to her. "He'll make Alissa destroy me. And she promised me she wouldn't."

Strell's breath shook as he exhaled. *It was still her,* he thought, finding the idea she could be one or the other more frightening than the idea she might be completely feral. He reached out, and after hesitating to be sure she would let him, tilted her chin to put her face in the faint light from Connen-Neute's ward. Puzzled, he searched her features. *They must be mistaken,* he thought. Alissa might have a second consciousness, but she was still herself. Why hadn't she told him? Was she afraid he would hate her? "Alissa?" he asked, feeling ill.

"No," Connen-Neute said. "It's Beast."

Strell forced his hands to drop from her and to take a step back. He searched her slowly blinking eyes for a difference. Apart from the way she said her words, there wasn't any. "You're still Alissa," he said as he turned to Connen-Neute and Lodesh. "That's still Alissa."

Connen-Neute shook his head. "Only on the outside. The one animating her is Beast."

The last of Strell's fears melted away. "No. I've seen the difference when Talo-Toecan animated Alissa. That's still Alissa."

"I'm not," Alissa said as she reached out to take Strell's hand.

He went willingly forward to steady her. She gave his hands a firm squeeze, and he looked up in surprise to find a warm, sultry expression simmering in her gaze. His heart pounded, and his entire body seemed to jerk in response. It wasn't that Strell hadn't seen that look directed at him before, but it was rather unexpected, considering the situation. "Ah, no," he said with a gentle refusal but not letting go of her. He couldn't just yet, not with Lodesh standing so near. "You have to go to bed so no one else will find out."

"I'd rather stay with you," she said, pulling him off balance and almost in to her.

Her hands went around his neck. Lodesh was positively green, and Strell felt a jolt of satisfaction, even as he disentangled himself from her. "Please, Alissa," Strell said as he gripped her wrists gently before him. "It's important no one else see you. They won't understand as I do. I—" He glanced at Lodesh, both glad and annoyed he was here to overhear. "I love you, Alissa," he said, knowing his face was flushed. "Even with a beast in your thoughts. Remember that when you wake up, all right? Please?"

Alissa's breath came out in a long exhalation, and she stopped trying to wiggle from his grip. "They think themselves so wise, but they forget they can see the wind." She pouted, allowing Strell to help her across the sand and back to the dark hut.

Knowing she would rather sleep in a chair than a bed, Strell pulled the bedclothes off and piled them on the hut's woven seat. He helped her sit, scowling at Lodesh when he got in the way. "I'll do it," he said darkly as he knelt to arrange the covers, his motions gentle as he tucked them under her chin. The memories it brought back forced his eyes closed in brief pain. She probably wouldn't remember this, either.

"Will you stay here?" Lodesh asked from the doorway, and she frowned.

"Please, Alissa?" Strell added as he rose to his feet, and her frown eased. She sighed her agreement, and he dropped the curtain over the door between them with mixed feelings.

"Let's get back," the Warden said tightly.

Thoughts churning, Strell turned and followed Connen-Neute's bobbing light. He felt ill. Alissa had kept her feral consciousness? Why hadn't he seen it before? He darted a sidelong glance behind him at the beach. But she was still Alissa. Though free with her emotions—unnervingly so—and though her voice had become as seductive as the desert wind, she was still Alissa. It wasn't his fault if Lodesh and Connen-Neute had never glimpsed the passion she hid behind her embarrassed stammering and hot temperament. He had known it was there since finding her in that ravine with a twisted ankle. Every time he pulled her desires into the light to surprise both of them, it was a joy.

"Are you sure that wasn't Alissa?" he asked, thinking perhaps she was simply drunk.

Connen-Neute shuddered at his elbow. "Yes. You can see it when she flies. She flies like a feral beast. With no fear of anything. And Beast sounds different in my head."

Deep in thought, Strell followed them. He would have breakfast with Alissa tomorrow. Make sure he understood it all. Make sure she knew this changed nothing and that he loved her all the more. The entire situation smelled like trouble simmering over a too-hot fire. And he didn't know if he could survive another one of her willful rebellions again.

Perhaps . . . he wondered as tugged at his short beard. Perhaps it was time to add his own wrinkle to the brew? A feeling of deviltry slipped through him, laced with a heavy confidence. It wasn't as if he hadn't come prepared, and there would be no better time. And since her adopted kin seemed so disappointed in her, Alissa had nothing to lose by saying yes.

A smile eased over Strell, and he felt his steps grow eager. He was not above taking advantage of the situation. If Lodesh didn't know enough to capitalize upon it himself, then he really didn't know Alissa at all.

The beginnings of a dance tune stirred in him, setting his

feet to move in time with its unheard rhythm. He pushed past Lodesh and Connen-Neute, not caring that they were glancing between themselves, probably wondering about his change in mood. He would keep the Masters dancing until dawn. They would sleep past noon. By tomorrow night, it would be too late.

And it would start with dinner, he thought, eager for the sunrise.

ב ב

The cord holding the corner of his tent made a soft twang as Strell tugged at it, and he frowned. "Too loose," he breathed. It had been ages since he set up a tent, but that wasn't why he was having trouble. The sand was loose. Jittery, he yanked out the post. That the sand was a beach and the flat horizon was water could be tolerated. A loose tent support could not.

He hammered the post in at a sharper angle. Testing the cord, he decided it would do. It wasn't as if she would judge him on how well he set up a tent. Not like a plainswoman would.

Not like a plainswoman, he thought, his stomach clenching. His village would have stoned him for marrying a woman from the foothills, but he didn't care. He loved her, and Alissa needed him. A smile warmed him. She needed him more now that her kin seemed so disappointed.

Strell tossed his makeshift hammer into the nearby vegetation and wiped his hands free of the sand. He glanced at the sun setting behind the hills and crouched at the small fire just outside the tent. Neugwin, the Master who reminded him of his grandmother, had made him a set of rugs in return for the promise of putting Connen-Neute's return to sentience into a song. Strell didn't think it necessary to tell her the ballad was already halfway written.

Strell had properly rolled the rugs and placed them to make a companionable V between the fire and the tent entrance. A pot lay simmering in the coals. The smell of what might be potatoes and the flesh of a clam mixed with the scent of the fire. Dumplings made from the starch of a thick-skinned root floated on top. Strell breathed deeply, nervous that Alissa might not approve. It wasn't the traditional dinner a plainsman made for a potential spouse, but she wouldn't know that, either.

His brow furrowed in worry that she might not come. Apart from the miserable breakfast where they had discussed Beast, Alissa had hidden herself in her hut all day. He imagined it was as much from her headache as it was from Keribdis's morning harangue. The angry Master had denied Alissa the relief of a healing ward, but he thought Alissa would have refused it anyway. She was determined to keep her tracings clouded as long as possible to avoid Keribdis's lesson.

The entire island had echoed with Keribdis's fury that Alissa had drunk her tracings into uselessness. He and Lodesh had disagreed upon whether they should interfere or not. It was only because Lodesh had used his physical strength and not his wards that Strell's dwindling esteem for the man hadn't disappeared completely. Strell was beginning to think Lodesh was afraid of the Masters, hiding his fear behind the word "respect." He gingerly ran a finger across his jawline and winced, glad his beard hid most of his new bruise.

But even Strell would admit Alissa had handled the verbal attack with a grace and dignity that seemed to have come from nowhere. She had stood and listened, and when it was clear Keribdis would say no more, Alissa walked away without offering a defense or apology. Strell grinned at the memory. Keribdis had nearly choked on her outrage.

Glancing up at the empty beach, Strell wondered if Alissa's conspicuous absence might simply be placed at the feet of the headache and uneasy stomach she was suffering.

He had thought an anonymous, unsigned note would pique her curiosity enough to venture forth, but the young woman's moods were as unpredictable as a colt in spring. A flash of worry went through him. What if she had taken the invitation as a command? He would never see her then.

Fidgeting, he held the long sleeve of his traditional, plainsman's robes out of the way and carefully stirred the thick concoction over the fire so the bread wouldn't sink. His fingers felt the outside of his pocket for the reassuring weight of the copper ring he had bought at the coast. The plains didn't exchange rings, but the foothills did, and so that was what he was going to give her. But not tonight. She wouldn't see her ring until later.

A faint tickle in his thoughts brought his head up. Strell swallowed hard. There she was, standing where the land met the ocean. Her back was to him, and she was unaware he was watching her. A panicked feeling raced through him and settled in his belly. Sand and Wind, she looked beautiful with one arm clasped around herself and her free hand gripping Redal-Stan's watch on its cord about her neck. The gesture had become a habit lately, showing itself more strongly when she was worried.

A pang struck him as the wind lifted through her hair. It was free and unfettered the way he liked it. And long. Long enough to show the status she deserved. She looked like the ghost he had found standing atop the rock at the mouth of the harbor: sad and melancholy. He had known it was a ghost when her hair and dress moved against the wind. He hadn't said anything to Alissa; it made his skin crawl that he could see things even she couldn't. He blamed it on his upbringing. It was said his grandfather had been able to see them, too.

Seeing her so sad, Strell stretched his thoughts out, wishing he could reach her mind. "Alissa," he whispered, but she never turned.

Grimacing, he dropped his eyes to her dinner. It was depressing that touching her thoughts at will was a skill Lodesh possessed that he never would.

When he found the strength to look up, she had seen him and was striding across the beach. Her awkward, too-long

stride of one not used to the footing of sand quelled his feeling of nervous anticipation. Her ineptness made her all the
more endearing. She beamed as she noticed his attention. A
stab of emotion went through him as he stood. Now, he would
know.

23

Alissa hesitated, her toes damp on the hard-packed, surf-wet sand. Frowning, she looked again at the note in her grip. She had found it this afternoon just inside her door. It said to be by the sand spit at sunset. She knew it was Strell's handwriting. His loops were cramped, a result of having learned to write when the air was cold from winter.

A slow breath slipped from her as she settled her nerves. Thanks to Connen-Neute and Lodesh, no one but Strell had learned about Beast last night. Strell had taken the news well, cornering her this morning on the excuse of bringing her a breakfast she couldn't possibly eat. His questions had been pointed but unaccusing, and she would be lying if she said she wasn't relieved that he knew the truth and still thought no less of her. Still, it had been embarrassing.

She flushed at the memory. Ashes, she had been stupid. She had risked Beast's safety to avoid Keribdis, and it had only bought her one day. The gossip, too, had worsened. But the fury on the woman's face as Alissa walked away without comment had made it all worthwhile.

It had only been since the sun began edging to the horizon that her stomach had settled. She hadn't eaten anything all day and was half starved. Clasping an arm about herself, she

looked out over the ocean toward the distant Hold. A wry
smile crossed her. It was so far, even the memory of it seemed
to have faded. She took a breath, hesitating at the smell of
something on the evening breeze. "Potatoes?" she whispered,
turning to look behind her.

The sight of a tent and fire pulled her into motion. Feeling
awkward on the loose sand, she slogged forward. The figure
hunched over the flames stood, showing he was dressed in
long robes of crimson and purple. The color flowed to the
ground in narrow bands of fabric. "Strell?" she called out, and
he looked up, waving to acknowledge he had seen her.

Alissa made her slow, bell-chiming way with her skirts held
out of the sand. She hardly recognized him, especially with
that beard of his. He was dressed in the traditional robes of his
homeland, with an odd, purple hat she had never seen before.
"You haven't worn a robe since we were in the plains," she exclaimed when she was close enough to be heard over the wind.
She squinted as she halted before him. "That's not the one you
brought back with you."

Strell nodded sharply, his attention lost in an unknown
memory. "I bought this special when we were out there."

"You brought it all the way from the Hold?" she said surprised. "Why didn't you wear it when you got muddy in the
salt swamp?"

He shrugged, extending a hand to help her sit down before
the fire. His fingers were warm, slipping reluctantly from hers
as he sat on the rug across from her. *Ashes, he looks good,* she
thought as she ran her gaze over him. She had forgotten how
exotic he was in his traditional dress. His tall, lanky height
was elegant instead of awkward. His lean, wind-scarred features now lent him the mien that he could confidently weather
any storm. The cut of his clothes hinted at a Master's vest, but
looked more authentic in its simplicity. It was like comparing
a jewel-bedecked bracelet to the beauty of a single band of silver. And Strell wore it extremely well. Realizing she had been
staring, Alissa snatched his hat in fun.

"That's mine!" he protested.

"Let me see," she said playfully, holding it behind her, and
he came to a curiously docile standstill. As he sat helplessly
across from her, she gave it a through once-over. Her eyes

flicked from the hat to him and back again with a teasing mistrust. The cap was made of colored leather cut into hexagons, sewn together with a darker stained leather between them. It was round, and so much like a bowl that she decided it wasn't much of a hat. "I can't imagine that would do much against the sun," she said as she gave it back to him.

Strell seemed unusually relieved as he took it. "It's not for the sun."

She arched her eyebrows. "I don't recall seeing a hat like that in the plains."

"It's plains," he said as he replaced it on his head.

Alissa waited for more of an explanation, tucking a windblown strand of hair out of her eyes as she thought it finished off the most fascinating outfit she'd ever seen. When it was clear Strell wasn't going to say more, she turned to the tent. "Did you put this up?" she asked, thinking he obviously had but feeling she had to say something.

"Yes." Strell's attention was on the fire.

Again he was silent, so Alissa got to her feet and poked her head in. It held only a thick bedroll and his dilapidated pack. "Oh, look!" she exclaimed, realizing the floor was substantially lower than the beach. "You dug out the floor." She stepped inside to find the rug was thicker than she expected. Wondering who had crafted it, she looked at the ceiling. It was two hand spans above her head and made the tent look larger inside than out. "Why did you dig the floor out?" she asked, thwacking the ceiling to find it properly taut as her mother had shown her.

"There's less temperature fluctuation that way," he said, his voice strained.

She was silent, hearing how the sound of the surf was muted through the thick fabric. Satisfied, she came out and resumed her seat on one of the rolled-up rugs beside the fire.

"Do you—" He hesitated. "Do you like it?" he asked, running a hand across his beard.

"The tent?"

He nodded, and she blinked.

"Uh—yes. I guess. It's a nice color."

Strell exhaled in a long, slow sound. Alissa glanced at him, wondering what was with him tonight. He was positively mysterious. "Are you going to sleep here in the tent?" she asked. "It would be nice to get away from everyone. I can't imagine what it's going to be like when they get back to the Hold." She bit her lower lip, having a pretty good idea and not relishing it.

"I might." Strell stood and shifted to kneel before the fire, and her breath caught at the image he made. "Uh, where's Talon?" he asked guardedly as he took the lid off the pot over the fire.

Alissa smiled as she breathed deeply of the fragrant steam. She hadn't known he was going to make them supper. "With Silla. She made the mistake of giving Talon a slice of meat."

"Good," Strell said. "I mean, it must be nice for her to have a pet to amuse herself with."

Alissa's smile went wry. "Yes. Good for her."

Strell dipped out a portion of the thick white slurry into a bowl and extended it to her. "Here."

She gave him a smile and accepted it, eagerly taking a spoonful of the creamy soup. Warmth, and a spicy taste of nuts, filled her mouth. Her eyes closed. "Oh, ashes," she almost moaned. "Bone and Ash, this is good. What's in it?" She looked up at his pleased expression. He was watching her, his hands empty. Her thoughts went back to the last time she had eaten something he had made for her. Her face went slack. "Strell?" she quavered, and he chuckled.

"No grubs," he said, grinning. "Nothing with feet. Promise. Not even those water animals with all the legs you can't decide about."

Flashing him a relieved smile, she took another bite. "Aren't you going to eat?" she mumbled around mouthful.

"I don't know," he said cryptically.

Her eating paused. Then she chewed rapidly and swallowed. "This is all for me?"

"Yes." He looked at her, his eyes glowing in an excitement she didn't comprehend.

She lowered her spoon, trying to figure it out. The tent, the clothes he had carted halfway around the world, the meal he wasn't eating. She knew it meant something. "I'm sorry, Strell," she finally said. "I don't have the slightest idea what's going on. I can tell this is important . . ." Her words trailed off into the sound of the surf.

He ducked his head to show the top of his round hat. "I'm trying to propose, Alissa," he said, and her jaw dropped. She went cold, then hot. "Didn't your mother tell you anything?" he continued, smiling. "The tent is supposed to show I can provide a home, though I'll admit it's to sneer at. And the meal is to convince you I can keep you and your children from starving through the spring. The robes and hat? They're just for show."

She blinked, her fingers going slack around the bowl. *Propose?*

"Dinner was supposed to be potatoes, goat, and apples," he was saying, the words tumbling over themselves. "But you don't eat meat, and I haven't seen an apple or potato since the crewmen stole what I had hidden. It's mostly roots and some of those clams that stick to rocks that Silla showed me. About the only thing right here is my beard and the sand."

She swallowed hard, her pulse racing as she remembered the comment Lacy had made. "You grew that beard for me?"

Strell ran a hand over it. "I couldn't propose without it. It's to give a man time to reflect on what he's doing. Sort of a waiting period."

She couldn't seem to keep her mouth closed; her jaw kept falling open. "What am I supposed to do?" she said, her voice high and squeaky.

"Well—uh—" he stammered as he dropped his eyes. "If you want to say no, then you eat everything and walk away. If you want to say yes, you—ah—leave me something."

"Leave you . . . what?" she questioned.

"Something to eat," he rushed. "Because you care enough that we will either eat or starve together." He reddened, and she could tell he was embarrassed that starvation was such a possibility in the plains that it had worked its way into even their wedding traditions.

"But . . . I can't get married," Alissa said as her cheeks warmed. "Useless said I have to adhere to foothill traditions. My mother must show favor."

Strell looked up, his brown eyes devious. "I already have her favor," he said softly. A slow grin spread itself behind his dark beard. "Remember this?"

Alissa felt her jaw drop yet again as he reached behind him

and untied his hair. His usual hair clip had been replaced with a familiar, copper-colored hair ribbon. Her eyes widened. "That's my mother's," she exclaimed. "The one she put around the map you bought from her."

He nodded. "She knew I might catch up with you, or hoped I might. At least, I think so. Why else would she give me a map for a paltry length of silk?"

A thrill of emotion rushed through Alissa, leaving her feeling as if she couldn't catch her breath. "But Useless said I have to adhere to foothills traditions, not plains," she said as her heart pounded. "Ribbons aren't a sign of favor in the foothills, just affection."

Strell smiled lopsidedly. "You don't need a sign of favor. I do. And as I'm plains and your mother is plains, the ribbon stands, regardless of what traditions *you* have to hold to."

"But is it enough?" she asked as she leaned forward. "Will Useless accept it?"

He tucked a strand of hair out of her eyes and his smile deepened. "I know it would stand up in a plains council. Your mother knew I was a Hirdune potter. That would be reason enough for most plainswomen to court a match for her daughter."

"Then . . ." She blinked several times, feeling unreal. "Then we can? You . . ." She bit her lower lip, afraid to believe he was serious. "You truly want to marry a—a half-breed?"

"Do I really want—" His voice cut off as if in disbelief. His face went serious as he took the bowl of food from her and put it upon the ground. Settling her hands in his, he leaned close. His eyes were deep in memory. "Alissa. I loved you when you were a foothills girl defying the mountains and an early winter. I loved you when you were a Keeper determined to not let Bailic dictate your future. I loved you when you were a Master, more wild than the mountains themselves. Nothing has changed." His eyes shone with unshed tears. "Nothing ever will."

His eyes flickered with an old pain, and her heart pounded. "I've made a place for myself in the Hold, but even so, Lodesh is much more deserving of you," he said without a trace of bitterness. "I don't care. I don't care that my kinsmen would stone me, or that the Hold will likely refuse to allow the marriage to stand. They can't keep you safe. I can."

His words began to get faster. "I love you," he said, and she couldn't breathe. "I think I have since finding you in that ravine, spitting mad and scared. I try and I try to keep you safe. But every time I see you clear of one danger, you find a new way to turn my life upside down. I can't take it anymore. The only way I can think to keep my skin intact is to marry you."

She couldn't say anything. Her hands trembled as they rested in his.

"I need you to decide between us," he said. "If only to keep myself sane. I have to know before I kill myself chasing a raku who doesn't need me."

Doesn't need him? she thought as she wiped the back of her hand across an eye. Didn't he know how she depended upon him? And as for choosing? Connen-Neute had been right. She had chosen a long time ago but was too afraid to admit it. Her heart said Strell. Not for what he had done, but for who he saw her as, as she truly was: a child of the foothills who jumped to conclusions and had too quick a temper. He was as simple and plain, as common and enduring, as honest and true as the sand he grew up amongst. And she loved him.

"Will you stay with me, always?" he asked, pulling her attention to him and the warmth of his hands. "At least as long as I walk the earth?" he said, sounding apologetic. "I know Lodesh will live longer than me, and after I'm gone, I'll understand if you—"

Making a cry that was both happiness and sorrow, Alissa dropped her head onto his shoulder. "Yes. Yes I will. I love you, too," she said as she took in the scent of hot sand. The tragedy of Strell's short span pained her, but she was fiercely determined to take what she could.

His breath came in a relieved, joy-filled noise. Strell pulled her close, his arms reaching all the way around her. Her eyes blurred with tears as he tilted his head and kissed her. Emotion coursed through her, seeming all the sweeter for knowing it was fleeting.

Then the dismal thought of Strell's short life was gone in a wash of heat. Tomorrow meant nothing. There was only now. His lips were warm, pulling her into prolonging the kiss. The softness of his beard was almost a shock. She reached up, drawing him closer by twining her fingers in his hair. There was a soft thunk as his hat hit the sand. Nothing existed but him. Nothing else mattered.

As her heart beat wildly, she absently noted her right hand drop from him. A wisp of alarm went through her as her fingers unexpectedly tightened into a fist. In slow motion, she found her arm pulling back. Her eyes opened wide in alarm. Beast was not happy.

"Mummph!" she mumbled, trying to draw away.

It was too late. Her fist slammed into his middle. Strell's breath whooshed out. Gasping, he clutched his stomach. He fell back to sit in the sand beside the fire.

Horrified, Alissa put a hand to her mouth. "Oh, Wolves!" she cried, realizing what had happened. "Strell," she said, her hair covering his face as she bent over him. "I'm so sorry. It was Beast. It wasn't me! Ashes, I'm sorry." She put a hand on his shoulder, not liking how red his face was. He still hadn't taken a breath, either.

"What did you do that for?" Alissa thought at Beast. She could feel Beast's anger at Strell curled up in pain on the sand.

"He wanted to bring you to ground!" Beast said in shock. *"I saw it in your thoughts!"*

"I love him, Beast. I want him to ground me," she exclaimed as she knelt beside Strell. "Here," she said, taking his shoulder. "Sit up. Come on. Sit up so you can breathe."

"Au-u-u," he moaned, waving weakly at her to go away. She fell back, guilt making her unsure what to do. Slowly Strell pulled himself from his hunched position into something marginally upright. He flicked a glance at her from under lowered brows, and she felt tears of helplessness prick. Still not having said anything, he knocked the sand from his hat and placed it upon his head like a helmet. "Cursed, burning-ash fool," he muttered, not looking at her.

"I'm sorry," she whispered miserably. "It was Beast. She won't do it again. I promise."

"No one grounds me. Ever," Beast said tightly, and Alissa went worried. Obviously she and Beast would have to have a very long chat. Perhaps she should also check to see if Beast's definition of bringing to ground was what she thought it was.

"How the burning-ash am I supposed to kiss you when you do that?" Strell said, his voice thick with frustration. "If it's not your ash-ridden bird, it's your teacher. Now I've got to worry about—about Beast?" He jerked in pain as he carefully felt his middle.

Going more unhappy, Alissa hunched into herself. Somehow in the commotion, her dinner had been spilled. "What does it mean when the woman drops the food on the sand?" Alissa asked, refusing to cry. Beast had ruined everything.

Hearing the misery in her voice, Strell visibly softened. Moving slowly, he came to sit beside her. The rug dipped as their weight combined, and she slid into him. He cautiously put an arm across her shoulders. Once sure she wasn't going to hit him, he turned her chin to face him with a single finger. She looked up, blinking at the wry humor in his eyes. There was no recrimination, and her chest loosened as she took a quick breath.

"It means she's from the foothills," he said, the forgiving tone of love thicker than his plains accent. "And the ash-ridden woman doesn't know the value of food."

She gave a hiccuping sob of a laugh, and he stood to pull her to her feet. "Come on," he said, his face suddenly grim. "Let's go tell everyone and get it over with."

She pulled back even as she stood. "They won't like it. They won't let me."

"What can they do? You have Talo-Toecan's permission. Besides, do you care what they think?"

Her gaze went distant over the incoming surf as she remembered Keribdis's scorn. "No," she said, her stomach tight and her mood frightened. "But . . . let me tell Lodesh first."

24

Craning her neck, Alissa held her hand against the lowering sun as she peered into the canopy of mirth trees growing wild outside the village. The interior of the island was covered in them in all stages of growth. She would love to see the island when they were blooming. "Lodesh?" she called, knowing he was somewhere but unable to pinpoint him exactly.

"Here, Alissa!" came a faint voice. A dusk-darkened bough shook high in the canopy.

She felt ill, and she was glad she had only eaten a spoonful or two of Strell's dinner. Hands gripped tightly upon her forearms, she approached a small mirth tree whose girth might be encircled by two people. Looking up, she anxiously licked her lips. How was she going to tell him? "Uh, can I talk to you for a moment?" she said loudly.

"Come on up," he sang out. "You'll like the view. It's a nice sunset."

"View," she muttered, staring at the smooth trunk as she wondered how he expected her to get up there. "I'm not a goat," she said, knowing her temper was a thin excuse for her guilt.

"There's a ladder on the other side."

She was silent, leaning over to see. Grimacing, she sighed

and started up. She was puffing by the time she reached the branch Lodesh was on. Her chiming bells gave her away, and he was by the ladder to help her make the transition to the wide branch. His fingers were warm, holding hers with a familiar grip. Immediately she sat down, as uncomfortable with holding his hand as she was balancing up here. She glanced down, thinking if she fell, she wouldn't have time to shift and catch the wind before hitting the ground. But yes, the sunset was nice.

Seeing her settled, Lodesh returned to his work. An open box rested in the crook of two branches. Small cuttings were in it. She watched him, deciding he looked right up in the treetops despite his fine clothes and tasteful Keeper's hat. He leaned to reach a distant branch with the balance and dexterity he displayed in his dancing.

"What are you doing?" she asked, not knowing where to begin.

"Collecting cuttings from the male trees to air-layer on my grove at home."

She was silent as he clipped another green twig as long as her hand and dropped it into his box. Her lips turned into a soft frown. "What for?" she finally said, and he smiled.

"I'm going to take these back and get them to grow on one of my trees. The next time they bloom, we will have both male and female flowers. That means fertile seeds."

He snipped another. "You don't happen to know how to run a preservation ward, do you?" he questioned. She shook her head, and he added, "I'll ask Connen-Neute. I would dearly love to see my city full of mirth trees."

Alissa's brow rose as she recalled the undergrowth of young trees she had slogged through to get here. "Too many might not be such a good thing," she warned.

"Nonsense!" He stepped onto a branch she thought much too thin. "And if they do, then beggars will have very fragrant fires, won't they?"

She managed a humorless smile, her eyes on the distant ground.

He turned at her silence. His head tilted and his posture slumped. "Ah," he breathed. "Guilt and happiness all at once? That can only mean one thing."

She flicked her gaze at him and away, angry with herself when her eyes grew warm with unshed tears. Ashes. How did she ever get herself into this?

"He asked, didn't he," Lodesh said, and she nodded miserably.

Lodesh scrubbed a hand over his chin and sighed in resignation. "I thought it would be soon. A plainsman grows a beard for only two reasons, and Strell's father died years ago."

Surprised, she looked up. She hadn't know what to expect, but not this. "You aren't upset?" she gulped, feeling useless as she sat on her branch and dangled her feet.

A heavy sigh slipped from him. Tucking his shears away, he walked confidently down the broad branch to sit beside her. There was a new distance between them. It was very slight, but her heart nearly broke seeing it.

"Of course I'm upset," he said, lifting her chin with a finger smelling of crushed leaves. "But I knew he would ask." He smiled, and her sadness took pause at the glint of mischief in the green of his eyes. "And I knew you would say yes. I only have one question."

"What?" she whispered, afraid of the hundreds of heart-breaking questions he might ask.

"What did Beast do when he kissed you?"

His question hung by itself for three heartbeats. Alarm trickled through her, pushing her sadness to the back of her thoughts. He wanted to know about Beast? Glancing at him, she rubbed the back of her neck. Her brow furrowed in that he might know something she didn't. "I—uh—she hit the breath out of him," she said, warming in embarrassment. "It's not going to happen again. I talked to her," she asserted quickly.

Lodesh smiled from under his yellow curls. He stood, confidence radiating from him. "Yes, it will."

"No, it won't. She just didn't understand. She does now."

He tilted his head, amusement dancing about him. "Oh, Alissa. My silly, bullheaded, so-clever-she-can't-see-the-forest girl. I love the way you insist on doing things the hard way."

Anger pulled her stiff. "What?"

Turning sideways, he pulled out his shears and snipped a twig. "You know you can't marry Strell. Talo-Toecan stipulated your mother must show favor. And I'm sure Talo-Toecan will keep you so busy the next decade or two that you won't have another chance to look for her. And even if you somehow miraculously manage to find her and she fancies a tradesman over the administrator of a city for a son-in-law, you will never be allowed to wed Strell."

She sputtered, not believing what she was hearing. Tradesman? Though he made his way as a minstrel, he had been born a Hirdune potter! Calling him a tradesman was an insult!

A twig dropped into the box with the rest. "You cooked your neighbor's goose when you came looking for the rest of the Hold," he said, his teeth white in the new darkness. "I think that's a large part of the reason Talo-Toecan let you search them out. One thing you can count on with rakus is that they will want a say in everything. Especially if it concerns a transeunt. They won't allow it." He shook his head in a rueful fondness. "Probably make a special law for you. And even if you do manage to pull off a wedding, you will never be able to consummate the marriage." His eyes went knowing. "A feral raku will not allow herself to be taken to ground. It's why the world isn't overrun with them. A proper Master might accomplish bedding you with sheer brute force, but Strell? The poor man won't even be able to steal a kiss."

Her face flamed at his frank words, but fear he might be right kept her unmoving.

Lodesh eyed her gleefully under the lowered brow of his hat. "The way I imagine it, by the time you manage to explain to Beast what love is, Strell will be feasting at the Navigator's table." He reached up to an overhanging limb. Using it as support, he leaned close to breathe in her ear, "What's a few decades more? I'm willing to wait."

She stared at him as he straightened. Snapping her mouth shut, she stood up, frantically catching her balance and fending off his help at the same time. "It just so happens, Warden of an empty city," she snapped as he fell back with an infuriating grin, "that Strell has already met my mother. She gave him a token of her favor before I even met him. We've fulfilled Useless's ash-ridden conditions. There's nothing they can do to stop us. And Beast will listen to me. She will!"

Lodesh bobbed his head to acknowledge he heard her

words, but his smile told her he didn't believe them. Infuriated, she hastened down the ladder, almost falling in her rush. She reached the ground as Lodesh started to sing. Furious, she pushed on the ladder. Satisfaction filled her as it crashed into the ground. But it was a short-lived emotion as his singing only grew louder. His voice raised in "Taykell's Adventure" dogged her like a second shadow as she stormed back to the village.

"I will marry Strell," she seethed aloud, swatting at a branch looming out of the encroaching darkness at the forest floor. "And Beast will listen to me. Lodesh will see. No one tells me what I can and can't do."

25

"You can't. You won't." Keribdis's emotions of outrage and anger were so strong, Alissa could almost feel them. Alissa's pulse raced as she struggled to keep from reacting the same. Talon's claws piercing her shoulder didn't help.

Yar-Taw stood between her and the rest of the conclave of Masters, and she pushed past the wall his gray Master's vest made. Strell stood beside her, his face as set as hers. The air was oppressive under the leaf-thatched shelter, as much from the smothering blackness of night as the arc of Masters staring at her in various stages of shock and disgust.

Yar-Taw put a calming hand upon her shoulder, and she flicked him a glance, relieved to have found an unexpected ally. The assembled Masters muttered among themselves, both verbally and mentally. A few were sitting on the benches, but the majority stood. Lodesh sat apart from all atop a table at the edge of the light. His elbows were on his knees, and he watched everything with a solemn quiet. Connen-Neute and Strell had reset his ladder and gotten him down. She didn't understand honor among men. Lodesh had *laughed* at her, and they didn't care.

"I like you, Alissa," Yar-Taw whispered as the uproar continued. "But you're making a mistake. Listen to Keribdis. She's right in this."

So, not an ally, Alissa thought bitterly. *Just the other side of the gate to the same fence.* "Marrying Strell is not a mistake," she said, her face warming at the implied insult.

"It is," Yar-Taw insisted, and Alissa stiffened at Keribdis's muttered expletive. "This is a fancy," he continued. "It's not love. Love does not happen over a winter."

Alissa's jaw clenched. "It does if you think you aren't going to live to see the spring."

Yar-Taw put a second hand on her other shoulder. She shrugged his long fingers off, feeling the oddness of them for the first time. She shifted closer to Strell. They were ignoring him as if he were nothing but a symptom to a larger problem. It infuriated her.

The background murmur of the Masters ebbed. Keribdis glanced over them. "She can't join with him," she said, her words clipped and short. "He's not a Master. Wolves, he's hardly a commoner. Nothing ever came from the Hirdune line. Nothing ever will."

A cry of outrage slipped past Alissa. Talon began to hiss in response to her anger.

Neugwin stepped close. The matronly woman glanced uneasily at Talon before taking Alissa's hands. "Alissa, dear," she said, and immediately Alissa took offense. "All children are precious. But to have a child who can't ride the wind? Always left behind? Lacking? Give us a few hundred years, and we'll have a suitable match for you. You must learn patience."

Alissa pulled her hands away. She took a slow breath to try to find a false calm. "I'm not asking for your permission," she said. "Strell has a token of favor from my mother. We met Talo-Toecan's stipulations. We fulfilled our end of the agreement."

At the word, "agreement," there were several groans. "All agreements aside," Keribdis stated, "you aren't officially an adult. Technically, you're still a child. A child as much as Silla is." A slow satisfaction eased over the woman. "You won't be marrying anyone," she said in a low threat. "Be on the beach tomorrow morning—student."

The entire congregation of Masters seemed to sigh in relief. The overwhelming tone of outrage turned to quick agreement: still a child, conflict ended, time for dinner.

Alissa hesitated. Keribdis called her a child, and that was

it? She glanced at Connen-Neute, then Yar-Taw. "What does she mean?" she asked as the Masters left.

Yar-Taw's silence made Alissa all the more upset. She turned to the disappearing crowd with wide eyes. Talon crooned as the tension under the shelter eased. The first faint inklings of panic went through her. "What does she mean, I'm not officially an adult?"

Connen-Neute dropped his gaze. "Masters are only given a verbal name when born," he said softly as he came close. "They don't receive a written word to represent their name until later. You inscribe it on the cistern to make it official. After that, you symbolically cleanse your old life away in the cistern, then fly from the opening of the holden as an adult."

She spun to Yar-Taw, her breath tight. "I've done that."

The Master's brow furrowed. "Alissa . . ." he said warningly.

"I've done that!" she insisted, ignoring the numerous protests of disbelief. The leaving Masters hesitated. "When I was trapped in the holden, I scratched a name on the cistern wall," she said breathlessly. It had been the word for "useless," but if it meant she could marry Strell, she would live with having that word represent her name.

Elated, Alissa turned to Lodesh. Her excitement died as he met her eyes from under his hat. "And I fell in," she said hesitantly. "And when I left, I didn't crawl up the tunnel, I rode out on wings." They had been Useless's wings, but she had flown. "Ask Lodesh," she said, her voice suddenly weak. "He was there," she warbled.

All eyes were on Lodesh. All thoughts were held still.

Lodesh looked at her with no expression. Her heart clenched. She had no idea what he would do. He slowly slipped from the table, tugging the cuffs of his shirt straight as he gathered himself. Her held breath escaped her, and she caught it again. A sly grin eased over him, and Alissa went colder. *"You will be with me someday,"* he whispered into her mind. *"I understand you love Strell, but you'll love me again, as you once did in the golden fields of my city."*

Alissa's knees felt weak, and she thought she was going to pass out.

"Yes," Lodesh said loudly, and the conclave exhaled in a

loud sound of dissent. A smile twitched the corners of
Lodesh's mouth. Apparently he felt secure in that she and
Strell wouldn't be able to consummate the marriage. "She
did," Lodesh affirmed as several voiced their doubts. "She
added a name to the list, fell in, and flew from the holden."

Alissa put a shaky hand to her head to hide her eyes. Talon
began calling in excitement as the crowd exploded into a furor
of noise. Keribdis stood stock-still, frustrated. "She still can't
marry him," Keribdis said above the babble. "We can't. We
can't let a Master marry a commoner. It just isn't done!"

"It's going to be," Alissa whispered. She looked at Lodesh,
trying to thank him with her eyes as she couldn't bear to touch
his thoughts again. She had asked for his help, and he had
given it. Before the moon had even risen on the day she chose
Strell, he had given it.

Keribdis sashayed closer. Her frustration had been replaced by a predatory gleam. "An adult," she said, and Alissa
blanched at the woman's bound fury. Talon gave a squawk at
how near the woman was, and Alissa plucked the bird from
her shoulder and covered Talon's head. "If you're an adult,
then you will be treated as such," Keribdis said. "You will
marry whom we decide. You're the Hold's transeunt. Your
very existence belongs to us."

Alissa's heart beat faster and her jaw clenched. She belonged to no one. Talon began an eerie crooning, her signal
she was going to attack. The beak worrying Alissa's fingers
became aggressive. Panicking, Alissa sightlessly shoved
Talon at Strell. The bird squeaked and fought, but Strell bun-
dled her up in the scarf Connen-Neute handed him.

"Be on the beach in the morning," Keribdis said, her black
eyebrows raised mockingly. There was a tug on Alissa's
thoughts as a red sash appeared in Keribdis's hands. The
woman dropped it at Alissa's feet. "Wear it. I will begin your
moral studies tomorrow. It seems you have—none at all."

Keribdis's eyes flicked to Talon screaming in Strell's grip.
Sedate and confident, Keribdis left. Several Masters trailed
behind her. Slowly the shelter emptied. Strell's breath slipped
from him as he sat down. Connen-Neute was the last to go,
giving her a pitying look, which she was too upset to take offense at. She never saw Lodesh leave, but he was gone.

Knees shaking, she sank down beside Strell. He released Talon, and the ruffled bird shook herself, starting to preen in short, abrupt motions. Her complaints never stopped.

"Perhaps we should wait until we get home?" he said, and she felt a wash of defiance.

Fingers moving, Alissa caressed Talon to help the bird put her feathers in order. She felt her breath slip in and out of her in an easy motion as she gathered her resolve. "I don't want to wait," she whispered.

26

The wind was brisk atop Silla's cliff, damp with the moisture of the afternoon's rain. Alissa sat on an outcrop of stone by the drop-off with her arms clasped about herself as she looked over the edge. Talon was perched on her shoulder. The bird's eyes were closed, and she was leaning forward as if delighting in the wind. Far below, the *Albatross* rode in the lagoon where they had left it. Alissa wondered how Hayden and the captain were doing.

To her other side was the unseen village under its canopy of mirth trees. A faint plume of smoke showed where the shelter was. By the shadows, it was almost noon. And if Alissa was honest with herself, she would admit she was too frightened to go back down.

She had stood Keribdis up.

Alissa's breath came and went in a quick heave of worry. This morning she had told herself it was defiance. Now she wondered if it hadn't been fear. Putting herself on Silla's cliff had sounded like a grand idea at the time. The air had been cool, almost damp enough for a fog as she had made the tedious climb upward. Her thoughts had been simmering with revolt, making her strides long and her mind set. How dare Keribdis give her a scarf! She was Useless's student. As far as

Alissa knew, the sash still lay where she had left it. But with the sun hot upon her shoulders and her middle rumbling from hunger, Alissa's rebellion had burnt itself to an ash of worry. She couldn't just go down as if she had forgotten.

A small scuff on the path behind her brought Alissa spinning around. Frightened, she sent a questing thought out to find Silla. Immediately she slumped. "Hi, Silla," she said as the purple-clad young woman puffed her way up the last steps.

Silla gave Alissa a small smile of greeting and went to stand at the edge. The wind tugged at the ribbons in her hair and the hem of her skirt to make her into a picture. Alissa felt a moment of sour self-consciousness. *She* would never be that beautiful.

"You really love him?" Silla said softly as if trying to understand. "A commoner?"

"I thought I was a commoner when I met him," Alissa said, surprised at her question.

Silla's thin shoulders shifted. Clearly she didn't understand. But there was no disgust in her eyes, and Alissa would be satisfied with that. "Is Keribdis upset?" Alissa prompted.

A wry look came over Silla. "I'd say."

Alissa frowned, wondering if her defiance would be worth the fallout.

"She took it out on me," Silla added defensively.

"I'm sorry," Alissa gasped.

"She had me doing first-decade wards all morning." Silla looked down the drop. "I am so bored with fields, I could chew nails and spit rust."

Alissa winced. "Sorry."

Silla turned back, a wide smile on her. "Don't be. No one could find you. Keribdis was quite vocal with her opinion of the situation. Which is how I found out it was possible to block a mental search." She grinned. "I learned a new ward today, thanks to you."

"So, how did *you* know where I was?" Alissa asked as she set Talon on the rock and held her hair out of her eyes.

Silla's eyes dropped. Taking the ribbons from her hair one by one, she tied them about her wrist so they wouldn't blow away. "Connen-Neute told me," she said softly.

Alissa stiffened in a pang of angst until she remembered that Connen-Neute could find her whether she had set up a block or not. "Blocks don't work between us because we've pickabacked," she said. "I can't hide from him, and he can't hide from me. I'm not so sure I like it anymore."

Silla made a small sound of surprise. "That's what he said." Pulling the last of the ribbons from her hair, she shook her head to let the wind take the black mass and stream it behind her. With the single gray ribbon she had kept in hand, she bound her hair in a simple tie. Looking almost embarrassed, she came to sit by Alissa.

"What was it like?" she said, her eyes scrunched from the bright sun. "Having Connen-Neute's thoughts so close to yours they could mingle as if one?"

Alissa smiled as she heard the interest in Silla's voice. "Scary at first. I almost burnt his tracings to a crisp before I got control of myself. I'd never had anyone that close before. It's a shock, an assault, really, though it gets easier with trust."

"Weren't you afraid he would see all your thoughts, the secrets you never told anyone?"

Silla's eyes were wide, and Alissa gave her a mirthless smile. "Yes, but I had no idea what the risk was until I had actually done it. I was innocent, and it was foolish. Now, I wouldn't pickaback with anyone. Anyone but Connen-Neute, I mean." She shook her head, then smiled a secret smile. "Strell, perhaps, if it was possible."

Silla shuddered. "I could never do that."

Alissa turned back to the view, thinking that might change someday. Though trust wasn't interchangeable with love, you couldn't have love without it. Her gaze went unseeing on the waves below. Perhaps trust was total understanding. She was unable to fly because she couldn't find it within herself to trust the wind. By the same path, Beast couldn't trust Strell, not even allowing a kiss now. Was it because Beast was unable to understand love? Alissa sighed. How was she going to teach Beast to understand something so basic?

"I wish I could fly properly," Silla mused aloud. Scrambling to stand upon the rock, she closed her eyes and held her arms wide as if they were wings.

"You told me you could fly," Alissa said.

"I can," Silla said around a laugh. "I can fly in my sleep. I do fly in my sleep. Every so often, I wake up on a cliff edge or one of the other islands. Keribdis says it's all right. That I shouldn't worry. That I'll outgrow it, like, uh . . ." She flushed. "Like night terrors. I just can't do it very well, yet." She shivered. "I don't like updrafts."

"Me neither," Alissa said, eager to have found an understanding ear.

"You can fly." Silla sounded hurt that Alissa might lie to make her feel better. "Connen-Neute said he broke his foot chasing you through a waterfall. Now that's flying!"

"He didn't break his—" Alissa bit back her words. If Connen-Neute couldn't admit he had broken his foot tripping over a cliff's edge, it wasn't her place to bring it to Silla's attention. "Do you want to practice?" Alissa suddenly offered. "Flying, I mean? The wind is perfect."

"What, now?" Silla turned, her golden eyes wide and her arms clasped about herself.

"Beast? Up for a lesson?" Alissa asked, and a slow shiver filled her. A grin came over Alissa, pulled into existence from Beast's eagerness.

"Yes," Beast whispered. *"I'd like another playmate."*

"Why not?" Alissa took off her string of bells and went to stare down the drop-off. "I can't stay up here forever. I'm hungry."

Silla fidgeted as she joined her. "I've always wanted to jump from here. I usually start from a run on the beach, using the updraft from the offshore breeze."

"Like an albatross?" Alissa said, appalled, then winced as Silla flushed.

"Let's fly," Beast promoted. *"You're wasting good updrafts with your mouth chatter."*

Silla glanced over the edge again. "I don't know. Keribdis and Yar-Taw have been trying to teach me, but I'm not supposed to fly on my own."

"So who's alone?"

Silla thought about that, smiling. "All right," she said with a sudden determination.

A flash of anticipation went through Alissa as Silla vanished in a white mist and grew to her proper form. Alissa took her in with her human eyes, better able to estimate size that way.

Silla was very sleek as a raku, almost gaunt. Her tail wasn't nearly as long as Alissa's, but her hide had a pearly iridescence that Alissa lacked. Her wings were flawless, not a scratch on them, and Alissa felt a flash of coming shame for the ugly scar on her wing. The sun shone through their perfection to put Alissa in a golden shadow. Silla shook them in the wind before settling them against her properly.

Alissa squinted up at her, thinking she could almost forget the arm-long teeth and the talons that could span a ship's wheel. Talon gave a call and launched herself from the rock. Jolted into action, Alissa shifted.

Her eyes closed in bliss as the wind went from a bother to a welcome companion. The ground seemed to tremble beneath her feet, and she realized the booming rumble she now heard was from the surf pounding the beach below. She opened her eyes to find the sky waiting for her, swirling with shades of darker blue and hints of purple to show her the updrafts.

"What happened to your wing?" Silla gasped into her thoughts, and Alissa started. She had forgotten she wasn't alone.

"Uh, I ran into a tree," she said. Her entire body went pink as she blushed, but she wasn't going to blame her scars on anything but the truth. Alissa picked up Redal-Stan's fallen watch. It fit snugly over the knuckle Bailic had broken. She shook open her wings, and with Beast in control, she lifted off the cliff's edge as if stepping into the air.

"Bone and Ash," Alissa almost moaned into Beast's thoughts. *"It's been too long since we've flown."*

Beast said nothing, shunning her usual barrel rolls and sudden dives. She simply glided, glorying in the feel of the wind pushing on them. Perhaps, Alissa thought to herself, she should fly every morning so Beast would have some time to be herself.

"How gracious of you," Beast said wryly, and Alissa cringed.

"Where's Silla?" Alissa questioned, and Beast made an elegant turn. Alissa blinked in surprise as she spotted Silla standing at the drop-off, her wings awkwardly half open.

"*She can't fly,*" Beast said. "*Look at her. Her wings are wrong to rise up on the updraft, and she isn't bunching her strength in her haunches for a launch.*"

"*She's just learning,*" Alissa admonished.

"*She isn't learning anything,*" Beast said back. "*Not crouched on that cliff as she is.*"

"*Well, what should I tell her to do?*" Alissa thought, tingeing her tone with irritation.

"*The same thing I've been telling you to do. Cup your wings about the air and let it pick you up,*" Beast said dryly.

Alissa sighed, thinking this was going to be like the lame leading the blind. Talon dived from the higher reaches, calling aggressively as she tried to entice Alissa into a game of chase. Beast casually rolled on to her back and caught the startled bird in a gentle grip. Talon's scream cut off in a shocked peep. Alissa, too, was surprised—not for having caught her but for the casual way Beast had done it.

"*Go fly somewhere else if you aren't going to be a help,*" Beast thought as she rolled upright and released the ruffled bird. Talon dropped for a heartbeat, then found her wind, rising up higher than before. Alissa turned back to the cliff.

"*You're better than even Keribdis, I'd wager,*" Silla thought, her wistful tone clear despite the distance. "*I'll never be able to do that.*"

"*Of course you will,*" Alissa thought encouragingly.

"*I can't even soar,*" Silla was saying. "*I can't find it within me to—to . . .*"

"*To trust the wind?*" Alissa said, almost afraid when the young raku nodded; it sounded so familiar. At Alissa's subtle suggestion, Beast angled them back to the cliff and landed. Wings snapping sharply, she folded the unwieldy spans of canvas tight against her. She couldn't read raku emotions very well, but if it had been her, she'd be depressed. "*Let's start from the beginning,*" Alissa said. "*Open your wings.*"

Silla did, looking as hesitant and ungainly as fledgling balancing on the edge of a nest.

"*Tell her to arch her back,*" Beast said.

"*Arch your back a little more,*" Alissa relayed.

"*And bring the tips of her wings forward.*"

Thinking relaying everything was going to get tedious, Alissa opened her own wings. *"Like this,"* she said, demonstrating. Silla mimicked her, seeming nervously encouraged.

"Now lean forward," Beast said. *"And close your eyes so you can taste the wind."*

Silla did, and Alissa stiffened. Beast had said that directly to Silla, but the wisp of a raku hadn't seemed to notice the difference.

"The wind is a force as much as the ground beneath your feet," Beast said, and Alissa knew Silla was hearing as well. *"You can see it. You can feel it. It won't drop you unless you refuse to let it carry you. Keep it flowing over your wings, and it will never fail."*

Silla's breath was slow and deep.

"Let it lift you," Beast said. *"It's the only thing you can trust."*

Silla's lips curled back over her teeth. Grimacing, she leaned forward. Alissa held her breath as Silla left the cliff's edge with hardly a shift in her wings. Alissa hastily followed, thrilling in Silla's success. *"You did it!"* Alissa shouted, and Silla's flight bobbled.

"Don't talk to me!" the young raku exclaimed, her thoughts thick with excitement. *"Don't talk! I can't listen."*

The wind was cold against Alissa's teeth as she grinned. Slowly she came up alongside of Silla in a gentle glide. It felt good to help someone for a change instead of causing trouble. *"See the updraft billowing up along the beach?"* she said, smiling as Silla darted a quick glance up, and than back down. *"Let's ride it all the way around the island. We can end up on the beach in front of the village."*

"All right."

"Just watch what I do," Alissa encouraged, and Beast put them on a slow glide that would get them to the beach with the fewest upwellings of forest heat to contend with. Alissa's first flash of pride for Silla slipped slowly from her, replaced with a cloud of self-pity. Silla was a better flyer than she was. At least Silla was being honest, doing it on her own.

"You'll learn to fly as soon as you trust the wind," Beast soothed. *"I don't know why you don't. It will never betray you. It's so obvious."*

"*Yes,*" Alissa thought sourly back. "*As obvious as love. Trusting the wind isn't in me, Beast. I can't do it.*"

"*I don't think it's in Silla, either,*" Beast said, a hint of warning in her tone.

Alissa felt her balance shift as Beast settled them into the updraft over the beach. Silla was right beside her, mirroring her exactly. She held her wings too tense but managed all the same. Together they followed the line of the beach, the salt heavy in the air. "*What do you mean, Beast?*" she questioned. Beast was conspicuously silent, and it stuck Alissa like a cold slap out of the dark. Silla retained her feral consciousness. That was why neither of them could fly properly. And why Silla was the only one Alissa could reach halfway around the world.

Suddenly the sun wasn't enough to warm Alissa. Silla didn't know. If she was waking up on cliff tops and nearby islands, then it followed that her feral consciousness was spontaneously taking control at night when Silla lay asleep. But why hadn't she gone completely feral?

"*No Master destroys their feral sides at first transition,*" Beast thought, and Alissa's heart pounded. "*They suppress them, thinking they're destroyed. And I did not evolve from nothing. I've always been here. The first time you shifted form, we got separated.*"

Alissa went cold, seeing the truth in it.

"*The raku-child is balancing on the edge,*" Beast continued, speaking of Silla. "*She's suppressing her beast so far that she can't fly. If she doesn't allow enough of it to surface, she'll probably die from a flight accident. If she brings it too close, she will go feral.*"

"Wolves," Alissa breathed, hearing it escape her in a rumble. She looked to see they had wound around nearly the entirety of the island. The village beach was before them, empty but for Yar-Taw fishing in the surf. He was in his raku form, thigh deep in the salt water. He looked up at the shadow of wings over him. His neck arched in surprise.

Silla snaked her head to look at her. "*I don't want to stop,*" she said, pride radiating from her. "*I'm not tired. Let's go around again.*"

"I-I have to sit down," Alissa stammered. "Silla. I don't feel well."

There was a sudden burst of half-heard mental communication, and Alissa turned to the village. Her stomach knotted, and she felt herself stall.

"Silla!" Keribdis's mental shout was far too loud, and the young raku beside Alissa faltered. She lost her concentration, and her wings collapsed.

"Angle your wings!" Beast shouted.

Silla beat her wings wildly, managing to set down in an ungraceful spray of sand. She shook her wings free of it. Her head was high in excitement, and her eyes glinted in success as she looked first to Alissa, then Yar-Taw.

Alissa landed next to her, frightened as Keribdis came to a wind-snapping halt before them. Keribdis was alarming as a woman, but to see her as a raku was enough to panic Alissa.

"Did you see me?" Silla bubbled. *"Keribdis! Did you see? I flew all the way around the island. I started from the lookout and went all the way around!"*

"I saw you, winglet!" Keribdis snapped, and Silla's eyes went wide. *"I told not to fly alone. You could have killed yourself!"*

"I wasn't alone," Silla said with a faltering thought, and Alissa's fear solidified into a sour lump. *"Alissa was with me. She can fly wonderfully. She was helping me."*

Keribdis let her second eyelid fall, turning her eyes from gold to bloodred. Alissa took a shocked step back. Frightened, she curled her long tail twice about her body, the tip trembling.

"Where were you this morning?" the furious raku wedged deep into Alissa's thoughts.

Alissa shifted. Flustered, she ended up reappearing in the first outfit she had managed to fix into her thoughts: Keeper garb. It probably wasn't the best choice. Yar-Taw had waded out of the surf but was keeping in the background. "I was on the cliff, meditating," Alissa said, hearing her voice tremble. Her gaze flicked to Yar-Taw. He shook his head in warning, and she belligerently added, "And you aren't my teacher. Talo-Toecan is."

Keribdis dipped her head down until her breath shifted Alissa's hair. *"I'm your teacher. Be on the beach tomorrow, or I'll drag you there whether you're in your human shift or raku."*

Cheeks warming, Alissa opened her mouth to protest, halting as Keribdis turned to Silla.

"And you!" Keribdis exclaimed, and Silla's golden head drooped. *"I can't believe the lack of common sense you have shown in allowing yourself to be taken advantage of by this . . . this—"* Keribdis hesitated, furious. *"By her!"* she finished.

Silla's great eyes were round with a shimmer of unshed tears, and the last of Alissa's fear grew to anger.

"You never said I couldn't," Silla protested. *"You only said I couldn't fly alone. I wasn't alone. Alissa was helping. She wasn't teaching me. She wasn't teaching me at all!"*

Keribdis's tail whipped in an arch to smooth the sand flat. It piled up a dune almost as tall as Alissa's knees. *"I am so angry with you right now that I can't bring myself to give you any instruction for a week,"* she said, her thoughts hard.

"But you said—"

"A week!" Keribdis thundered, and Yar-Taw winced. *"And the next time you're in the air without me or Yar-Taw, I will double your punishment. You could have killed yourself jumping from that cliff!"*

"Yes, Keribdis." She was on the verge of tears.

Alissa's anger simmered. "It wasn't her fault," she heard herself say, going more angry as Keribdis ignored her, shifting back into her human form and striding back to the village. "It was my idea!" she shouted after her, but Keribdis never slowed. Beast stirred to anger, sobering Alissa quickly. Having Beast voice her opinion would be a disastrous mistake.

"She only said I couldn't fly alone," Silla whispered.

Alissa turned in time to see Silla coalesce down into her human shift. Her misery was obvious by her small chin trembling. "Silla, I'm sorry," Alissa said, her anger turned to guilt. But Silla turned away. Head bowed, she walked in the opposite direction Keribdis had taken.

Helpless, Alissa stood with her arms at her sides. Yar-Taw brushed by her in a whisper of gray cloth. "I don't know whether to make you dinner or to spit at your feet," he muttered, then hastened after Silla.

Alissa's eyes warmed, and her throat tightened. Angry and frustrated, she wiped a hand under her eye. Yar-Taw matched

Silla's steps as he came even with her. He put a comforting arm over her shoulder and waved an extravagant hand in the air. Silla seemed to brighten.

Vision wavering, Alissa stared at the incoming waves. Talon dropped from the sky, startling her with her sudden appearance as the sound of her wings had been lost in the noise of the surf. Sniffing, Alissa ran a finger over the bird's faded markings, taking strength in the smell of the wind on Talon.

Alissa crouched to retrieve Redal-Stan's watch from the warming sand. Spinning the band of metal between her fingers, she vowed she wouldn't be on the beach tomorrow.

27

"Alissa."

Someone was whispering her name. It dragged through her uneasy dream of running through the Hold, searching for something in cupboards and under rugs. She slowly separated herself from the dream, hating it when she wasted her imagination on something that useless.

"Alissa. Wake up."

"Strell?" she mumbled. Her eyes flashed open as his hand went across her mouth. Alissa's breath caught in surprise, but she stayed silent. He was crouched beside her chair with a pack beside him. The curtain had been pulled from her door, and the moon shone bright on the sand outside. The surf seemed louder than usual for the lack of any other noise.

"What time is it?" she whispered when he lowered his hand.

He put a finger to his lips. Glancing at Talon asleep on her perch, he held up two fingers. "Two in the—" she started, but he threatened to cover her mouth, and she desisted.

Strell got to his feet. He held out a hand to her, and she took it, silently rising. Her feet were bare, and she scuffed her shoes on without showing her toes past the edge of her nightgown. Strell glanced at Talon again before he snatched up the pile of clothes beside her sleeping chair and shoved them in his pack.

"What—" she began, and he gestured for her to be silent. By moonlight, she could see an amused urgency in his eyes. He placed a bowl of fruit on her unused bed. Hunched and furtive, he picked up his pack and gestured for her to follow. Mystified, Alissa let Strell draw her outside. He eased the curtain down over the door before pulling her into the shadows of the nearby trees.

Alissa followed him, wondering what was going on. The air seemed chill as it passed through her lightweight nightgown, and she held Redal-Stan's watch hanging about her neck to keep it from swinging. Her bells were still on the cliff top, and her steps were silent. She made a light, letting it go out when he waved wildly. "Stop," he breathed in her ear, causing shivers to fill her from the inside out. "I'm trying to steal you."

She stared at him, and he grinned, his teeth glinting in the moonlight. "In the plains, if the bride is of higher standing than the groom, the son-in-law-to-be has to steal her, leaving a symbolic token of worth in her place. It's an arranged affair, but the tradition stands."

Her eyes went wide as she looked back toward the unseen hut. "That's why—"

"Yes." He ran a hand over his beard and turned away. "I never thought I'd see the day when a Hirdune potter would have to leave a bride-price behind on a pillow." He grimaced. "So, will you come with me willingly, or do I have to carry you?"

A grin stole over her. "You're going to have to carry me."

His face went slack. "All the way to the lagoon?" A puzzled frown came over Alissa, and he added, "The captain is waiting. Connen-Neute, too. He has to be in on it, seeing as he can find you and all, and besides, he's the perfect witness. We're going to put to sail and—"

"I can't leave!" she exclaimed in a hushed whisper.

"—have the captain perform the vows," Strell soothed, taking her shoulders and starting her into motion. "Then he will drop us on one of the smaller, nearby islands. We will have a few days before they realize we aren't on the main island and start searching."

A titillated feeling bubbled through her. "Run away?" she said, knowing Useless would be furious. But they'd met his stipulations, burn it all to ash. "I should change . . ." she said.

"You look fine," he said absently. "And we have to hurry. That is, unless you'd rather stay and have lessons with Keribdis this morning?"

That did it. Alissa shook the hair from her eyes, refusing to let her fear of the woman intrude on her excitement. Strell took her hand. She thought it was trembling, and he gripped her more firmly. Keeping under the shadow of the trees for as long as he could, he led her to the dark beach and the *Albatross*'s remaining rowboat.

Her heart pounded as he carried her over the black waves and set her carefully in the middle of the boat. "Here," he said, dropping his pack beside her and opening it up. Her blanket, the one gone missing yesterday, was pulled out and draped over her.

A smile crept over her. "Thanks," she whispered, though no one could possibly hear them over the sound of the waves. The night air was balmy, but she let the blanket stay where he had put it. His attention made her feel warm and needed. And it covered her nightgown, too.

He said nothing, his smile confident as he levered himself in to sit before her. The boat rocked violently, and after a tense moment, settled. Strell blew his breath out in relief and awkwardly pushed them into the surf with an oar. The boat scraped free of the bottom, and he resettled the oars between the tholes and began rowing.

Alissa watched him for a moment before reaching into his pack and pulling out her clothes. She could put them on over her nightgown. Unable to bring herself to do it where he could watch, she rose into an unsteady crouch to make her way to the bow and behind his back.

"What are you doing!" Strell gasped, dropping the oars and clutching the boat as it tilted.

Face flaming, she pushed past him. "I'm changing," she said. "Don't turn around."

"You can do that when we get there!"

Her jaw clenched, part embarrassment, part bother. "I'm

not going to let everyone see me in my nightgown," she said tightly. "Don't turn around!"

"It's not everyone. It's only Connen-Neute and the captain. And maybe Hayden." She said nothing, and Strell's shoulders shifted in a heavy sigh as he hunched his back over the oars.

Keeping one eye on him, she tugged her clothes on over her nightclothes. They were thinner than her real underthings, and it felt like she was only half-dressed. Face still warm, she returned to her seat, unable to look at him. "What else is in here?" she said as she took her seat, desperate to get Strell thinking about something other than her getting dressed behind him.

"This and that," he said mysteriously.

"Hey!" she said as she found something familiar. "My mother's hair ribbon?" she asked, pulling it out and letting it dangle. "I mean, the one she gave me! You took it off my pack?"

He nodded as she used it to tie her hair out of her way. "Mine's in there too," he said. "Careful. Don't break the globe."

Her fingers felt something smooth and cool. Shadows blossomed in the bottom of the rowboat as she made a small light to see the fist-sized ball she brought out. It was shockingly light, and her eyes widened as she realized it was glass. It was a glass ball!

"Be careful!" Strell warned again. Letting go of the oars, he clasped a hand about hers.

"When did you get this?" she said in awe. It must have come from the coast, seeing as he could buy it for a song there but spend a lifetime's income anywhere east of the mountains.

"Our first day on the coast," he said. "And don't break it. I plan on using it tonight."

"What's it for?" she asked, nestling it back where it had been.

Strell smiled lopsidedly at her. "You'll see. The captain only knows the coastal wedding vows. That's what the ribbons are for. He's going to want to tie our hands together. But I asked him to have a bucket of sand, too, so it ought to be legal in the plains as well, and I'm going to use that glass to satisfy the Hold."

"All right," she said, wondering what sand and a glass ball had to do with anything. As Strell rowed, she anxiously scanned the moonlit night for wings and thoughts, finding none but Connen-Neute waiting for them at the bow of the *Albatross*.

"Hurry," the tall Master said loudly from the bow as they grew close. "And put your light out, Alissa. The captain says we have to leave now in order to get back before he's missed. If the boat isn't back at anchor when the sun comes up, they'll know you're off the island."

"Hoy, *Albatross*!" Strell called, waiting until Hayden's black silhouette and wave showed against the stars before he helped Alissa up the clammy ladder. A long, thin hand was extended, and Connen-Neute pulled her over the side.

"Connen-Neute," she said, her voice brimming with expectation.

"Alissa," he said solemnly, but his eyes glinted mischievously in the light from the oil lamp by the wheel. "You know this will create problems?"

She nodded, her stomach in knots. *Create problems?* Connen-Neute had a knack for the understatement. "But we met Useless's stipulations, yes? You agree?"

His expression grew wicked. "It's why I agreed to be the Hold's witness." He leaned to help Strell over the side. "That, and to make sure your vows are up to the Hold's standards. I won't let Keribdis call your marriage null on a petty point of law."

"Thank you," she whispered, deeply appreciative.

The stomping of the captain's feet echoed over the deck. "Get the anchor up!" he shouted. "Hayden, stop your gawking! Haven't you seen a woman without her bells before?"

Connen-Neute gave Alissa's shoulder a squeeze, and he went to the windlass to help Hayden. Strell joined him, and Alissa looked back at the shore in worry as the harsh clanking seemed to echo against the wall of vegetation. The captain gave a grunt of acknowledgment, then stomped to the wheel. Hayden looked up from his work to give her a quick nod of greeting, his gaze flitting to her silent, unseen ankle. There was a rustle of canvas as the sails lifted. Immediately they filled with wind, and the boat began to move.

Alissa looked over the shadowed deck, wondering if there was something she should be doing. Strell had spread a square of leather on the planking and seemed to be starting a fire, of all things. She glanced at the oil lamp burning by the hatch and back to him.

"I can do that for you," she said, and Strell shook his head. He didn't look at her, and feeling put out, she went to the recessed deck where the captain stood with his feet braced and his hands gripping the wheel. Hayden had disappeared belowdecks.

"Captain," she said guardedly, not sure what his reaction would be.

"Ma'hr," he said, nodding at her. He flicked his gaze from her to Strell, frowning. Strell had managed a small flame, which he then used to light an oil lamp. Rolling everything but the lamp up in the leather, Strell shoved it in his pack and vanished under the deck.

Alissa sighed before turning to the captain. "Thank you for what you're doing."

The captain snorted, spitting carefully downwind so it would clear the boat. "I'm not doing it for you, Ma'hr," he said. "I'm doing it because *he*"—he gestured with his chin to Connen-Neute at the bow—"said it would vex that sea wolf of a woman."

Alissa winced. "Yes. It will. I'll likely spend the next century trying to make amends."

"Aye," he said gruffly. "Mind my words. You're going to live to regret it."

"I hope so," she muttered, thinking Keribdis would likely want to kill her by the time the sun rose a handbreadth above the horizon and she found the beach empty.

A scuff drew her attention to the hatch behind her. Strell rose into view, one hand gripped tight on his light, the other clenched on the boat. He had his round purple hat on again. "Where's the sand?" he said tersely as he hung his lamp from a hook. "I said I needed sand."

"Tighten your halyards, desert man," the captain said. "Hayden has it. You get any on my deck, and you'll be washin' my boat." He spat again, and Alissa grimaced.

"Are we far enough out?" Strell asked as he lurched to stand beside her.

The captain's eyes squinted. "Aye. As long as we aren't in a harbor." His eyes went to Strell. "Are you sure, lad? You've got a good heart. You aren't much on the sea, but I'll take you on if you're marrying her for her money."

Alissa's breath caught in a huff. Her ire eased as Strell took her hand and gave it a squeeze. "Thank you, Captain," he said. "Your offer is more than generous, and I'll likely live to regret turning it down, but I have plotted my course and will see it to its end."

The captain sighed, his entire body moving with his exhalation. He glanced up at the flag waving from the tallest mast. "If you're sure, then." Strell nodded, and the captain whistled sharply. "Hey!" he called. "Come back! Come in! We say farewell to a man today!" He hesitated, then shouted, "Get your scrawny, no-account dockman arse up here, Hayden!"

Alissa frowned, the curve of her mouth deepening as Strell seemed to find something humorous in the captain's words. It was a wedding, for the Navigator's Hounds, not a wake.

Connen-Neute made his sedate, unhurried way back from the bow, his shadow looking tall in the dim light. Hayden appeared at the hatch, and Strell's shoulders eased at the sight of the covered bucket in his hands. A thrill of excitement went through Alissa. It settled in her middle to grow. They were going to be married, and no one could stop them. In a moment it would be done and immutable.

"All right, then." The captain stepped from the wheel and let Hayden take it. "Where's the ropes?" he said sourly.

Strell started. "Here," he said, fumbling in his shirt pocket to pull out a ribbon. Alissa took the one from her hair with a flush of embarrassment. Strell had kept his in perfect condition. It shimmered in the faint light as if her mother had pulled it from her hair and given it to him yesterday. By comparison, Alissa's ribbon was dingy and stained. There were frayed patches, and a clean, warped spot where it had been tied to her cup.

"Ribbons," the captain muttered. "Damn fool woman's fancy. I should have known I was in for a wolf ride when my wife bound me with ribbons. Give me a sturdy rope. A sturdy woman chooses a sturdy rope."

"It's what we want," Strell said, staggering as a wave ran under them.

"Aye," the man grumbled. "Tie 'em on your wrists, then. His left, her right. Hurry up. The wind is freshening, and Hayden won't be able to hold the boat, skinny dockman that he is."

Hayden grunted. It was obvious he had no problem with the boat.

Alissa's fingers trembled as she tied her ugly ribbon about Strell's left hand. The waves were larger out from the shelter of the bay, and it was getting hard to keep her balance. Her heart beat fast. Strell's hat made him exotic. The lamplight made his eyes shine. The beard made him look dangerous. She wished she had taken the time to put on something nicer.

Her fingers lingered on his hand as she finished the knot, and as the wind pulled through her hair, Strell smiled at her with a warmth to make her breath catch.

Strell placed her right hand atop his open palm. She stared at them, seeing the obvious differences in skin tone and shape. By lamplight, he meticulously laced the ribbon about itself and into a secure knot using only one hand. It was obvious he had practiced as he made the difficult task look easy. When done, he pulled her closer. Her eyes widened as she looked up.

"Yes. Yes," the captain grumbled. "Let me look at the *ropes*."

Alissa held out her hand as Strell did. Her mother's ribbon draped from it. Grimacing, the captain took both strips. "Ya sure, lad?" he questioned.

Strell gazed at her, his brown eyes almost black in the starlight. Looking eager and somewhat afraid, he nodded. "More sure than anything I've ever been sure about before."

"Aye," the captain sighed. "I was, too." Brow pinched, he placed Alissa's and Strell's hands together. With no fanfare, he took the ends and tied them to leave a short length of free ribbon between them. "All right. You're married. Strell, if you leave her, she gets everything. Alissa, if you leave, he gets everything." He frowned at both of them. "Agreed?"

"I agree," Strell said softly.

"Me, too," Alissa followed quickly.

The captain dropped their bound hands, and Strell raised them to his lips, kissing her fingertips. "All right," the older man grumbled. "You can kiss her proper, now."

Alissa turned to Strell in surprise. "That's it? We're married?"

"On the coast," Strell said, his eyes gleaming in the low light. "Where's my sand?"

The captain muttered something and pulled the bucket close. Never dropping her gaze, Strell kicked it over. "Hey!" the captain shouted, red-faced. "I told you no sand on my deck!"

"I'll sweep it up," Strell said as he pulled Alissa forward. The grit ground into the decking as she stepped on it, and Captain Sholan made an ugly noise.

"What do I do?" she whispered.

Strell smiled. "Do what I do." He bent to crouch, and awkward because of their bound hands, she did the same. The sand was cold as she scraped a handful into her bound palm. They rose together, smiling at the angry captain. With his free hand, Strell took off his hat and held it under their bound hands. Alissa wasn't surprised when he sifted his sand into it. She did the same. The tightness of threatened tears took her.

Connen-Neute stepped forward and took the hat from Strell. "May you be as productive as there are grains of sands on the dunes," the young Master said, and she saw Strell mouthing the words with him, as if to insure he said them properly.

"No!" the captain cried in a panic as Connen-Neute flung the sand across the upper deck. "The Navigator's Wolves will eat you!" he shouted, choleric. "You will get every last grain! And then you'll paint her!"

Alissa didn't care. "Now?" she questioned, pulling Strell closer. "Can I kiss you now?"

"Not yet," he answered as he took a teasing step back.

As the captain fumed, Connen-Neute adjusted his Master's vest, becoming even more official looking. "It is customary," he said, his voice taking on the cadence of tradition, "that two rakus joining their lives should demonstrate their will by merging two wards of light."

Alissa glanced between Connen-Neute and Strell in alarm.

"But Strell can't make a ward of light—" she began, her words cutting off at Strell's mischievous grin.

"Watch me," he said, leaning to reach his pack. Being tied to him, Alissa almost fell as the boat shifted and she caught her balance. He drew out his glass ball and handed it to her. She held it as he awkwardly took the ceramic jar Connen-Neute extended. Careful because of his one-handed state, he dribbled a swallow of fragrant oil into the small opening in the top of the glass ball. Her eyes widened, understanding why he had taken the time to light a flame by himself earlier. She set her tracings to make a light, not yet setting the ward into motion.

Strell smiled, managing to look both sheepish and devious. Alissa held the glass globe as Strell used a dry stick of what smelled like mirth wood to transfer the flame from the lamp he started earlier to the globe. "Let me have it," he whispered, taking the glowing ball from her. "And hurry. There isn't enough air in there to keep it going for long."

Alissa's breath came in a quick sound. "Make a field?" she questioned Connen-Neute.

"Yes!" he exclaimed. "Put your light over his. Quick! Before it goes out!"

Heart pounding, Alissa made a field of light no bigger than Strell's mundane globe of fire. It took shape in her free hand. She held her breath as she placed it over Strell's concoction of glass and flame. The captain and Hayden watched with wide eyes, but Connen-Neute sighed in satisfaction as the sphere glowed all the stronger. She flicked her gaze from the ball of light to Strell as it dimmed. She let her ward drop, and the night darkened.

"Enough?" she breathed, feeling her body ache to be closer to Strell.

Connen-Neute chuckled. "There's more, but the entire ceremony takes three days. The only part mentioned by law is the wards of light. It's the oldest."

"That's not what I meant," Alissa said, just wanting to feel Strell's arms about her.

Strell shook his head. "One more thing," he said. Her knees felt weak as Strell handed the smoke-blackened globe to Connen-Neute. Fishing in his pocket, he shyly brought out a small ring of shining copper. Alissa's eyes widened, and the warmth of tears trickled down one cheek. A ring. He had gotten her a ring.

"How did you know?" she whispered, not trusting her voice to hold steady.

He grinned behind his beard. "Legal and binding no matter where we go, Alissa. You aren't going to slip my snare in any shape or fashion."

"But I don't have one for you—" she said as she wiped her cheek. Then she stopped. Redal-Stan's watch. Awkward because of having only the one free hand, she ducked out of the cord she kept his ring on about her neck. The captain stooped forward, and flicking his eyes to hers for permission, cut the cord in two. Heart pounding, she faced Strell.

He seemed unable to meet her eyes as he slid the copper ring about her finger on her free hand. Hands shaking, she put Redal-Stan's watch on his finger. It didn't fit him either. Strell looked down at the oversized band of metal, then smiled at her with bright eyes.

"Are we done and legal-like?" the captain grumbled. "We're coming to the first island."

"Yes," Strell said, pulling her close. She looked up at him, and he kissed her with a relaxed tenderness, as if there was nothing—now or ever—that would stand between them again. His emotions of fulfillment flowed through her, easing every thought away. She leaned into him, reaching up to pull him closer. Her eyes opened as the boat shifted to throw her off balance.

"No!" she exclaimed, pulling away as she realized the boat held steady. It was her knee coming up to Strell's groin that had thrown her off balance. *"Beast!"* she shouted into her thoughts, shocked at the fierce determination she found herself running into.

"Gotcha," Strell whispered, catching her knee with his free hand. He had been expecting it. Alissa was wide-eyed and grateful. As she stood unbalanced on one foot, he leaned forward and gave her another, teasing kiss. Alissa gasped a warning as Beast shifted her hand to slap him. But it was the one tied to him, and she couldn't move fast enough.

Grinning, Strell pulled her closer. Her face flamed as the

captain made a loud guffaw. "They all turn into contrary beasts once they know they've got you, my lad. I tried to warn you."

Strell searched her eyes carefully as he released her and took a step back. "I expected that, Captain. Can I borrow your rowboat?"

28

"Ow!" Strell cried. Holding his nose, he leaned from Alissa with a hurt, resigned look.

Humiliated, Alissa loosened the fist her hand had clenched into. "Strell, I'm sorry," she pleaded. Deep in her thoughts, she could hear Beast seething. Alissa said nothing to her feral consciousness. There was nothing left that she hadn't already said. "Just—just stay away from me!" Alissa exclaimed, turning her back on him with a sudden frustration. He had only been holding her as they watched the sunrise. He hadn't even tried to kiss her.

Strell sighed and moved a shade down from her on the fallen tree they were leaning against. They had been here most of the night watching the stars move behind the main island where the rest of the conclave lay sleeping. But now the stars were gone, washed away in the light of the sun like her hopes in the cold slap of reality.

Their evening had been mostly talk as they had set up a rude shelter against the daily rain. Talk was all Beast would allow now. It was frustrating, especially when the more conscious Strell was about not triggering Beast's anger, the more aware of him Beast became. *"He is trying to ground you,"* was all she would say, her thoughts tinged with an unreasonable fury.

Alissa sniffed at Strell's heavy sigh. He glanced wryly at her as he ran a hand over his beard. "It's all right, Alissa," he said. He dabbed at his nose, tucking the cloth away before she could decide if she had bloodied his nose or not.

"It's not all right," she moaned. "It's my wedding night, and . . . and . . . nothing happened!" She felt the tears prick, and her head drooped. "Lodesh said Beast would do this," she said miserably. She had been awake most of the night, and she was sleepy and weepy from her fatigue and unfulfilled anticipation.

Strell chuckled, making her more depressed. "Lodesh knows only half of it," he said, and she looked up through her wavering vision. Smiling, Strell wiped his wide thumb under her eye. His shoulders eased when she didn't hit him. "He forgets I'm a minstrel," he murmured.

"What do you mean?" she asked, sniffing loudly.

"I mean we're going to figure this out. Or Beast is going to go to sleep. Or perhaps when things calm down, I'll be able to charm her, maybe?"

"I will not sleep," Beast vowed.

Alissa ignored her. "Do you think so?" she said, hope making her voice quaver.

"I'm sure of it. Why don't you get some sleep? I'll be there as soon as the fire is set."

A flush of emotion went through her at his words. "I'll be there," he had said. Together. Under the same roof. Married. Ashes, what if their feet touched? "All right," she said, rising to her feet and brushing her skirt free of sand.

A fluttering of wings drew her eyes up to the trees. She went cold as a kestrel landed, bobbing on a long leaf. "Talon," she whispered. "We forgot about Talon." The bird dropped to her fist, calling loudly and worrying her fingers. There was a slice of red fruit in her claws, and she seemed insufferably pleased with herself as she shoved the sticky thing into Alissa's grip.

Alissa's brow pinched. "Go away!" she shouted, waving her hand. Talon took flight with an indignant squawk. She perched in a nearby tree to chitter accusingly as the fruit fell to the sand, spoilt. Alissa turned to Strell, desperation making her stomach clench.

"I'll just tie her up," Strell said, grinning. "I'm more worried about Beast."

"No," Alissa cried, backing up into the shade of the trees. "They'll follow her!"

Strell's face went slack. "Wolves," he swore, standing up and kicking sand into the fire.

But it was too late.

Howling like one of the Navigator's Wolves, Keribdis landed on the beach. Sand gouted into the air to land in knee-high drifts. Terrified, Alissa froze. The raku shifted, and Keribdis stood before her, dressed in crimson and stiff with fury. "It is sunrise," the woman all but hissed.

Alissa's mouth moved, but nothing came out. A hundred, flippant answers died in fear.

"Get in the air," Keribdis said coldly, her voice leaving no room for debate.

"No," Alissa stammered, backing up until she found Strell gripping her shoulders.

Keribdis took a step closer. "Get—in—the—air."

Frightened, Alissa shook her head. Keribdis was the Hold's best flyer. Alissa wouldn't go into her element. Keribdis wanted to prove her dominance, and in the air, she could do it.

Keribdis shifted in a swirl of gray. *"Get in the air!"* she shouted into Alissa's mind.

"Go," Beast whispered privately, and Alissa started at the feel of her anticipation and eagerness. Panicked, Alissa shifted. She heard Strell's cry of warning, but she couldn't think. She could only react. She had to flee.

"Now we will begin our lesson," Keribdis said as Alissa coalesced. The Master's thoughts were tinged with bloodlust.

Alissa leapt into the air. Beast took control, and Alissa welcomed it, almost weeping. *"She's a fool to think she can outfly us,"* Beast thought. Alissa said nothing, frightened at the strength of Beast's desire to best Keribdis.

Wings straining, they flew. Beast rode the wind, acutely aware of Keribdis behind them. As Alissa panicked in a distraught frenzy, Beast confidently raced forward. Heart pounding, they rose. It was a game to Beast. She lived to fly, and at last had found a worthy playmate.

High above the ocean, Beast casually craned Alissa's long neck to find Keribdis effortlessly keeping up. Keribdis's lips pulled back from her teeth. The older raku lunged. Her teeth snapped on air as Beast darted to the left, anticipating her.

A whining growl of annoyance came from Keribdis. The raku angled to rise above them. Beast let her. Howling in satisfaction, Keribdis dropped, her talons spread.

Beast folded their wings and they fell like a stone. A wave of fright assaulted Alissa at the strength of the wind. *"Fly!"* she cried into Beast's thoughts as the water grew close.

"I am," Beast said, her thoughts humming with a savage passion.

Keribdis followed. Her intent thoughts spilled into Alissa's. Keribdis had to catch her. It was all the older raku existed for. The water grew close. Alissa felt a stab of doubt creep into Keribdis's thoughts. Alissa, too, tensed. *"Now!"* she shrieked. *"Beast, now!"*

Almost as one, the two rakus spread their wings—Keribdis a telling heartbeat sooner. Pain arched through Alissa's shoulders as the wind slammed against the canvas of her wings. Beast roared in satisfaction as she sped horizontally against the waves. She spun in a glorious barrel roll, dipping the tip of her tail in the water so as to maintain her awareness of how close she was to the trap it could be.

Howling as if insane, Keribdis lunged. Beast darted. There was a grunt of pain as Keribdis's foot hit the water. The raku behind them put on a burst of speed; Beast matched it. Keribdis swung her tail to hit her; Beast tilted her head and nipped it. There was a cry of rage.

And then Beast turned her attention to the sky and climbed. Alissa knew Beast's intent even before Beast did. She was going to fly higher than Keribdis, proving to everyone watching that she was stronger than Keribdis.

They rose higher, and Keribdis took an audible, gasping breath. It sounded ragged. She was struggling to maintain the steep ascent. The raku's sudden panic was clear and unmistakable. A wave of gratification poured from Beast into Alissa, pooling to swallow her fear. Alissa looked behind them, hope and relief making her brave.

Beast was the better flier. She couldn't be dominated by physical strength as Keribdis had done to everyone else. Age and Beast's instinctive reactions had brought the old matriarch to a shocking realization. She was old.

"No!" Keribdis shrieked into their thoughts. Anger, jealousy, and frustration slammed into Alissa and Beast. Shocked at the mental assault, Beast faltered. She knew how to fly; she had no understanding of this. Beast's hesitation was only for a heartbeat, but Keribdis saw it.

"You're mine!" the old raku growled into their thoughts. A phantom pain exploded in Alissa's mind, shocking through her and Beast to send their wings into spasms. An echo of pain, real this time, came from her tail. Alissa gasped as Beast staggered in flight. Her feral consciousness was unable to cope with the mental assault.

Alissa felt the terrifying cessation of speed. They were going to stall. *"This is my pain,"* Alissa said. Steeling herself, she opened her thoughts. She took the entirety of the agony to free Beast from her confusion. Alissa heard herself cry out as Keribdis's illusion of pain burned through her mind, unfettered. She felt her eyes bulge and her lungs ache as she screamed to find a release, but Beast was free of it.

"Let go of my tail . . ." Alissa heard Beast whisper savagely, pushing her feral thoughts deep into Keribdis's. *"You are old. You are done."* A snarl rolled. *"And you cheat."*

Alissa's agony vanished with a shocking suddenness. The sensation was so quick and somehow violent that Alissa gasped, almost passing out. Beast flipped them end over end, doubling back. Her talons were spread wide. Keribdis hovered in midair, clearly stunned at having recognized the feral beast in Alissa's thoughts.

Beast slammed into Keribdis, raking her lower claws into her. Beast fought, aiming for Keribdis's eyes. Pain jolted Keribdis into action. Screaming as Beast found her face, Keribdis bit down. Fire exploded from Alissa's wing. She took the pain, leaving Beast free of it.

Golden wings beat against each other as they dropped. *"I don't like you,"* Beast seethed. And then they hit the sand.

They broke apart from the fall. Gasping for air, Beast rolled them upright. Alissa panicked as she couldn't breathe.

Hunched into a crouch, Alissa struggled to make her lungs work. Her wings lay in a disarray, mixing with the sand.

Keribdis stood on her haunches, her wings spread awkwardly. Blood ran from her leg and from under her eye to stain the sand. *"I don't care if you like me or not,"* she said. Snarling, she swung her tail, whipping it in a power-filled strike to hit the back of Alissa's head.

Alissa fell without a sound.

29

"Another one," Strell said tersely. He impatiently held out a hand for Connen-Neute's mentally crafted scarf. His eyes were on the sky. Alissa was toying with Keribdis. *Or Beast was,* he thought, feeling helpless on the ground.

A shimmering length of red silk appeared in his palm, and he broke his gaze from Alissa for the heartbeat it took to tie it to the end of the makeshift rope.

"It's long enough," Connen-Neute said. "Get in the boat."

Strell lunged for the surf. Fingers fumbling, he knotted one end of the scarf to the ring at bow. He crouched in the bottom of the dinghy, his brow pinched as he searched the sky. His breath caught as Keribdis lunged at Alissa, missing.

"Where are they going?" he shouted, but Connen-Neute had already shifted and couldn't answer. The young raku grasped the other end of the scarf in a hind foot and leapt into the air. Strell gripped the gunwales against the expected jolt as the slack was taken up. The jerk rocked his head back. Strell's eyes widened as water sloshed over the bow. "Slow down!" he cried, torn with the need to follow her and the fear of drowning.

Connen-Neute checked himself. As they sped across the waves to the main island, Strell watched the twin golden forms flying in chase. One dropped upon the other, forcing the lower one into a fall. "Alissa!" he cried, rising to a crouch. Muscles tense, he watched them dive to the water. "No!" he shouted, his breath escaping him in an explosion as wings flashed open.

Strell watched the two rakus speed over the waves, grateful Connen-Neute had come to fetch him. Guilt swept him. He could do nothing to help her. This was his fault. He should have told her to swallow her pride and accept Keribdis's teaching. He should have told her Keribdis was a fool and to pretend to respect her. He never should have asked her to marry him. "No," he whispered. He would not feel guilty about that. "I should have tied up her stupid bird," he said, hearing his voice catch.

A wave broke over the side, and Strell wiped the salt water from his face, his gaze on the sky. He tensed as Keribdis lunged, then lunged again. She kept missing, growing more and more angry. Alissa was keeping herself maddeningly out of reach, taunting her. But then Alissa began to climb. Slowly the twin forms became smaller. A gap opened between them, then more. His heart pounded. Keribdis couldn't do it. Alissa would win!

Then Alissa faltered. Writhing in a pain he could see no reason for, she stalled. Strell gasped as she began to fall. Keribdis dove with a cry of success, her talons outstretched. Strell watched in panic, helpless as she grasped Alissa's long tail.

His heart seemed to stop as Alissa shuddered violently. Keribdis unexpectedly flung her wings open, slamming them into the air to stop dead in flight. Alissa pulled free of her grip, smoothly flipping head over tail to dive at Keribdis.

"No!" he shouted as they tangled into one body and dropped. He watched, not breathing as they fell to the island.

"Faster!" he exclaimed as Connen-Neute surged toward the rapidly approaching beach. The two rakus fell lifeless onto the beach ahead of him. Neither moved.

He lurched forward as the rowboat scraped the beach. One raku stirred, rolling to a crouch with her wings awkwardly splayed. Nearly mindless with fear, Strell tipped the boat over, falling into the surf. He tried to run, but the water pulled at him. He fell, crying out in frustration. As he pushed himself upright, the larger raku, bloodied and savage, rose up on her hind legs. Strell felt his stomach twist as she swung her tail to hit the smaller behind the head.

"Alissa," he whispered as one fell senseless to the sand. It had been her. He knew it.

Keribdis reared up with a fierce snarl, spittle dripping from her. Strell felt his face go bloodless. She was going to tear Alissa's throat out. He'd seen that look on a pack of dogs before they fell upon a wounded rival.

"Keribdis!" Connen-Neute shouted. His voice was thick with fear. Strell found him by the forest in his human shift. The larger raku spun, snarling as she realized she had witnesses. Strell blanched as the winged beast spread her bloodied wings and pushed once upon the air. Her one eye was red with blood; the sand was speckled with it. She was out of her mind with rage.

"Keribdis!" Connen-Neute exclaimed louder, pleading. Strell came to a stumbling halt beside him. There was a whoosh of air behind them, then another. Strell wouldn't look from Keribdis to see who had landed.

Bellowing in rage, Keribdis reared over Alissa. Her jaws opened in a roar of denial. Terror flashed through Strell. She was going to kill her. She was going to kill Alissa!

Strell crouched at the roar of protest exploding over his head. Keribdis faltered, and Strell almost collapsed from relief. His knees were weak, and his hands hurt from clenching them. Tearing his gaze from Alissa, he found Yar-Taw swirling back into reality as a man.

Keribdis rumbled a response. Strell spun back around. The raku had returned to all fours. Her head was high as she surveyed the incoming rakus. Her second eyelid slid shut to cover her damaged eye, and she shifted in a swirl of nothing that was almost black in the afternoon sun.

Heart pounding, Strell ran to Alissa. The sand slid as he came to a halt beside her triangular head. *She's breathing,* he thought, a cry of relief escaping him. His hands were spread wide, not knowing how he could help. He gently touched an eye ridge to feel the sun's warmth on it. Angry, he looked up, hatred suffusing him as he fastened upon Keribdis.

The old woman stood in obvious exhaustion. It was as if
only her rage was keeping her upright. Blood had quickly
stained her dress, and one eye was swollen shut. Savage
scratches marred her face. "You hurt Alissa," he said, his
voice carrying a deep hatred.

Keribdis gave him an icy look. "I let her live."

It was the first thing she had ever said to him. "You're an
animal!" he cried, lunging at her. Before he moved three
steps, his feet were pulled out from under him. He fell, spinning to find Connen-Neute's long fingers about his ankle.
"Let—go!" he shouted, kicking in time with his words. He
scored on the young Master, and his tight grip fell away.
Connen-Neute's pupils were so large, his golden eyes looked
black.

Strell scrambled to his feet. His breath came fast as he realized Connen-Neute had probably just saved his life. Wolves,
he was so helpless.

Keribdis haughtily pulled her red scarf tighter about her
narrow waist. She waited with a mocking expectancy, wanting an excuse to ward him to death. *Alissa,* he thought, fear
replacing his anger. Panicking anew, he fell to his knees beside Alissa's head. Fingers trembling, he reached out to touch
her. *Please,* he thought. *Please, Alissa. Be all right.*

Yar-Taw strode quickly to Keribdis. "Are you all right?"
he asked, reaching to support her as the woman shakily nodded. "Perhaps you should have used another method to bring
Alissa in line. Knocking your student out for willful disobe-
dience is hard." Yar-Taw glanced at Alissa. "On both of you,
it seems."

Strell stood. His hands were clenched at his sides. The
bulk of Alissa lay behind him. "You gave her a concussion,"
he said, ignored. "She might never wake up!"

Keribdis turned to Yar-Taw. "It wasn't as if I could control
her by withholding information," she said bitterly. "Talo-Toecan
made her untenable." An ornate bench grew from a shadow,
and Keribdis wearily sat down. She took a breath and steadied herself, arranging her dress to try to hide the seeping
blood. The shadows of incoming rakus fell over the sand.
"And it was necessary," the woman said. "I didn't bring down
Alissa. That—" She pointed at Alissa. "That is feral."

Strell felt the blood drain from his face. Keribdis knew. Connen-Neute had said she flew like a feral beast. Keribdis had seen it.

"Feral!" Fear pulled Yar-Taw's face tight as he glanced at Alissa. "She went feral?"

"Yes." Keribdis dabbed at her eye with a fold of cloth that hadn't been there a moment ago. "We were fortunate I managed to bring her down myself. No one but me got hurt."

Yar-Taw's face was stark with horror. He backed up a nervous step. The beach was rapidly getting crowded. Strell felt his helpless anger grow as more and more rakus landed and shifted. They clustered about Keribdis, bombarding her with questions she didn't answer. Connen-Neute came to stand beside him as if ready to accept punishment.

Lodesh and Silla stumbled out from the undergrowth. Eyes wide, the young woman clutched Lodesh's hand for an instant, then dropped it and ran to Alissa.

"Stop!" Keribdis shouted, jerking the young woman to a halt. Slowly Keribdis got to her feet. The unanswered questions died away. "I know you think I overreacted this morning."

"You knocked her out, Keribdis. No student deserves that."

"Did you see her fly?" someone asked. "I've never seen anyone drop like that before!"

"And she flipped head over tail!" another exclaimed. "I didn't know you could do that!"

Keribdis pursed her lips. "That wasn't Alissa in the air," she said, then swallowed as if in pain. "Alissa has gone feral."

"Feral!" someone exclaimed, immediately hushed.

With Yar-Taw's help, Keribdis took a limping step forward. Strell wondered how much of the pain showing across her face was real and how much was for effect. "Do you honestly think my husband could properly bring about a first transition? Alone? With a rogue transeunt?" Keribdis said, and Strell seethed.

Keribdis gestured at Alissa. "Her thought signature changed. I saw an echo of a second consciousness in her last night. It was only a matter of time until she went feral. I'm sorry," she said, dropping her gaze in what Strell knew to be a false sadness. "I think it was my anger that tripped her across the edge."

Neugwin rushed forward with consoling words spilling from her. The Master's soothing voice sent Strell into a wash of delirium. This could not be happening! It was all Strell could do to not stride across the sand and slap her. As if sensing his hatred, Keribdis pulled her eyes to his. The corners of her mouth curved upward, and she raised a hand to cover her smile.

Connen-Neute took Strell's elbow as he rocked forward. Strell fingers trembled as he pried Connen-Neute's grip from him. Lodesh said nothing as he stood beside Silla. His eyes darted everywhere. *Assessing the political situation, most likely,* Strell thought bitterly.

Keribdis coughed, clenching in upon herself. Waving Neugwin's concern away, she straightened. "She will be chained here. There's no other way to keep her grounded without the holden. When she recovers, we will force her to destroy her feral consciousness. She has not flown under starlight yet. We may be able to reclaim her."

"No!" Strell cried, unheard over the buzz of conversations that erupted. Silla clenched Lodesh's arm. She looked terrified.

Keribdis's gaze went distant. "It will be executed properly this time," she breathed as if eager for it. "I will have my student. She will respect me. By the Navigator's Wolves, I won't let Talo-Toecan win this."

Strell jerked with understanding. Lips parted, he looked at Connen-Neute. The young Master's long face was gray. Clearly he heard her as well. Keribdis cared nothing if Alissa lived or died. This was to prove Keribdis was better than Talo-Toecan. To show the Hold that she was the one they should follow, not him.

Connen-Neute leaned toward Strell. "I will explain to Yar-Taw the pact Alissa made with Beast." His voice was soft and level, but his hands shook.

"Now," Strell said urgently. "Tell them all now. Alissa will kill herself before being forced to destroy Beast. You know it! I almost killed her myself doing the same thing."

Connen-Neute's grip on his shoulder tensed. "I won't let them tie her to a post. Let me do things the way that will get the best result. If Alissa wakes sane, as we know she will, she has the right to a trial before they force her to destroy Beast. I can get her that, but if you inflame them with the truth in one breath, they won't slow justice down enough to listen."

Strell's stomach knotted. He watched the assembled rakus break up in ones and twos. Finally he nodded. "All right. Your way. One of us should tell Lodesh not to say anything."

Connen-Neute glanced at the Keeper. He had Silla's elbow and was trying to draw her away from the blood-splattered sand. The young woman was pale and shaking, clutching his arm with a white-knuckled grip. "Lodesh won't say anything," Connen-Neute said. "He thinks with his head. You, though, think with your heart." A very brief smile crossed him. "You're the most dangerous to her, but you're probably the only one who can save her."

A hard lump fixed itself in Strell's throat. Alissa, his love, lay unconscious on the sand. He took a breath as he forced himself to see past the "now" and into the "what had to be done." "Can you get me a tent to shade her from the sun?" he asked. His joy of last night had become bitter ash as he resigned himself to the task of keeping Alissa alive while the world exploded around her. That's what he was good at. Picking up pieces and putting them back together.

Connen-Neute bobbed his head. Giving his shoulder another firm squeeze, he strode to Yar-Taw. Strell watched, satisfied when Connen-Neute pulled him from Keribdis with the air of an equal, not a cowering student asking a favor.

Lodesh came up alongside of him. For a moment, they said nothing as they looked at Alissa. "How are we doing?" the Keeper said, his hands on his hips.

Strell stiffened at his light tone, then relaxed as he saw the shared pain behind Lodesh's green eyes. "The same as always," Strell said, gesturing for him to help him move a wing back into a normal position. "The same as always."

30

Her head was a thick haze of muzzy agony. "Not again," she whispered, hearing it come out as a guttural sound instead of words and remembering she was in her raku form. Alissa swallowed hard, nausea surging through her. She was tired of waking up like this. Her mouth felt as if she had been eating feathers, and she couldn't open her eyes.

Screwing up her courage, she tried to visualize her tracings but was unable to. *The ale,* she thought, deciding this wasn't the way to avoid Keribdis. But then a feeling of dismay filled her. The ale had been ages ago. She had flown against Keribdis and won.

Alissa held her breath and wondered what it felt like when one lost. Ashes, she hurt all over. A slow throb of pain came from her tail and left hand, and she cracked an eyelid upon remembering Keribdis had bitten her. Light stabbed into her, making her head feel like it was going to turn itself inside out. Moaning, she buried her head into the huge cushion her head was propped on. The fabric was damp. "Urg," she grunted, realizing she had drooled on it.

"Beast?" she whispered into her thoughts.

"She cheated," Beast muttered. *"They're all fools. Go away and let me sleep."*

Satisfied Beast was all right, Alissa opened her eyes again. The light was almost tolerable this time. A band of red fabric was wrapped tightly around her throbbing left hand. She pulled her head up from the pillow to find a band of metal snapped around a hind foot. A length of chain ran from it. She blearily followed it to where it was attached to an outcrop of stone. *Where had they found the metal?* she wondered before thinking an occasional ship must maroon here. Her stomach roiled, and she held her breath lest she vomit. She felt too ill to be outraged at being chained to the earth.

"Alissa?" whispered a gray voice. Concentrating, she blearily focused upon Connen-Neute. He was in his human shift, sitting cross-legged on the sand to put himself at her eye level. The afternoon sun shimmered on his Master's vest, and he held himself at an unusual ramrod stiffness. They were under a huge black canvas shelter open on two sides. The up-wellings of heat over the sand looked reddish from the salt swirling through them. Talon was perched nearby on a stick jammed into the sand, surprisingly quiet and subdued.

"Ashes," she moaned into his thoughts. *"Make it stop. I can't concentrate to find my tracings. Please. Run a healing ward for me? My head hurts."*

Connen-Neute's long face was frighteningly worried. "Alissa. Don't try to free yourself. And for the Navigator's sake, don't talk to anyone but me. They're watching."

"I can't free myself. I can't even sit up. Do something. Please?" She shut her eyes, unable to take the light any longer. How could light hurt so much?

She heard Connen-Neute's sigh. "All right. But don't do anything."

Alissa waited, feeling as if she might die at any moment. Warmth filled her as his ward eased over her, pushing most of the pain and confusion away. It was replaced with a wave of heat, and she basked in it as her tension eased. The headache retreated to a faint memory, whispering a promise to return someday. Her tail seemed almost normal, but her hand had no improvement at all. A blissful sigh escaped her. She could hear the surf pounding on the shore and the cry of gulls. Slowly she opened her eyes.

"Thank you," she thought, feeling her muscles ease. Her

brow pinched, and she swung her head up and back as she recalled the chain. *"Why am I tied up?"*

Connen-Neute's face was pinched and white. "Alissa, remember. No freeing yourself, and no talking silently to anyone but me. You promised."

Anger flashed through her. *"I did not!"* she exclaimed, struggling to sit up, awkward because she was clutching her left hand close to her chest. It was sending stabs of pain all the way up her elbow. Her wings half-opened for balance and her head began to pound again. Alissa glared at Connen-Neute as if he was at fault. Immediately she unfocused her attention. She would shift right now to get rid of the band of metal about her ankle.

"No!" Connen-Neute stood up, frantic. "I told them you would do what I said."

"That's your problem, not mine," she said, furious.

His brow pinched as he grasped her jaw with both hands. "No, Alissa," he said, gazing into first one, then the other of her eyes. "I vouched for you. If you don't do exactly what I say, they'll burn both our tracings to commoner status. Right here. Right where we stand."

Her breath caught. Reading the truth of it in his frightened eyes, she licked her beak. Slowly she nodded. He let go of her head, and she followed his gaze to Silla's cliff. Three human figures were up there. Beast sent a low, guttural growl of satisfaction through their shared thoughts, and Alissa knew one of them was Keribdis.

"Now," Connen-Neute said with a puff of relief as he took a step back. "No shifting. No freeing yourself. And no talking to anyone in their thoughts."

Scared, she asked, *"Are they angry—"* She hesitated. *"I hurt Keribdis."* Alissa felt a moment of panic. What would Useless do to her for hurting his wife?

He looked past Talon at the waves as he fingered the edge of his red sash. "You temporarily damaged her eye and gave her a permanent scar on her leg. That might be forgiven, as she forced the conflict. But that isn't why you're restrained."

A feeling of nausea came over her. *"They're angry about me marrying Strell?"*

"They don't know, yet," he said.

She swallowed hard. *"What, then?"*

Connen-Neute took a slow breath. "I told them about Beast."

She stared at him, tensing. *"You said you wouldn't!"* she wailed, struggling until she managed to lurch into an upright position. The chain tightened and a link snapped. Alissa lurched and fell, almost passing out at the pain in her hand as she hit the sand.

"It was an accident!" Connen-Neute shouted frantically in his thoughts as he spun to the cliff, and Alissa knew he wasn't talking to her. *"An accident! Let her take the ash-ridden chains off. It's her! You know it's Alissa. If she was feral, I would be dead and she would be gone!"*

Alissa froze, terrified. The tips of her wings trembled. There was a buzz of half-heard conversation, and Connen-Neute eased. "Go ahead and shift," he said. "You're lucky Silla's with them. They're afraid to show their fear in front of her."

Fear? Alissa thought. She was the one shaking. Alissa took a steadying breath, then shifted. She took a long time, concentrating on making sure she reappeared in her best out-fit. Immediately the pain in her hand grew worse. Nauseous, she fell to sit on the sand.

Her stomach clenched as she looked at her hand. The wrapping had vanished when she shifted. Ugly purple and yellow discoloration patterned her skin between the red gashes where bones had been slid back under the skin. Alissa's breath came in short pants to keep from passing out. She would never be able to use it again. She knew it.

"Here," Connen-Neute said, holding out a sling. "Yar-Taw set it. He gave you a ward to dull the pain, too. He said you should regain most of its movement. He'll bind it again for you, I'm sure. But you ought not shift anymore until it's healed further."

Alissa's stomach was roiling. Why had he bothered? Why were they talking as if she had a tomorrow? They were going to make her destroy Beast. What did it all matter?

But she let him help put the sling over her shoulder and arrange her hand in it. The pain besting the ward made her grit her teeth until she saw spots, but she wouldn't pass out. Kerib-dis was watching. Alissa wouldn't give her the satisfaction.

She was almost panting when they were done. The wind was suddenly chill, and she shivered. "You promised you wouldn't tell anyone," she whispered.

Connen-Neute exhaled long and slow. He glanced up at Silla's peak and back again. "Keribdis recognized Beast in your thoughts. If I hadn't told them, you would have awoken ringed by the entire conclave with them thinking you were feral."

"They're going to make me kill her anyway!" she exclaimed, dropping her head as the edges of her vision started to go black. "I won't," she whispered. "I won't, and you know it." She tried to stand, failing. The pain in her hand was almost too much to bear.

Connen-Neute's eyes were hard with determination as she fell back. "I got you a chance, Alissa." He hesitated. "There's going to be a meeting," he said quieter.

"It's a trial. Call it what it is!" she demanded, her heart pounding. She had to get away. She could fly back to the Hold. She could make it. Why had she ever come looking for them?

"It's not a trial," he said uncomfortably.

"I'll be standing alone?" she asked bitterly. "I'll be justifying my actions?" Connen-Neute wouldn't meet her eyes. "Then it's a trial," she said.

"It's a meeting where you will try to convince the majority of the conclave that Beast is not a threat to you or anyone else. You don't have to convince Keribdis, only half of them—"

"Keribdis owns all but a handful!" Alissa exclaimed.

"If you can do that, you'll be allowed to remain as you are," Connen-Neute finished.

"And if I can't?" she asked, her stomach clenching.

He said nothing, not even looking at her.

Silence settled over them. She looked at her hand in its sling. Heartache went through her as she realized she had lost her ring. "Where's Strell?" she said. Her ring—her wedding ring—gone.

"Close, but out of sight so they won't make him leave."

A cold feeling went through her. She touched the back of her head, making a small noise when she found a lump. She must have been knocked out. She didn't remember that.

"I do," Beast muttered, and then Alissa did as well.

The sound of approaching voices pulled her attention down the beach, and her anxiety flowed back tenfold. Connen-Neute extended a hand to help her rise. His smooth face was pale and worried. She stood, wavering. Her knees felt as if they wouldn't support her. Alissa brushed her good hand down her Master's attire, wishing she had something nicer to wear to her lynching. Her hand trembled as she reached for Talon. The bird chittered comfortingly, worrying Alissa's fingers until she put Talon on her shoulder. "I'm ready."

31

Alissa walked beside Connen-Neute, feeling like a pris-
oner. Her hand throbbed under the pain-deadening ward.
The Masters they passed paused their conversations, turning
them into a buzz of private mental communication hazing the
edge of her awareness. She stiffened, touching Talon's silky
feathers for reassurance.

Connen-Neute subtly guided her to a table and three chairs
waiting in the shade above the high tide mark. They looked
out of place on the sand, the impression strengthened by the
woven mat under them. The odd trees arched overhead to provide relief from the sun, and the wind off the water made it
cool. Her heart pounded as she saw Yar-Taw waiting. His
trousers, long sleeveless vest, and shirt were black; his yellow
sash went to the ground.

"Still think it's not a trial?" she said bitterly to Connen-
Neute as she took in the semicircle of empty cushions surrounding the table at a respectful distance. Behind them
were benches. They were all alike, the elegant, detailed
carvings making it obvious that someone had made them
from their thoughts. The table held a pitcher and set of cups.
Alissa felt a pang of worry when she found her small, rude-
looking cup of stone amongst them. *One more thing to have*

to explain, she thought sourly. One more thing to set Keribdis against her.

"It's not a trial," Connen-Neute muttered. "Yar-Taw promised me it wasn't a trial."

They came to a stop before the older Master. He looked tired. She saw no horror for her having made a pact with her feral nature, just a tremendous weariness. "Alissa," he said as he helped her with her chair. "Are you always this much trouble, or are we just lucky?"

"She's usually worse," Connen-Neute said brightly, clearly trying to lighten the mood.

She managed a smile. "Thank you for setting my hand," she stammered as she sat.

"You're welcome." Yar-Taw settled himself and reached for the pitcher. She reached for her cup and proffered it as he topped off his own drink. His eyebrows rose as the water went tinkling into the stone vessel. "I thought that was your cup," he said. "You haven't been here long enough to make it by hand." He shook his head. "Thought-form, is it?"

To answer him, she set her tracings alight and made another. He picked it up and blew the dust from it. "I'd like to know how you managed that," he said softly as he looked it over.

Alissa felt numb, unable to find the strength to care anymore. "No one told me it wasn't possible to craft thought-forms out of stone until after I did it," she said.

Connen-Neute shuffled nervously, finally settling himself on a nearby cushion.

Yar-Taw was silent, fingering the second cup. The sound of approaching people pulled his head up. "It is a trial," he said, and Alissa tensed. "But you can walk from here as you came if you fly the right updraft." She went to speak, and he held up a hand. "This arrangement between you and your feral consciousness . . . You know it isn't the only issue Keribdis has?"

Alissa nodded, glancing past him to the brightly colored figures moving through the brush. They were all dressed so nicely. She looked like a beggar, even in her best clothes.

"Keribdis is fighting her own personal war," Yar-Taw said, bringing her attention back. "It started long before you were born. Wolves, I think it started before the Hold was built. Talo-Toecan is on the other side, and unfortunately you have become a point of contention."

"That's not it," Alissa protested, going silent as he raised his finger again.

"Whether it is or isn't doesn't really matter," he said, his words quickening as the people grew close. "The only way you can win this is by not arguing with her. She is a dramatic, spoiled old woman who has the backing of most of the Hold. Don't get me wrong; she earned that backing fairly. She is intelligent, devious, and has no mercy when she is protecting something dear to her. I expect she will rant and rave, and if you respond in kind, her dramatics will be seen as being justified and not as the method of persuasion they are. Only by letting her rage alone will the rest see how irrational she is being."

He pressed his lips together and leaned back as the first of the Masters took their spots. "I don't agree with what you've done with your bestial consciousness, but maybe . . ." He hesitated, glancing at her second cup. "Perhaps some good can come of it."

"Thank you," she said, relieved she seemed to have someone on her side.

"Or perhaps I simply don't like a bully," he added.

Alissa's stomach dropped. Unable to meet his gaze, she turned to the surrounding crowd. Silla had seated herself beside Connen-Neute. The young woman was pale, and Alissa wished she had been able to explain to Silla about Beast. Who knew what lies Keribdis had told her?

Alissa turned to Yar-Taw. "Where are Strell and Lodesh?" she questioned.

"Keeping themselves at the edges where they ought to be," Yar-Taw said seriously.

Stifling a surge of annoyance, Alissa ran a mental search, startled to find both Strell and Lodesh up a nearby tree like boys at a village hanging. Peering closer, she spotted Strell's hat, the one she had given him ages ago. She gave him a weak smile, and a large leaflike frond moved contrary to the breeze. It made her more confident. She took a sip of water, but her fingers trembled as she set her cup down. Her hand hurt through the ward, and she cradled it.

"Wolves," Yar-Taw muttered, his gaze on the sky. "Here she comes. I imagine this is going to be one of her more dramatic entrances."

The crowd became noisy as everyone found his or her place. Alissa squinted into the noon-bright sky. She brushed a strand of hair from her eyes with her good hand. Looking as if it was coming out of the sun was a golden form: Keribdis.

Beast stirred at Alissa's alarm. Together they watched Keribdis circle and land far enough away that the sand and spray she kicked up would hit no one. The older raku surveyed all from her higher vantage point, nodding to several on the benches. Alissa's brow furrowed at the discoloration about her eye. It had clearly been subjected to a three-day accelerated healing. *It hardly seemed right,* Alissa thought with a stab of irony. When in the past, Alissa had taught Redal-Stan the tricky ward, who in turn taught it to everyone else, Keribdis included.

There was a swelling in the subliminal buzz of private conversations. *"I'm not afraid of her,"* Beast said into their shared thoughts, and a wash of prideful satisfaction went through Alissa as they gazed at the tender-looking scar on her thigh.

"I am," Alissa thought back sourly.

Beast harrumphed. *"She can't bring us down. Look how dull her hide is. She's thin from age, not strength. She hasn't the stamina."*

"Perhaps." Alissa pushed her cup away. *"But it didn't do us any good, did it?"*

"She cheated. This one can't catch us," Beast added, and Alissa felt a glimmer of hope. She could always flee. Leave Keribdis to sulk on her island. Beast could get them back to the coast. But even as she thought it, her thoughts turned to Strell. She couldn't leave him.

There was a pull upon Alissa's tracings as Keribdis shifted to her smaller size. Smaller, but no less formidable, Alissa decided, blinking in surprise as she took the woman in.

Keribdis had appeared in an extravagant dress of patterns and colors the likes of which would take Alissa years to make. Gold and red interwove with dark greens and bronzes. Her obsidian hair shone, piled atop her head as Silla's often was, the ribbons holding it in place trailing in the stiff breeze. Her scarf was the only thing unchanged, and it drew Alissa's eye like the sun. The stark crimson was surrounded by so many colors and shapes that at first it seemed the only place Alissa could look at. But the color was so vibrant, she finally had to look away.

Alissa squinted at her, suddenly seeing the woman's extravagant clothes as an overdone costume worn to appease someone's idea of self-worth. Looking down at her own attire, she saw it in the same way. Her hair blew into her eyes, and she wished she had cut it to a proper foothills length. She wished she had worn her old clothes. She wished she hadn't tried to be anything other than a farm girl. What the Wolves was she doing here?

Keribdis made her sedate way across the hot sand to Silla, ignoring Alissa completely. "Silla, dear," she said gently as she drew the young woman to her feet. "Why are you here?"

Silla's chin quivered, but her eyes grew determined. "I want to stay," she said.

"But until you scribe your name on the cistern, you have no voice in the council," Keribdis said persuasively. "There's no reason for you to have to witness this. Go wait on the overlook. I'll tell you what happens. Every little detail."

Silla's lips parted in disbelief. "Alissa is my friend," she said. "I want to stay."

Alissa felt a surge of relief. Silla was still her friend.

Keribdis drew Silla stumbling out of the conglomeration. "Silla." Her voice was harder. "This is nothing you need to see. Nothing that concerns you."

"The sanity of my friend doesn't concern me?"

"Student—" Keribdis started, her eyes holding a severe look of reprimand.

"Let Silla stay," Yar-Taw interrupted. "She's a member of the conclave, whether she has scratched her name on some fool wall or not. If you want to keep with Hold traditions, then I suggest we go back to the Hold so we can."

There were muttered agreements, and Alissa watched with satisfaction as Keribdis forced her brow smooth. "You're such a dear," she said to Silla as she gave her a quick hug. "If you're that concerned for your new friend, of course you should stay. There is a spot in the back."

"I already have a seat," she said. Not waiting for a reply, she strode to her cushion beside Connen-Neute and sat in a huff of nervousness and determination.

Keribdis was left standing alone. She looked shocked. Her eyes narrowed as she met Alissa's gaze, and Alissa looked away. Silla's defiance hadn't helped in the least.

"About time we saw some backbone in that girl," Yar-Taw said, making Alissa feel somewhat better. He gave Alissa an encouraging smile, then stood. "Keribdis," he said loudly, gesturing. "Come and sit with us."

"I prefer to stand," she said, moving gracefully forward despite a small limp.

"Your preference, of course." Yar-Taw poured her a cup of water.

Alissa listened carefully to his tone and decided to take his advice on how to confront Keribdis. His words were slightly sarcastic but still polite. She snuck glances at the surrounding Masters, seeing several with amused expressions. Hope made her sit straighter.

Keribdis took a stance in the shade midway between the table and the assemblage. She hesitated as if gathering her thoughts, her head bowed in concentration. The crowd grew quiet. Looking surprised at the sudden silence, Keribdis brought her head up. The wind blew upon her ribbons, fluttering her long skirt and sash.

"I have spent much time in meditation," she said softly, "thinking how best to confront the problem that has come before us." Keribdis looked at Alissa, and Alissa stared back. "She has willfully maintained her unlawful feral consciousness. We thought it couldn't be done," she said into the uneasy silence. "But her transition from Keeper to Master was not executed properly."

"Still think it's not a trial?" Alissa said silently to Connen-Neute, and his ears reddened.

"It's a situation that can be remedied, and I say we should," Keribdis finished.

Alissa opened her mouth, but Yar-Taw shook his head. "Not yet," he said softly, then louder to everyone else, "We meet today to talk over Alissa's well-being. As has been correctly stated, she has made a pact with her bestial consciousness instead of outright destroying it. We need to determine if this has a detrimental effect, and if so, begin to explore remedies."

Keribdis took a step toward the table. "That is what I said," she accused as she raised her cup and took a sip. Her eyes fell upon the stone cups. They widened as she realized there were two now where there had only been one before. Clearly they were thought-forms. Alissa mockingly picked one up, silently claiming her accomplishment.

Keribdis's shock vanished, and her face went hard. "I want to talk to it," she said, and Alissa blanched at the force behind the simple request. "I want to talk to your bestial consciousness. Let us see it so we can decide if it's safe. See if you control it, or it controls you."

Alissa's chin trembled as her shock turned to anger. It? Beast was not an it. She lowered her eyes, swallowing the insult. "Her," Alissa said shortly, and Keribdis paused.

"Her what?"

"Beast is a her, not an it."

Keribdis looked over the surrounding people, a mocking arch to her eyebrows. "Her, then," she drawled patronizingly.

Alissa seethed, taking another sip from her stone cup.

Keribdis gracefully folded herself onto a chair with her hands on her lap. "Well, where is—Beast? Or are you not really in control? Is it a mistake that brings her on?"

"No," Alissa lied. She glanced at Silla and then away. The girl looked frightened, and Alissa wondered again what Keribdis had told her. "But Beast promised she wouldn't take over my actions, and she won't, unless I pass out or I'm in danger."

Keribdis's eyes bore into her, but her words were for the crowd. "How convenient. A moral beast. But you are in danger. Tell your beast you're in danger for your very life."

Alissa took a slow breath. Her heart pounded, and she felt ill from the pain in her hand. *"Think on the wind,"* Beast said, confusing Alissa. *"I'd like to be entirely me to answer her, so you must relax and trust me to give yourself back to you when I'm done."*

Aware that everyone had gone silent, Alissa nodded. An odd feeling of detachment slipped over her. She clenched, her fingers gripping her cup tightly. Then, with Beast's admonishment, she relaxed, finding herself wondering why she couldn't see the updrafts any longer and why the sound of the surf was muted. Her fear of Keribdis shifted to contempt. How dare the old female try to outfly her. To succumb to the strength of youth was the way of the world.

Alissa felt a shiver pass over her, and everyone gasped. Talon left her, hopping to Silla. The young woman didn't seem to notice as she clutched Connen-Neute's arm. "You're old," Alissa heard herself say, the words enunciated with more care than she ever took.

Keribdis went ashen, covering her sudden shock by standing up. *"She's putting distance between us,"* Beast said into Alissa's thoughts. *"She knows we can outfly her."* Alissa felt a bewildering spin as she tried to look at the crowd, finding she couldn't. Beast was concentrating on Keribdis with the intentness of a predator and wouldn't allow it. "But I won't talk to you," Beast said to Keribdis. "You're a child and would misunderstand anything I might say."

"Child!" Keribdis exclaimed. Her fright was gone or hidden very well. She tossed her head to send her ribbons fluttering in a blatant attempt to pull all attention to her. Beast adjusted their posture slightly. It was a small move, but the men in the crowd suddenly had slack faces. Beast understood now she was encouraging them to try to bring her to ground, but as long as she was free to fly, filling them with a desire they couldn't satisfy gave her power over them.

"I am not a child!" Keribdis said, gaining at least the women's attention. "I am older than you by seven hundred years, you ash-ridden foothills spawn."

Alissa felt her breath leave her in a languorous sigh. "I remember the birth of the wind," she said slowly. "You only ride it."

Keribdis blinked, her lips slightly parted. But her jaw returned to a clench long before the Masters behind her remembered to breathe.

"Maybe that's enough, Beast?" Alissa questioned, not liking the lack of control she had. No wonder Beast liked to fly. It was the only freedom Alissa gave her. Perhaps she wasn't being fair to her feral consciousness.

"Are you sure?" Beast said as she breathed in the sweet air,

and Alissa smelled for the first time the difference in the mirth trees. *"I could end this quickly if you would shift. This should be settled in the air as it has been for thousands of years."*

"No!" Alissa cried aloud, and snatched control back. The world seemed to hiccup, and Alissa blinked, startled to find herself seeing everything in the mundane way she always had.

The Masters exchanged uneasy glances. It was obvious they knew Beast was gone. "What did she say to you?" Keribdis asked, her predatory gleam shaken. "There at the end?"

Alissa allowed herself a smirk, though she was shaking inside. "She suggested we should settle this in the air as has been done for thousands of years."

Keribdis drummed her fingers together as if to point out Alissa's shorter digits. "Perhaps we should," she threatened.

Beast surged forward. "You cheat," she said through Alissa. "But you would still lose, winglet," she added, then vanished.

Yar-Taw raised a hand to ease the soft murmuring. "Enough," he said, taking a nervous glance at Alissa. "We've seen Beast, heard her speak. What say you, Keribdis?"

"I want it dead," Keribdis said flatly.

Alissa jerked her head up. Swallowing, she went cold. The Master was playing no longer. The flamboyant dramatics were gone. Keribdis's fear of losing control of the conclave, of her inability to control Alissa, had burned all emotions from her except an unbreakable determination. Even Keribdis's fear had been destroyed. This was what everyone had warned Alissa of, and she hadn't understood.

"I want it dead," she repeated, loud into the shocked hush. "The feral consciousness that evolves upon first transition must be destroyed. Talo-Toecan failed. It must be done now."

Keribdis stepped forward, and Alissa shrank back in her chair, her bravado vanishing as if it had never existed. "She is a dangerous mix," Keribdis said. She leaned over the table so her trailing ribbons nearly touched it. "Not feral, not sane. She's a carrier of disease, unable to succumb but infecting those around her. She made Connen-Neute feral. She might do the same to Silla." She stood up and faced the crowd. "She might do the same to one of you!"

"No!" Connen-Neute shouted, standing up. "That's not what happened."

"Sit down, Master Connen-Neute!" Yar-Taw exclaimed over the rising murmur. Alissa looked from Connen-Neute's anguished expression to Silla's horror-struck one. Keribdis knew Silla was balancing on the edge, and she was going to make Alissa take the blame if she fell.

"Beast is not a disease," Alissa said over the talk both aloud and unheard. "She isn't something that evolved during my first shift to Master. She isn't something foreign to be destroyed. She's always been there, just mixed up with the rest of me." The Masters stilled themselves, listening, and Alissa took a steadying breath. "I believe Beast was separated into her own being the first time I shifted to a raku. Beast isn't evil, just out of place. Just like everyone else's beast. None of you have destroyed your beasts. You only suppressed them."

For a heartbeat, there was silence. Alissa became afraid when horror washed over the faces staring at her. Then the crowd roared denial. Keribdis looked satisfied. "I want it dead," she said over the noise. "I want it dead, now. There's no both. There's one or the other. I do not have a beast in my thoughts!"

"You do!" Alissa exclaimed.

"Kill it!"

Frightened, Alissa stood, her pulse pounding. "You can't make me kill her."

Keribdis's face went ugly. "Then I will rip your sentience from you and return you to what you really are: an animal."

The noise fell to nothing. Alissa's breath came in a panicked gasp. Then, realizing what Keribdis was proposing, she slumped. Relief poured through her so quickly and strong, she had to support herself against the table. It was over. Almost she laughed, catching it as they would think she had snapped. Keribdis had come out with the worst she could think of, and it was a threat that couldn't harm Alissa.

A smile, unhelped and honest, came over her. Keribdis blinked, and Alissa let it grow. She dropped her eyes, almost embarrassed for the woman's misunderstanding. "You can't take my sentience," Alissa said softly, her eyes on her stone cup. "You can suppress it, perhaps, but Beast won't take control as your crushed, bound feral selves would." She felt her pulse slow as Beast laughed within their thoughts. "I'd stay as I am. You can't hurt me, Keribdis." Alissa straightened, taking a clean, deep breath of air. "You can't. There's nothing you can do to me."

Alissa looked over the assemblage, reading the fear on some, the awe of understanding on far more. Her questionable pact with her beast had made her untouchable by their severest punishment and immune to their greatest fear of becoming feral.

"I'm going back to my boat," Alissa said, supporting her weight on the table with her good hand. Her knees were weak, but it was from realizing her position of power, not her fear. "As soon as the stores are restocked and the boom mended, I'm leaving. I hope some of you will return with me. Talo-Toecan is tired of being alone."

Feeling more in control than she ever had before, Alissa turned and headed down the beach to the village. Her hand throbbed, and she held it close. Beast was silent, thinking.

"She's insane," Keribdis whispered. "You see?" she said louder, and Alissa continued on. "She is rogue when herself," Keribdis raved. "She is an abomination when feral."

Alissa shook her head and sighed. She had been called worse by her own townsfolk.

"An animal!" Keribdis shouted, and Alissa felt a pricking on her neck. "Dangerous and uncontrollable, like a half-tamed wolf. Bringing her in among us was a folly. It will turn and tear out our throats even as we feed it! We must destroy it now!"

"Keribdis!" Yar-Taw said in warning and Alissa spun.

The fear and hatred in the woman's golden eyes shocked Alissa to a standstill. The woman's proud face twisted, and she pointed. "You're a—a—"

"Half-breed?" Alissa said, finding strength in the word. "In more ways than one. It's why I can accept the truth, and you can't." She sighed. She would have to tell them the entire story. She knew they wouldn't like it.

"Your numbers have been dropping since you learned to shift to human form," Alissa said softly. "It's because you're suppressing your feral side instead of blending it back into your consciousness where it came from. I'll admit I don't have it quite right, but it's better than what you have done, suppressing it so strongly that half of your children die trying to learn how to fly and the other half go feral to keep from becoming insane." She looked at Keribdis, feeling pity at the hatred pouring from the woman. "I can help Silla find the balance where you cannot," Alissa said to her alone. "And you know it."

Having won, Alissa turned away.

3 2

"You will not walk away from me without leave!"

Alissa turned on the path to give Keribdis a look she tried to keep from being mocking. There was a flash across Alissa's tracings as a ward snapped over her, shocking her with its strength and quickness. Alissa gasped, finding herself warded to stillness. She had beaten Keribdis at her game of words, so the woman was changing the rules. Again.

"Keribdis . . ." Yar-Taw protested as he stood.

"Catch an updraft, Yar-Taw," Keribdis warned, her gaze locked upon Alissa. "All of you. You're too weak and naive to see what she is. I'll take care of it. Like I always do."

Alarm jolted though Alissa. Steadying herself, she sundered the ward. Fear flickered over them all. Alissa's head thrummed with the unheard comments bandied between the Masters at her show of strength. Keribdis's surprise was replaced with a savage determination. Too late, Alissa realized her mistake. By showing everyone wards couldn't contain her, she had backed Keribdis into a corner. The proud woman wouldn't accept Alissa unbroken and defiant. Keribdis needed to crush her to maintain her grip on the conclave. They both knew it.

"She will change the rules again," Beast warned, almost

sounding eager. *"But if she takes this into the air, she will lose."*

Apparently Yar-Taw knew it as well, as he came out from behind the table with his hands raised soothingly. "Keribdis . . ."

Keribdis ignored him. "You were to have been my student," she said, seeming to spit the words. "You will either respect me or you will be dead."

"Keribdis?" Yar-Taw questioned, his face suddenly slack as Keribdis blinked slowly, clearly settling herself for something difficult.

Alissa's resolve stiffened as Beast—always confident, always wise—grew fearful. "You can't hurt Beast," Alissa said loudly. "Only I can suppress her, and I won't!"

Keribdis's pupils widened to nearly cover the unreal Master's gold. The lines in her face deepened. "You will kill that beast in you before the sun moves," Keribdis whispered, "and you will beg me to forgive you for your reluctance."

Yar-Taw moved, halting at Keribdis's outflung hand. "Keribdis!" he warned. "Any action to be taken needs to be discussed."

"You are too weak to see the truth!" Keribdis shouted, her face flushed. "You are too afraid to make the choice!" She took a breath. "I'll make it for you."

"Keribdis, no!" Yar-Taw exclaimed.

Alissa staggered as Keribdis's thoughts crashed into hers. Anger, rage, jealousy, all hammered at Alissa. She stumbled to find her balance. Fighting back was not an option. She could only struggle to separate herself from the close mental contact Keribdis was forcing on her.

The woman's thoughts freely mixed with her own. Alissa couldn't move, shocked to find Keribdis was deathly afraid of being found lacking. The Master was consumed with her fear for Silla and the thought she might lose the girl's love. The shame and doubt that Talo-Toecan might never come for her hounded her days, making everything she did seem inadequate.

Keribdis's fears poured through Alissa with the unstoppable force of a wave. It was akin to raping the soul, and Alissa stood, too shocked to respond. "I will have your respect," Keribdis whispered, and Alissa mouthed the words. "Until you give it to me, I will have your source."

"No!" Alissa shrieked. Jolted into action, she expunged Keribdis from her thoughts with a frightened surge of mental force. Agony flared through her. Staggering, she clutched her chest. Keribdis was gone from her thoughts, but something was wrong!

A savage feeling of loss racked her. Helpless, she fell to her knees. She clutched her arm to herself. Struggling to breathe, Alissa pulled her head up and looked past her falling hair. What had Keribdis done?

The Master stood proud and savage above her as if she were the Navigator's mouthpiece. A white sphere too bright to look at, too bright to be real, hovered above her outstretched hand.

"That's—mine," Alissa whispered, falling forward to catch herself with one hand. Her broken hand pressed against her chest as if to keep her soul from spilling forth. Keribdis had fastened about her source during their close contact. In forcing her out, Alissa had unintentionally expunged her source as well.

"Keribdis!" cried Yar-Taw in horror. His hand was on Alissa's shoulder. "What did you do!"

Alissa knelt, gasping, wondering why she hadn't died. Her soul lay within her, torn and ravaged. The bright glow of Everything was gone, leaving ragged edges where death began to consume her from inside. Her eyes closed. It was over. She could do nothing.

"She can't be controlled!" Keribdis cried wildly. "She shouldn't have a source! Talo-Toecan is wrong! *I* will do it the way it should have been done! She is *mine!*"

A tiny shriek of rage came from above. Alissa turned to the sky. "Talon! No!" she exclaimed, holding up her good hand in warning. But her bird dropped, talons spread.

Keribdis's face became ugly. There was a flash of resonance across Alissa's tracings. Talon's cry ceased with a frightening suddenness.

Alissa felt her life end as Talon fell to the sand. Not wanting to understand, Alissa reached out and touched a disarrayed wing, tracing the familiar lines. "Talon . . ." she whispered, her vision blurring as she realized the bird was dead. "Talon?"

The Masters stood behind Alissa, too stunned to move. Alissa felt her lungs press against themselves as she lost the will to fill them. A blur came before her eyes. Keribdis's shoes. Blinking the tears from her, she looked up to see Keribdis's harsh face outlined against the sky.

"Your source is mine," Keribdis said, the bitterness in her voice making Alissa think her words were like the black stains the gulls etched across the sky above her.

Keribdis didn't care, Alissa thought. She had killed Talon without thought and had forgotten it already. Despair forced Alissa to take a breath. "No," she said, but it was a futile gesture. The woman had changed the rules and won.

Alissa's source lay in Keribdis's hand, a carrot to demand obeisance. And Alissa knew to the depths of her soul she would take it when offered. It was only the shock of Talon's death that kept her from crawling even now to beg, to grovel, to promise anything to get it back. She would agree to be dominated forever by Keribdis even as her bird lay murdered at the woman's feet. Her wounded soul cried out to have that warm glow of power and comfort within her again.

And Keribdis knew it, standing above her with a hard satisfaction mirrored in her stance.

Alissa closed her eyes. Catching her breath against a sob, she drew upon Talon's memory to find the strength to steel her soul for what she was going to do.

She would not allow herself to belong to Keribdis, to anyone. She lacked the strength to wrestle her source back, but it was close enough to use. Still—close enough—to use.

Alissa slumped until the warmth of the sand brushed her brow. Only if her source was gone would she not beg for it. To use it up might mean her death, but she would rather be dead than belong to this woman.

Finding peace in the loss of hope, Alissa willed herself deep into her unconsciousness. She could feel a small part of herself crying, hunched in pain over Talon. Nothing mattered anymore. She sat up, and lifting her gaze unseeing to the sun, she set her thoughts on a mountain fortress—cold with night, peaceful with silence—and an old raku sitting atop it, waiting, listening at the point where night balances on the cusp of time before becoming day.

"Useless!" she cried, drawing, pulling, running every glimmer of strength from her source in Keribdis's hand through her mind.

A blinding wave of force shot from her in a concentric, flat pulse. The surrounding Masters fell to the sand with hands pressed to their ears. Her eyes on the sky and her thoughts on Talon, Alissa felt the clean energy of her source race through her mind a final time. The light in Keribdis's hand vanished to nothing, spent.

Alissa slumped to the sand. It was done. There was no need to do more.

The glow surrounding her tracings went out.

33

From behind Yar-Taw came simultaneous cries of surprise and pain as Alissa's mental scream tore through his mind. Clutching his head, he lurched to catch himself against the table. His breath came in a haggard gasp, and then the unheard shriek was gone. "Wolves," he panted.

The harsh afternoon light stabbed deep behind his eyes to set up a soft throb in time with his pulse. "What the ashes was that?" Swallowing the last of his vertigo, he pulled his head up. Slowly the light became tolerable. He squinted to find Keribdis at the center of her impromptu stage, staring at her empty palm in shock. His stomach twisted in horror. Keribdis had torn Alissa's source from her while the girl was alive and watching.

Then Yar-Taw went slack in awe and understanding. The mental shout. Alissa had used her source before Keribdis could claim it. The child had used her entire source in one final defiant gesture. "Useless," Alissa had cried. A last show of rebellion.

Heart pounding, he spun to Alissa. His chest clenched in helplessness as he found her slumped in the plainsman's arms as they sprawled on the sand. She had to be dead. No Master could live without a source. Strell desperately rocked her, whispering. How had he gotten to her so fast? he wondered. Everyone else was still picking themselves off the sand. Then Yar-Taw remembered that Strell was a commoner and hadn't felt her mental shout.

Close beside them was Lodesh. His hair was in disarray, and he carried an unreal mix of grief and helpless anger. His lip was bleeding. Yar-Taw glanced at Strell, wondering what had happened in the moments he had been incapacitated.

There were several tweaks on his awareness, and his tracings began to resonate in response to others setting up healing wards. He decided to live with the bruise across his tracings until it healed on its own. He might have a more dire need for the ward later.

"Stay with me, Alissa," Strell whispered, and Yar-Taw started. She was still alive?

Tensing with a righteous anger, Yar-Taw turned to Keribdis. She was stock-still in bewilderment. "What?" she stammered, staring at her empty hand. "What happened to it?"

"She used it before you could," he said, surprised to find his voice hoarse. "Damn you, Keribdis." For the first time in his life, Yar-Taw saw Keribdis struggle for understanding.

"But—I was going to give it back," she said, dazed.

"When?" He straightened, his motion slow as he felt the weight of two decades of folly fall upon him. He had waited too long, and now it was too late. "After she groveled at your feet for it?" He glanced at Alissa, his breath quickening. "After you hammered her into submission? After you broke her down to what you have made the rest of us? You ripped it from her soul!"

Keribdis shook her head as if clearing her thoughts. "I was teaching her humility."

Yar-Taw laughed. It was a bitter, mirthless sound. "You taught her the power of self-sacrifice. You taught her you were vengeful and cruel, moved by jealousy. And you taught us the same."

Keribdis stiffened, jolted back to her usual self. "I just saved everyone's life."

"You killed us," he said with a false calm as he took a step closer. "Alissa was the Hold's transeunt. She was our future."

"Silla is our future." Keribdis haughtily adjusted her sash, her face twisting with a savage satisfaction as she looked at Alissa slumped against the plainsman. "That"—she pointed—"was an accident. I can bring six like her up in two centuries. And do a Wolf-torn better job of it than Talo-Toecan did."

Jaw clenching, Yar-Taw took another step forward. "We don't have two hundred years," he said tightly. Beso-Ran slipped behind him, giving him strength.

"She's still alive," Strell said raggedly, and Yar-Taw heard by the pain in his voice how deep their unfortunate bond went.

Keribdis pursed her lips, and Yar-Taw's frustrations swelled. "I think giving you the privilege of teaching the next transeunt was a mistake," he said, gratified when Keribdis's face went slack in surprise. "I think if you hadn't done this, you would have crushed her slowly so we couldn't tell," he added, his jaw aching from clenching it. "I think you were afraid of her."

Despite his efforts, his words got louder. "I think you wanted a transeunt that you controlled," Yar-Taw said, coming nose to nose with her, not caring that she was white with rage. "And when Talo-Toecan," he shouted, "nurtured one better than you could have, making her into someone you couldn't manipulate, you killed her!"

"She's not dead!" Strell cried desperately. "Someone tell me how to help her!"

Yar-Taw said nothing, focused on Keribdis. That Alissa was still alive was a miracle, but no Master could live without a source. And to tell the plainsman that was beyond him right now.

Keribdis's mouth snapped shut. "She was insane. You saw her! You all saw her!" she cried as she took a step back. "She still had her feral consciousness! Are you blind?"

"Not anymore." Yar-Taw tugged his sash straight as he felt the support of the Masters coming to stand behind him.

Keribdis sputtered in disbelief. "She bruised everyone's tracings while I was holding her strength in my hand!" she raged. "You would not be alive had she held her source at the time!"

"None of us would be hurt if you hadn't ripped her source

away and dangled it before her like her still-beating heart."
Yar-Taw heard Strell's horror-filled intake of breath as the
man finally understood what had happened. "She could have
done far worse. She didn't." Yar-Taw took another step forward. "*You* are the beast, Keribdis. You tore Alissa's source
from her soul. The punishment for such a crime has been
written."

For a heartbeat, Keribdis stood with incredulity in her eyes.
"She was going to destroy us all!" she exclaimed. "Didn't you
see?"

Yar-Taw steadied himself, forcing his feeling of illness
away. He could feel the rest of the conclave behind him, their
agreement brushing the edges of his bruised tracings. His
breath was slow and even. "The punishment for taking another's source while alive is to be made feral, Keribdis," he
said evenly.

Keribdis blinked in disbelief. "You wouldn't," she
breathed. "You can't. I was right for what I did, and you know
it. You're cowards!" she said, pointing. "Afraid to make the
choices that must be made. She was a mistake! She never
should have been allowed to be engendered!"

"She was a Master, Keribdis. And you took her source."

"She was a foothills half-breed that Talo-Toecan dressed
up and played pretend with!"

Strell took a ragged breath, and Yar-Taw tensed. "She
was—*a Master,*" Yar-Taw said, hammering at the word. "One
you couldn't control, and that's why you killed her." His eyes
went hard. "You're tried and sentenced, Keribdis."

Keribdis went white. For an instant, Yar-Taw saw fear. She
lost her arrogant stance as he felt a collective nod from the
Masters behind him. Then she pulled herself straight, her
mouth curving upward into a mirthless smile. "Who will do
it?" she said, her voice mocking. "The law says I must lose
my sentience. Will you take it, Yar-Taw? Beso-Ran? Neugwin?" The proud lines returned to her face as her gaze went
over Yar-Taw's shoulder and among the Masters.

Yar-Taw stiffened. She was right. There were so few of
them now, even her crimes could be overlooked to keep them
one step further from extinction.

"No," she said caustically. "None of you will because you

know I'm right. I saved you, and you're too cowardly to admit
it. She was a blasphemy. An abomination. A putrid caricature
of what a Master is."

There was a gasp from Strell, and Yar-Taw's breath came
quick in anger. "Leave, Keribdis," Yar-Taw said. "Leave, and
don't come back to the island."

Keribdis laughed. "You know I'm right, or you'd take my
sentience right now."

"It's called mercy, Keribdis. Leave."

"It's cowardice!" she asserted. "And you can't make me
leave. Not any of you alone. Not all of you combined. But I'll
be damned before I stay with such ungrateful, shortsighted
fools." She turned her back to them and walked away, confident they wouldn't harm her. Yar-Taw's mouth twisted, knowing her trust was well-founded.

Once more in the sun, she gave them a disparaging look
ripe with disgust. Her hair glinted, and she pulled her ribbons
from it as if divorcing herself of an unwanted burden. "Go
back to Talo-Toecan with your tails tucked," she said caustically as the last fluttered from her. "And when he calls you
fools, come back, and I'll accept your apologies."

Yar-Taw spun at a blur of motion. It was Strell.

Lodesh was quick behind the man. "Stay out of it!" the
Keeper shouted, lunging to bring Strell to a halt two man
lengths before reaching Keribdis.

Strell rose with a frightening determination. Lodesh
yanked his arm, throwing him spinning back into the crowd.
Keribdis watched, unafraid and uncaring. Lodesh dabbed at
his lip again. "I will not stand before Alissa and try to explain
why I'm alive and you're dead!" he shouted at the incensed
plainsman. "Stay where you belong. You can't do anything!"

Frustration and rage, quickly followed by hopelessness
and grief, passed over Strell. Shaking off the hands supporting him, he stood protectively over Alissa. His hands were
clenched to make his neck and arms like cords. "They're letting her get away with it," he said bitterly, and Yar-Taw felt a
twinge of guilt. "That—*animal*—hurt Alissa. She's dying, and
your precious Masters are going to let her go. Without even an
acknowledgment she did wrong!"

Keribdis made a patronizing sound and shifted. Golden

and shimmering in the noon sun, she leapt into the air. The backwash from her wings threw dry sand into the air. When Yar-Taw dropped his arm from his face, she was gone. He felt ill. She had been right, though. They were cowards: cowards for not following through with her sentence, cowards for allowing her to tell them what to think for so long, cowards for not stopping her before she did—did this.

Sick at heart, he turned to face the aftermath of Keribdis's jealousy.

34

"Help me," Strell said. His face was so grief-stricken that Yar-Taw cringed. "Help me get her somewhere," Strell insisted.

"Strell," Yar-Taw said. "I'm sorry. A Master can't live without a source."

Crouching, Strell pulled Alissa into a sitting position to better grip her. "She isn't dead yet," he snarled. "Damn you all to the Navigator's hell."

"Piper . . ." Lodesh warned, glancing uneasily at Yar-Taw.

"Shut your mouth, Lodesh," the plainsman said, struggling to pick her up. "You may be frightened of them, but I'm not."

Yar-Taw bowed his head. There was nothing he could do. He stood unmoving as the rest of the Masters began to slip away. Silla was already gone, probably frightened by Keribdis's bloodlust. Alissa should have never come. She should have let them stay lost. She should have let them languish into nothing.

"Someone needs to find Silla," Yar-Taw said, catching Beso-Ran's thick arm as he passed. "I can't sense her. She's using that new block of hers."

The heavyset Master nodded. He glanced at Alissa before walking away.

"Connen-Neute?" Neugwin called. "Connen-Neute? Are you all right?"

Yar-Taw turned, alerted by the worry in the woman's voice. Her long-fingered hand gently shook Connen-Neute's shoulder. The young Master was sitting where he had been during the trial, Silla's cushion empty beside him. His face was slack in concentration. His eyes were closed. His breathing was slow and deep. Clearly he was in a deep trance. Then Connen-Neute's head tilted as Strell lurched to his feet and Alissa's head thumped against his chest.

Yar-Taw's face went cold in understanding. "Stop!" he shouted, causing Neugwin to straighten in alarm. "Don't touch him. Strell, don't move."

The Masters within earshot hesitated, looking back. He strode to Alissa, peering at her cradled in Strell's arms. Instead of showing pain, her face was as blank as Connen-Neute's. "They're linked," he breathed.

Neugwin gasped. "How?" she stammered, going pale.

"Connen-Neute said they've pickabacked," Yar-Taw said. "He snatched her consciousness up and is keeping her alive." Yar-Taw reached for Alissa.

"Stay away!" Strell exclaimed as he backed up. "You were going to let her die."

The plainsman's face was angry and desperate, and Yar-Taw held his hands up in placation. "Don't—don't move!" he said. "Please. Connen-Neute has pickabacked her consciousness on his. He's keeping her alive, breathing for her, keeping her heart beating, but if you move her too far away, it might kill them both.

"Please!" Yar-Taw cried as Strell took a mistrustful step backward. "If she dies, Connen-Neute dies with her. He might not be able to separate himself from her."

Yar-Taw felt ill, proud of Connen-Neute but cursing the young Master's sense of responsibility at the same time. Around him, the conclave dispersed, their faces and motions subdued with understanding at the double tragedy. Neugwin stood helpless over Connen-Neute. Tears slipped down her cheeks, unremarked upon and without shame. Wyden stood beside her. It was only a matter of time. They would lose two children today, not just one.

"Then, she's—she's all right?" Strell asked, sounding as if he was afraid to hope.

Yar-Taw shook his head. "How long can this last?" he said, gesturing weakly as Wyden helped Neugwin to a bench. "An hour? Until sunset? A day? Connen-Neute is strong, but when he fails, they'll both die."

Neugwin huddled into herself. Wyden sat beside her and rocked the adult Master like a child. "He looked so like his mother," Connen-Neute's aunt whispered, and Yar-Taw felt a stir of anger as he realized they were all to blame for this.

Strell closed his eyes. He buried his face in Alissa's tumbled hair. When he looked up, Yar-Taw was astonished at the determination, not despair, in his eyes. "Someone put a cushion in front of Connen-Neute," Strell rasped, and Lodesh's eyes widened at the tone of command in the plainsman's voice. "I want to set her down in front of Connen-Neute," he said louder, frowning until Lodesh put a pillow on the ground.

"Strell . . ." Yar-Taw protested.

"You were going to let her die on the sand," he said bitterly. "You will do what I want. If Connen-Neute is keeping her alive, it might be easier for him if she is sitting up as he is." He awkwardly knelt with Alissa. She slid to the ground, half supported by the plainsman. "Forgive me if I'm wrong, Alissa," Yar-Taw heard him whisper as he propped her awkwardly up like a doll. Strell's breath came in a hopeful gasp as her posture straightened. "It's working!" he whispered as she took on a more normal appearance.

Neugwin pulled her head up. Her tear-streaked face was utterly blank. Strell put Alissa's hands in her lap, mimicking Connen-Neute. Her fingers curved to match Connen-Neute's, broken though they were. Carefully, Strell pulled his supporting hand away. Alissa sat firm.

Face tight with anger, Strell rose. "I want that tent moved," he said belligerently.

"I'll do it," Neugwin said abruptly.

"I'll help you," Wyden added.

Strell's anger vanished. The heartfelt look he gave the two

women overflowed with gratitude. Used to such quick transitions of emotion, Yar-Taw nevertheless grunted in surprise. Neugwin rose with Wyden's support. The two passed in front of Yar-Taw. Neugwin's hand reached out, but she didn't touch Connen-Neute.

Yar-Taw blinked as he found Strell staring at him with hot accusation. The man was holding one of the chairs for support. The fatigue of the last few days clearly pulled at Strell, gnawing at him like a cur. "Put a preservation ward on Talon," Strell said bluntly.

"Strell . . ."

The plainsman's eyes narrowed. "I have sat and done nothing," he said. His hand was shaking as he held it out to keep Lodesh from saying anything. "I'm done with it. Every time I let one of you Masters near my Alissa—"

"Your Alissa?" Yar-Taw questioned.

"My Alissa," Strell said, his voice hard. "Every time you tell me what's best for her, she ends up unconscious, burned, under a ward, or nearly dead. I'm tired of saving her. Now, listen. And do what I say." Pulling himself upright, Strell poked a finger into Yar-Taw's chest. "And before you get uppity with me, I'm not a student. I'm not a Keeper. I'm Strell Hirdune, the Hold's piper with a room in the tower. You will treat me with the respect that comes with that."

Yar-Taw's jaw dropped. He could kill the man with a thought. How could Strell presume he was an equal? His gaze darted to Lodesh. The Keeper stood with shock and alarm on his face. "Piper of the Hold?" Yar-Taw questioned.

"Piper of the Hold," the agitated plainsman snarled. "Do you understand?"

Yar-Taw was at a complete loss. It was like a little dog yapping at the heels of a bull. But what would it hurt to give a little? To placate him would do no harm, and the man certainly had the courage of a raku. "What do you want?" Yar-Taw asked.

Strell picked up Alissa's bird. Never more than a step from Alissa, he faced Yar-Taw. His face was lined with grief and anger, and he cradled the small bird as if it were a child. "Put a preservation ward on Talon," he said, his voice cracking.

"When Alissa wakes, she'll want to say a proper good-bye, not one to a mound in the sand."

"Strell . . ." Yar-Taw began, then hesitated as Strell's jaw clenched. "All right," Yar-Taw said cautiously, putting the ward in place and wincing at the hurt from his bruised tracings. It was a small thing, not worth arguing over. And easier than telling the man she wouldn't wake to say that good-bye. Not when Strell was so raw with pain.

The plainsman slumped as if a hard knot of emotion had loosened. "When I'm sure Alissa is getting no worse, I'm going to the boat. Lodesh? You're coming with me. I'm going to need your help sailing it."

"The boat?" Lodesh said wonderingly. "You can't make it to the Hold in time."

His gaze went accusing. "I'm not going to the Hold. I'm going to find Keribdis."

"What!"

Strell's fists clenched. "Someone has to tell her what she did was wrong. And since none of you seem to be *capable* of it, I will."

Lodesh moved to stand beside Yar-Taw. His face was creased, and his green eyes looked dead. "She'll outright kill you, Strell. Just like Talon."

Strell's breath came in a quick sound. "I'm a shade more durable than a bird. And I wasn't planning on walking up and asking if she would like to discuss it over tea."

Yar-Taw felt a stab of guilt. It was an emotion he was becoming uncomfortably familiar with. Though the man's understanding was woefully inadequate, his bravery wasn't. "Strell," he said reluctantly. "Keribdis needs to be punished for what she has done. But it's not that we don't want to. It's that we can't."

"You outnumber her!" Strell shouted.

"She would have shifted and flown. No one here can catch her." Yar-Taw moved uneasily from foot to foot. "And as for carrying out the judgment? I can't do it. Perhaps once, but not now. Not anymore. I've been complacent too long."

Strell's arms were stiff at his sides. "You're afraid. She was right. You're a fortress of cowards, hiding from your mistakes."

Lodesh reached out to restrain him, and Strell shook him off. Yar-Taw swallowed his anger, knowing Strell wasn't in his right mind. "Am I afraid of the horror of taking someone's sentience?" Yar-Taw said stiffly. "Yes, I'm afraid. But that wouldn't stop me if I thought I could do it." He went to the table, sitting so he could see Alissa. Slumping, he looked away. Ashes, he was tired. "Strell," he said reluctantly. "I physically cannot take Keribdis's sentience away." He glanced at Lodesh, embarrassed for speaking aloud of such things.

"Why not?" Strell demanded, and Yar-Taw blinked at the man's attitude.

"None of us can," Yar-Taw said. "Her grip on us is too sure, too tight. To take someone's sentience—or suppress it until the feral consciousness takes over, if Alissa is right—requires that the one carrying out the verdict is stronger of will than the condemned. Keribdis would have fought, and the stronger-willed Master would have won." Yar-Taw frowned, not liking the feeling of inadequacy and liking even less having to admit it to a commoner. "She would have taken my awareness instead of the other way around."

Yar-Taw felt his face go slack in a sudden thought. "That's why Keribdis was so storm-bent on dominating Alissa. . . ." he whispered, thinking it was the ugliest thing he had said in a long time. "Alissa had proved she was stronger willed, in the air as a raku and on the ground as a Master. Apart from Talo-Toecan, she was the sole person capable of bringing Keribdis to justice. Perhaps," he wondered aloud, "that is the real reason Keribdis left Talo-Toecan."

"Then Alissa is right," Strell said, startling Yar-Taw from his revelation. "You believe her. Your feral sides are suppressed, not destroyed."

Yar-Taw's gaze went to the stone cup Alissa had made with her thoughts. "No. I do not have a beast in my thoughts. But now I will never know why Alissa did."

"She won't die."

He grimaced at the sound of certainty in Strell's voice. Lodesh, too, had lost his look of despair and was brushing the sand from Alissa's face with the corner of his sleeve. His motions held a positive feeling, not one of last rites. Hope was one thing. Blindness was another. "We can't prevent her death," Yar-Taw said. "A Master can't live without a source."

"She did for the first twenty years of her life," Strell said bitterly.

Yar-Taw shook his head. "She won't survive. She would be dead now but for Connen-Neute. He bought you time to say good-bye. And he's likely to pay for it with his life."

Yar-Taw turned as Beso-Ran padded down the path, graceful despite his large size. He had several long poles and stakes. "I'll be back with the canvas," he said shortly. Handing them to Lodesh, he gave Yar-Taw a look before walking away, telling him more clearly than words not to say it was a useless gesture. It seemed the conclave needed misplaced hope. Lodesh and Strell fell into motion, deciding where the poles should be placed.

"Such a will she had," Yar-Taw said, more to himself than them. "She would have been a marvelous Master." His eyes dropped. "She was a marvelous Master. Imagine, expending all her source in one last cry of defiance."

"Defiance?" Lodesh said, puffing as he hammered a stake with a large nut. "That wasn't defiance. That was a cry for help. That's what she calls Talo-Toecan." He paused as he let the nut drop to the sand with a thump. "Useless."

Yar-Taw went still, only now realizing where their hope had come from. The breeze from the ocean ruffled his sleeves. "Useless? She calls Talo-Toecan, Useless?" Yar-Taw frowned. They were halfway around the world. He couldn't have heard her. But then recalling the strength of the shout, he swallowed and looked over the empty beach.

Strell and Lodesh worked together with little comment. Their desperation was gone. It had been replaced with action, action they clearly thought would make a difference. Yar-Taw licked his lips. Talo-Toecan wouldn't be pleased with him for having allowed things to get so out of control. Wolves. Not only had they killed Connen-Neute, miraculously returned to them, but Talo-Toecan's student as well. "Do you think he heard?" he asked.

Lodesh wedged a second stake deep into the sand. His eyes

met Yar-Taw's with a frightening refusal to accept the loss of hope. It sent a chill deep into Yar-Taw. He had seen it only once before, when an army thirsting for revenge hammered at the gates of Lodesh's city.

"If I know Alissa," the Keeper said, "he heard."

35

Talo-Toecan flew. The sun was setting before him later than it should; he was chasing the failing day and gaining on it. Alissa's terrified, soul-rending scream had torn through his mind almost three days ago, shocking him into immediate, undeniable motion. He had been listening to the night as was his wont, hearing it echo with its familiar emptiness. And her cry of anguish had reached him. He was coming. Like an insane dream-demon, he flew.

Below him was only water. His wings faltered at the thought of it, then resumed their steady cadence. Someone had hurt Alissa. He would find out why. He never should have let her go alone. He instinctively knew she had found the conclave. And someone had hurt her.

Why? he wondered, feeling the breeze cool as the sun set. True, Alissa was stubborn and bullheaded. She often made mistakes while trying to prove herself. But she was always contrite when her error was shoved under her nose, even if it took several days for her to see it. Her temper had much improved. She shouted at him only on the rare occasion now. And it had been ages since she had outright said "no" to him. There was nothing in Alissa to find fault with. She was the archetype of a young raku, full of promise and in desperate need of a gentle hand.

And then Talo-Toecan went cold. *Keribdis*.

His breath came fast at the thought that his wife might be behind Alissa's pain. But upon searching his emotions, he decided she probably was. Feeling the potent rush of anger and worry, he forced his wings to move faster. All too soon, fatigue forced him into a glide. Cursing himself for having gotten old, he slowly descended as he gave his wings a rest, the sun seeming to rush to set as he lost altitude.

The water grew closer, and his anger shifted to self-preservation. He had followed Alissa's call, but the nearer he got, the harder it became to pinpoint exactly where her cry had originated. And he had no idea how far he had yet to go.

Settling his mind, he listened. All of last night he had listened. Listened until the pounding of his heart thundered in his ears like the pulse of time. Now, as the sun set, he closed his eyes and listened again. With all his being he sought her presence, trying to believe he could be heard beyond the curve of the earth. Alissa could. Why couldn't he?

"Alissa . . ." he called, willing his heart to slow as he was confined to listening between its beats. A faint response jolted him, and his eyes flew open. *"Alissa!"* he called, scanning the sky. His breath came quick as he found a shadow splayed awkwardly on the swells. Golden wings caught the last glint of the setting sun. Fear, unfamiliar and shocking, struck through him.

Her wings were outstretched, with her neck curled back upon itself to prop her head on her shoulders and out of the water. Her tail hung beneath her, almost lost in the blur of water. Even in the fading light, he could see her golden hide was red from the sun. A white crust of salt rimmed her. Large, dark shapes circled below.

"Alissa!" he cried, angling downward. *"Trying to fly back? You silly, brave fool!"*

"My fault," came a whisper of ailing thought.

Talo-Toecan hesitated. That wasn't Alissa's thought signature. There were no other young rakus. It had to be . . . *"Silla,"* he thought, both elated and dismayed. What was she doing out here dying on the swells? Then a low rumble escaped him. Perhaps the question was, What had Keribdis done to frighten her student this badly?

Clamping down on his returning anger, he descended until the sound of the wind on the water came to him. A noise of dislike slipped from him at the sensation of water running under his hind feet as he landed. He held his wings up until deciding he floated high enough to keep them dry, then carefully folded them. The dark shadows fled, and relief went through him.

"Silla?" he thought tentatively, reaching a hand out to run the back of a claw across her head. The dark shadows beneath her returned, and he tensed. *"Silla, wake up,"* he said, trying to keep his worry from spilling into his thoughts. *"You have to shift so I can carry you."*

Her lids fluttered. *"All my fault,"* came her faint thought, and his brow furrowed. Her thoughts were like a steady breeze scented with woodsmoke.

More confident, he chanced jiggling her head. *"Silla, I'm Talo-Toecan. Look at me. I have to get you back to the island. You have to tell me where it is."* He leaned forward, and as his shadow fell over her, she opened her eyes.

"No!" she cried. *"I have to find Talo-Toecan. I have to find him!"* Her golden eyes struggled to focus. She was dehydrated and not in her right mind.

Talo-Toecan tensed in frustration. What had Keribdis done? Desperate for answers, he looked up at the pristine blue of the sky, remembering why he hated the water. It was worse than a desert, and just as deadly. *"Silla, listen,"* he thought firmly. *"Alissa is real."*

"I know," Silla warbled, her thoughts weak. *"She and Beast are real; I'm not."*

Confused, Talo-Toecan splashed a rivulet of water on her. It had the desired effect.

"Who?" the young raku cried, snapping awake. Rearing her head back, she struggled to take flight, crying out in pain as her wing canvas cracked from the sun and salt.

"I'm Talo-Toecan!" he cried, alarmed. *"Alissa called me. I'm here!"* Still she thrashed, making red foam where her wings had cracked. *"Stop!"* he thundered, frightened she might drown right in front of him. *"I want to help!"*

His thought cut through her panic, and she came to a half-submerged halt, panting. *"You're Talo-Toecan?"* she whispered, her fright mixing with hope. Eyes glazed in hurt, she struggled to fold her wings against her, then gave up.

Blood stained the swells, and Talo-Toecan grew more worried as he glanced below to the dark shapes. He had to get her out of the water. *"Yes,"* he said. *"Where is Alissa?"*

"Please," she whispered. *"Do you know a healing ward, Master Talo-Toecan?"*

His eyes closed briefly as he imagined her agony. *"Yes, child. But I don't think I can run one on you. How long have you been in the water without food and water?"*

"Two days in the water, three without food," she whispered, her gaze falling. *"I thought I could make it,"* she finished, crying now. *"I didn't know it was so far."*

Talo-Toecan shook his head. *"You've already used up a good fraction of your body's reserves. It will likely cause you worse pain."*

"All right," she said bravely, her focus weaving. *"I'll try to fly without it."*

"Fly!" Talo-Toecan said he ran his gaze over her salt-cracked, dehydrated wings. She was nearly dead from exposure, and she wanted to fly. *"Silla, I'm going to carry you. I can at least dull your pain, and then you can shift."*

Alarm tightened her, and she opened her eyes. *"I'll drown if I shift!"*

"I won't let you drown," he said, lunging a hind foot at one of the shadows to warn them away. At her nod for permission, he ran the ward. He knew it took effect when her eyes opened wide at the sudden easing of pain. A sliver of cautious fear had come into her gaze as the curtain of pain was removed and she really saw him for the first time. He tried to give her a confident, comforting smile, but she looked so bad, he knew it was a useless attempt.

She took a slow breath and disappeared in a swirl of pearly white, reappearing much faster than Alissa ever had. He lunged forward as her head threatened to slip under the waves, trying to be gentle as he pulled her dripping from the water. Her involuntary cry of pain shook him as the salt bit deep at her burns and the hurt broke through the ward.

"Are you all right?" he asked, cursing his claws and thick skin.

"Yes," she said aloud, then hunched as her voice cracked into a fit of coughing.

He waited until she stopped. Cradling Silla against him, he shook the water from the tips of his wings. Her hair was as black as Keribdis's, and he wondered whose child she was. *"Bear with me, Silla,"* he said, eyeing the darkening sky. *"The worst part will be getting airborne."* He hesitated, wondering how he was going to manage the extra weight. *"Which way do I go?"*

Silla closed her eyes. Her lips were cracked. Two days in the sun had turned her a savage red, the skin so tender, her salt-soaked clothing brought grimaces of pain through the ward. Perhaps . . . he wondered, feeling the heat radiating from her burns. Perhaps he should risk a healing ward. If he only let a trickle run the pattern, it might do more good than harm.

"That way," she said, vaguely pointing. She let her head fall against him, accepting his protection, and his heart went out to her. "That way."

Talo-Toecan's anger slipped into a steady burn. He used it to force himself back into the air. *Keribdis,* he thought, feeling his muscles pull as he beat his wings and ran atop the water like an ungainly albatross. He never should have let the woman out of his sight. He never dreamed she could cause so much damage away from the Hold.

With a final lunge, he made it into the air. Three more heavy beats, and he began to gain altitude. He glanced at Silla, both relieved and worried that she had passed out.

If the truth be told, he had goaded Keribdis into leaving, letting her believe it was her idea. He had reached his breaking point, and it was easier to distance themselves than resolve their disagreement. And he had said nothing when the entire conclave went with her, glad for it.

Talo-Toecan felt a wash of bitter satisfaction. With them gone, the decision as to what to do about the escaped recessive alleles had been delayed for an additional two decades. In that time, the people had mixed so thoroughly that, by doing nothing, they had unwittingly put the beginnings of his plan into action.

As he struggled for height, Talo-Toecan's eyes narrowed.

There was a faction of Masters that believed as he did, their agreement made known only by their silence when others protested. Had they known how close he estimated the populations were to a true breakdown of barriers? Had they willingly left so his plan would have a chance? Why hadn't they stayed?

He had no way of knowing. Perhaps they went with Keribdis to keep her from doing something foolish. If so, they had failed. For if Keribdis had hurt Alissa, the woman had changed the rules so far as to be playing a different game. One he wouldn't allow her to win.

36

Strell finished one tune and slipped into another with the same breath of air. The sand was cold under him, and the sunrise felt good on his shins through his thin trousers. He sat at the base of a palm tree just outside the tent's shelter. Lodesh sat beside him. The Keeper yawned and ran a hand over his stubbled cheeks. Strell stifled a grimace as he realized the three-hundred-year-old man had no gray in his infant beard and likely never would.

It doesn't matter, Strell thought with a stab of satisfaction. Alissa was his. His eyes closed in heartache. She would be all right. She had to be.

Lodesh stretched, sighing from a fatigue born from no sleep. "She can't hear you playing," he said softly as they watched Alissa breathe.

Never missing a note, Strell stretched his right foot out, and with the toe of his boot, awkwardly wrote in the sand, "She can."

"Oh, clever." Lodesh gave him a wry look. "I can write my name in the snow, too."

Struggling not to laugh and ruin his music, Strell added in raku script, "So can I."

"Two languages?" the Keeper said. "All right. Now I'm impressed."

Strell lowered his pipe. "Alissa taught me the Hold's script our first winter together," he said into the new quiet. "In case Bailic ever asked me to read anything."

Lodesh nodded. "Did he?"

Strell shrugged. "A few times."

"Hm-m-m," Lodesh mused. "You don't know how she writes her name, do you?"

Strell smoothed a piece of sand and sketched in the Master's script the small figure consisting of a smooth, unbroken line weaving amongst itself. He considered adding the name Hirdune after it but desisted. Now was not the time to make it known they had eloped.

"Luck?" Lodesh's brow furrowed in disbelief. "Her parents gave her the word *luck?*"

He smiled. "Uh-huh. I think it's appropriate. She gave my name the word for *stone.*"

The Keeper's face went slack. "As in hard as?"

"As in dense," Strell corrected, and Lodesh seemed to relax. Taking his pipe up, Strell began a soothing tune. Lodesh closed his eyes and leaned back until his head hit the tree. The Keeper had been awake all night watching Alissa; tonight it would be Strell's turn.

Lodesh's breath turned slow and even. Strell noticed his eyelids twitching as Lodesh found sleep. It pleased Strell. At least the cursed Keeper had to sleep.

Strell continued playing, turning his attention to the gentle swells and the flat horizon. He liked the visual distance. It reminded him of his home in the desert. The mountains were captivating, but with a flat horizon before him, he felt he could do anything, go anywhere.

Nearby, just beyond the swells' reach, stood Yar-Taw. He was balancing on one foot, reaching out as he slowly shifted his position. Strell had seen Connen-Neute do the same thing on the boat, and he wondered what use that kind of a skill was.

Yar-Taw abruptly dropped his outstretched limbs and stood straight. Deathly still, the Master stared out over the water. The wind fluttered his long vest. Following Yar-Taw's gaze, Strell lowered his pipe and stared as well. A golden shape was approaching, flying just above the water. *Keribdis?* he thought, then took a quick breath. It was too big.

"Wake up," Strell said, nudging Lodesh's foot. "He's here."

Lodesh stirred with a grunt. "Already? It's only been four days."

Strell rose and brushed himself free of sand. "It will be five come this afternoon."

"But it took us weeks."

"We weren't in a hurry." Strell went to stand beside Yar-Taw. The Master looked none too eager, his expression pinched as he looked out over the water.

Yar-Taw's eyes widened. "Silla," he whispered. "Bone and Ash. He's got Silla!"

Strell squinted, unable to make her out.

"There, in his arms!" The Master had gone white. "She hasn't been hiding. She ran away!" He looked at them, then returned his attention to the incoming raku. "She's unconscious. Back up. Back up! Give him room to land."

Talo-Toecan grew close quickly. Tensing, Strell backpedaled with Lodesh and Yar-Taw. The large raku landed. Sand and spray went everywhere. Dropping his arm from his face, Strell took a gulp of air. Talo-Toecan looked angry. Even worse than the time Alissa had accidentally pulled the pendulum from the great hall's ceiling.

His wings made the air snap as he folded them. His golden eyes were almost black, as his pupils were wide. His tail was quick and sharp as it whipped about for balance. In his arms was Silla in her human shift. She tried to sit up, reeling as her sunburn scraped. Blinking as she struggled to focus, she struck out at Talo-Toecan's grip, pointing to the ground.

Yar-Taw held a hand to his head. "Not so loud!" he shouted. "My tracings are bruised."

Talo-Toecan lifted his head and roared. Hunching, Strell covered his ears and peered up. He had forgotten how large Talo-Toecan was compared to most rakus. Just his hind foot was as long as Strell was tall. The sound of approaching voices came from the new trail to the village.

"Please?" Silla whispered.

Talo-Toecan's head whipped around. Dropping it submissively, he puffed a breath of air on her before he slowly, gently, set her on the ground. A lumpy brown cushion materialized on the sand, and Silla gratefully sat on it. Huddled to little more than a ball, she held one hand to her head, the other to her middle. Her black hair lay in lank strands to cover her face. Yar-Taw stepped forward, jerking to a stop as Talo-Toecan slapped his tail into the sand between them.

"We thought she was with Keribdis," Yar-Taw said defensively, his hands on his hips as he scowled up at him. "We would have looked for her if we had known."

Talo-Toecan vanished into a swirl of pearlescent gray. Strell's shoulders eased as the raku reappeared as a man. "Where is she!" he shouted the instant he took form.

Strell glanced at Yar-Taw, glad Talo-Toecan wasn't angry with him. Yar-Taw licked his lips. "Uh . . . Talo-Toecan. It's good to see you. Keribdis is—"

"Not her. Where is Alissa? Where's my ash-ridden student!"

"Oh." Yar-Taw looked behind him at the rustling sound of Masters approaching. Strell thought they looked more afraid than pleased as they gathered into grim-faced clusters. Strell jiggled Yar-Taw's arm. "Uh, at the tent," the Master said, seemingly not aware Strell had touched him.

"Tent?" Talo-Toecan said, seeing it. "What the Wolves is she doing in a tent?" He bent to Silla, whispering, "Can you stand yet?"

Strell felt a pang of sympathy at her slow shake of her head, remembering Talo-Toecan asking him the same thing one winter's afternoon. Taking a steadying breath, Strell strode across the sand. "Talo-Toecan," he said shortly, giving the Master a nod as he took Silla's other arm. "I'm glad you're here. We need your help."

Talo-Toecan's face became empty. "What did they do to her?"

Strell tried to answer, but his voice unexpectedly caught. The last four days of hope and fear welled up. He couldn't say it. Shaking his head, he led Silla away. The young woman was crying. Strell wished he could carry her, but her sunburn wouldn't let him.

Neugwin came close.

"Get me that nut oil Beso-Ran puts in his ale," Strell said tightly. "It might soothe her skin."

Neugwin nodded, her gaze going distant before matching his pace again. Wyden turned and left, and Strell was satisfied she would soon show up with what he wanted.

"Why is Alissa in a tent?" Talo-Toecan asked, ignoring the following behind him.

"Didn't Silla tell you?" Yar-Taw walked a touch behind Talo-Toecan. Strell thought it looked submissive, and he felt a jolt of satisfaction.

"Silla has been unconscious all night," the angry Master said. "Half-dead from exposure. How could you not know she was missing? Are you that careless with your children?"

Talo-Toecan's wrath vanished with a shocked suddenness as he came upon Connen-Neute and Alissa. Alissa's hand lay bound under a splint, her fingertips purple and white. Even though the morning was cool, Connen-Neute's face had beaded with sweat. Quiet and still, Talo-Toecan stepped into the tent. "What did that ash-ridden wife of mine do?"

Yar-Taw flicked an uneasy glance behind him. "Alissa . . . Keribdis . . . When—"

Strell interrupted lest they lose what little time they might have in conversation designed to slide blame rather than remedy the problem. "Excuse me, Yar-Taw," he said as he helped Silla down onto a cushion. "Connen-Neute is pickabacking Alissa's consciousness upon his, keeping her alive after Keribdis took her source in an attempt to dominate her."

"Her source!" Talo-Toecan said, lines of horror making him look older. "How?"

Steeling his voice, Strell added, "Apparently Alissa then used it up to call you."

"The Wolves will hunt her." Talo-Toecan's eyes closed, and pain etched his face.

Yar-Taw cleared his throat. "You left a few parts out, plainsman."

Talo-Toecan's eyes opened, and Strell stifled a shudder at the bound anger in them. "I'll hear the rest from Alissa," the Master said as he knelt beside her. He reached to touch her cheek with the back of his hand. Strell saw his long fingers trembling, and he wondered if the Master was afraid. The surrounding people had halted at the edge of the tent, but the large space seemed small with Lodesh, himself, Yar-Taw, Silla, and Talo-Toecan in it.

Moving his head back and forth in denial, Yar-Taw sighed. "She won't come back from that. I've tried to reach both of them. They've retreated too deeply."

Strell took a step back as Talo-Toecan whipped about and rose to his feet. "She will. They both will," Talo-Toecan said.

Yar-Taw's eyes carried a deep sympathy. "I'm sorry, Talo-Toecan. Connen-Neute might, but your student is lost. To return from such a hurt knowing there's nothing to come back to? No. I might be able to find her, but I couldn't make my way back. Neither could you."

Talo-Toecan's jaw clenched. Long fingers curled into fists. He stepped toward Yar-Taw. "She already knows the way back," he said. "And she's taught Connen-Neute the same path. Didn't she tell you she has come back from Mistress Death's garden before?"

"No." Yar-Taw was red with anger, refusing to back up. "Did she tell you she retained her feral consciousness after her first transition?"

Talo-Toecan's mouth opened. Blinking, he shut it. He looked behind him to Alissa, then back. "No!" he whispered urgently. "She . . . but she destroyed it." Slack with confusion, he stared at Lodesh. "You were there. You saw."

Lodesh shrugged. "That's why Keribdis took her source."

"No, it isn't," Strell interrupted hotly. He would not let the truth be buried in the sand like an unwanted newborn. "Keribdis took it because she knew Alissa would agree to anything to get it back. That's why Alissa used it up. She wouldn't belong to that woman."

Talo-Toecan didn't seem to hear. A distant memory seemed to flicker behind his eyes. "I thought it was wrong she could fly right away," he said. "It was her feral consciousness."

"And why she wouldn't let you pickaback to reach Silla by dream," Lodesh added. "She was afraid you would see Beast as Connen-Neute did."

Talo-Toecan shifted his gaze to Connen-Neute as the Keeper had probably intended. "Beast? Her other consciousness has its own name? You all knew?"

Strell paled under Talo-Toecan's intent gaze. "No," Strell said. "I didn't know until a few days ago. But, Talo-Toecan. They're wrong. Beast is still Alissa. I'm the only one who knew Alissa well before she learned how to shift, *and Beast is still her.*"

"You think it's—" The old Master seemed to steady himself. "It's still there?"

Strell shook his head. They still didn't understand. "Beast is Alissa," he said patiently. "You Masters have it wrong. The feral consciousness you think you destroy at first transition isn't something that evolves on its own. It's always been there. It just separates from the rest of you when you learn how to shift." Strell ignored the angry voices his words pulled into existence.

"Get him out of here," Yar-Taw growled. "I don't have a feral beast suppressed within me. No one does."

Beso-Ran stepped forward, and Strell tensed. "No!" he shouted. "You let Keribdis all but kill Alissa when she said the same thing. Is it because it might be true? Are you afraid?" Beso-Ran took his arm, and Strell struggled to not strike him. "Talo-Toecan!" he exclaimed as he was pulled away. "Let me tell you what Alissa said!"

"Let him talk." Talo-Toecan's eyes never moved from Alissa.

Beso-Ran hesitated. Strell's heart beat fast, and he jerked away from the heavy Master. "She says that's why your numbers have been dropping since you learned to shift to a human form. Young rakus who suppress their feral side too much die from flight accidents. Those who suppress it too little go feral from the strain. It makes sense. It fits. Alissa hasn't figured out how to blend her feral consciousness back into the rest of herself, but she's closer than anyone else is. It might explain why she was able to shift through time, reach you across half a world, craft objects of stone from her thoughts, talk to both Keepers and Masters, return Connen-Neute to sentience, and all the other things she manages that none of you can." His gaze flicked from Talo-Toecan to Yar-Taw, pleading for a whisper of understanding to show itself.

The gathered Masters seemed to hold their breath as Talo-Toecan's eyes widened. Then he shook himself. "We can discuss it at length with Alissa herself," he said roughly.

Strell took a heaving gulp of air as the tension broke. At last. Someone was going to do something. "Can I help?" he said, surprised when Talo-Toecan nodded.

"Stand here," he said, pointing beside Alissa. "Lodesh, you have Connen-Neute. The rest of you—" He hesitated, looking up at them irately. "Go away. The last thing Alissa wants to see is you staring at her as if she were a cripple." Expressions ranging from anger to understanding passed over the crowd. Talo-Toecan's face creased. "Get out of here!" he shouted. "She came to find you, and this is what you do to her?"

Silla looked up. Her face was streaked with tears, and a white film of salt colored her black hair. "I want to stay," she quavered. "Alissa is my friend."

Immediately Talo-Toecan's anger vanished. Kneeling beside her, he carefully took a burn-swollen hand in his. "Then stay until Alissa regains consciousness," he said.

She smiled weakly, and he stood. No one had moved, and he frowned at them. Slowly, in twos and threes, they left with the exception of Yar-Taw and Neugwin. "He is my kin," the woman said—her soft face looking wrong under so severe a mien—and Talo-Toecan nodded.

"What are you going to do?" Strell asked, his relief swinging back to worry.

"Go in her thoughts and shake her up," he said, his brow furrowed. "Connen-Neute would have likely pulled her out himself, but he's too involved in keeping her alive. Once I take over that, he can bring us all out. On the count of three I want Lodesh to give Connen-Neute a slap. Make it hurt. Piper?" He turned to look at them. "The same with Alissa."

Strell swallowed hard, trying to imagine hitting Alissa. Talo-Toecan hesitated. "Can you do that?" he asked, the wrinkles in his face becoming deeper.

"Will she remember it?" Strell asked in worry, and a vague smile passed over the Master.

"If we're lucky? No. But I think she will."

Strell nodded, recalling Bailic had done the same to bring Alissa awake the first time she had retreated this far into her unconsciousness to escape an unbearable pain.

"Ready?" Talo-Toecan said, and Strell nodded. "All right.

I want you to count to three slowly. That will give me time to find and explain to Connen-Neute what to do."

Yar-Taw shuffled closer. "I'll count."

"If you feel you must," Talo-Toecan said caustically, then closed his eyes. Strell shifted nervously, unnaturally conscious of his hand. He glanced at Lodesh. The Keeper was grim.

"One—two—three," Yar-Taw said slowly, and Strell started.

His hand met Alissa's cheek in a shocking sound. "Alissa!" he exclaimed, staring at the ugly handprint on her cheek. "Oh, Wolves, I'm sorry," he said, bending close. "Alissa?" His breath came tight as her eyes opened. They were horror-filled and unseeing.

"Gone!" she shrieked, the sound frightening him. "It's gone!" she cried again. She flailed out with her good hand as Strell tried to take her in his arms. Curling into herself, she rocked, clutching her broken hand to so tightly it had to hurt. Strell fell back, shocked.

"What are you doing—Keeper?" came a cold, dark voice, and Strell's gaze darted to Connen-Neute gripping Lodesh's outstretched arm in a white-knuckled grip. His strike had never landed.

"Uh, nothing," the Keeper said, three shades whiter. "Can I have my hand back?"

Yar-Taw was staring at Alissa in repugnance and fear. "Silla," he hissed, gesturing. "Come here. You shouldn't see this."

Strell spun to Alissa as she sobbed violently. He reached out only to have Talo-Toecan intercept him. "Give us a moment alone, Piper," Talo-Toecan rasped, an air of tired resignation about him. He glanced at Silla. "Take Silla with you," he added. "This may take some time, and Alissa is likely to hate whoever sees her like this."

"I—I want to stay," Strell said, alarmed at the ragged look of the old Master. Something had happened in those three heartbeats. Something he would never comprehend.

"Go," he said, waving a hand in dismissal. "All of you. Find her something to eat. And water. Lots of water. Ashes, I'm thirsty."

"Water, yes," Strell said, reaching to help Silla to her feet. The young woman looked stunned, rising willingly to take

Yar-Taw's offered arm as she darted frightened glances at Alissa rocking in a tight ball.

Connen-Neute groaned in pain as he got to his feet. His long face was creased in hurt as he forced his arms and legs to move after four days. Leaning heavily on Lodesh and Neugwin, he gave Talo-Toecan a unreadable nod before limping out. Neugwin's gaze became distant as she probably sent word ahead to prepare for them.

Food, Strell thought, desperately wanting to do something for Alissa. He could get her some food. He knew Alissa better than all of them combined. If anyone could find her a reason to go on, he could. And it would start with food.

37

The fire was small. It was ready to go out, losing the battle to keep back the night. Alissa's hand throbbed under Useless's pain-dulling ward. Before her, Talon lay on a square of black cloth. The bird's plumage showed dark drops of color where tears had fallen. "I'm sorry, Useless," Alissa whispered, numb and rife with apathy. "I should have let Keribdis have her way. I can't shift now. I can't—" She forced the words out, telling herself she couldn't feel anything. "I'm worthless. I—" Her throat closed, her body betraying her will.

Useless sat where he had been since noon, beside her on one of his lumpy cushions on the sand next to Strell's offered plate of untouched food. "I shouldn't have let you come out here alone," he said, more to himself than her. The darkness seemed to soak up his low voice. "And you aren't worthless, Alissa. You will have another source."

"No," she protested. "I don't care anymore. I'm done." Her eyes were on Talon, wondering when he would go away like the rest of them. Even Strell had left.

"Alissa," he said, softly pleading. "You will get a new source."

Her face twisted bitterly. "When? When someone dies? I don't want another."

"Don't be a martyr," he said. It was obvious he had tried to make his tone sharp, but pity hadn't let his voice make the jump.

"I'm not." Her breath slid in and out, soundless against the hiss of the fire and the night-hushed waves. "I tried to be something I'm not. It's time . . ." She took a steadying breath. "It's time for me—to go home," she finished, the words squeaky toward the end. She was a crippled half-breed. A mix of everything that amounted to nothing. She would return to the foothills where she belonged. She would be shunned and reviled, but she wouldn't stay in the Hold. Her view of Talon became blurry as the tears threatened, and she couldn't imagine where she was finding the strength for them.

"You need to fly, Alissa."

"I don't," she said, holding her breath to catch a sob.

"Beast does."

Jolted, she looked up. His eyes held a questioning hurt. Then her alarm broke apart, torn by apathy. She slumped, and her gaze returned to Talon.

"Why didn't you tell me?" he asked.

She shifted her shoulders. "You would have made me suppress her until she might as well have been destroyed. I like her, Useless," she said, her voice low so it wouldn't break. "She's hiding now. So far I can hardly sense her." Looking up at his silence, she was surprised at his calm expression. "You aren't angry?"

He grimaced. "Later, maybe." He gave her a mirthless smile. "Actually, I think your notions concerning feral awareness are worth considering, no matter how uncomfortable they are. We may have been making the same mistake for thousands of years, too afraid to admit we are closer to our feral kin than we would like to be. But if you don't help us understand what you've done, we can't change anything. I—" He hesitated. "I don't like the idea that I might have a feral beast in my thoughts, waiting for me to falter so it can take control."

"Beast isn't like that."

"I was talking of mine. And everyone else's."

Alissa's thoughts swung to Silla. Softly she whispered, "Silla needs help."

Useless blinked. "Silla? She . . ." Face ashen, he shook his head in denial.

Alissa nodded. "She's having a difficult time finding a balance. She's close to going feral. That's why I could reach her across the ocean. And why Keribdis hates me. She knows Silla is balancing on the edge. Keribdis will blame me if she goes feral, saying Beast is a sickness I gave Silla." Alissa pushed one of Talon's feathers straight. Her throat tightened.

For a long time, Useless was silent. Only the sound of the water and the waves broke the stillness. Even the gulls had gone, sleeping on the sand in rows and columns.

"None of them wants to believe," Alissa said, not looking at him. "It doesn't matter. Let them think what they want. Just help Silla. Help her suppress her feral consciousness until she all but destroys it, like I should have." A feeling of helplessness welled up in her, making the blood pound in her head and broken hand. "And I won't have another source," she said louder. "If I do, I'll belong to whoever gives it to me. I can't do that."

"I wouldn't ask anything of you," he said, the firelight flickering deep on his wrinkles.

Alissa believed him, but she knew the feeling would haunt her nonetheless. "And what can I do without a source?" she said, not wanting to acknowledge she had heard him.

"You can do fields," he said with a forced brightness as he brushed the hem of his vest.

"Fields." She made a helpless noise. "Stopping stones and moving feathers? Protecting my thoughts from burns that no longer matter?"

She was bitter, and she jerked away when Useless reached to turn her chin to him. "You're still a Master," he said, a hint of iron in his voice. "Your voice will be heard in the conclave whether you can work wards or not. And you will have a source again. I promise." She made a miserable sound, and he leaned closer. "Don't mind their looks and whispers," he said. "You're not a cripple. We will get you another. The looks will stop. You will go on."

"It's not that," she breathed, losing her will to even speak. "I've been stared at before." Useless was wrong. She would never fly again. Beast would wither and die. Already, her awareness had begun to fade as the promise of flight turned to ash.

For a long time he was silent, then he asked, "Are you ready to go back to the village?"

Alissa's eyes closed. The sound of the breeze in the palms was too much like the sound the wind made in her ears when she flew. The silence grew expectant, and remembering he had asked her something, she nodded, fully intending to stay where she was.

Useless forced a smile. "Strell is just over the dune, waiting for you."

"Strell?" A spark of emotion flickered, then slid down to nothing. She should tell Useless what they had done but couldn't bring herself to. What did it matter?

"Search him out, Useless prompted. "You don't need—you need only your own strength for that. And you will fly again."

Alissa managed a false smile. He was trying to make it better. He didn't understand. Wanting him to leave, she cocked her head and made her gaze distant. She nodded as if she had done a search and found him.

"There," Useless said overly cheerful. "He'll walk you back to the village. He probably has something else for you to eat, too. Go on. I'll join you before sunrise. I have—an errand."

Alissa's gaze dropped to Talon. The bird's feathers were soft against her fingertips. *Keribdis*. There was no fear in the name. There was nothing. No hate, no anger, nothing. "It doesn't matter," she whispered. "It's done. Let her be. I have no outrage left to avenge."

"I do," he said shortly as he stood and brushed the sand from his yellow trousers. She heard the determination in his voice and decided it would be easier to bend to his will. "Go on," he added. "Strell is waiting. Join him before he has a conniption fit trying to decide if he is doing something wrong by trying to get you to eat."

Alissa forced herself to rise, ignoring Useless's outstretched hand. She had no intention of finding Strell. Seeming satisfied, Useless moved a few steps away. The lines on his face were deeper than she remembered. Giving her a nod, he shifted. Alissa froze in misery as her tracings resonated with a ward she could no longer do. She slumped to the ground. Her head drooped until her chin almost touched her chest.

There was another pull on her thoughts, and Useless shifted back. Saying nothing, he returned to the fire. "You aren't going, are you," he said flatly, his white eyebrows bunching.

"No." Alissa wouldn't look up. "I want to—" She swallowed, her eyes on the small kestrel. "I want to take care of Talon." Her vision swam. Her friend was dead.

Useless sighed. "My errand can wait," he said as he sank down beside her.

A lump filled her throat. Grateful for his presence, she brushed a finger over Talon's graying markings as Useless added wood to make the fire high and hot. Alissa's eyes closed against the new heat. She would miss Talon. Even her habit of plying her with her catches, snakes included. A faint smile stirred her to open her eyes. "Did you know Talon once spent an entire week bringing me snakes?" she said, and Useless's eyes softened.

Alissa clutched her good arm about her knees as the warmth of the fire went through the thin fabric of her dress. Her broken hand lay like a dead thing in her lap. "It wouldn't have been so bad," Alissa said, "but she brought back one that wasn't dead once. Talon dropped it in the kitchen. My mother killed it by throwing a knife at it. I didn't know she could do that. I had to sit with my feet off the floor for three months until she was sure Talon hadn't brought back another that we didn't know about."

"Did she? Bring you another, I mean?" Useless asked, his voice gentle.

"Only one other time. I made such a face, I think Talon realized I'd never eat it."

Useless pushed a stick into the fire, his fingers almost amongst the flames. "I've never known a bird to do that."

Alissa glanced down at Talon, then away. "Talon never did anything normal," she said, finding it easier to talk than she would have imagined. She picked at the binding about her wrist.

Seeming to understand, Useless took on a more casual air. "What I don't understand is how she could fly at night. She was a fine flyer. The only thing I couldn't catch."

Alissa looked up. "I thought you always won those games of hers."

Useless shook his head, a veil of memory coming between her and his eyes. "No. And I've been able to catch everything, Keribdis included." He grimaced, then forced himself to be light. "That's not entirely true. I was never able to catch Redal-Stan. He was the one who taught me to fly. For a transeunt, he was more of a raku than most born to it."

Alissa nodded, edging back from the flames as they grew higher. Wiping her bleary eyes, she wondered if the fire was hot enough yet.

"Yes," Useless said as he made a platform of the old coals, almost as if he read her mind. "When you're ready. She lived an extremely long life for a bird. It's time she returned to the Navigator." His golden eyes shone. "I'd wager you'll find her waiting on the back of your chair at the Navigator's table when you get there," he said, and Alissa choked back a sob.

Tears dripping from her unchecked, she awkwardly picked Talon up with one hand. The small bird was light, almost as if she wasn't in her hand at all. Eyes closing, Alissa buried her nose in the silky neck feathers, breathing in Talon's scent for the last time. The wild smell of clouds coursed through her, almost covering up something she had never noticed before.

Book paste? she thought, hesitating. Why did Talon smell like book paste?

Her eyes opened, unseeing. She had smelled it before; she knew it.

Alissa's tears hesitated as a faint thought struggled to solidify. Visions of her chair before the fire in the Keepers' dining hall and of Redal-Stan's pillow flitted through her mind. "No," she whispered, not believing the two were connected with Talon. But the scent of book paste delved through her thoughts, tugging them into order.

"Redal-Stan?" she whispered, her eyes widening as she looked frantically at Useless.

She had given the old Master a memory of Talon. She remembered that, she thought, her pulse quickening. Could

Redal-Stan have figured out how she crossed the patterns to shift through time after all? Had he used her memory to shift forward?

Feeling numb and unreal, Alissa cradled Talon close. But why shift into a bird? He had known birds didn't have complex enough tracings to shift back to human or raku with.

Her breath caught at the answer. "He knew he would go feral," she said aloud, not caring that Useless was bending over her in concern. "He knew he would go feral from shifting too far through time and losing his reference points, so he purposely shifted into a bird, where it wouldn't matter if he was feral or not." She looked at Useless, seeing the sudden alarm in his eyes.

"He was feral!" she said, not caring he might think she had snapped. "Right up until the last few years when he found new reference points. But he was a bird. He had no tracings to shift back with! He knew he would be trapped as a bird. Why? Why did he do it?"

"Alissa?" Useless's hand was tight on her shoulder. "What are you talking about?"

The tears welled up as she realized why. He had done it for her. To help her when there was no one who could. To keep her from being alone as she struggled to become herself.

Alissa shook in huge racking sobs, crying for understanding come too late and the love the old Master must have held for her. Unable to see the fire through her tears, she let Useless take Talon and place the bird on the fire. Knees drawn up to her chin, she rocked herself as she struggled to pull her will together. Redal-Stan had a gift other than his love to give her.

Slowly, her field took shape in the flames that flared up from burning feathers. It was small, but as her heartache swelled so did her field until the entire fire was encased. The heat inside the field grew, seeming to warm her from within. Still weeping, she bowed her forehead to her knees, clutching her broken hand between her legs and her chest, sobbing, rocking, feeling the difference in the flames.

"Alissa?" Useless whispered. The weight of his long hand rested upon her shoulder. Then it fell away with a quick intake of breath. "Wolves, Alissa," he said, his voice suddenly full of awe. "What are you doing?"

Alissa looked up. She wiped her eyes with the back of her hand. Her breath came in a ragged sound as saw her field was not red with flame but white with the shadow of infinity. "Talon was Redal-Stan," she whispered. "She was a he after all. I only said she was a girl because of her size. When she was younger, her markings were much darker."

"Redal—" Useless stammered.

She sent a tendril of thought past her field. Her eyes widened with unbearable emotion as something eased from the field and began to settle in her thoughts.

There was a sliding of sand, and she felt both Strell and Yar-Taw's presence behind her. "What do you want?" Yar-Taw said tightly. "I said I was busy with Silla."

"Look at the fire," Useless said, and she heard Yar-Taw gasp.

"What the Wolves!" the bewildered Master exclaimed, taking a step back.

"Help her, Yar-Taw," Useless said harshly. "It's a pyre field. But I don't know if this is right or not."

"But how . . ."

"Talon was Redal-Stan," Useless explained tersely. "We knew he was experimenting with tripping the lines when he went missing. He helped Alissa get back from the past. Obviously he shifted forward to help her when there was no one else who could—when you abandoned the Hold. Now tell me, Yar-Taw! What is she doing wrong? Why is she crying?"

"She's doing nothing wrong!" Yar-Taw said, and Alissa shook with a racking sob. "But it's so concentrated. Usually it's within a field a hundred times larger. I think . . . Alissa?-I think you should bind some of it now."

"I am," she wept, feeling the strength of the old Master course through her until finding the empty spot within her and making her whole again.

Without warning, her field collapsed in on itself. Alissa convulsed as a wave of emotion crashed over her. Her eyes shut as a word echoed in her thoughts. *"Squirrel,"* came a soft whisper, and tears streamed from under her closed lids.

Strell's hand touched her shoulder, trembling. She opened her eyes. The fire burned only wood. The three men were staring at her, their expressions tinged with alarm. Feeling self-conscious, she straightened. There was grit on her fingers, and the breeze coming off the water was chill upon her damp cheeks. Her broken hand hurt, helping to bring her back to herself.

Embarrassed by their witnessing what had happened, she took a steadying breath. The tears were utterly gone, lost in wonder. "It's—it's different," she said, conscious that she was the first Master in existence who could possibly know sources carried a whisper of their previous owners. She searched herself, tasting the subtle distinctions of strength settling deep inside her mind. "It tastes like—book paste."

38

The wind lifted Alissa's hair, trying to tug it free of the copper-colored ribbon glinting in the sun. Smiling, she leaned against the railing of the *Albatross* and watched Hayden ferry Silla, Lodesh, and Connen-Neute from the island to the boat. Strell stood beside her. Alissa leaned to run a finger down his jawline. He had shaved off his beard, and she wasn't sure she liked it.

Her smile grew as he ran a hand through her hair, taking the copper-colored ribbon out and tucking it away. Alissa's hair billowed behind her. Beast didn't mind the touch, and for that Alissa was grateful. Her feral side's definition of bringing-to-ground didn't include small, random shows of affection as apparently feral rakus were not that subtle.

"Ready to go home?" Strell whispered in her ear, causing a chill to fill her from the inside out. Beast did take notice of that, and Alissa mollified her with a bitter thought that they were not going to roll about on the deck of the ship.

"Go home? In a way," she said as she remembered what he had asked.

"In a way?" Strell's eyes were wide in incredulity. His gaze flicked to her hand in its sling and back to her. "I would've thought you couldn't wait to leave."

She shifted her shoulders and gestured to the island. "It's warm. I like the water. There's lots of fish to eat."

He grunted as he turned back to the shoreline. "But it rains every day."

She made a face, turning as Captain Sholan raised his voice at Yar-Taw. The captain had become quite bold when dealing with Masters, deciding if they were going to eat him, they would, but he would not cower like a cur in the meantime. Apparently the water barrels Yar-Taw had constructed weren't up to the captain's standards.

Captain Sholan's final acceptance of Masters had happened this morning when Neugwin, Beso-Ran, and Connen-Neute rowed out shortly after she did and silently fixed a new boom to the tallest mast. Neugwin had fastened the rigging, Connen-Neute had fixed the hardware, and Beso-Ran had held it in place while standing armpit deep beside the boat in his raku form. Through it all, the captain had stood at his wheel and watched, his brow furrowed in thought. Alissa hadn't even known they had been making a new boom.

Later, she had seen Captain Sholan running a hand down the boom's length to gauge the strength of the dark, fragrant wood. She knew it was a well-appreciated gift, and could almost see his thoughts circling about the possibility of what else could be made out of the dense wood.

The sound of Hayden's oars pushing against the water came faintly over the wind and the cry of the gulls, and she turned back to the ocean. Silla and Connen-Neute could have flown over, but the captain understandably didn't like it when his boat nearly swamped every time a raku landed on it. She pushed away from the railing and made her way with Strell to where the ladder snaked over the side.

"Oh, here," Strell said as they crossed the deck. "You should probably have these back. I think the captain and Hayden would appreciate it, even if no one else does."

Alissa's gaze dropped to his hand as she recognized a faint jingle. "My bells!" she exclaimed; she had forgotten all about them.

"Not just your bells," he said softly as he pulled her ring out of a pocket.

"My ring!" she cried, then looked to see if Yar-Taw had

heard. "Oh, Strell," she said, her voice shaking as he strung it on her hair ribbon and put it around her neck. "Thank you. I thought I had lost it."

Strell gave her a quick squeeze, releasing her before Beast could take offense. "I went to find it right after making you something to eat yesterday. I would have gone sooner, but I couldn't leave you. Not until Talo-Toecan was with you and I knew you would be all right."

"Ashes," she breathed, her eyes bright with tears. "Thank you."

He said nothing, dabbing at her eyes with the hem of his sleeve. "Not a word," he said as he turned her to the railing and the upwelling noise of the rowboat's arrival. "We should tell Talo-Toecan what we did before we tell anyone else."

She glanced at Redal-Stan's watch hanging about his neck like a pendant. Nodding, she tucked her bells into her pocket to put about her ankle later. Her heart clenched as she looked to the rigging for Talon, but then she pushed her heartache away. She missed her, or him, or both.

"Alissa!" Silla cried as her ribbon-strewn head appeared over the railing. Strell offered the young woman a hand, and she found the deck safely. "How did you get out here before me?"

"I've been here since sunup," she said, returning the young woman's impromptu hug.

"Eager to get home?"

"I suppose." Alissa glanced at Strell. It would be nice to find a new pattern of days.

Connen-Neute was next, fidgeting as he took up an uneasy position beside Silla. "We're going to make the trip entirely by boat," he said as if expecting them to protest.

"Really?" Alissa glanced between them, wondering. "I'd have thought you would fly ahead with the rest."

Lodesh's fair head rose above the railing. "No," he said, answering her question. Smiling impishly, he vaulted over the railing to find the deck with a dancer's grace. "Captain Sholan needs a crew, so Connen-Neute volunteered to make the trip with us humans."

Alissa glanced at Silla. The young woman's influence was obvious. She wasn't strong enough to make the journey by wing. "Well," Alissa offered. "It isn't as if they're going to make the trip in one go either. That's why we're leaving now: to give them a place to rest halfway there."

Connen-Neute smiled at Alissa gratefully. Silla shifted a touch closer to him, and the rims of his ears reddened. Oblivious to Connen-Neute's fluster, Silla put her hand on his shoulder to balance herself as she leaned over the railing to see Hayden struggling with the packs in the dinghy. "And Neugwin said I shouldn't see the Hold until they have a chance to put it in order," Silla said, her eyes on the waves slapping the boat.

Lodesh grinned. "I'm sure she'll drag all the furniture out of the annexes," he said.

"And restock the pantry," Strell said.

"And weed the gardens . . ." Alissa moaned, glad she was going the long way.

"And she'll probably want the rugs freshly beaten, too," Connen-Neute added sourly, causing Alissa to wonder how much of his desire to crew was to avoid a spring-cleaning.

As one, they sighed, clearly smug in having nothing to do for the next few weeks but haul on ropes and take direction from a sullen captain instead of a demanding teacher.

The cold shadow of wings covered them, and Alissa squinted up to see Useless spiraling about the boat in wide circles. The captain's gaze rose from his discussion with Yar-Taw. "I said no landin' on my boat!" he shouted. Alissa held her broken hand against her chest in alarm as Useless back-winged, miraculously missing the rigging. He vanished into mist a good two man lengths above the deck, dropping to land in a comfortable-looking crouch as a man.

"Ashes," she whispered, and Connen-Neute made a small sound of agreement.

"You haven't seen the half of what he can do," the young Master said as he edged to make room for him in their circle. Captain Sholan grimaced and turned back to Yar-Taw, gesturing at the barrels of water and demanding six more.

"Come to say good-bye?" Lodesh said, squinting at Useless past the rim of his hat.

"No." Useless tightened his black sash. "One flight across the ocean is enough. I'm taking up Captain Sholan's offer to serve as crew. Besides," he grumbled, "if I go with the rest of them, Neugwin will have me putting new slates on the roof before the end of the month."

Alissa's first feeling of delight hesitated. Useless as crew? She glanced worriedly at Silla. Seeing their disbelieving looks, Useless frowned. "Masters can see the wind, Alissa. It flows over a sail exactly as it flows over wing canvas." He harrumphed. "I can lift a sail and navigate a straight tack better than our good captain. And someone has to keep an eye on you."

She smiled at that. Her pack came arching over the railing, followed shortly by a substantial basket of dried fruit. Hayden's head poked above the railing, his brow furrowed for having to unload the rowboat by himself, no doubt. He scowled at Lodesh and Strell, then shouted across the deck, "Hoy, Captain! Where do Alissa and the piper's things get stowed?"

Busy with Yar-Taw, the captain didn't look up. "Put them in the bow bunk!" he exclaimed. "I don't want to listen to them carryin' on when I'm on night watch. If I had wanted to be a nuptial boat, I would'a painted her white. Damn fool business this is."

His grumblings tapered off into half-heard complaints. Alissa froze. They had forgotten to tell the captain to keep quiet. Eyes wide, she held her breath, afraid to look up as Useless took a hasty breath. "Alissa?" he drawled.

Licking her lips, she glanced up at him and away. She couldn't look at Lodesh, but his boots weren't moving. Wincing, she fidgeted with the hem of her sling. "Uh . . ."

Silla took her hand and pulled Alissa to face her. "You didn't!" the young woman cried, her eyes alight with mischief and delight.

"We did," Strell said, and Alissa looked up in relief as he moved to stand beside her. He very carefully put a slow arm about her waist and pulled her close.

Beast snapped awake. *"You touch him,"* Alissa threatened, *"and I will keep us out of the sky for the entirety of the trip."* Beast restrained herself with soft mutterings.

Yar-Taw stormed across the deck. "We forbade it!" he shouted, then glanced at Useless as if remembering he wasn't the ranking male Master anymore.

Guilt, and perhaps shame, kept Alissa from looking at Useless. She couldn't bear his disapproval. Besides, it had been done four ways from springtime and couldn't be reversed. Useless straightened, and she cringed. *Here it comes,* she thought to herself.

"Well, that's where you made your first mistake," Useless said, and she jerked her attention up at the wry humor in his voice. "Telling Alissa she can't do something will insure she will do nothing but that." He smiled, his white eyebrows arched. "Nautical vows?" he said dryly, glancing at the captain as he came to direct Hayden where to put the rest of the cargo.

"Took Hayden two days to get the sand off the deck," the captain grumbled as he passed them. "I warned him. I warn them all. But they never listen. Never," he said, his voice going faint as he stomped to his quarters with a small, carefully wrapped package.

"Coastal," Strell said, his voice even and calm as he took a firm stance. "We also exchanged vows from the plains, foothills, and those of the Hold, too."

"Got them all, eh?" Useless cocked his head as he looked at her and Strell's rings with a new understanding. Alissa wondered at his attitude. She had thought he would be furious. She was surprised to find Lodesh grinning as if it were a grand jest as well. Her eyes narrowed. Somehow Lodesh knew they hadn't been able to consummate their marriage, and his amusement irritated her, vastly overshadowing her embarrassment.

"You couldn't exchange raku vows," Yar-Taw said. His face was red, and he looked a mix between annoyance and disgust. "He can't make a field, much less a ward of light."

A half smile came over Strell. "I made a sphere of light. It was made of glass and glowed with burning oil, but Connen-Neute seemed to think it was sufficient."

Yar-Taw's eyes narrowed. "Wolves take it. A witness," he muttered, giving Connen-Neute a dark look. "The marriage can't stand," Yar-Taw said. "The vows should be annulled."

"Annulled!" Alissa cried, suddenly afraid. "You can't! It's done!"

"He has no tracings," Yar-Taw asserted. "That's why we forbade it in the first place."

Useless reached out, and Alissa jumped as he put a long hand on her shoulder. "What do you care what she does?" he intoned, the amusement in his voice replaced by a dark threat. "You already let Keribdis kill her once. I'd say that removes any claim the Hold might ever have had on her. She deserves a fifty-year sabbatical at least for that. Besides, as my student, she doesn't need anyone's permission but mine."

"But—" Yar-Taw stammered.

"All I need to know," Useless said as he turned to Strell, "is what, under the ash-ridden moon, you think gave you the right to marry her, Piper."

Strell grinned. He confidently ran a finger under the ribbon Alissa's wedding ring was laced upon, and Useless's eyes crinkled as if in pain. "Her mother's?" Useless asked, and Strell nodded. "I had forgotten about that," Useless added, his voice strained. "Fine. Providing you can consummate the marriage within the year, the vows stand." Ignoring Yar-Taw's protests, he gave her a wry look. Alissa felt a stab of worry. Had he talked to Lodesh or come to the same conclusion by himself that they were having trouble?

"Year?" Silla whispered, looking up at Connen-Neute in confusion.

"I'll tell you later," Connen-Neute said, the rims of his ears reddening.

Still, Yar-Taw shook his head. "Talo-Toecan," he persisted. "He's not a Master. He's hardly a commoner. He won't live but a few decades more. What kind of a life is that?"

Alissa tensed, dismayed that her private heartache be displayed so blatantly. Useless's grip on her shoulder tightened. It wasn't fair, she thought. But if a few decades were all she had, then a few decades was what she would take. She'd deal with the pain later. She wouldn't let it spoil her time with Strell. Still, her throat tightened, and she blinked to keep the tears from showing.

"She is *my* student! She has *my* permission!" Useless exclaimed, as if reaching his limit. Alissa blinked, shocked out of her misery. "He can read our script," Useless continued. "Trace his lineage back to the Warden line. He knows our secrets, including how a Master can come from a human, and he rescued me from the holden while *you* were on an ash-ridden holiday. We had better give him something to keep his mouth shut or kill him."

Alissa gasped, and Useless added, "And none of you are laying a thought on my musician." He held Yar-Taw's gaze, his eyes fiercely determined. Alissa shivered, feeling the force behind his stare, glad he wasn't looking at her. "I suggest we install Strell Hirdune as the Warden of Ese' Nawoer," Useless added. "Give him a visible show of his status."

There was a heartbeat of silence. Alissa's mouth dropped open. She looked first to Strell—who appeared as shocked as she was—then to Lodesh. The elegantly dressed Keeper slowly backed away. His face was utterly blank. Not looking at anyone, he spun on a slow heel and vanished belowdecks. Her breath caught in dismay. They couldn't do that to Lodesh. It was all he had left.

"No," she said, pulling the hair from her face. "Lodesh is the Warden. I don't care that you struck the title from him. Lodesh is the Warden." But her protests went unheard.

Strell took her elbow as Yar-Taw began talking in persuasive, pleading tones. Other rakus were flying in from all over the island. It looked like an impromptu meeting was going to take place. "Don't worry," Strell whispered. "They won't make me the Warden. I don't want it, and I'd make a poor leader for a city of ghosts, even if I do see them now in my sleep." He shuddered, trying to disguise it as he moved her to the back of the boat. "I think Talo-Toecan is asking for the stars so they will be satisfied to give him the moon. There isn't even a city anymore. The Warden position is only a bargaining point."

Alissa's steps were slow and reluctant as Strell led her away. She glanced behind them, unsure if they should be leaving. Useless gave her a slow smile over his shoulder, then turned back as the Masters began landing in the water to cluster before the *Albatross* like ducklings about their mother. He stood at the railing as if it were a pulpit, his hands raised in placation and his voice soothing. Silla and Connen-Neute stood beside him. They looked happy and content, fully cognizant they were in a position where their opinions would be heard despite their youth.

Alissa leaned back against the railing of the boat as her

feeling of unease built. "We met his stipulations," she said slowly. "But he gave in awfully easily." She squinted at Strell. "I thought he would be more angry than that."

Smiling, Strell tucked a strand of hair from her eyes. "I think he wants you to have a little joy, Alissa. You never really had a raku childhood. Perhaps that's how he's looking at it."

She frowned. "I don't like the idea they think of this as a spring love, a piddling dalliance until I—I grow up!" she finished fiercely.

His smile was sad. "It's not a dalliance to me, Alissa. It's a lifetime. You will never grow old to me, always as beautiful as you are today. How could I be that lucky?"

She could say nothing. Miserable, she turned back to the water. And all of this hinged on whether they could teach Beast what love meant.

Strell sighed as he turned with her. "So, Alissa," he said as he pulled her closer. "Which side of the bed do you want?"

"The side that you're on," she whispered, wiping the last of her tears away.

39

Talo-Toecan's eyes were closed as he held the wheel. The sun was well down, and not even the light of the moon stained the back of his eyelids. Standing on the deck of the *Albatross* with the water thrumming under his feet and the wind doing the same in the sails, he felt the peace instilled by the forces running through him. Motion. He liked to be in motion. And this blending of wind and wave was intriguing, especially at night. Flying only used one elemental force. Sailing used two. It added a delightful sensation to the mix.

But while the boat made a connection between the two dissimilar forces, it also added a large measure of restraint upon his direction. Perhaps he might take a decade or two to study it further, somehow find a way to use the wind and water to a greater extent. It might be only a different cut of sail or arc of hull that would increase the span of direction or speed.

His eyes opened at the thought that Alissa was much like the *Albatross*. She, too, had forged a connection between two dissimilar forces: the feral and the sane. Her range of motion was greater than theirs, and she was able to do much that they couldn't. He wondered if it would ultimately be worth the risk.

A wry smile came over him as Strell and Alissa excused themselves from Connen-Neute's late dice game. He didn't watch as they headed down the fore hatch together. He couldn't bring himself to. The boat was too small for his liking. Especially at night.

Actually, he mused as the sound of their voices grew muffled and vanished, Alissa had only exchanged one set of problems for another. Having a feral consciousness too close apparently had a drawback—or two.

A faint tug of unease pulled his gaze to Lodesh, standing at the railing and staring at nothing. The Keeper seemed accepting of Alissa's choice, saying, when Talo-Toecan questioned him, that he believed because Strell and Alissa would never be able to maintain a true marital relationship, she would ultimately turn to him. But it still had to be difficult.

Talo-Toecan looked from Lodesh's hunched back to Connen-Neute. The young Master had put his dice away to fall into a ramrod-straight, meditative stance right where he had been sitting against the mast. He would probably be there all night, making Hayden nervous and edgy. Silla had vanished belowdecks. Everyone was settling in for the night. High time he stop procrastinating and take care of his last task.

A small scuff at the hatch behind Talo-Toecan drew his attention over his shoulder. "Captain," he said shortly, taking a firmer stance at the wheel.

"Master Talo-Toecan," Captain Sholan responded as he stood beside him. The man followed Talo-Toecan's gaze up to the night-lost top of the mast. "You sail a straight tack," the man said. "Do you have any nephews who need a profession?"

Talo-Toecan smiled, releasing the wheel and taking several steps to the side as the captain reached for it. "Only Connen-Neute, and his path is already charted."

Captain Sholan grunted, settling himself into a relaxed tautness as he gripped the wheel. The wind held steady, but Talo-Toecan felt the boat slow under the captain's touch. He looked up at the mast again, estimating his chances of tangling the rigging if he jumped from the top.

"Leaving?" the captain said sourly, apparently having guessed why Talo-Toecan was eyeing the sails. "Be back by sunrise, or I dock your pay, same as if you're too drunk to crew."

A smile came over Talo-Toecan. He hadn't been under anyone's constraints for five centuries. Real or imagined. "I have to finish something," he said softly. "We're far enough away that—" He hesitated. "I wanted to be far enough away that not even Alissa could hear an echo. This isn't her argument to finish. She'd try to convince me to let sleeping rakus lie, and I can't do that anymore. Keribdis is my wife. I should be the one to do it."

"Aye," the captain said, his gaze on the bow where Alissa and Strell had gone. "I know about unhappy wives. I think those two will have better luck than we had, eh? They seem to have a knack for it. Bringing out the best in each other, I mean." He sighed, and Talo-Toecan realized that though their weaker kin had a shorter span, they loved as deeply. Perhaps more so.

Talo-Toecan's shoulders lifted and fell. He looked up to find Connen-Neute watching him with solemn, knowing eyes. "I'll be back before dawn," he muttered to the captain. Saying nothing to Connen-Neute, he went to the railing. Levering himself onto it, he dove cleanly into the waves, enjoying the warmth of the water. He shifted before finding the surface. With some surprise, he felt an odd, not uncomfortable surge from his source as it bound the extra energy it found in breaking down the small amount of salt water around him.

He bobbed to the surface as a raku. It would be difficult to get into the air, but easier than trying to explain why he had tangled himself in the rigging and swamped the boat. His heart heavy, he shook his wings free of water and forced himself into the air and among the stars.

Again, his eyes closed as he rode the wind, feeling the similarities and differences from standing on deck of the *Albatross*. All too soon the outline of the island showed a darker patch against the water and sky. Faint tugs on his awareness gave hints to the preparations the conclave was making below. They wouldn't leave for several weeks, but would still arrive at the Hold nearly that same span of time ahead of those on the *Albatross*. Talo-Toecan thought distancing the youngest members of the Hold from the rest would be a good thing. Too many personalities had been dominated for too long. They needed time alone to realize who they could become.

His thoughts were despondent as he ran a faint, very tentative search. Guilt, and an even older emotion of betrayal, surged through him as he found her on the island at the end of the chain. A large fire winked and flickered on the widest cove, and it was here that he landed, shifting into his human guise.

She stood before the flames, posing so that the amber light flickered against her face and hid the faint lines. Her hair was bound in ribbons. He had given them all to her: signs of his love, tokens of his desire to understand her. His muscles tensed as he steeled himself against her wiles. It had been so long. And he had desperately wanted them to find common ground.

"You're late," she said, hitting the two syllables with precision.

"I didn't want to come."

She sniffed, her eyebrows arched mockingly. "I can see why. You ruined her, Talo. She was supposed to be mine, and you ruined her."

His resolve hardened. "She was supposed to be everyone's and entirely herself."

There was a twinge on his thoughts as she made a cushion. Folding herself gracefully, she sat down. "You gave her almost everything," she accused. "How were you expecting me to mold her into something we could use when there was nothing left to force her obedience with?"

"I thought you were dead." The words came from him unbidden, and he belatedly decided there was no harm in having said them. He stood with his arms crossed, watching her features shift in the upwellings of heat from the fire between them. "And Alissa needed a Master's repertoire of skills to survive."

Keribdis's face twisted, the high cheekbones he had once thought beautiful making her look severe. "All the skills you gave her did her no good," she said, satisfaction permeating her as she tossed her head and touched her ribbons as if to be sure they were in place.

Talo-Toecan's stomach clenched. She didn't care. The woman thought Alissa was dead. She didn't care she had torn Alissa's source from her soul and left her for dead. Keribdis had more empathy for her long-dead horse than she did for Alissa. "You think so little of her," he said with a harsh satisfaction. "Have you searched out her presence lately?"

"She's dead," Keribdis stated, her lips pressing tightly together.

Talo-Toecan willed his hands to stop trembling. How could he have ever loved her? Had she changed so much, or had he been blind? "Look for her," he said.

Keribdis's gaze cleared. Wide-eyed, she stared at him. "On the water? She's alive?" Then she stiffened. "Silla is with her!"

She rocked forward to rise. Talo-Toecan started. Once he moved, his body took over. Striding around the fire, he put a heavy hand on her shoulder and forced her down. He wouldn't let her take to the air. He would be unable to carry out the Hold's justice if they flew.

"Alissa is alive. Yes," he all but hissed, an unexpected satisfaction jarring him when her face turned to his went startled. "Yar-Taw gave me the memory of what happened. She bested you in the air. She bested you with words in front of the conclave. You tried to kill her, knowing she was stronger of will than you and therefore could force you to obey our laws."

Keribdis's gaze was bewildered. "She has no source," she said, mystified. "How can she still be alive—" Then her confusion vanished. Talo-Toecan could almost see the winds of her thought shifting her path. "She's an abomination, Talo. How could you presume that you alone could manage a transeunt's first transition to raku?"

"She came to the Hold. You were gone. The choice wasn't mine," he said flatly.

"You couldn't even tell she had retained her feral consciousness!" Keribdis berated. "She has a beast in her thoughts waiting for the chance to kill us all, destroy our way of life!"

"So do you," he said, giving her shoulder a small push as he stepped from her in disgust.

"You maggot!" she shouted, her face going white. "I do not have a—a *beast* in my thoughts. I am not an animal! *She* is a worthless guttersnipe of a human. A mistake. And you will let her drag us down to wallow where she is."

Heart pounding, Talo-Toecan forced himself to take a step away from her. "Alissa is right," he said, hearing his voice tremble. His head hurt, and his arms ached from keeping them unmoving. There was no compassion in her anymore. It was gone, driven away by fear. "She's right. She's right in her theories, and I think you know it."

"She poisoned you, too," Keribdis said, her voice rife with scorn. "It doesn't matter," she gloated. "Your little dress-up doll has no source. She won't survive the trip back across the ocean. It's a long way. Too long to live without hope. She'll go insane from the loss." Keribdis made a cruel-sounding laugh. "No, that's right. She already is insane."

Talo-Toecan tensed. He wanted to shout that she was wrong. That he loved her but that she was wrong to treat their weaker kin as if they were sheep. That he couldn't look the other way again. That he was here to bring her to justice. That he was sorry. That he was angry. That she had caused more pain and suffering than a thousand winters, and why couldn't she be different? A score of things needed to be said, but what fell from his lips was simply, "She bested you. She has Redal-Stan's source."

There was a heartbeat of silence. "Redal-Stan—"

He pulled his eyes up to her, feeling his gaze harden. "I'm not going to waste my breath telling you how. I didn't come here to give you answers. I came to carry out a judgment."

Sitting on her cushion before her overindulgent fire, Keribdis went white. Now there was the barest hint of fear, Talo-Toecan thought. Only now, knowing he hadn't come to forgive her, was there a glimmer of emotion. "You wouldn't," she whispered. "You can't."

He said nothing. Part of him buried under his resolve and anger was crying no. He sealed it off.

"You can't!" she exclaimed again frantically. "I'm your wife!"

His breath came in a ragged sound, and he held it. "I can't look the other way anymore, Keribdis," he finally said. "You're hurting too many people."

"They're just humans!" she protested.

"That doesn't make it right," he said as his faint hope she might be repentant died. "The divided groups of people are mixing. The alleles have escaped. We're no longer in control. We shouldn't be. Over the next few centuries, we're going to be up to our wing tips in Keepers and transeunts, not to mention the shadufs and septhamas. We won't have time for your games."

"Games!" she shouted, her cheeks spotted with red.

"I'm asking you to stay here." He met her eyes, despondent. "Forevon."

Her jaw clenched, and she stiffened. Looking magnificent, she stood. "I won't!"

She vanished in a gray mist. He stumbled back as she reappeared in her raku form. The fire glowed against her, making her golden and young again. *"I'm done with this,"* she thought savagely, crouched for flight. *"You're going to ruin everything. Everything! You never cared about me. You only cared about your precious Keepers and your Hold!"*

Talo-Toecan's guilt was black and bitter even before he acted. She'd never understood. How could she be so brilliant, yet be so blind? "Keribdis," he pleaded. "Please. Just tell me you'll stay here."

She snaked her neck down, breathing on him. *"I'll let you in on a secret everyone but you seems to know, Talo. We are nothing like them! Humans are fodder. Raw materials. They're not our equals. Not even our transeunts!"* She raised her head to look toward the island where the rest of the conclave was. *"I'm taking them home. We're going back to the old ways. We will take back the foothills and the plains. The humans should never have been allowed past the coast. The Hold will be taken apart and thrown over the cliff, and you!"* She shouted the word into his thoughts. *"You will never—never—be taken seriously again. Your idea of equality is worthless tripe. The last five decades prove it!"*

Talo-Toecan was riveted by her magnificent fury. She was

beautiful when she was impassioned, and perchance that was why he hadn't stopped her sooner. Some of this was his fault. Most, probably. *"I'm sorry, Keribdis,"* he whispered, caressing her thoughts one last time.

She drew back in surprise, and he struck.

Her body stiffened as he dove deep into her thoughts, taking advantage of her shock to slip past her defenses. He saw her fear that she had lost the grip she maintained on the conclave. He pitied her terror that she might not be superior to humanity, then recoiled at her frantic need to keep them ignorant to maintain her self-worth. His heart clenched in grief at her needless jealousy of him for his easy companionship with humans, and he wept at her loss of hope that he might still love her. And somewhere, deep within her, almost lost amongst her fears and the terrible needs those fears demanded be met, he found her joy of flight.

With a savage vengeance, he fastened on that. Pushing everything else away, he gave it room to grow, to expand. Her joy flickered, seeming to hesitate. Stark terror filled him, and he recoiled as he realized Alissa was entirely right.

Keribdis's feral consciousness had been curled up about that joy as if it were a starveling curled about a dry crust of bread. As he watched in a horrible fascination, her feral consciousness saw him. For an instant, he stared at the face of instinct. Then it exploded, pushing him from Keribdis's thoughts as it struggled to be free.

Again before the fire, he reeled backward, falling. Keribdis towered above him, straining as if chained to the ground. She screamed aloud and in his thoughts. Staring at her with his hands pressed to his ears, he realized he had done it. Horror twisted his stomach, and he cried her name in heartache. She was feral. It couldn't be undone.

The raku that had once been his wife shrieked, rising up on her haunches with her wings spread wide. The firelight enveloped her in an unreal glow. Talo-Toecan scrambled to his feet. "I freed you!" he shouted, knowing her feral consciousness would understand. "I freed you. Go!"

And the raku went. The force of her single wing beat scattered the fire. Talo-Toecan covered his face, quickly patting at his trousers where an ember had landed. When he looked up in the new darkness, she was gone.

For a moment, he listened. He sent a thought after her to find nothing.

Slumping to the cooling sand, he put his head in his hands and wept.

40

"Love is not anything like dominance," Strell was saying, his resonant voice swirling into Alissa's dream of hoeing beets like cream through tea.

"You're mistaken. It is. Everything I've seen says so," Alissa heard her voice say, her tone unusually precise. In her dream, she straightened from her work and leaned on the mirth-wood handle. Someone was coming over the field. They were little more than a blurry shadow, and she wondered who it was. "This is too hard," she found herself saying, and her dream shattered as she realized Beast was speaking directly to Strell. Startled, Alissa jerked awake.

She found herself sitting upright on their small V-shaped bunk. The underside of the top deck was a handbreadth above her head, and a soft glow filled the low-ceilinged cabin from a gimballed oil lamp. A wisp of fright from Beast went through her, and Alissa wasn't surprised to find Beast had jammed herself against the wall. Alissa clutched for a hold with her good hand as the bow of the boat rose and dropped with a thick whoosh of water.

Within an arm's length, but as far from her as the small cabin would allow, was Strell. He watched her carefully from the other side of the bunk. His hair was mussed, and his nightshirt was in disarray. He looked softer, gentler. She liked it. "Why are you talking to me?" she said, confused. "I was asleep."

"I was talking to Beast." His brow pinched. "She said she didn't think you'd mind."

"I don't." *Sort of,* she added silently. "What happened?"

"The boat shifted tack. You rolled into me. I put my arm around you. Beast woke up."

Alissa's eyes widened, and she searched his face for any sign of pain. "Did I hit you?"

He smiled. "No. I told you I loved you, and Beast decided she would rather talk. It was either I talk to her or the ghost of that sailor who died hitting the deck above us."

She went uneasy, not sure if he were joking or not. Seeing her wide eyes, he added, "I think I frightened Beast. I'm sorry."

Concerned, Alissa searched her thoughts to find Beast in the unusual state of bewilderment. *"Beast? What's the matter?"* Alissa asked.

Slowly her second consciousness took shape. *"It can't be true, what he says."*

Alissa looked at Strell. Her lips pursed, not liking to see Beast's usual confidence shattered. "What did you say to her?" she asked again.

"You don't know?" he asked in surprise.

"I told you I was asleep."

His brow furrowed, and he stretched his long legs. His bare toes brushed against her leg in passing, and she pulled her leg closer to herself. Yes, they were married, but still . . .

Strell ran a hand over the stubble on his chin. "I—ah—told her I loved her as I loved you. See, we were discussing the difference between love and lust. She seems to equate the two, which may account for . . ." He shrugged, wincing.

Alissa's face pulled into a sour expression. Reaching to tug the blankets more securely over her bare feet, she paused in thought. A feeling of titillation, of daring, set her fingertips tingling. "Well . . ." she said as she put the back of her hand to her warming cheeks. "If Beast thinks love is dominance, perhaps we're going about this the wrong way."

Strell's face went slack. "What do you mean?"

She gave him a wicked half smile. "Hold still," she said, scooting across the V-shaped bed. Her broken hand hurt out of its sling, and it was awkward holding it close to her.

He put out a protesting hand. "Wait. You're going to hit me again."

"No, I won't," she protested as she knelt beside him on the bed.

"You will!"

His eyes were wide in trepidation, and she felt a wash of bother go through her. "Hold still . . ." she grumbled, edging closer. "I'm just going to kiss you."

"No. Alissa, wait!" he exclaimed as she put her arms about his neck and pressed close.

Their lips touched. The fingers of her left hand grasped his hair at the back of his neck, overriding the pain of using them. "Mumph!" he mumbled in warning as she held him unmoving and punched him in the stomach with her good hand.

Strell grunted in pain, and she let go. "Oh, Strell!" she cried, almost beside herself with frustration and guilt. "I'm sorry! I thought it would work. I thought if I was the one who—"

"'S all right," he said, his face red. "I was expecting it." Eyes watering, he glanced up at her. "Hounds, it was almost worth it."

She miserably put herself back in her corner, shamed. At least he wasn't gasping for air. "I'm sorry," she whispered, her broken hand throbbing with pain. "I thought it would work."

"I, uh, am going to get some air." Strell carefully edged the to the end of the bunk and the tiny floor space the cabin had just before the door. "I'll be right back."

She said nothing, knowing air was not the reason he was leaving.

Strell jammed his feet into his boots. Not looking at her, he fumbled at the door and gently closed it behind him. The awkward clumps of his unlaced boots grew distant, and she heard him stumble under a wave.

Alissa looked about their small room and tried not to cry. *"What's wrong with you, Beast?"* she accused. *"Why can't you understand?"*

"Why can't you fly?" Beast said sourly.

Alissa uncurled herself, searching Beast's emotions, feeling her feral side's honest desire to grasp the concept of love. Beast knew she was lacking something and truly wanted to understand. It just wasn't in her. Just as it wasn't in Alissa to understand and trust the wind.

"Lodesh is going to laugh at us," Alissa thought bitterly, her motions sharp as she arranged the bedclothes with one hand. *"He's going to laugh and laugh, and when Strell dies, he's going to try to bring us to ground as well."*

"I'll hit him, too," Beast said.

"Is that so?" Alissa turned sullen. *"In the meantime, he's going to laugh at us. If you would just trust him . . ."* she pleaded.

Beast's feeling of shared dislike of being laughed at vanished. *"I'm trying,"* she protested. *"Just as you try to trust the wind. I think we're too far apart."*

Alissa settled herself cross-legged at the very center of the bed where the ceiling was the highest. The boat's motion had eased into a gentle rocking, and Alissa shivered. *"I want to understand,"* Beast whispered. *"He said he loved me, but I don't know what that means. I can't imagine why you will allow him to bring you to ground. Love must be—a very strong reason?"*

A tremor went through their shared body. *"Tell me,"* Beast demanded suddenly. *"Tell me what love is. I'll understand this time."*

Alissa's shoulders shifted in discouragement. How could she explain? It was a lifetime of memories, of feelings. Soft nuances, mixed with hopes and desires. Compassion, empathy. A willingness to trust absolutely with no regard for safety. Reckless abandonment. It wasn't possible to simply tell her.

"Show me how to trust the wind," Alissa thought glumly, and she felt Beast falter.

"I can't," her feral consciousness whispered. *"You just do—or do not."*

"And that's what love is," Alissa said, miserable. *"You just do."*

"Perhaps," Beast said, sounding frightened. *"Perhaps if we let our thoughts mingle as one, I could show you how I trust the wind. And you could show me love."*

Alissa balked. *"You mean like pickabacking?"* she thought, and she felt Beast's agreement. *"Aren't we already doing that?"*

"Yes," Beast agreed. *"But what if instead of sharing our thoughts we . . . let them mix?"*

Alarm went through Alissa. *"Redal-Stan said not to. We might hate each other!"*

"I can't hate you," Beast said, sounding almost scornful. *"I am you. You already know my thoughts and fears. I know yours. Where's the risk in that?"*

Alissa's fright eased. Let go completely? She didn't know if she could.

"I trust you," Beast said, shaming Alissa into a hesitant agreement.

Procrastinating, Alissa looked around her. Everything was as it should be. Her and Strell's gear was jammed into the tiny shelves. The light flickered from the lamp to shift the shadows in time with the boat's motion. Unreasonably cold in the balmy night, she pulled the covers around her. Beast patiently waited.

Embarrassed at her hesitancy, Alissa snatched up a pillow. She clutched it between her broken hand and herself as she closed her eyes and took three breaths, willing herself into a light trance. A stab of anticipation shivered through them as Beast's presence grew substantial in her thoughts. Alissa hadn't been this acutely conscious of Beast in a long time. Fidgeting, Alissa lowered her defenses, feeling Beast do the same. A fear not hers washed through Alissa. Startled, she pulled back and opened her eyes.

Beast grew impatient. *"It's only my fear,"* Beast thought as Alissa glanced over the quiet room. *"Taste it, then let it go."*

"Taste it," Alissa grumbled, cautiously allowing Beast's fear to brush the edges of her awareness. Alissa let it seep through her as if she were slipping into a cold stream. Slowly their fears eased to permit more sophisticated emotions to flow between them—a wary anticipation from Alissa and an eager curiosity from Beast.

Alissa's pulse pounded. Fear was one of Beast's rarer emotions. Her feral side was more inclined to wild states of enthusiasm. That Beast's high passions might surge through

Alissa as if they were her own was frightening. Her stomach clenched, and anticipation set her fingertips trembling. Again, she closed her eyes, allowing Beast's eagerness to pull them unsettlingly deep within themselves. With a rash quickness, Alissa consigned herself completely to Beast's thoughts.

An unexpected, almost unbearable rise of feeling went through her, and she tensed. Beast's emotions were stark and shockingly brutal in their strength, not having been couched with the self-imposed shackles of decorum Alissa bound herself with. She felt her lungs heave with a ragged gasp as Beast's emotions poured through her like a raging torrent through a narrow pass.

Stunned at the magnitude of Beast's thoughts, it took Alissa a moment to realize Beast was afraid of losing the wind. Only now did Alissa see why Beast wouldn't allow herself to be grounded. Beast truly lived to fly. Her joy was in motion. She existed for the now, and only for the now. She had little comprehension of tomorrow. It was both her strength and downfall.

That is why she can't understand love, Alissa realized with a surge of compassion. One had to have a grasp of the future—and the hope that springs from it—to understand love. A pang went through Alissa as she realized Beast would never understand. She couldn't.

"I can't teach you, and you can't teach me," Alissa said, her sorrow weighing so heavily, she had to force her lungs to move.

"Then we failed," Beast whispered.

Beast's disappointment melted into Alissa's, doubling it. It was almost crippling. *"No!"* Alissa exclaimed. *"There has to be a way. We're still separate. If we can become closer, then you'll have to understand!"*

Refusing to give up, she dove into Beast's thoughts. Wild emotion seemed to buffet her. Panicking, Alissa forced herself deeper into the passion and wild independence that made up Beast. Beast's fierce desire to fly, her willful freedom, and the trust Beast held in the wind, all swept through Alissa—leaving her intact. It hadn't worked.

She couldn't make the jump. Balancing on the cusp, she was unable to lose herself, to make their thoughts one. Bad things happened when she lost control of her will, and she was afraid to let go of herself, even for an instant.

Alissa's will collapsed in a disconsolate heap surrounded by Beast's thoughts. They seemed strong compared to Alissa's shallow emotions of self-pity. Disappointment coursed through Alissa, unshared by Beast. Alissa would have nothing, cursed with a half-life.

"I can't," Alissa said, hopelessness filling her. *"I can't let go of my will."*

"I can," Beast said. *"I do it every time I fly."*

Alissa's tension slammed back into her. *"Beast? Wait!"* she cried, seeing Beast's intent. If Alissa couldn't do it, then there was a reason. *"It's too close a mixing. I don't think we will be able to separate again. It will kill you!"*

"But he said he loved me. I want to understand," Beast said, and with no fear, no thought of tomorrow, Beast willfully, independently, and passionately, dissolved her being into Alissa's.

"No!" Alissa cried.

Beast's violent, chaotic thoughts blew out like a candle. Alissa stiffened as the black shadow from her absence seemed to pass through her. Silver and icy, it found the edges of her awareness and eased into the corners of her being. Alissa gasped in wonder as an unexpected longing to be free filled her. It was accompanied by a sublime confidence in knowing she was. The twin emotions rose to become everything. Still they multiplied until Alissa felt as if she was going to pass out. She couldn't breathe. She couldn't cry out.

Then, as unexpectedly as they came, the wild emotions collapsed inward to something familiar she could exist with.

Alissa took a shuddering breath, snapping out of her trance with a suddenness that left her shaking. A crushing heartache took her as she hunched gasping over her pillow. What had she done? Instead of finding understanding, she had destroyed Beast! The place where her feral consciousness had rested was empty. There were no thoughts in her mind but her own.

Loss crashed over her, and Alissa curled in on the pillow still in her grip. Rocking back and forth, she shoved the pillow against her so no one would hear her cry. Beast was dead. It was her fault. She should have stopped her. With a bitter pain, Alissa realized Beast had understood love. She had understood it all along.

"Alissa?" came Strell's careful call from the other side of the door followed by a light tapping. "I brought us something to eat."

"Go away!" she said, hearing a hiccup. She turned to the wall as the door opened.

"Oh, Alissa," Strell said softly, his voice thick with compassion. "It's all right. We'll figure this out. And I was expecting it. You didn't hurt me." She heard a clatter as he set his plate of food down. It was followed by the sound of his hand slapping his middle. "See? Tight as a plainsman's tent rope!"

"I took her over," Alissa sobbed. "Beast is gone. She wanted to understand love, and she killed herself to do it."

Strell's breath came in a quick intake of understanding. For a heartbeat there was nothing, then Strell whispered, "Sh-h-h-h." She felt the bed shift, and the last of her resolve melted as his arm went around her. The scent of hot sand was familiar and comforting. "Hush," he soothed as she wept all the harder. "It's going to be all right."

"It isn't!" Alissa wailed. "She's gone! I promised I'd never hurt her, and she's gone!" Wiping her eyes, she hesitated. Her hands seemed wrong, but she couldn't tell why. The one was broken, but that wasn't it. Blinking the tears away, she looked up. The heat from the oil lamp streamed upward in a mist of blue, pooling at the top of the small cabin like bubbles under ice. The sound of the boat's timbers groaning seemed louder but soothing.

In wonder, she turned to Strell. Her breath caught. He was different: fiercely independent but stronger for having bound his independence with hers. She could see it so clearly it was a feature almost as much as his softly curling hair and his bent nose. He wasn't trying to ground her, he was trying to free her. "Strell?" she questioned, afraid.

He stiffened, pulling from her. "You sound like Beast," he said.

From the cradle his arms made about her, she searched her feelings, recognizing his acceptance of her—of everything about her—and that he loved her. And she understood what that love was. Her eyes closed as she heard the wind in the rigging. A keen pain went through her as she understood what the wind was, too. She hadn't destroyed Beast. Beast had blended herself back into her. They were one. As they should have been before.

"Alissa? It is you, isn't it?" Strell questioned, and she met his eyes. His face went ashen. "Wolves," he swore, tilting her chin so that the light fell upon her face. "Alissa. Your eyes . . . They're gold!"

41

L odesh stood on the dew-wet deck with the wheel in his grip. The boat was entirely in his hands as Talo-Toecan had yet to return, and the captain was still asleep. Connen-Neute and Silla were somewhere above the predawn fog having what a red-faced Connen-Neute had called "flying practice." The sky might be clear far above them, but here, it was foggy. It made Lodesh uncomfortable—the thick, cloying gray. It seemed a personification of his awareness of what had been going on belowdecks.

A frown, unusual and not welcome, passed over Lodesh. He had been at the wheel almost the entire night, part from crewing duties, part from personal preference. He didn't want to be belowdecks. Not tonight. Perhaps never again. It had been a very quiet evening. Strell had emerged from his cabin shortly after he and Alissa had retired, claiming to be looking for something to eat. Even worse, he had come out again a few hours later looking for more. The reasons might be many, but Lodesh had a very uneasy feeling.

Brow pinched, he looked to where Strell now sat against the mast with his back to Lodesh, his head slumped in sleep. He had appeared only a few moments ago, his nightshirt in disarray and his hair wild, blinking as if he had never seen fog before. The sun wasn't up yet, and Strell was making tea. At least he had started tea, setting a pot of water over the tiny fire in the galley before stumbling out to fall asleep before the water warmed. *Not good,* Lodesh thought.

Lodesh brushed the dew from his stubble as he flicked a gaze to the mouth of the galley hatch. Someone ought to take the pot off the flame before it boiled dry. He could use a bracing drink to throw off the damp that had settled into him. Where, he wondered, was Hayden?

A gust of wind shifted his hair, and Lodesh looked through the lifting fog to the monstrous silhouette curving about the mast. Talo-Toecan. The Master was back. Lodesh shifted his grip on the wheel as the raku underwent an impossible landing, somersaulting to fall to an easy stance balanced on the railing as a man. The sails barely stirred.

"Lodesh," Talo-Toecan said softly in greeting, and Lodesh nodded. Padding across the deck in his slippers, Talo-Toecan eased himself down to the bench beside Lodesh. A sigh slipped from him as he arranged his Master's vest about his knees. He seemed weary from more than a lack of sleep.

"Are you all right?" Lodesh asked tentatively, guessing he had been to see Keribdis.

Pulling his questioning gaze away from Strell sleeping against the mast, Talo-Toecan grimaced. "No," he said shortly. "I won't talk about it."

Fear jerked Lodesh straight. Keribdis would not be arriving at the Hold. Ever. He closed his eyes against the thought of what Talo-Toecan had done—had been required, had been forced—to do. From the depths of his soul, Lodesh knew he lacked the strength to hurt someone he loved. Not again. Once, standing atop his city's walls, had been enough. Telling himself the pain would eventually be swallowed up by a greater joy was a lie.

Unbidden, the memory of Kally's upturned face—first tear-streaked and pleading, then lost in madness as she murdered her children—swam before him. He should have done something. Killed her in mercy as she asked before the madness caused her to tear her children apart and decorate the stones of his damned wall with their sundered limbs and insides.

"Has he been there all night?" Talo-Toecan said softly.

Lodesh jerked, remembering where he was. Taking a steadying breath, he followed the Master's gaze to where Strell was slumped.

"No." The flatness of his voice surprised him. Hearing it, Talo-Toecan arched his white eyebrows. "He's only been there long enough to boil his tea water," Lodesh finished.

Talo-Toecan made a noise of disbelief. "Alissa asleep at sunrise and the piper awake?"

"Not awake," he muttered, his eyes back on the thinning fog. "He's asleep sitting up."

"Hm-m-m," the Master murmured.

A slow burn of worry went thorough him. It was not possible the piper could have managed to convince Beast to let him touch Alissa. She was feral. She wouldn't allow it.

Talo-Toecan broke his silence with a groan. "Let me take the wheel," he grumbled as he stood, reaching for it. "Before our good captain docks my pay."

Lodesh's hands fell away without thought. He took several numb steps backward, hesitated, then muttering, "Tea," he went belowdecks. Intentionally missing the last step, he landed hard on the planking. Strell's pot of water was steaming violently, and Lodesh moved it from the flames. Moving by rote, he listlessly made tea.

The day brightened around him as the fog lifted and the fragrant leaves steeped. He fingered the notches Hayden had cut in the ceiling support, and the mind-jolting scent of tea shocked him from his apathy. "Tea," he whispered decisively. "Alissa wants a cup of tea." Suddenly smug that he was awake and Strell was asleep, he decided to finish Strell's errand. Why was he assuming the worst? Strell was asleep on deck because of a fruitless night spent trying to convince Beast he was not going to hurt Alissa. And Alissa would undoubtedly appreciate an understanding set of ears after a frustrating night alone on her side of the bunk.

Yes, he thought. He had planned everything to perfection. Nothing had changed.

Feet shifting to the memory of a dance tune, Lodesh poured two brimming mugs of tea. He easily balanced against the boat's motion as he made his way down the narrow aisle, dodging the packages the Masters had wanted them to ferry back. The ceiling gradually lowered as he reached the bow. Almost hunched, he tapped at the door with his foot.

"Alissa?" he called softly. "I have tea." Heart light, he waited, hearing nothing.

Wedging one cup out of the way among the clutter surrounding the door, he knocked before easing the door open. He poked his head around the frame to find her slumped asleep among her pillows and blankets. Smiling, he set their cups down where they wouldn't spill. Eager to wake her, Lodesh came closer. His smile slowly faded.

Alissa's hair lay strewn across her pillow, not hiding her faint smile. An arm lay carelessly tossed, bare to the shoulder. She slept peacefully, content, smiling as she recalled a memory he would never share with her.

Lodesh went cold at the sudden wash of truth. Throat closing, he stood frozen, unable to take his eyes from her grace. *The piper has won,* he thought, shocked to find he could even think it. Somehow he had won her. His eyes traced the pale, lissome angle of her arm to find the copper ring loose upon her broken finger. *Another man's wife,* he thought, his chest clenching, *dreaming dreams of Strell.* His breath came in a quick rush, and he frantically backed out of the room. Almost unaware, he shut the door. How could he have been so blind?

He would never have her as his love, he thought. She loved Strell. Even when the plainsman died, she would love him. And though she might choose to be with Lodesh, perhaps even take his name when she learned to live with her loss, Lodesh knew when she smiled she would be thinking of Strell. And that's the way it would be, whether Alissa lived for a hundred years or a thousand.

Grief shook him. Unseeing, he stumbled down the aisle. He had put his trust in the belief that time would work for him, and now he had lost. Lost it all. Lost everything.

Lodesh found the galley bright with sun and busy with Hayden making breakfast. Connen-Neute and Silla were clustered together at the long table, laughing about her improving flight skills and their unexpected swim when Captain Sholan refused to drop the jib so they could land on the boat.

Not meeting their eyes, Lodesh retreated to the deck, not

caring he left an uncomfortable silence behind. The sun had burned away the fog, and the morning was hot. His body cried out to run, but there was nowhere to go. Talo-Toecan stood silently watching him from the wheel. Alissa lay in slumber in the bow. Strell slumped against the mast, sleeping.

Strell, he thought, gritting his teeth until his jaw ached and his pulse hammered.

The sudden hush he left in the galley seemed to mock him as he made his slow, sure way across the sloping deck toward the plainsman. He would sit with Strell for a moment.

Acutely aware of Talo-Toecan's suspicious scrutiny, Lodesh eased himself down beside Strell as if for casual talk. The man never woke, and Lodesh's chest tightened as he saw the bemused contentment in him. Jealousy pulled Lodesh's shoulders until they hurt. *She should have been mine!* he thought bitterly. He had patiently waited. Gave her time to make up her mind. He had done everything right. Why wasn't she his?

Throat tight, he stared at the lanky, unassuming plainsman. Strell had won. Hurt, rage, and malice ran hot through him, building upon one another to make his head pound. He wanted to hurt Strell, to make him feel the same pain. How could she not be his? He had done everything right. How could Strell have taught a beast what love was?

Lodesh's breath caught in sudden understanding. *The Wolves should hunt me. It had been love,* he thought, his eyes closing as the depth of his folly crashed anew over him. He had answered his own question. Strell taught a beast what love was because he loved both Alissa and Beast. Strell called them one and the same. He loved them both—but Lodesh loved only Alissa.

Lodesh's breath shook as he exhaled. His urge to punish Strell evaporated, leaving him empty. The hollow it left behind throbbed in his soul like an open wound, cold and aching. He couldn't hate Strell for loving Alissa more than he did. He could only curse himself.

Anguish bowed his head as he looked ahead through the coming centuries. He had failed three times over. Alissa would be cursed as much as he, forced to live a hundred lifetimes without the love of the man she desired.

"I'm sorry," he whispered, his heart clenching in grief as

he thought of her smile, soft with sleep. "I only wanted to see you happy." He closed his eyes against his misery. He had only wanted to see her happy. And with that, he knew.

"My curse," he breathed, feeling as if he was being torn inside. He could give Strell his curse. "Yes," he whispered, hearing it come out harsh and ugly. Strell was a Hirdune, born to his sister's children many times removed. He was entitled to it. And as Lodesh was sure the Hold would ultimately make him the Warden, it only seemed fitting.

There was a perverse satisfaction in knowing the guilt would hurt the man, coloring everything he did in a gray shadow. He was sure Strell would carry his curse for a thousand years so as to remain with Alissa to the end rather than the paltry three hundred he had carried it. Strell would suffer, but Alissa would be happy.

Lodesh pulled his head up, almost shocked to find the sun was still bright and shining. His jaw was tight, and his neck hurt. His mind cried for him to get up and walk away before he could do it: to let Strell have her for a time, then be happy with what Strell left him. But Alissa . . . Alissa would cry when Lodesh couldn't see. It would shape her days and haunt her thoughts until she was a shadow of the woman he loved. For Alissa, he would give Strell his curse.

Grieving, he closed his eyes, searching his feelings for the way to give his curse to Strell. It had been laid upon him in despair and grief, and he would have to use the same to give it in turn to Strell.

Lodesh went cold, unable to feel the strong morning sun. The memory of the bitter taste of ash at the back of his throat from burning bodies coursed through him. Eyes closing, he cast his mind back to when he had stood atop his dammed walls, weeping as he watched Kally die, then again as Ren brought his shame and grief to rest within Lodesh. *This,* he thought. *This will be my gift to you, Strell.*

Heady and strong, his emotions poured through him. His breath caught at the strength of it, and as he exhaled, he willed his curse away from him and onto Strell.

He felt his curse shift, then gasped as pain clenched his heart. Lodesh's eyes flashed open, and he reached for the support of the boat. He caught his breath as a delicious agony struck through him. The curse was peeled away like a scab, and three hundred years of guilt lifted from his soul.

The clean beam of innocence struck deep within him, cold against the exposed patch of soul. He felt wounded, ripped apart, as he stared unseeing. As nebulous as a dove in the rain, the guilt was—gone.

Slowly the band about his chest loosened. Slowly Lodesh regained his senses. Sweat ran from him, and he stared at Strell.

The man had woken as the curse intended for an entire city fell upon him. His eyes were wide, and his mouth was open, reaching, gasping for air. "It will get easier," Lodesh rasped, putting a trembling hand upon the man's shoulder. Then his hand dropped. "No. I lie. It never gets easier, but you'll learn to carry it so it doesn't color everything you do."

"What . . ." Strell gasped, pain etched over his brow. "What did you do to me?" Understanding, black and angry, flashed over him. "You ash-ridden, twisted son of a—"

"No," Lodesh interrupted. He dropped his eyes, knowing he would be unable to hide his sudden upwelling of bittersweet joy. It was gone. His curse was gone, leaving him free. His joy mixed with heartache, and he suddenly knew how Sati must have felt. *Sati,* he thought, his gaze going distant. He had never understood her until now. He had loved her, too, and it had nearly killed her. Alissa, though . . . Alissa would live. Alissa would love.

"I can't breathe," Strell said, dropping his head into his hands. "I can't think."

"You will." Lodesh rose and stumbled to the railing. He felt ill. Unable to look at Strell, he gazed sightlessly over the fog-flattened water as his thoughts drifted to a memory of Sati in the moonlight, her eyes bright with laughter as she whispered giggles and threw dandelions at the citadel guards. He had tried to love her even as she saw his death over and over again. Would she remember that as she sat at the Navigator's table? Had she waited for him?

There was a scrape, and he turned to see Strell struggling to move his legs. The plainsman looked about as strong as a starving kitten. "You gave me your curse," Strell whispered, his eyes haunted. "This guilt." He looked desperate. "It's not mine. Take it back!"

Lodesh's jaw clenched. "No. I gave it to you for Alissa, and you're going to carry it." He forced himself to look at Strell. "Because I love her, too," he finished, choking on his words.

Strell blinked several times. "Alissa?" he breathed.

Lodesh turned, unable to bear the sudden hope that crossed Strell's face. The next few weeks trapped on this boat were going to be a living hell. "She needs you more than I need her," Lodesh whispered to the waves. He swallowed hard, his chest hurting. "Go away."

He heard Strell stumble to his feet, and Lodesh spun. "Wait," he said, then hunched in surprise as a cough shook him. His face went slack as he recognized the sound. It had been over three hundred years, but it wasn't easy to forget. He swallowed, feeling ill at the coppery taste. *So soon?* he thought. *The Navigator help me.*

Shaking inside, he faced Strell. "Don't tell her," he said, praying the man would do as he asked. "Wait until we get to the coast. The next few weeks—" He steadied himself, gripping the railing as a wave ran under the boat. "I can't bear her pity," he whispered.

The tall, ashen-faced plainsman before him nodded. Saying nothing, he walked away. Lodesh wasn't surprised to see him move easily across the gently tilted deck, not using the railing as support for the first time. Empty and drained, Lodesh turned back to the fog. His breath slipped in and out of his lungs. He listened for the rattle of blood. Waiting.

42

It was hard to have a proper honeymoon with your friends around, Alissa thought in cheerful resignation as she leaned over the railing of the *Albatross* to watch the foam stream. It was even more difficult when your father was there as well, and that's what Alissa had begun to see Useless as. She squinted into the dusk to better see the lights on the dock. The moon was hidden behind thick clouds, which was why they were coming into port without the Masters hiding their eyes and hands. The stored heat of the day rose from the water like a violet mist, visible now whether she wore skin or hide. She could fly now, too, frightening Useless the first time she had shimmied up the mast and jumped from it, shifting in midair.

A smile came over her as Strell put a hand on her shoulder. "Ready to go home?" Strell whispered, his finger tracing the curve of her cheek.

She shivered and leaned into him. "Yes," she said. It wasn't that she hadn't enjoyed their trip back—far from it—but the boat was frustratingly small, and she was growing weary of the ribald jests at her expense. If she rose early, it was noted. If she rose late, it was noted as well. She was eager to move her things into Strell's tower room and find a new pattern of lessons and chores.

Lights blossomed on the dock as Hayden shouted across the dusk-stilled water. It was unusual for a boat to sail into dock instead of dropping anchor or being towed in, especially at night. The dock people were grudgingly moving their boats to make room. That Captain Sholan was attempting to sail in proved he was an excellent seaman who liked to show off.

The captain stood at the wheel, alternating his gaze from the flag on the mast to the approaching dock. Alissa could feel the tension, relishing it. There were advantages to having a small boat. "It'd be easier if one of us would shift and just push it to shore," she said.

"Perhaps you could do that in a few centuries," Strell said. "The captain seems to have accepted rakus. I don't think they're as frightened of Masters as Talo-Toecan thinks."

Alissa glanced across the flat deck at Captain Sholan. The forced contact had desensitized the man. It would be nice to see rakus and humans working side by side someday, but the fear on his face the first time Connen-Neute had shifted was a very strong deterrent.

"Hayden! Drop the jib!" Captain Sholan shouted suddenly as they came within hailing distance of the dock. "Neute!" he called, and the young Master jumped to his feet. "Take the bow rope. Cast it to the largest man on the dock. No, wait until we get there! Talo-Toecan, if you would take the stern line, please. Wrap it round a piling as soon as you can. Lodesh, fend us off. Use an oar, not your arm, man! You want to break it? Hayden! Help the piper. He's got no strength in those skinny arms. Only able to lift a mug, he is. Alissa!" he shouted, and she jumped.

"Get your hind end in the wheel pit with Silla before you get knocked down. The girl is the only one of the lot of you with any sense. Here!" he exclaimed as Alissa obediently jumped into the lowered deck. "Take this rope and drop the mainsail when I tell you."

Alissa meekly took it in her good hand, thinking integrating the two cultures might not be such a good idea after all. At Captain Sholan's direction, she unwrapped the rope and let it slide through her fingers. They were still some distance from the dock when the mainsail fell with a sound of sliding canvas to make a white puddle on the deck.

Within the shadows of the flickering oil lamps and the hush of excited conversation, they drifted in on their momentum. Excitement thrilled through Alissa at the tricky maneuver.

"No! Wrap it twice, wind-torn fool!" Captain Sholan shouted. "Let the piling stop the boat, not your back. You'll break it, and then what good will you be to me. Bone and Ash, you would think you never brought a boat in before!"

There was a flurry of tossed ropes and shouts, and they came to a creaking, reluctant halt. Alissa took a quick breath, feeling the finality of the boat ceasing motion. Unthinking, she looked to the top of the mast for Talon, her shoulders slumping as she remembered she would never hear Talon's scolding chatter again but in memory.

Calls went down the dock with the name of the boat. Apparently their arrival had caused a stir. She was glad it was dark enough to hide her eyes. Silla stood beside her, gaping at the dock. "Look at all the people!" the young woman exclaimed softly. "See? Some are children!"

"Watch your hands," Alissa whispered back. "Tuck them in your sleeves. And wear a hat to hide your eyes if you go off deck. You don't want to start a panic."

Silla absently nodded. Her lips moved as she counted the lights on the dock, her amazement growing. Her foot jingled with several bells on loan from Alissa: two from Useless, and the one from Connen-Neute. It had been Alissa's idea, though Connen-Neute had promised to get Silla her own bell as soon as they made landfall if she wanted.

Alissa frowned as an uneasy buzz started on the dock. It surrounded the man Connen-Neute had tossed his rope to, and she wondered if the dockman had noticed Connen-Neute's fingers or that he had left as a blind man and returned whole.

"Hoy, Sholan!" a strong voice called merrily out from the dock.

"My brother-in-law," the captain muttered, then louder to Hayden, "Get the plank out."

The plank slid into place, and the man strode eagerly aboard. Captain Sholan sighed as he went to meet him, his entire body moving with his exhalation. Connen-Neute and Useless vanished belowdecks. The older Master beckoned to Silla, and she reluctantly joined them. Alissa refused to drop her eyes, knowing she was safe in the dusk. Still, she stayed in the wheel pit while Captain Sholan went to greet the man.

"Sholan!" the man said, pounding him on the back. "Where've you been? No one has seen you for months."

"The Rag Islands," Captain Sholan said gruffly, clearly pleased.

The man bobbed his head, not giving Alissa a second look after hearing the few bells on her ankle. Alissa smiled, glad for the lack of notoriety. "You found them? Imagine that," the man said in a preoccupied way. "And what did you do to my sister's boat?" he asked, walking quickly to the boom. He ran a hand over it, grunting when he found the wood smooth and strong. "Oh, I like this. What kind of wood is that? You get this on the Rag Islands? They have hardwood there? Who would have thought that? Is there more?"

"Get yer grubby hands off my boat," Captain Sholan said loudly, and several people on the dock shouted cheerful agreements.

"Aye, your boat again," the man admitted. "My sister sent me spying. I'm here to appease her, the scrawny witch. But tell me about the Rag Islands. Is there much good timber? How long does it take to get there? Do you use the current?"

Alissa followed Strell with her eyes as he passed with his arms full of packages. She wondered if Captain Sholan might be going back to the Rag Islands sooner rather than later. His brother-in-law seemed as impressed with mirth wood as the captain was.

Strell dropped his load at the bottom of the plank and crossed back in front of her. Connen-Neute was handing bundles up to Lodesh, who was making a surprisingly high pile on the deck. "How are we going to get all that back to the Hold?" she whispered as Useless came out the second hatch to stand behind her in the shadows.

Useless harrumphed, keeping a close watch on the two coastal men discussing the boom. "We only need to get it out of town," he said, careful to keep his eyes down and his hands hidden. "Everyone will come and collect their things before sunup. Yar-Taw said he's finished the sling for the piper. Between us, we can get Strell back safely."

Strell shuddered dramatically as he passed them, his arms loaded down.

"We'll be home by sunrise," Useless continued in a satisfied voice. "The Hold looks the best at sunrise. Silla should see it then."

Alissa thought the Hold would look good in snow, sun, or fog at this point. Then she hesitated. "What about Lodesh?"

Useless rocked back on his heels and said nothing. Still silent, he spun on a heel and went belowdecks. Alissa frowned. She could get an answer from him, but it would be easier to go right to the source. Looking across the deck for Lodesh, her eyes narrowed. Lodesh wasn't going to run away just because she and Strell were married. She was going to make sure of that!

She stomped over to him, her emotions high. The bells about her ankle jingled to give her away, and Lodesh straightened from his crouch before she was close. Connen-Neute took one look at her, stammered an excuse, and vanished into the more-certain dark of the boat's hold.

"What's this about you not coming back with us?" she demanded, her hands on her hips.

Lodesh pushed a lengthening curl out of his eyes. "I'm staying with Captain Sholan," he said evenly. "He told me yesterday he's going back to the islands for mirth wood. I'm going with him to make sure he doesn't harvest the island into a desert."

"That's not why you're staying with him," she accused. "You're running away."

Can you blame me? his raised eyebrows said, but his words did not. Alissa flushed. She shifted from foot to foot, then darted to stand in his way. "Ese' Nawoer will soon be filling up with people," she said. "We need you. The Hold needs you."

He took her shoulders and moved her gently out of his way. "You don't need me," he said, but his smile held no recrimination.

"Lodesh," she protested, guilt making her voice high. "You can't just leave!" She furrowed her brow, thinking. "I—I do need you. You know everyone at the Hold. You have to smooth things out, or I'll end up on everyone's work list."

Lodesh ducked his head, making a small cough to hide his laugh. But it turned real. Harsh and deep, his breath raked from him. Alissa reached to touch his shoulder as he hunched under the force of the coughs. He had a red handkerchief at the ready to cover his mouth, and he took a step to pull out from under her hand. The cloth looked black in the dim light. He had been carrying it the last few weeks. She stared at it, seeing a wet smear as he tucked it casually away and resumed stacking packages. "Strell will keep you out of trouble," he said, his voice breathy.

Worried, Alissa came closer. "Lodesh. What's wrong?"

He said nothing, silent as Strell took an armful of packages from him and walked away. Strell's steps were subdued, and Alissa grew more worried. Lodesh had been different on the way back. Quieter, less inclined to jest. She had attributed it to her and Strell, but now, she wondered. She thought of how he had been avoiding her, his increasing coughing spells impossible to hide on a boat, and the way he held the railing as his uncanny balance seemed to be gone. Frightened, she glanced at Strell, carrying an armful of packages down the plank with an unusual ease. He hadn't been ill the entire trip back, walking about the boat with the sureness of being on dry land.

"Lodesh?" she asked, a new tremor in her voice.

He straightened, pushing his hat back so she could see his eyes. "I'm dying, Alissa."

Panic washed over her, and she reached up to grip his arm. How could he say that with his voice so calm and even? "No!" she demanded. "You're cursed! You can't die."

"I gave my curse to Strell," he said, never dropping her gaze. Alissa's throat closed up. Tears welled as she saw the love in them. "I gave it to Strell for you," he whispered. "I promised I'd see you happy. My mistake was assuming that meant you would be with me."

Her heart clenched. She took his hands and pulled him a step closer, not caring if anyone was watching or not. "You can't die," she said urgently, feeling as if it were her fault. "I won't let you run away like an old cat to die in the woods. I'll—I'll just bring you back again." she said, her voice loud with a false threat.

Lodesh smiled from under his hat. His eyes were tired, and she could see lines about them. "No," he said, running a finger under her eye. "Not without the curse to help, and besides," he said, glancing beyond her to Strell. "You didn't bring me back the first time."

Alissa blinked, and her eyes overflowed.

Lodesh's gaze flicked back to her. "Strell did."

"What?" she breathed.

"He's a septhama, Alissa. And I think he knows it. He's been seeing ghosts ever since he smoothed out the scar tissue across his tracings to bring you back from the past. Ask him. A Master can't bring a ghost to life. Neither can a septhama. But together . . ." His eyes crinkled in heartache, which he hid with a false smile. "Together you can. Strell has the pattern of tracings that made it possible, but it was you who woke me, my sweet Alissa. And gave me substance when you drew on a memory you hadn't yet lived."

She was crying again, resigned that she would be leaking tears for weeks. Useless came up behind her, and she caught back a sob as he put a steadying hand on her shoulder.

"But it was Strell," Useless said, seeming to know what they were talking about. "Strell's tracings, even scarred as they were, made it possible?"

Lodesh nodded, taking a step back. He looked tired, and her heart was breaking all over again. "But how?" she pleaded. "How can he be a septhama?" She turned to Strell, seeing nothing in him as he gave a man with an empty wagon a coin. "I've seen his tracings. They're a shambles. And Redal-Stan said you don't get a septhama without the warning of an upsurge of Keepers in the family line. Nothing has ever come from his."

"But it should have," Lodesh said. He gave Useless an un-repentant look, hard with an old anger. "You were going to let my sister's children go shaduf. I couldn't let that happen. So I had a pipe warded to gently burn an infant's tracings, pre-venting their development."

Useless's face went red with anger. "Connen-Neute!" he shouted, and there was a crash from below.

"Strell's grandfather's pipe . . ." Alissa breathed. "Strell said it gave him headaches when he played it too long. His pipe was scarring his tracings?"

"Him and all his kin," Lodesh said. "I had no idea the ward would last this long." His hand reached out, dropping before it could touch her. "I gave my curse to Strell for you. I couldn't bear your smile, Alissa. Not when it wouldn't be for me."

She hung her head. She couldn't look at him. She couldn't.

Useless was in a state. "You can't just give Strell your curse," he said irately. "That's not what I had intended at all. You had this all planned out, did you?"

"No." It was flat, and Alissa wiped her eyes and looked at him. "I didn't plan on dying quite so soon. That was a sur-prise, but perhaps it's for the best."

"Lodesh!" she cried in misery. "You can't." A loud stomp-ing turned her attention to Captain Sholan coming toward them from where he had left his brother-in-law at the ramp to the dock. Quickly she wiped her eyes and dropped her head, not wanting him to know she was upset.

"Neute!" the squat man bellowed, his voice echoing against the distant houses. "Get your long-fingered hand up here if you want me to put some money in it!" He turned to Useless, his eyes respectful.

"Thank you for crewing on my boat," Captain Sholan said. "You sail a straight tack, brought us in right where I wanted to be. I'll give you the same advice I give all my crew." He leaned close as he dropped a paltry few coins in Useless's hand. "Stay away from the Red Skirt Inn. Their girls bathe too much. Makes for unclean living."

Useless blinked in surprise. Captain Sholan laughed, knowing his advice was worthless, which was why he gave it.

"Lodesh," the captain said, handing Lodesh a few coins. "I expect you to give word to the Three Crows where I can find you, eh? We ship out as soon as I can get the *Albatross* careened. My brother-in-law is going to back us." He smiled, his teeth glinting in the torchlight. "That will put her bells in a twist."

"Ma'hr," Lodesh said, pocketing the money. Alissa's heart broke at hearing the term of respect come out of Lodesh, but he didn't seem to find any shame in it.

Strell stood with his hand outstretched, and Captain Sholan looked at him in disgust. "I'm not paying you," he said. "You ought to be paying me. Lying abed most of the day . . . Turning a woman's eyes to gold. Wolves and hagfish. Damnedest thing I've ever seen."

Strell grinned as his hand dropped. "That's the Stryska in me," he jested, but it lacked feeling.

A very long and shaky hand gripped the hatch opening behind them, and Connen-Neute emerged to stand awkwardly next to Lodesh. He flicked a guilty look at him. Alissa frowned, not knowing what he was worried about. Useless grimaced in irritation. She watched an unheard comment pass between them, and Connen-Neute slumped in relief.

"Here," the captain said, pulling Connen-Neute's ear down to his level and dropping a few coins in his hand. "Spend it on her," he said, looking at Silla as she came up on deck. "Spend it *all* on her."

Connen-Neute flushed, glancing at Silla and away.

"Everyone but Lodesh off my boat," the captain said. "My brother is buying me dinner."

They all stared blankly at each other. Alissa panicked. How could she just say good-bye? Captain Sholan made an exclamation of disgust and flung his hands in the air. Stomping to the bow, he checked lines that needed no checking.

Alissa looked at Lodesh, her eyes wide as she refused to cry. Useless gripped Lodesh's arm in farewell and walked away. Connen-Neute did the same, hesitating to give the Keeper a look deep with gratitude and friendship. Silla pulled Lodesh down for a quick, inexpert hug, whispering something in his ear that made him smile. Turning, she hastened to catch up with Connen-Neute. The sound of her bells as she descended the bobbing plank made a lovely counterpoint to someone on the dock singing a lullaby.

There was only her, Lodesh, and Strell.

"Strell," Lodesh said, his face holding a frightening emptiness. "Once you're Warden, take my damned wall down. That's all I ask. I know you'll take care of everything else."

Alissa clasped her arms about herself, pinching her healing hand painfully.

Strell nodded. "I'll make a road out of it," he said solemnly. "All the way to the plains. And if there's enough left, I'll take it to the coast."

"A road?" Lodesh said in disbelief. "That will take a thousand years."

Strell pulled Alissa close, and her eyes closed against a tear. "That's what I have." He hesitated, his silence saying more than words ever could. "Thank you," he whispered. Strell took a step away, clinging to her hand to draw her with him.

Alissa couldn't move, unable to leave Lodesh standing alone on the deck of a ship—dying of a disease that killed him once before. "Lodesh?" she quavered.

Strell's grip dropped. She heard him move away. As if unable to speak, Lodesh took her in a last embrace. Feeling his strength for the last time, she didn't want to let go. The clean smell of mirth wood filled her. She knew she would never be able to stand in Ese' Nawoer's field and not think of him when the wind pushed against the autumn-gold grass.

"Here," Lodesh said as he gently pushed her away and pressed his box of cuttings into her hand. "Make my field a forest?"

She took it, choking on her sorrow. How could she just walk away?

Lodesh put his hand on the back of her head and drew her close. "Don't let him be alone," Lodesh whispered, and tears sprang into her eyes. "The guilt of the curse is terrible, Alissa. And now that I'm free of it, I find myself feeling guilty for having given it to him." He was smiling forlornly as he dropped his grip on her. Only a hint of his usual recklessness peeped through his melancholy. "Perhaps I've lived with guilt for so long, I need it."

"Lodesh . . ." she pleaded, her head pounding with the effort not to fall into sobs. Her fingers gripped the box so tightly that it hurt.

"Go on," he said, and she let Strell draw her away and down the plank.

She turned as her feet found the dock, but he was gone. The deck of the ship was empty. Miserable, she turned away. "I'm supposed to be happy," she said, hiccupping around a quick intake of breath, and Strell gave her a sideways squeeze. She had done everything she had set out to do. Wasn't she supposed to be happy?

"Come on," Strell said as they followed slowly behind Useless, Connen-Neute, and Silla in a wagon. "Let me get you something to eat."

"Something to eat," she said, sniffing morosely. She felt the edges of Lodesh's box of cuttings as her feet moved slowly. "Is that your answer to everything?"

"Yes!" he exclaimed with a forced cheerfulness. "Look," he said, pointing to where the wagon had stopped. "They seem to have read my mind. See? They stopped at an inn."

Alissa wiped her eyes. Nothing could make her feel any better right now. Nothing.

"I'll get you a cup of tea, and everything will be all right," he muttered grimly. It was obvious he knew tea would do no good but was determined to do something.

"Thank you," she said, not wanting it. "That would be nice."

It was a very subdued group that clustered inside the inn's stables about their wagonload of belongings. Strell was elected to go in and get a pot of tea and some biscuits to tide them over until Yar-Taw and the rest met them outside of town. Alissa sat miserably on a bale of straw and picked at the twine as she waited. She appreciated that everyone left her alone. The price Lodesh had paid for her happiness was like an anchor about her heart. It wasn't fair. None of it.

There was a small stir when Strell returned. The Masters

clustered about the impromptu table they had fashioned of two bales of straw and a torn horse blanket, fussing cheerfully as Strell made a great show of presenting the tea. Alissa had no choice but to take the cup as he came to her corner and proffered it with a hopeful smile.

She took a sip, making a face. "This is awful!" she exclaimed, looking up into questioning faces. "How can you drink it? It's bitter." Playacting to cover misery was one thing, but pretending that this swill was good was an entirely different matter. She hadn't had a good cup of tea for days, but this had to be the worst.

"Bitter?" Strell said, taking a hasty sip. His eyes were puzzled. "It tastes fine to me."

"Me, too," Silla interjected. Connen-Neute simply shrugged.

Useless took a sip, then another, saying nothing as his brow furrowed. Alissa watched as he started at a sudden thought, looking at her with wondering eyes. She shook her head. "Bitter," she affirmed, setting the cup aside, not wanting any more. "Worst cup I've had in days. And that's saying a lot."

Useless peered at her. "Alissa?" he questioned, and she looked across the dim stables as he hesitated. His head was cocked, and he had the most peculiar expression on his lightly wrinkled face.

"What," she said flatly.

"Would you mind if—" He cut his thought short, and she grew curious.

"What?" she asked again.

Useless put a hand to his chin and eyed her. He turned to Strell. "Been shrewish lately? Especially at sunup?" Useless asked him, and Alissa frowned.

"Yes," Strell answered cautiously. "It gets better after her morning flight."

Bobbing his head, Useless looked at Connen-Neute. "Is she tending to glide more in flight? Carrying her head higher than usual?"

Connen-Neute's jaw dropped, making his long face even longer. "Yes. As a matter of fact, she is."

A delighted grin came over Useless. He took three steps to her, his hand outstretched toward her middle. Frightened, she backed away. "What?" she demanded.

"Can I . . ." He hesitated, and a grin came over him. "May I be so bold as to run a search through you, Alissa?"

She felt her face go ashen. "What for?" she said, thinking she already knew.

Strell picked her up, spinning her around before plunking her down. Her hair flung into her eyes, and she cried out in surprise.

"What is it going to be, Alissa?" Strell asked, his sudden delight frightening. "You have to choose now, seeing as it's too dangerous to shift after the first few weeks. I asked Talo-Tocoan all about it. He told me everything."

Bewildered, she pulled her hair out of her mouth. "What?" she finally stammered.

"Strell is right," Useless said, his white eyebrows jumping. "You have a few weeks to decide before you need to chose a shift and stay in it for the term. Tradition would point to raku, but it's your choice, naturally. Just because human hasn't been done before doesn't mean it shouldn't. I'd suggest human, seeing as you'll have a hard time getting enough protein as a raku, and it takes three months longer as a winged monstrosity than a frail human being. And being able to talk silently to Keepers is a skill no raku-born Master can duplicate."

His voice prattled on, stirring Silla to an almost comical state of excitement as she whispered in Connen-Neute's ears nearly loud enough for Alissa to hear. "Months?" Alissa said, but nothing came out. Strell was a septhama. She didn't need to do a chart on her and Strell to know that she had a fifty-fifty chance of raku child, fifty-fifty for a human septhama. Her heart pounded, and she felt weak. Useless seemed to think he knew already.

"Don't unpack when we get home, Alissa," Strell whispered. His eyes were glinting as he slid a sly look toward Useless. "We have to go to the plains. Very, very soon."

"Plains?" she stammered.

Strell grinned, giving her a hug to leave her breathless. "I have to register you, my love, or my children will lose the chartered status of their name." Arms still around her, he beamed at Useless. "And I'm sure your teacher will want your children to have all the status they deserve. He can't say no now to a trip to the plains."

A low growl of discontent slipped from Useless.

Alissa felt sick. A child? So soon? "Oh, Ashes," she murmured. "I don't think I'm ready for this."

And Strell laughed.